THE RABBIT

THE JAGUAR

& THE SNAKE

ALSO BY JAMES NOLL

Tales of the Weird
(Short Stories and The Topher Trilogy):

A Knife in the Back
You Will Be Safe Here
Burn All The Bodies
Mad Tales (Compendium)
Don't Turn Around (Illustrated Compendium)
Thirteen Tales (Short Story Compilation)

The Topher Trilogy (Novels):

Raleigh's Prep
Tracker's Travail
Topher's Ton
The Topher Trilogy (Compendium)

Audio Books

A Knife in the Back
You Will Be Safe Here (Coming Fall 2017)
Burn All The Bodies (Coming Fall 2017)
Mad Tales (Coming Fall 2017)
Raleigh's Prep
Tracker's Travail (Coming Fall 2017)
Topher's Ton (Coming Winter 2018)
The Topher Trilogy (Coming Winter 2018)
Thirteen Tales (Coming Fall 2017)

The Rabbit,
The Jaguar,
& The Snake

JAMES NOLL

PULP!
Horror, Post-Apocalyptic, and Science Fiction

THE RABBIT, THE JAGUAR, & THE SNAKE. Copyright © 2017 by James Noll
All rights reserved. Printed in the United States of America. No part of this book may be used or reproduced in any manner without written permission except in the case of brief quotations embodied in critical articles and reviews. PULP books may be purchased for educational, business, or sales promotional use. For information, visit www.jamesnoll.net

Book Design by James Noll

Cover Art by Jamie Bronson

Cover Design by James Noll

Author Photo by Haley Noll

ISBN: 0692886621
ISBN-13: 978-0692886625 (PULP!)

For Fuck's Sake

CONTENTS

THE WIDOW

The Widow Mrs. Feldman leaned her elbows on the sill, her ample belly pressing against the radiator, testing the limits of her coarse, black skirt. She sniffed the early evening air, the wart on her nose quivering with each whiff. The neighborhood stank as usual: a bouquet of garbage perfumed with mildew and gutter rot, and riding beneath that, the musk of the homeless men who laid up in the alleys during the day. It had always smelled that way, for years and years. Sometimes worse, sometimes better. But the new century had brought with it new odors. Car exhaust and gasoline, bleach from the factories, chemical and stringent, with a soupçon of cancer. Not that The Widow Mrs. Feldman cared. She was there long before the white men constructed their towers and poisoned the land, and she would be there long after they were gone. She was an element of the earth, as timeless and indestructible as dirt, susceptible to nothing but the nuclear tides of the sun.

She looked up and down the block, scanning for any signs of trouble, then zoomed in on the old abandoned townhouse right across the street. It was in as poor condition as ever—the bricks were stained, the windows streaked with grime, and moss hung out of the leaf-choked gutters. She paused, peering hard at the door, searching, waiting for the slight shimmer in the air, the rippling that signaled that something had come over from the other side. Nothing.

Unsatisfied, she hawked up a lunger and spat it out onto the sidewalk below.

"Demon!" she snapped. "Demon! Come here you little . . . demon."

A thump sounded from some far off room above. Demon liked to hunt in the attic. The insects were juicy there, the rats juicier, and, if the crone had some leftovers from her own nocturnal adventures, he had his pick of the best vital organ meat in the city. Lungs

1

untouched by smoke, livers unsullied by alcohol. The Widow Mrs. Feldman pulled the stump of a cigar out from the folds of her sweater and plunked it into her mouth, lighting it with a snap of her fingers. Smoke carpeted her lips, and she watched the shadows loom over the street. The best time to use the door was right before the sun set, in the gloaming, the transition from safety to terror, and the gloaming was coming soon. That's when the beasts crossed over.

A city kid ran down the street in front of her, shouting "yeah you and what army?" over his shoulder. His voice reminded her of BG, King of the Goons. She thought about her last conversation with him and snorted.

"'Oh but they ain't coming over here,' he says. Oh yeah? Tell that to my Demon. He's gained five pounds in the last month, the little pig."

She took another pull on her cigar and blew out a heavy, gray cloud.

"Tells me to do my job. You do your job, I say! Pah. Stupid goon. The faces change, but they're always the same. Demon! Come here you brute!"

But Demon was a long time coming, and she drifted off into her memories, back, back, back, all the way to her beginnings. She didn't remember a father or a mother. She had no siblings. She just was. In those early times, she wandered the landscape, cold and alone. She spoke no language, had no tongue of her own. She sang to the plants and the water, and they provided for her. She drank from the streams, and they were cool and clean. She ate what she could catch, first the little creatures, the mice and the rats, the frogs and the fish, but it was never enough to fill her belly. In time she learned the songs of larger game, and she sent sweet sweels of melody out into the air, and they came to her, and she feasted on their flesh.

But with the bigger beasts came prodigious danger, horn and hoof, teeth and claw, and she didn't always win. Even worse were the things that walked upright. They made tools and knew fire. They were cagey and knew how to fight. She had only tasted a few before the rest came for her, chased her through the forest with bone clubs and spears. They cornered her in the foothills, and she cowered against an outcropping. She could still see the flicker of their bared teeth in the angry red flames of the torches, the thrusting spears. She reached up around her back to rub the old wound. The skin was shiny and smooth beneath her hairy hand.

"Demon!" she yelled again. "Oh!"

Something tickled the back of her legs just above her dirty brown hosiery. Demon. Or his tail, rather. He was a gray Bengal cat with black stripes and striking blue eyes, prone to mischief, yes, but sagacious and loyal. And powerful. He rarely used it, for the transformation drained him, but if tested, if threatened, he let it loose. And woe to the creature stupid enough to be on the receiving end. He wound his way in and out of her skirt, rubbing his face against the scratchy stockings and purring. The Widow Mrs. Feldman chuckled.

"There you are, you nasty little creature. Where you been, huh? Up in the attic? Get yourself a bellyful?"

He meowed, blinking up at her.

"That's what I thought. You're a good little demon, huh? A good little devil." She scratched his ears, then patted the sill. "Come on up here now. C'mon. Time for you to earn your keep."

Demon followed the sound, tail swishing, and jumped up, sinking his claws into her finger before she could pull it away.

"Ach, you demon, Demon!" she cried, and popped the digit into her mouth.

Then she took a few bits of smoked meat out of a fold in her sweater and sprinkled them on the sill. He sniffed them, wary. She'd tricked him before. When he was satisfied that there wasn't anything wrong with the meat, he chomped in. The old crone waited for him to finish, then sang him his song. He watched her, mesmerized and blinking, before turning toward the street and sitting down, his tail swishing back and forth like a pendulum, irregular at first, then falling into a steady rhythm—swish-swish, swish-swish.

The Widow Mrs. Feldman leaned over peered between his ears. She watched the air, waiting for the right moment. The shadows of the brownstones lengthened on the street. The air began to cool and . . . there! A shimmer in the door of the old abandoned townhouse. She took a pull from her cigar and blew a plume of smoke between Demon's ears. He didn't even flinch as it expanded in front of him, a dark gray cloud. The crone bored into it, concentrating, willing it to stay, to hover, to reveal what it was meant to reveal.

And it did.

The front door of the old abandoned townhouse flickered in and out, in and out, and then the passage opened and a monster leaped through, shrouded in shadows. Demon yowled and the smoke dissipated, and by the time it had all cleared, the creature had galloped halfway up the street.

The Widow Mrs. Feldman winced as she stood up, her spine popping. She put her hands on her back and stretched. Plonked the cigar in her mouth. Took a few puffs.

"Well, Demon." The cat looked at her. It blinked. "What do you think?"

She waited a moment for a reply, and when none came, she stubbed the cigar out on a black spot on the sill and hid it in the folds of her skirt. Then she grabbed a walking stick from its place next to the window and limped over to her front door, the heels of her boots clonking on the hardwood.

"C'mon you mangy beast," she said. "Time to sing for your supper."

THE RABBIT

Hey, how's it going?

Lemme tell you the story about the time I saved the world.

Looking around right now at the burned out buildings and the churned up streets and the bodies in the gutters, I know what you're thinking: "This is how you save the world?" So I guess my answer is that I don't really know. And I don't really care. I kind of look at it as something that happened to me, like jury duty or a colonoscopy. But hey, that's jumping ahead now, ain't it? Let's start from the start. And there ain't no better place to start with than my Ma and Pop.

Pop came to America from the old world before the Model T, if you can believe it. Met my dear old Ma on the boat on the way over, and even though I knew it wasn't the truth, I like to think that the whole thing was a whirlwind romance. Love on the high seas. A jealous suitor. Fist fight in first class, a triumphant right hook followed by a wedding on the main deck, with the ship's captain and the clear blue skies and the icebergs floating by. In reality, pop was a penniless Jew from Minsk, and ma, she wasn't no better off. Their getting together was probably more like a scrum and a moan behind a crate in steerage, a pauper's union at the neighborhood temple, and nine months later, me.

I grew up in the slums of the Bottom with about five million other street rats. Living in a place called the Bottom was exactly like what you'd think it'd be like living in a place called "the Bottom." The one room tenements, the baking hot summers, the midnight bum-rolls, the cholera, the TB, the dysentery. Ah, the golden years. Ma toiled long hours as a seamstress in a heat box deathtrap, and Pop worked a whole bunch of miserable jobs. He was a fish monger, a ditch digger, a stone-cutter. He buried gas lines. Dug subway tunnels. I don't know how he did it, but eventually the old codger saved enough money to buy his own business. A newsstand. Established himself as a true entrepreneur.

Me, however, I was free as a bird. Lived like a king. I hung out the usual gang of gutter punks. Skinny Pete. Squinty. Slappy. The Mangler and the Jew. We got up to all kinds of hi-jinx, me and them. Alley smokes. Heel hacks. Knife fights. But then Ma died in a factory fire, and Pop didn't know how to put up with me. Granted, I was a bit out of control, and short of drowning me in the river, there wasn't nothing he could do to keep me in check. Plus, he'd just got that newsstand off the ground, and he couldn't have a liability running around, that liability being me, so his only option was that free school them papists run.

And by that I mean Catholic School.

And Catholic School was Catholic School.

I know what you're thinking. You're thinking, "ain't you a Jew? Them papists don't let no Jews in Catholic School."

Well, you're right, you're right. But pop, he wasn't no dummy. About three months before he signed me up, we started attending mass. Every Sunday morning, every Sunday night. Pop got himself in thick with the priests, told them that he wasn't no religious type, that it was too late for him but that he didn't want his only son to go to Hell. Next thing I knew, they're swinging that censer all over the place and tracing the sign of the cross on my forehead with water. And just like that, I was a mackerel snapper, with all the privileges and blessings and hope of heaven.

He packed me off to Our Lady of the Bleeding Hands and Slit Throat that very fall, and then my education began in earnest. And boy oh boy did it suck. Sure I got me a nifty uniform and three squares a day, and oh yeah, they taught me how to read, rite, and rhythmatic, but I also got myself a hefty backhand whenever I done anything to offend anybody, which, given my natural constitution, equated to a considerable amount of backhanding. I'd always thought I was pretty clever, a real yuk yuk guy, you know? I even got The Mangler to laugh on occasion. In my opinion, my mouth was the best part about me, but them priests didn't seem to share my sentiments. (Well, they did and they didn't, but more on that in a sec.) They hit me so much their knuckles'd swell up just looking at me. Unfortunately the kind of behavior in which I specialized also drew a different kind of attention, the kind ain't nobody want, and from there my story went from pitch black to pitch blacker.

Satan black.

Ninth bolgia of Hell stuff.

I don't feel like going into all the details cause there ain't no point in grossing nobody out. The only thing you need to know is this: all the things that happened to poor kids with no resources in Catholic School happened to me. Pretty unconceivable a century later; run of the mill back then.

I got my revenge, though, right? Not after they fucked me up permanent, and not until I was much older, old enough for everybody who hurt me to forget about who I was and what they done, but revenge was got. I won't go into the particulars. That story's been told already anyhow. Some jerk wrote it up in some dumb book he published. *A Stick in the Eye* or . . . what's that? Oh yeah. *A Knife in the* Back. Anyway, it's a good read. A real pot boiler. Seven short stories and a novel. You should check it out. Especially the one about me.

Go ahead.

I'll wait.

Okay, maybe we ain't got the time for that kind of thing right now. For those of you who don't want to, or who ain't got the time or the patience, or who can't read, think of it this way: That priest's head looked good up there on my wall, didn't it? Not as good as them two goombahs, dumbass Basilio and fat little Arko, but good enough for government work.

So look, enough with the exposition. Here's where the story really begins.

About a year after that, I was killing time at Pop's newsstand, selling the typical newsstand type stuff, like newspapers, and magazines, and chocolates, when The Widow Mrs. Feldman stuck her head out her window.

"Howzit," she said.

It was a slow day. The war'd been over for three years, and the twenties was roaring like a lion. After the morning rush, ain't nobody was interested in the good news, so I sat back and put my feet up on a stack of City Sentinels to read the science section.

"Fuck you, you old witch."

"Hey, language, language. Is that any way to talk to your elders?"

"No. But it's the way I talk to you."

She laughed that chuffy laugh of hers. Half phlegm, half soot: "Huh huh huh. Huh huh huh."

"Jesus," I said. "You inhale a smoke stack or something? You gonna be alright?"

"You're a funny one," she said. "Real wiseass. You get that from your pop or your ma?"

Ma'd been dead for centuries, but Pop, he kicked it only a few months before. Lasted pretty long, him. Ninety-five years. Not bad for a time when most people died at half that age. It's fantastic, actually, unless you consider how he died, because he died kind of shitty, if you ask me, with the cancer eating away at his lungs until there wasn't no lungs left. I was already irritated before she reminded me of all that, but now I was irritated considerable more. I took my feet off the papers and plonked them on the sidewalk.

"You need your attitude adjusted?"

She waved me off.

"You don't scare me. Mr. Feldman was the last one who tried and look at what happened to him. Plus," she nudged her chin at the old abandoned townhouse. "I know what you done over there. And I like it."

I gave the old place a glance. It was all blackened at the base from when them two idiots tried to burn it down, and the windows was still cracked and grinning at me, but it was still standing, proud and unbeaten. I returned my attention to the article I was reading.

"Oh yeah?"

"Yeah. You got style, kid. And I know you been thinking about expanding your services."

Now that one shocked me a little. How the fuck she did know about that? She wasn't wrong, but, well, after I finished "The Unholy Triumvirate," I ain't had no inclinations to carry on. I felt I'd done my duty, purged my demons. Lived along with the knowledge them fucks who did what they done to me and mine would never be able to do it to somebody else and theirs. Until recently.

I'd heard things about what was still going on at that school. Good old Ronnie Resnick told me about it, and let me tell you something, I was none too pleased. In fact, I was so unhappy that I was actually thinking about giving them a little taste of my scalpel and bonesaw, add a few more trophies to my wall. But that was as far as I got, just the thinking about it, and as far as I knew, thinking about a crime wasn't a crime. That wasn't the problem, though. The problem was that The Widow Mrs. Feldman knew about the crime I was only thinking about.

"You know fuck all about it," I said.

"About what?"

I stared at her over the top of my paper. She wouldn't look me in the eye. Looked everywhere but, mumbling and muttering to herself. Dead giveaway. Finally, I said, "You know fuck all about fuck all."

"You're a laugh riot. A gaggle of giggles. I don't know fuck all? You just told me everything I needed to know."

"Ah you're a crazy bitch," I said.

But she wouldn't let it go. Kept laughing that hoarse laugh. I won't lie to you. It pissed me off.

"The fuck you laughing at?" I snapped. She laughed harder. A little ball of energy swirled up in my chest. I tried to keep reading, but it wasn't no use, so I folded the paper and slapped it down on the stand. "Can I help you with something?"

"No, but I can help you with something."

"Not interested."

"No, really. Listen. You look in the mirror lately? You look good for a guy your age."

"Watch it, you old hag. I might be horny, but I ain't desperate."

"What are you? Thirty-three? Thirty-four? You don't look a day over twenty."

"Sorry, you're not my type."

"I heard that about you."

Sometimes a body just got to absorb the insult. That was one of them times.

She said, "I know you know what I'm talking about. I know you seen it, too. You're in your prime. You'll never look better. I'm just trying to help you out a little. Give you a boost." I pretended to read again. "Look. I'm on your side here. You wanna stop them fucks from doing what they do?"

Fine. Fuck it. She knew. How she knew what she knew, I don't know. But she knew. I put the paper down.

"Yeah," I said. "I do. I'm gonna kill every last one."

The Widow Mrs. Feldman nodded.

"That's what I thought. C'mere a second."

"Fuck that. I ain't going nowhere. You come here."

"Got a bad hip." Her cat jumped up on the sill next to her and arched its back against her shoulder. She pet it. "Hey there, Demon. You come out to say hello?" Demon meowed. The Widow Mrs. Feldman reached behind her and put a glass of something on her sill. "Demon made you something to drink."

I looked at it. It was tall and skinny and filled up with something green and goopy looking.

"I ain't drinking that."

"It's cool and fresh, and it's a hot day, no?"

"Yeah, but I ain't drinking that."

She seemed to take that in, studying me, reading me, but she finally shut up so I was able to get back to the news. Whoo boy, the world was in a ton of shit. The Great War really fucked things up good. Unemployment rising in Germany. Some asshole in Italy and his black shirts. The old lady started to hum a tune. I didn't notice it at first cause she sung it under her breath, but then it seeped into my head, into my bones. I'd heard me a lot of music in at that point in time. "I Ain't Got Nobody." "Ain't We Got Fun?" "I Ain't Nobody's Darling." Streets was positively filled with that new jungle bunny shit. But this was something different, eerie and earthy, like the trees and the rocks and the wind all got together to start a band. It was the most beautiful thing I ever heard, and I felt transported by it back to a time when there wasn't no bricks or buildings, no assholes or asphalt, just the sky and the ground and the oceans and the rivers, and the next thing I knew, I felt something rub my calf, and when I looked down I seen Demon winding his way around my ankles. I got dizzy. And out of the haze came The Widow Mrs. Feldman's voice.

"You sure you don't want that drink?" she said.

And you know what? I did get a thirsty right then. Parched, even.

Years passed, and it was around that time that I started noticing something different about me. My old friends, Slappy and the like, they got older. Fatter. Sicker. Slappy caught a case of the Nationalism, enlisted in the Army, and ended up a corpsesickle when he tried to fight the Bolsheviks in Siberia during the Russian Civil War. The Mangler was too smart to sign up for any government sham but dumb enough to get himself killed in a drunken pub brawl. I heard Squinty went blind, which anybody with half a brain could of predicted, and then I never seen him again. The Jew was the only one who made it out somewhat prosperous. Owned himself a pawn shop near the Industrial District. I seen him every now and then, always alone, muttering to himself, stooped over and worn, like the trials of life weighed on his shoulders so heavy that he couldn't take it no more.

But me?

I stayed the same. Like my body got to the ripe old age of twenty two and said, "Fuck it. I'm done." And that's when I knew. I knew what I was going to do. I was going to follow through on all them thoughts I'd been thinking.

Look, I got a lot of regrets in my life. Who don't? I regret not running away from them fucks at the Our Lady of the Bleeding Hands and Slit Throat before they got to me. I regret not taking on extra work somewhere so Ma didn't have to work in that heat box deathtrap. But one thing I don't regret is drinking the potion old Mrs. Feldman made me that afternoon. Changed my life, it did. Or at least I think it did. Who knows? All I know is that once I realized what was what, all them ideas that'd been swirling around in my head solidified, and the guy I was after wasn't the guy I was before, and everything I'd ever known, the fear, the pain, the helplessness, vanished, replaced forever with an anger that nearly consumed me.

So I expanded my services. And by that I mean killing any fucks what fucked with the well-being of a helpless kid. This took some creativity. You know, before you start in on the judging, you should remember who I was going after. I wasn't duping no co-eds into helping me carry my groceries up a flight of steps. I wasn't leaping out at grandma from alley corners. I went after the kiddie diddlers, the pedo-pokers. Remember what I told that priest?

"I wish I had someone like me around when I was a kid."

Well, I took that serious, and for a while, it worked out pretty well. I find you been diddling kiddies, I hunted you down and slit your throat. Worked out well for about five or six years, but unfortunately, no matter how skilled or careful or sneaky or creepy, there comes a time in every great killer's career when he ends up caught. Well, not every one, because has anybody ever heard of Jack the Ripper?

So, yeah, this was some time around '51? '52? I got wind of a local cop whose tastes ran unconscionable. First some kids started spreading rumors. Scumbag took Jerry Blumczech for a ride in his cruiser. Gave Arnold Gold an option in an alley. Then this new cop showed up, lo and behold, fresh out of nowhere, young guy, slicked-back hair, square jaw, and a bit swarthy in the palms if you know what I mean. I seen him talking with the kids on my street, and then he's walking them to school, buying them ice creams. Classic profile. I also noticed that little Robby Resnick—Ronnie Resnick's grandson—wouldn't go near the guy, avoided him at all costs, ran across the street when he offered him a chocolate, took the long way to school. Once I seen that . . . there ain't no words for it. I felt an anger I ain't never felt before, and not for me, but for that poor kid. I didn't save Ronnie Resnick's ass from a priest way back when just to have his grandson get his plowed by no cop.

If only I'd known.

Them kids was paid to spread them rumors.

Robby was paid to act like he was afraid of the jerk.

Blumczech never took no cop car pleasure cruise.

Gold remained just as pure as his name.

And I fell into it like the sucker I was.

One night, returning home drunk from a date with one of The Widow Mrs. Feldman's bottles, an opportunity presented itself. I seen that sonofabitch pedophile cop walking across the street a block in front of me, and the dark twirlies descended. I didn't normally snatch nobody on the spur of the moment, and I definitely didn't do it when I'd been drinking, but up until that point I'd enjoyed a string of successes and I let it go to my head. Isn't that always the case with people like me? They call it a cycle or something; we plan and we stalk and we kill and we drink to forget it, even if we're not supposed to be bothered by it, and then we plan and we stalk and we kill again, a little sloppier this time, and a lot sloppier the next time, and worse and worse and then you're spiraling out of control like an idiot. So yeah. Pedocop spotted. Dark twirlies descended. I don't remember what happened after that. One second I was walking behind the guy, the next I'm surrounded by a bunch of dicks screaming at me to hold up my hands, goddammit or they'll shoot.

"Alright, alright," I said, and did what I was told.

Unfortunately for me, my hands was covered with gore. So was my face. And my chest. And them cops is shining the lights in my eyes and I can't tell if it's real or fake, can't see nothing, really, except them lights, and suddenly I realized I was straddling somebody, and when I looked down I seen a busted open chest cavity between my legs.

"Oh shit," I said.

"Oh shit's right," someone said, and slugged me solid right in the temple.

What'd they do? What do you think they done? They dragged my ass to the station and worked me over with a rubber hose. Ripped out my adenoids. Showered me with the old lead sprinkler. They could have saved their breath. I had no intention of lying. I wanted them fuckers to know what I done. Maybe they'd see the light. Maybe they'd understand that I was actually trying to help them out. So that's why when the beatings stopped and my face had time to unswell, and they hauled me into a little room with a bright light overhead and a two-way mirror (you seen TV), and the one cop was breathing down my neck and the other acting all official and polite, and they asked me "Did you fucking do this shit?" I said, "Yeah, I fucking did that shit" and that was that.

I don't think the cops expected me to do that, kill their boy so soon. I think they thought they were going to do some serious investigating, whip up the media, maybe fabricate an event, something they could use during an election year. They certainly didn't think any of theirs was going to die, and if they did, they didn't think it'd be as unpleasant as the way I made it. The guilt must have been phenomenal. The one I killed was fresh out of the academy. Top of his class. Asshole tighter than a corncob. True blue, him, and his dumbass superiors set him up to be gutted like an animal.

I seen the realization dawn on them right then and there in the interrogation room. Their eyes went dead, and they broke out another round of rubber hoses and wooden clubs and brass knuckles and beat the ever-loving shit out of me, punched my half-swole eyes until they was fully swole, pummeled my bread-basket until it was mush. When it was all done and I wasn't nothing more than a bloody pulp, they drug me down to the deepest, darkest, dankest part of the jailhouse, threw me in the moldiest cell, slammed the door, cut out the lights, and marched off, slapping each other on the back and giving each other hand jobs. Okay, maybe they wasn't giving each other hand jobs, but they was jerking each other off. I'd like to say I took it all professional, but I was scared out of my mind. I soiled myself silly. Them fuckers threw away the key. I was gonna die down there. I curled up on the thin mattress in the corner and cried myself to sleep.

The main think I had was "what happened?" Why didn't they parade me around in shackles? Publish my picture in the newspapers? Slap me in the chair and let me do the electric jiggle on live television? I'll tell you why. Because things didn't turn out the way they planned. Because I didn't do it the way they wanted me to. Because I didn't follow the rules, didn't fit into a box, and that makes normals itch, and no matter what anybody tells you, no matter how many times they say "live your dreams and be an original," they don't mean it true. Sure, live your dreams. Sure, be an original. But don't do nothing too dreamy or original or you'll freak us the fuck out and we'll throw you in the dungeon.

And that's all it was, them sticking me in that cell. Fear. Pure fear. I educated them on the limits of all that freedom they said they loved so much, and all the sudden they started to think maybe too much of it wasn't such a good idea, that were was people like me who took them serious, took them at their word, who didn't give a fuck. That scared the crap out of them more than anything else, because where there was one dumb enough or sloppy enough to get caught doing the kinds of things I done, there were probably a hundred more waiting in the wings, just itching to cut and slash and slaughter, and once they seen what the people in charge had in store for them, who do you think they'd be coming for?

Well that wouldn't do.

That wouldn't do at all.

Fortunately, there was another group of people that'd took notice of my talents. Powerful people. People like me. Violent, ageless. Better than that, they were from the Neighborhood. Not the neighborhood, the Neighborhood. There's a difference. What's the differ . . . ? Just give me a minute. You'll see.

One morning after breakfast (a rotten orange and moldy bread) I got a knock on my cell all polite like, like I had a choice not to answer.

"Yeah?" I croaked.

The voice on the other side sounded like the streets. Asphalt and brick. Dumpsters in alleys.

"That you?"

I worked my jaw and it clicked.

"Yeah it's me."

"Lemme in."

"What do you mean, lemme in'? I'm in here. You're out there."

"No. You're in there, and I'm out here."

"Six to one, and go fuck yourself." A pause. "Please."

Another pause. Then the guy said, "You gonna let me in or what?"

Seeing as I'd just spent the last few weeks getting my adenoids ripped out, I really didn't feel like screwing around, you know?

"Remember what I said before about 'go fuck yourself'?"

He laughed. Can you believe that shit? Laughed.

"That's a good one," he said. "Good to maintain a sense of humor. But you know what? You ain't got no manners."

"I got plenty manners. For example, I said, 'Go fuck yourself,' then I added 'please'."

The silence on the other side of the door hung thick in the air. A mausoleum at midnight.

He said, "Maybe I'll come back another time."

His footsteps clopped away down the hall.

"Hey, I can be good!" I cried. "You come in here and I'll give you a shot of my bologna, how about that!" I couldn't stop laughing. "Oh sure, I got some cheese to go with it, too. And a little grease for extra flavor!"

After that, nobody came to visit no more. They stopped everything, the beatings, the food, everything. The former was a relief, the latter, a problem. I got creative. You ever eat a spider? It's not as traumatic as people think. I mean, sure, you gotta, you know, actually eat a spider, but then the stomach acid burns it to bits and you're ready for more. I became quite the arachnid connoisseur. Never reached Renfield status, but after ten days, twelve days, thirty days—who the fuck knew—I decided that, yeah, there really wasn't going to be a trial, and, sure, there really wasn't going to be no electric chair, neither, but the cell? The cell was my sentence. Twelve feet by twelve feet of eternal punishment. Four water-stained walls, a gray, concrete slab, a metal bed bolted into the wall, and that slate iron door.

So I ate spiders.

And flies. And silverfish. And cockroaches. And ants. And anything else that showed up. Catching a rat was like Christmas dinner.

Years passed, I guess. I stopped keeping track. Toward the end there, though, I couldn't really tell what was what no more. I can't remember when I started seeing things, but I started seeing things. Entire cities demolished by a ball of fire. Houses swallowed by earthquakes. Children snatched from porches. At first, I knew it wasn't real, then I thought it might be real, then I wasn't sure no more, and at a certain point, it didn't matter. There it was, and I was seeing it, so it was real.

And then one day the guy came back.

I was standing on my bed trying to coax a roach into my cupped hand when the knock came at the door again. I eyeballed it. Thought for a second. Almost had the fucker. Just. One. More. Second.

Another knock came and I said, "Just a minute."

The third knock came harder, and my hand shifted and the roach scurried up and away into a crack in the mortar and I pounded the cinderblock with my fist, crying "Motherfucker!" I turned my anger at the door. "You sonofabitch! You just cost me my lunch!"

"Tsk tsk," the guy said. "I see we haven't learned our manners yet, have we?"

I stared at that friggin door a long, long time. Sometimes when things started talking to me, if I stared at them long enough without saying nothing, they went away. So I stood there kind of hunched, my hands held up like I was about to pounce, my stringy hair covering my eyes. What was left of my prison uniform hung in tatters off my shoulders, and I didn't have no hips left, so I had to make a belt out of a strip of one of the pant legs to keep them from falling off. Not that it mattered. When the guy didn't speak again, I relaxed.

Phew, I thought. *He wasn't rea—*

"Hello?" he called. "You still there?"

"Oh," I said. "It's you."

He snickered.

"Yeah. It's me. You want to let me in now?"

"We gonna have this conversation again?" I sat down on my metal bed.

"I guess we are. So what's it gonna be?"

"Let's see. How's it go again? You want me to let you in, but you're out there and I'm in here."

"Noooo . . ."

"Yeah, yeah, I know. I'm in here and you're out there. Still don't change nothing."

"I don't begrudge you your bitterness."

"Bitterness? Bitterness? You got any idea how long I been down here? Because I don't. You should get a look at me. I'm a ghost. A fucking wraith. And all for what? Getting rid of the scum who did what they done to them poor kids? I was helping them out! And they locked me away!"

There was a long pause after that, and ice started to form in my belly. Did I scare him off? Right when I was about to plead with whoever it was not to go, he said, "You mind I can ask you a question?"

Oh thank fuck.

"Go ahead."

"You ever wonder if there was other people out there like you?"

I thought for a minute.

"Like scraggly macs who's been thrown in a hole until the sun explodes?"

"I think you know what I mean."

I took a deep breath.

"Yeah," I said. "The thought did cross my mind from time to time."

"That's good. That's real good. So you wanna let me in or what?"

"I can't," I whispered.

"What's that?"

"I said I can't!"

"Oh yes you can. Yes you can. All you go to do is stand up and open the door."

"But it's locked! They locked me up! They threw me down here and melted the key!"

"So you won't do it?"

"The door. Is. LOCKED!"

"Is it? You ever try opening it?"

The fuck was he talking about? Of course I'd tried opening it. I hung on the handle until my fingers broke, kicked it until my toes bled. Or maybe not. Who knew. One second oozed into the next down there. I could cup my hands against the wall for hours, waiting for a beetle to crawl into it, or lick at the water trail until my jaw ached, and I wouldn't know if it was the next day or the next week.

"I dunno," I said. "Maybe I haven't."

"Well, why don't you give it a shot? If it opens, great. If it don't, well, I ain't like you'd be any more disappointed than you already is."

That was some hot logic right there. Couldn't even start to think of an argument against it, so I said, "Okay."

I stood up shaky and shuffled toward it, and the whole time I'm thinking, "It's a joke. The fucking fuck is fucking with me." I knew that when I grabbed it, I'd feel the metal in my fingers, the same icy handle that I'd been yanking on for years (or hadn't been), and once again I'd push on it, and once again it'd creak and whine, and once again it wouldn't open. And then that son of a bitch on the other side would laugh and laugh, and I'd scream until my voice gave out.

Well. No time like the present, right?

I put my hand on the handle.

I pushed down.

You can imagine my surprise when, with a rusty squeal, the frigging door swung in at me.

THE JAGUAR

Wheeler stood topless in front of her spotted bathroom mirror. The scar on her chest had faded so much that she could almost believe that it wasn't there at all. She ran her fingers over it. The skin was dull but smooth. She turned to the left and covered her breast, trying to see it, to imagine what it might look like with it gone. After a moment she stopped and faced the mirror again, letting her hands drop to her sides. She stood there for a long, long time.

Later.

She was getting drunk at the bar under her apartment, Harvey's, when her asshole alarm went off. It was something on which she prided herself. She wasn't sure how it had gotten so keen. Maybe it was her academy training. Maybe it was the fact that she'd been a woman her entire life. Whatever the case, it was as honed and accurate as ever, and when the guy in the rumpled Banana Republic suit sidled up to the bar next to her, all four alarms rang. Five if he wasn't wearing socks. She tucked her head down and peered at his feet.

The fifth bell rang.

He knocked on the bar.

"Hey, Issac from *The Love Boat*! Un muy grande cerveza! Pronto!"

Jesus.

She tried to ignore him, she really did, but then Twan, the bartender, passed by, clearly too busy to pay attention a racist jerk acting, well, like a racist jerk, and the racist jerk snapped his fingers three times in a row, leaning over the bar as he did so. That wasn't so bad. Well, it was bad, but it wasn't terrible. The terrible part was that he elbowed her arm and made her spill her drink on her jacket.

"Watch it, dickhead," she snapped.

He barely glanced at her.

"Sorry, honey. If this porch monkey ever does his job, I'll buy you a new one." He snapped his fingers again. "Hey! Hey! Hey!"

"Don't bother," Wheeler muttered, and got up to move to a different part of the bar.

Crap. It was packed.

When had that happened? The place was empty when she got there. She'd been watching a Single Corp infomercial for, what, about an hour? First the demonstration of the Viddy Viewers™ and the Nimble Digits™. Then the slick talking head brought in a dozen construction workers and a couple of office stiffs to demonstrate their new body modification, something called Barrel-arm Biceps™. They were lifting sofas with one arm, ripping doors off hinges. Buy now on your mobile device, or better yet, use your Single Corp Cochlear ConNext™ and get 10% off our skin tone matching upgrade! That's a $400 deal! It must have been some deal. She lost an hour in it.

No, actually she lost four hours because when she looked at the clock behind the bar, the one with pool balls for hours and cues for hands, it was almost ten. No wonder the asshole was so aggressive. He'd probably been drinking as long as she had. Now he was leaning with his back on the bar, smiling at her.

"Why so salty, baby?" he said.

Christ. This wasn't worth it. She could get a bottle and drink at home, alone, where nobody would bother her.

"Fuck off," she said, and started to leave.

He grabbed her wrist, and she spun around hard, yanking it out of his grasp. She was about to slam her half-empty tumbler of whiskey into his face when someone stepped in between them. Luis. The bouncer. He towered over the guy, keeping his muscular back to Wheeler in case she tried to follow through with her punch.

"Hey buddy," he said. "Nobody's allowed to talk to my regulars like that. Not even me."

Wheeler pushed him from behind.

"I can handle this myself, Luis."

He half-turned to her, saying, "I'm just trying to cool everybody down, Wheeler."

"I am cooled down."

"Uh huh."

"Fuck you, Luis."

"Don't make me kick you out of the bar again." He turned back to the asshole. "Are we going to have a problem here?"

The asshole held up his hands.

"Whatever, Sanchez. I just want this boy to get me a drink." He turned around, muttering under his breath that sounded like "Fucking wetback."

Luis paused. He'd heard it, and he was trying to figure out the best course of action. Wheeler could tell he wanted to beat the shit out of the guy, but she also knew he had to calculate the danger and the damage. Did he have a weapon? Were any of his friends here? How many glasses would break? How many barstools? He took a deep breath, flexed his hands, and stepped away. She watched him, dumbfounded, as he walked back to his post by the door.

"Seriously?" she mouthed

He leaned up against the door jamb and flicked her off. Wheeler turned her attention back to the asshole, who was leaning over the bar, still trying to get Twan's attention by snapping at him. She tossed back her drink, sidled up to him, and wrapped her arms around his chest.

"I think I'll take that drink now," she purred, letting her lips graze his earlobe.

"Yeah. I bet. What do you want?"

"How about Pappy Van Winkle?"

"Not a chance. How about some Old Fitz?"

She fondled his tie.

"Jack Daniels?"

"I'll think about it."

Wheeler flagged down Twan. He purposefully didn't make eye contact with the asshole.

"What do you want, Wheeler?"

She handed him her empty tumbler and gave him a look.

"Right," he said.

He grabbed a bottle of the rail and put it down on the bar in front of her. Then he turned around to look for a clean glass.

"You gotta be fucking kidding me," the asshole said. "Hey Sambo. I'm the one who's buying here."

Wheeler smiled. She was waiting for him to say something like that. She looped his tie over her hand and yanked. His chin cracked against the edge of the bar. Then she grabbed him by the back of the head and slammed it down. It bounced and he reeled back, his hand covering his nose.

"Fuck!" he yelled.

Wheeler spun around in front of him and acted like she was about to give him a hug. Then she brought her knee up into his groin. He keeled over and she grabbed his shoulders and shoved, sending him sprawling. By the time Luis made it over, she'd already kicked him in the ribs three times. In the chaos that followed, she grabbed the bottle off the bar and put it in her jacket. She was laughing when Luis scooped her away and carried her to the door.

"Assholes shouldn't wear ties!" she cried.

Luis grunted as he threw her out into the street.

"Es una perra estúpida," he said. "How many times I gotta tell you not to do that kind of shit here?"

"C'mon, Luis. El tipo es un cabrón. He called Twan a porch monkey."

"Uh huh. What got in your jacket?"

"None of your business."

"Don't make me hurt you, Wheeler."

"Fuck off, Luis."

He took a step toward her.

"Wheeler, I swear to god. If you stole another bottle . . ."

"It's not a bottle."

"I know what I felt."

"Yeah, my tits."

"Not my type."

"Oh yeah. I forgot."

He crossed his arms.

"You gonna open up and let me see?"

"I thought you said I wasn't your type."

He took two more steps forward, but she held out her hand to stop him.

"Okay, okay," she said.

She opened up her jacket, exposing a Glock in a shoulder holster.

"You brought a gun into a bar?"

"It's not loaded. I'm a cop."

"Yeah, well, then you should know better."

"You saw what that guy was like. Nobody'd blame a woman for carrying protection."

"You still can't do that here."

"Why not?"

"You know why not. I'm banning you."

"What about that asshole?"

"Don't worry about him."

She groaned.

"Luis, not now. I've had a shit day, and I got a whole lot more shit days in front of me."

"One week."

"What's the point? I'm just going to come back."

"The point is so I don't have to put up with your ass." He held up one finger. "One week."

"What're you going to do without me?"

He pulled the door open, and the sound of the bar—the music from the jukebox, the noise of the customers—poured out into the street.

"Not have to clean up your shit anymore, that's what."

She flicked him off as went back inside. Then she the bottle of Jack out of the other side of her jacket.

"Vete a la mierda, asshole."

Wheeler had always wondered what it was like to get drunk in an alley. She'd lived in the city her entire life, and as a child she saw plenty of men squatting next to dumpsters, tipping bottles in brown paper bags up to their lips. For a while the bottles were replaced with pipes, then the pipes were replaced by needles, and then it all circled back to the bottles again. She thought briefly about taking her sorry ass up to her apartment, but she just wasn't ready to do that yet. The mirror was up there. And the letter from the lab. She needed a couple of shots, a couple of stiff belts to steel her nerves so she could face all of the things she was going to have to face. Asking for time off. Calling her sister to come and stay with her again. Loading up her phone with audiobooks and podcasts. So she copped a squat against the slimy bricks beneath the fire escape about halfway down the alley.

She let her head loll to the left. A dumpster sat at the far end, half in shadows, overflowing with garbage from the bar. A few murky puddles dotted the concrete. No time like the present, she thought, and took a long pull. She rested like that for a while, thinking "I'll just take one more. Just one more." But one more became another, and another, and another. The more she drank, the easier she found it to make excuses to stay. I'll just drink until I get to this line on the label, then a little lower, and a little lower. Soon she wouldn't be able to stand up let alone make it all the way back to her apartment, and that would put her in an even more dangerous situation than she already was. A woman drinking alone in an alley was one thing. A woman passing out in an alley was something entirely different. Not that she cared. Her hand wandered up to her chest. Before she let it go any further, before the tears that had started to well up, she took a deep breath, let it out, and, still holding the bottle, pressed herself back against the wall, using the leverage to rise to her feet.

The ground tilted and her vision quadrupled. Yep. She was a lot drunker than she thought. When a functioning alcoholic realized how drunk she was, she was really drunk. Really, really drunk. Good thing the door to her building was maybe twenty-five yards away. All she had to do was make it out of the alley. Turn to the right. Navigating the turn might present issues, but if she could control her legs and maintain a hold on the wall, maybe by leaning on it . . .

What was that noise?

She turned around, head bobbing, and squinted into the dark alley. It didn't help. Her vision blurred and doubled, and when it finally came back into focus, she saw a black form hunching at the end.

And it was watching her.

"Shit," she whispered.

She smashed the bottle against the bricks and stumbled to the middle of the alley. She swayed there, wondering if she could reach into her jacket and pull out her gun without falling over. If she could, could she click off the safety? Aim? Pull the trigger, even? The black form clicked like an insect, rhythmic and staccato. Never a good sign. Two amber orbs lit up. Also never a good sign. Wheeler pulled her gun out of her jacket, her thumb fumbling with the safety, and backed away, unsteady, hoping to reach the sidewalk before whatever that thing was attacked. The noise of the bar thrummed through the bricks, laughter and loud voices just below the deep bass of the jukebox. Save for the odd taxi rushing by, the streets were empty. Nobody would hear her scream.

The thing at the other end galloped forward, and Wheeler pulled the trigger. The shot went wide, pinging off the dumpster, and the monster leaped for the wall and stuck there, its talons anchored deep in the bricks. The light of the moon spotlighted it, a headless, muscular thing with two long legs that ended in six-toed talons. It had cannons and hocks turned backward like a horse's, but instead of a torso, a mouth gaped in its chest. Its eyes were embedded in its muscular shoulders, and its arms reached nearly to the ground.

She barely had time to take it in before the thing lunged for her, arms and legs wide, teeth extending as she fired again. It squealed when it hit the ground, then, anticipating the next shot, jumped back to the wall and ran along it, tearing chunks out with each stride. Wheeler followed it the best she could, missing, and when it was five feet away she turned and ran but it shot forward struck her from behind, sending her sprawling on her face. Her gun clattered away.

Wheeler flipped over just in time to block the beast's teeth with her forearm. She screamed. It bit into her shoulder next, and through the pain she felt something sting her muscle, pumping in and out, over and over. She gathered her rage and plunged the jagged glass of the broken bottle into one of the eyes bulging out of its shoulder. The thing roared and released her and she scrambled back, searching for the gun. It was right there, just out of reach. She lunged for it just as the beast bit into her thigh and pulled her back with a lurch, once, twice, and the gun was finally too far away.

This was it. This was the way she died. She adjusted her grip on the bottle neck as it dragged her back in the alley, her palm tacky with blood and fluid. If she was going to die, she'd make it pay. Take a deep breath. Count down from three. Two. One.

"Hai you sonofabitch!" someone yelled. A deep gruff voice. "What you got there? A little toy?"

The monster spun around, startled. As soon as it did, Wheeler sat up and scrambled away, putting as much distance between her and it as she could, which wasn't much. She could barely move.

"Tsk tsk, little *herif*," the voice said. "Who said you could play on this side of the door?"

All Wheeler could see was a hooded figure standing in the middle of the alley. It was squat and hunched and not at all menacing, and though the thing that had attacked her bared its predator's teeth, it seemed to have lost a little of its bark.

"Remember me?" the figure asked. "No? Maybe this'll jog your memory."

It removed its cowl and stepped into the light of the moon, revealing the ugliest woman Wheeler had ever seen. A bulbous, misshapen nose loomed over her hairy lip. Heavy eyebrows sat like caterpillars over her crooked eyes. Her hair was long, black, and stringy, and she tucked it behind an ear with a missing chunk.

The monster growled.

"Aww," the woman said. "You're not trying to throw a scare into a helpless old woman, are you?"

A cat appeared from under her skirts and wove its way around her ankles. The monster's growl escalated, and it even took a half step back. The old woman chuckled.

"Scared of my little Demon? Scared of a little kitty? You should be."

The beast took another step back, the growling louder. One more step and Wheeler might be able to stab it. Blood rushed to her head when she sat up, making her dizzy and ill, and she hated it. It made her feel weak, and weakness made her angry. She blamed it on her father, her military upbringing. And with the anger came that old, familiar rush of adrenaline, the same stuff she used to fight off her brothers when they were growing up, and her bastard of a stepfather two years after her mother and father split. She leaned up against the wall and got to her feet, leaning heavily on the bricks. The old crone pinned her down with her eyes. They were glowing yellow, shot through with red.

"You gonna stab the fucker, or do I have to do everything?"

The beast spun around as if it understood, gnashing its teeth. Wheeler pushed off the wall with her good leg and buried the shard in its eye. Now completely blinded, the thing squealed and shook its body back and forth, clawing at the glass. It tripped and fell on its back. Then the witch was there.

"Who said you could eat that pretty young girl?" she said.

She pointed at it with two fingers.

"Phfft! Phfft!" she said, drawing them back and forth.

A gash opened up in its midsection, deep and wide. Blood drained onto the concrete, and then it was dead.

"Well that's done," the witch said. She took a long, ugly knife from inside her sweater and shuffled over to where Wheeler lay.

"Wait," Wheeler croaked.

"For what?"

"I'm a cop."

"So?"

"Call an ambulance."

The old woman laughed.

"Ambulance? Ain't no ambulance will save you from what this sweet puppy did."

Wheeler pushed back with her good leg, trying to escape. She had to make it to the entrance. Maybe someone would see her, help her. She made it about two feet when a cracked leather shoe clomped down next to her head. Then the old woman's face was in hers.

"Where do you think you're going, pretty?"

And she struck her in the temple with the butt of her knife.

The Widow Mrs. Feldman muttered to herself as she finished working, happy that Demon was too preoccupied with the blood to bother her with his mewling. He got so impatient when he was hungry. She didn't blame him. He'd done his part, earned his keep, sang for his supper.

She whistled as she sawed through the bone, carefully avoiding the teeth. They held a kind of anesthesia in them, something to numb the area and so its victims barely felt the stinger that put the poison.

"Nasty little swimmies," she muttered. "Nasty little beasts."

She outlined the thing's torso, plunged her hands into the cut, and pulled the exoshell open, revealing the secret chaos of its dark biology. First, she severed the stinger and threw it away, disgusted. She snapped, and it burst into flame. Then she cut off a small hunk of meat and tossed it to Demon, who pounced. Now it was time for the real work. She made a makeshift net out of her skirt and started to cut. When she was done, it was nearly bursting with organs and meat. She struggled to her feet and tied it into a knot.

"C'mon now, Demon. That's enough."

The cat ignored her and continued to eat. She chuckled.

"You'll ruin your supper."

She toed him away, but he circled back to gnaw on a different part.

"Fine. Have it your way."

Then she stooped over, grabbed the monster's foot with one hand and Wheeler's arm with the other, and started to drag them both to the other end of the alley, away from the sidewalk and deeper into the city. In a moment she started to whistle again, a familiar verse, something she heard over a half-century before. When she got to the part with the only lyrics she remembered, she began to sing.

"The ice age is coming, the sun is zooming in. Meltdown expected, the wheat is growing thin. Engines stop running, but I have no fear. Cause London is drowning, and I live by the river."

Demon didn't look up from his meal until the witch had melted into the shadows. He stopped then and meowed, his muzzle red with blood, his blue eyes searching the blackness. She'd be gone soon. Without a second thought, he ripped off a chunk and zipped off down the alley, streaking around the dirty puddles and under the dumpsters. There was more food where the old witch was going, and better. If he didn't catch up to her soon, she might keep it all for herself.

She'd done it before.

THE RABBIT

I guess I could plant the particulars of how I got from point A to point B between your ears, but info-dumps is boring. Plus I remember fuck all about it anyway. The door swung in at me, and the next thing I knew I woke up in a room about the size of a closet. It was all decorated for a kid, too. Wall paper with ponies and butterflies on it, bedspread with ponies and butterflies on it, and a little wooden dresser with—actually, the dresser didn't have nothing on it. It was just a dresser.

Everything was painted blue, too, or shades of it, even the dresser, so I assumed it was a boy's room. The first think I thought was "are they trying to turn the kid into a faig?" because, seriously, baby blue? Have some balls. I grew up with a whole lot of nothing in my room because you know why? I DIDN'T HAVE A ROOM. Ma and Pop and me, we lived in a tenement, remember? Most I had for privacy was a sheet pinned to the ceiling, and half the time it was gone because Ma was using for something: hauling potatoes or laundry or potatoes and laundry. You can bet there wasn't no ponies and shit and no baby blue nothing in my corner of the room neither. It was all brown and gray. Brown and gray.

Anyway, the guy who saved me from the hole? His name was BG. As in "Bill Grimes" or "Barry Gold" or "Bartholomew Griffin" or "I don't know what the fuck his real name was" because he only answered to the two letters: 'B' and 'G', and then only when you said them simultaneous, like BG, because if you said the one, like "Hey, B!" he'd probably mistake it for a warning and think he was about to get stung by a . . . okay, that was kind of a lame joke. In fact, I'd really appreciate it if you forgot I said that altogether. Ain't nobody wanted to play no pranks on BG anyway. I won't go into too much detail, but look at this way: the last guy who pranked him did the thing where he pulled his seat out right when he was about to sit down, and that guy don't have full use of his mouth no more. Because he don't have a mouth no more. Or arms. So what'd we learn here today? BG and pranks mix together as good as orange juice and toothpaste.

Anyway, I was lying there, feeling terrible, and BG opened the door and it hit the corner of the dresser and he said, "Crap." Then he looked up at me. "I always do that."

I tried to say something, but the most I could manage was a croak, and even then it got stuck in my craw. He wasn't listening, anyway. He was too busy doing the "Where do I sit?" dance. Twist to the left, nothing. Twist to the right, nothing. Wasn't no chair, wasn't no couch, just the bed and the dresser and a bedside table with a lamp on it. (Did I tell you that lamp had pictures of ponies all over the shade? Fuck yeah, it did.) When he realized he was going to have to sit on the bed, he winced. He tried to hide it, but I seen it. He pursed his lips as he sat down, the legs of his pinstripe pants riding up, exposing a hairy ankle.

"Howzit?" he asked. "You hanging in there?"

Didn't even look at me. Couldn't blame him. I was little more than a sack of bones. Sunken eyes. Sunken cheeks. Sunken chest. My legs was twigs with sticks poking out the end. Could've poured a full bucket of water on my stomach and made a nice-sized koi pond. I cleared my throat until I could talk better, but even then it was hoarse and weak.

"I'm all fucked up."

"Yeah, you are. They fucked you up real good. I'm surprised you ain't, you know, even worse off."

"Can't get no worse off than this. I'm a twig, BG. Used to play football. Unload the news truck. Now look at me."

I shook my head, and a tear tumbled down one sunken cheek. A tear! It'd been a long time since I had enough water in me to cry. I wanted to leap out of the bed in joy, but BG got all embarrassed and looked away. I let it roll down into the corner of my mouth. I hadn't seen it before, but there was a cup of water on the bedside table. Half empty. I took it and sipped, and it zinged on my tongue, traced its way down my throat. Damn that felt good. Not that it meant anything. The only water I'd drank for years was what drippings come out of a rusty old pipe in the ceiling of my cell. The water in that cup could have been dirty toilet munge and I'd have swore up and down it came straight from Puerto Williams itself. BG looked like he had something to say but didn't want to say it.

"So I guess you know," he said.

"Know what?"

"What you are."

"You been talking to The Widow Mrs. Feldman?"

"You know her?"

"Know her? She lived on my street when I was a kid. Used to hand out licorice to us for Halloween."

"Licorice, huh?"

"Yeah. It was terrible. Like Chinese candy terrible. We threw it in the gutter before her door even closed."

BG looked like he was about to burst.

"I knew it!" he said. "I knew it was you. I told them 'It's gotta be him. Gotta be,' but none of them believed me. Well they can eat my ass now."

"Yeah? Huh."

"So how old are you? Sixty-five? Seventy?"

"Seventy-five."

"When'd it start? Twenty-four? Twenty-five?"

"About that."

"You got lucky, you. I didn't start until I was fifty. My best days behind me. Some of us it don't happen to until we're sixty, seventy, eighty years old. I knew one poor fuck it ramped up like two seconds before he died. So there he was, couldn't get sick and didn't age no more, but what does it matter when you can't wipe your own ass?"

"That sucks."

"Yeah." He tapped his foot nervously. "Well, I got news."

"What kind of news?"

"Good news. Good news. And other news. Other news, too."

"Okay."

"Wanna hear it?"

"Fuck's sake, BG. Spit it out already."

"Alright, alright. The good news is that we got a war going on."

"Ah, fuck you!"

"No, listen. Them tecuani is getting out of control. Going over to the other side, infecting people."

"Tec-what? You remember where you just got me from, right?"

"Right, right. Shit. Sorry. Look. Them tecuani's is like the worst monster you never seen. They don't fuck around. They, uh, well, put it this way: if enough of them get over, that's the end of the human race."

"So I gotta kill all them tec-whatevers?"

"Not necessarily. See, the Widow, she kind of guarded the world against them. Any of those fucks tried to get through, she done the old 'Phfft! Phfft!' and dragged their asses back to her place."

"The old 'Phfft! Phfft!' huh?"

"Oh yeah. She's really good at it. Cuts them right in two. Don't get me started on that cat of hers. Friggin' monster, him. Anyway, I think something happened because we ain't heard from her in a while, and knowing how much that old bat likes to jaw, well, not hearing from her's got us a little spooked."

"Okay."

"So, seeing as you know her so well, I was hoping you'd help us find her."

"I don't know her that good."

"This is serious business. You got to do it. Without her, we're cooked."

"So why do I got to go to war? Just let me look."

"It ain't that simple. We think maybe one of our own had something to do with it."

"Who?"

"His name's Zoot. He's in charge of BT."

"Oh, like a general or something?"

BG laughed.

"No. No. Zoot ain't no general. That ain't the way the Neighborhood works."

I didn't say nothing.

"Look. I think you'll like it here. The Neighborhood's got some fantastic perks. We got pizza. And pasta. And dental insurance."

"Seriously? You broke me out of jail just to put me in the Army?"

"Look at it as an opportunity."

"For what?"

"Not eat bugs for the rest of your life, stuck in that cell."

"I won't do it."

"Fine. Then back in that cell you go."

"I ain't going back in that cell."

"And I ain't here to argue. You got two options: this or that."

I let that sink in a little. Of course I didn't want to go back to that hole, who would, but I didn't want to get involved in no Neighborhood bullshit, neither.

"This gig come with benefits other than pizza?"

BG laughed.

"Don't get ahead of yourself. We need to do this correct. You need to look like you're just some dumb schmuck recruit."

"I thought you said—"

"I know what I said. But Zoot's in charge of BT, so you gotta go through BT."

"Aw c'mon."

"You'll be fine. There's only three parts anyway. Golgotha, Hell, and The Battle Royale. Guy like you? You'll be fine."

"That's the good news?"

"Yeah."

"What's the other news?"

"You fail any part of the test, you're dead."

"Fuck's sake, BG."

He got up, slapping my knobby little knee in the process. I'd have winced, but I could barely feel my own dick.

"You'll be fine. Listen, I gotta go. Morgellons is freaking out again. And don't get me started on them pyramid people."

"Oh, right. Them pyramid people."

"Rest up. You got yourself a hard row to hoe, my friend."

"Not the reference I'd use."

He laughed.

"You're a bit of a smart-ass, aren't you?"

I wanted to spread my hands, but all that talking wore me out, so I settled for a grin.

"I call it like it is, BG. I call it like it is."

The next morning I woke up to a pair of sweaty mitts shoving up under me. I protested with a groan, but that only seemed to make them hard hands harder. Then I felt stubble scratch my cheek and hot breath in my ear.

"Rise and shine, sweetheart."

Is that any way to wake a body up? How about a gentle shake? A little violin?

I opened my eyes and there he was. Morty. I didn't know his name at the time, of course, and he don't factor in much in this story, not yet, but you'll meet him again in a little while. The point is this: ever meet someone you didn't like right off the bat for no reason? Biologists cry "pheromones!" Psychologists cry "guilt!" Sociologists cry "hierarchical constructs rooted in tribalist survivalism and perpetuated by a tenacious religious infrastructure!" Whatever the cause, that's how I felt about Morty. Fucking asshole.

"The fuck you doing?" I said.

Morty picked me up off the bed with a, well, I'd like to say that he groaned or grunted with the effort, but remember that time I told you I spent a thousand years in solitary confinement with nothing to eat but bugs? I didn't weigh more than a buck ten, so the only grunting Morty let out probably had to do with, I don't know, a raging case of syphilis, not me.

"Shut up," he said, and whisked me out the door like a bride on her wedding night. Except for the part where my groom don't pay no attention to where he's going and hits the bride's head on the jamb. Morty laughed when he done it.

"I guess the struggle started early for you today, huh?" he said.

He carried me down a flight of steps and out into the day. The bright morning light hit me full on, right in the face, and I blinked and winced. I should've been ecstatic. Them was the first rays of the sun I'd seen in years. But instead, I was pissed off and irritated.

"Golly me that is a bright sun this morning," Morty said. "Kind of hits you right in the skull, don't it?"

"Ugh."

If I could've shrouded my eyes, well, I'd have made a fist instead and punched him in the face, because what's the use of blocking the sun when someone treats you like that? Instead I tried my best to enjoy the moment proper. I let the sun warm my skin, fill my pores, sink into my veins. Every nerve ending prickled awake, and I smiled.

"What're you smiling about?" Morty asked.

"I'm enjoying something. That's what people do when they enjoy something. They smile."

"Psh. You even know where you're going?"

"Psh."

"Well, where you're going, you ain't gonna be smiling very long."

And he was right, too.

I smelled it before I seen it; the worst smell I ever smelled in my life. There ain't one thing in the whole world I could compare it to, it was that bad. I guess the best I can come up with was that it smelled like a mix of burning hair and busted guts, like someone was, uh, burning hair. And busting guts.

Boy that was a terrible analogy.

How about "It smelled like someone took a crap in a hole and set it on fire"?

Eh. A little better.

Oh, I got it. "It smelled like someone extinguished a mountain of flaming pig guts with a dump truck of diarrhea."

Yeah. That's the one.

But even something as disgusting as that couldn't distract me from how stupid I felt being carried like a baby by a grown man to what was in all likelihood the second most horrific thing that ever happened to me (the first being when my pop enrolled me in Catholic School). I tried to brace myself. What'd BG call it? Golgotha? What the fuck was a Golgotha? It sounded like the sound a cat made when it puked.

Unfortunately, it was worse.

I seen a lot of things in my life. Sceels. Snats. Sniders. Not to mention a military-grade robotic werewolf. Who do you know who can say they seen themselves a military-grade robotic werewolf? Not many. Just me and Sal the Butcher. Just saying it out loud is nuts. Say it out loud three times and it's even crazier. Military-grade robotic werewolf. Military-grade robotic werewolf. Military-grade robotic werewolf. See? But Golgotha was even crazier than that.

Not to be ironical or nothing, but the setting itself wasn't so bad. It looked like any other neighborhood in The Neighborhood. Townhouses and row houses, brownstones and redstones and graystones. A couple of produce stands, a bodega on the corner. But lining the street four solid blocks deep was scaffolds, six feet by eight feet, four columns of them spread curb to curb. And strapped to them scaffolds was people. All kinds of people. Black people, white people, kid people, old people, men people, women people, yellow people, brown people, tall people, short people, skinny people, fat people. People with long hair. People with short hair. People with big tits. People with little tits. People with big cocks. People with little cocks. The rhythm was mesmerizing. So was the tits.

Look, I'm a horny bastard even when I been getting laid steady. I can't get laid, I jerk it like a madman until I do. And being cooped up like I had been for the last thousand years didn't do nothing to put the kibosh on my urges. Sure, maybe the dehydration and the starvation made it a little more difficult to finish, and I guess there's some might think that getting a little stank on the hang-lows ain't the most important thing in the world when your body's eating itself, but clearly they ain't never met me. I've gone balls deep in the throws of some serious Spanish Flu. I got a hard on in the middle of my appendectomy. I mean, I ain't never seen no pictures of an anorexic with an erection for obvious reasons, but that's missing the point, which was that I seen some live tits for the first time in years, and I liked it. Couldn't stop staring. I felt like a paraphiliac at the Paralympics. Too bad all them tits was all chained up. If I'd been into BDS&M? Goodness gracious. But I wasn't. Morty shifted me in his arms.

"Take a gander, kid. Your future."

"Bullshit."

"No bullshit. This is Golgotha. Your first stop. Hopefully your last, too."

Christ on a pony that guy irked me.

"You know, I ain't always gonna be like this," I said. "And when I'm not, when I get back to like I was before, we're gonna have a nice chat, you and me."

"Oh yeah?"

"Yeah. And we won't be talking about the weather." He didn't say nothing. "What I mean to say is I'm gonna kick your head in."

"I'm shaking in my wingtips. Pardon my bluntness, but you know fuck all from fuck nothing." He nodded at one of the ladies in the front row, a scarecrow with nipples. "See that bitch right there? That's Sophia Esposito. Weighed a 220 plus when she got here. Thighs full of cream cheese. Gut full of olive oil. She's made it two months so far, longest I ever seen." He bounced me in his arms, and I could feel my bones rattle in my skin. "You weigh maybe a ninety-five cents. Do the math."

"Not my best subject."

"Then foreshadow the ending."

"I don't think you know me that good."

"Oh, I know you. I know you like I know your mom's asshole, which is to say intimate because I banged your mom last week. In the asshole."

"Hey Morty, that's fucked up. My ma's been dead and buried almost fifty years."

"Psh."

Morty carried me into the first row. It was eerie quiet, not a peep, not a cry. Everybody just hung there, limp and lifeless. If any was awake or alive, I didn't see none. But that wasn't the worst thing. The worst thing was what was dug out in front of each scaffold: a bed of coals. The heat relative to the newness of the crucifixee. That's to say, some was dead cold, and some was white hot, and the rest all measures of degree in between. Morty glanced at a little scrap of paper he took out of his pocket.

"Let's see. Ten two three. Ten two three." He stopped and counted the rows, counted again, then squinted ahead. "Oh, there it is."

He carried me up to two open scaffolds side by side, both bleached raw and white, with fresh, red coals sitting in front. The heat radiating off them burned my skin even at ten feet away.

"Imma put you down now," Morty said.

"I can't stand! You crazy?"

"You see them coals right there? You're gonna walk across them and strap yourself to the scaffold.

"The fuck I am."

He laughed at me.

"I can drop you or I can put you down gentle. What's it going to be."

What could I do? Wasn't like I had a choice or nothing. I chose the latter. At least he was true to his word. He set me down on my feet, and he done it real gentle. Not that it mattered. My legs was more skin than muscle, and I tried to hold on to his shoulders, but that was like tying a cow to a post with a piece of grass. And I swear to fuck that when my feet touched the ground, I could feel my bones grind together. Like needles shoved into every tendon. So that hurt. I hung on to him with all the strength I could muster.

"Leggo," he said.

"Not a chance."

"You don't leggo, I'm gonna drop you."

"You drop me, I'll shatter."

"Promise?"

"Look, don't do this. Just take me back to that bed, okay? Just carry me over there and nobody will be the wiser. I promise I won't tell."

"No can do, my friend. BG's orders."

BG, you fuck. What kind of rescue was this? I was only half-serious when I said I wanted to go back, but now . . .

"You gonna walk or what?" Morty said.

"No."

Morty shrugged. "Fine," he said, and then he dropped me. "You don't wanna walk? You'll fucking crawl."

So yeah. I had to crawl across them hot coals. It was a ball, a blast, a gas gas gas. You might be asking yourself, "Why didn't you just not do it?" Because Morty would have just thrown me face first on them, that's why not. It ain't like crawling on my hands and knees across a bed of hot coals was on my bucket list. And if I could have stood, I would have. Burning your feet sucks, but you know what's worse? Burning your palms, your knees, your toes, the top of your feet. You know what's worse than that? Burning your chin and your face when you lose all your upper body strength and collapse, oh yeah, and also your chest, and your thighs and, wait for it, your cock and balls. Not my best moment.

But I did it. I crawled across a bed of hot coals. And when I was done, did Morty even clap or give me a trophy? No he did not. He just scooped me up and tied me up on that scaffold like the rest of them putzes. The weird thing was, once it happened, once he tied that last knot, once I was hanging there like a moth on a mounting board, I didn't feel like me no more. It was worse than being in that cell. In that cell, at least I knew I was alone. The only person I had was me, and that made me real. But out there strung up to die with hundreds of others, I was just another sap. Nameless. Faceless. And that was more terribler than anything.

A couple days passed. Then a couple more. Then I lost track of time again. I seen me some shit, though. Ever seen a man get scalped? I did. Some guy in my row. Three goons dressed in white robes, I don't know if they was male or female, came strolling all peaceful through the scaffolds, one in the front, two behind, and glided to a stop in front of him. There was a pot of something boiling on his bed of coals, and the one in the lead gestured to it and one of the ones in the back wrapped the bottom of his robe around it and picked it up. (I'm saying it was a 'he' because I seen his hairy legs, but that don't mean nothing, I guess.) Anyway, when they did the thing, the guy didn't react or nothing. Just took it. Then they dumped that little bucket on his head. And you know what was in the bucket? Sand. Hot sand. They dumped a pile of hot sand on an open scalp wound. Still, he didn't do nothing. Must've been close to the end, I guess.

And that ain't the worst of it. Them white robes came at different times every day, and every day they brought some fresh, new horror with them. They stuck people in the sides with sharpened sticks. They beat people in the face until you couldn't hardly recognize their faces no more. I was terrified at first, but after a while, truth to tell, I actually looked forward to it. It was kind of like listening to a good story on the radio or watching a flick in the theater. First there was the conflict: Man verses man—what batshit crazy thing would they bring today? Then there was the initiating moment: Three freaks in white robes appear out of nowhere. The build up of suspense: Who's next? Culminating in the climax: Let's rip this dude's eyelids off! But only half-off, you see, because ain't nothing worse than ripping something all the way off than ripping it half-off, so it just dangles there, all weird and inconvenient.

Every now and then they did something nice, you know, just to mess with people. Like they'd walk down the row, heavy and solemn, their hands hid in the arms of them robes. They'd pick their victim. They'd surround her. Then they'd start chanting or some crazy shit, and then, slowly, very slowly, they'd pull out . . . a tall bottle of water and take turns feeding it to her.

Then came the day Wildcat showed up. I didn't know her as Wildcat then. She was just some poor schmuck they strapped up to the scaffold next to mine. We didn't say much to each other. There wasn't much to talk about. Can you imagine how that one would go?

"Hey, howzit?"

"Not too great."

"Yeah, me neither."

Plus, she wasn't in no condition to say nothing. Her hair was burned down to the scalp in some spots, stubbly in others; her clothes hung off her in strips. Her skin was bright red, too. Come to think of it, maybe she'd been in a fire or something. After they marched her across the bed of hot coals and strapped her to her scaffold, she didn't do much of anything except hang there. When she was awake, she stared at the ground. Mostly. She had something in her right hand, too. How she snuck it in ain't nobody knows. It was long and bone white, and I'd say it was a key but it didn't look like no key I never saw. It had a leather strap at the end, and she wrapped it around her fingers. Sometimes she'd stare at it for hours on end, like a mental patient. Sometimes she'd flip it between her fingers, over and over and over. Her shoulder was branded, too. Three spirals, two on the bottom, one on the top, running counter clockwise.

Anyway, my point is she wasn't doing too good, and even if she survived all this nonsense, I didn't think she'd be much longer for this world. Why? Because people with injuries like that don't last very long. Plus she was kind of hot, and being hot don't get you nothing but attention. In civilized society, that's fine. Free drinks, a modeling gig. At the Golgotha, though, Jesus. Not to beat a dead horse, but being hot at the Golgotha was like being a little boy in Catholic School. Here's an example of what I'm talking about.

About a week after she showed up, Morty came back. He had some other big bastard with him. And when I say 'big bastard' I mean 'big bastard'. Buffalo head, tree trunk arms, sausage roll fingers. Biggest bastard I ever seen, and I seen me some big bastards. He was such a big bastard that he looked like he swallowed two other big bastards, that's how big a bastard he was.

Both of them was all dressed up nice in their white zoots and two tones. They strolled up to her scaffold and stood there, eyeballing her. Being new and all, there was plenty of her to eyeball. What was left of her clothes hung off her in strips, and for some reason that was worse than being naked. Trying to cover yourself with a strip of cotton was as pathetic as a misdemeanor; if you're going to do something stupid, have enough sack to go full frontal felony. Morty and his friend didn't seem to mind. Morty plunked a cigarette into his lips and lit it with a flick of his zippo. At least the tried to, but after three or four strikes the thing just wouldn't spark, so he swatted his friend on the shoulder.

"Hello?" the big guy asked.

"My lighter's broke."

"Oh, jeez, Morty. I'm sorry."

"I'm not looking for empathy, asshole. Gimmie yours."

Asshole's face fell all troubled, like someone just told him his cat just died. He patted around all over his parts. His chest pockets, his pants pockets, his secret pockets, his double secret pockets, which, if you don't know, is the secret pockets inside the secret pockets. This took a while, too, because like I said, Asshole was a big bastard, and being such a big bastard, he had him a lot of pockets. Funny thing about him and all his big bastardness was that for all that space in that moon-sized head of his there wasn't too many brains to fill it up with, because after a while, even though it became apparent that he didn't have his lighter, instead of saying anything, he stopped groping himself and stood there, staring at Morty.

"Well?" Morty said.

"Morty, I don't have no lighter."

"Yeah you do. It's right there in your breast pocket."

Asshole dipped two of them sausage roll fingers into the one on his right.

"No, it's not. Morty? I don't think I smoke."

"Not that one, you idiot. The other one."

Asshole searched the other one and pulled out a pack of Pall Mall's and a silver zippo. He stared at them, mystified. Morty blinked, equally mystified, though I'd hazard a guess that his was more sarcasm than anything else.

"You gonna give me that lighter?" he said.

"Oh, sure Morty. Here you go. That's for you, Morty baby."

"Don't call me that."

"But Morty's your name."

"Don't call me baby, asshole."

"Oh, okay Morty."

Morty flicked the wheel of the lighter once, twice, three times, but it wouldn't spark neither.

"Hey, dummy," he said. "It's out of fluid."

"Oh yeah. I ran out yesterday."

Morty caught me looking and he held out this arms, palms up, shaking his head as if to say, "Can you believe this shit?"

No I could not. It was better than *The Fred Allen Show*.

Then he looked around him, and kind of joking he said, "Anybody got a match?"

Wildcat broke out laughing. It was wild and hoarse, and she glared at them while she did it, grinning ear to ear, and with her head hanging forward and her eyes shining, she looked demonic.

"Yeah, I got a match," she said. "My ass and your face."

Then she fell to laughing even harder. Asshole joined in kind of uncertain like, not because he got the joke, but because, you know, of how hard she was laughing. It was—what's the word? Contiguous. Asshole was laughing because her laughing was contiguous. Like herpes. Morty though, he didn't appreciate the humor.

"You think you're fucking funny?" he said.

Wildcat didn't miss a beat.

"You think you're fucking funny?" she repeated, mocking him.

Morty looked at Asshole, even more dumbfounded than before, then back at her.

"You think this is a joke?"

"This? This? This isn't a joke. This is torture."

"Damn right it is."

"But your assface is even worse!"

Asshole laughed out loud this time. Even I smiled a little bit. That bitch was crazy.

"Do you know who I am, you numb cunt?" Morty said.

"Um, Assface Cocklefuck?"

Assface Cocklefuck? The fuck is an assface cocklefuck?

"Alright. That's it."

Morty snapped his unsmoked smoke onto the cold pile of coals sitting at her feet and marched right up to her face. "You fucking bitch."

She smiled that succubus smile at him, all bared teeth and pulled back lips. At this point Morty (and based on the outcome of the current confrontation, I was thinking I should stop calling Morty Morty and rechristen him "Assface Cocklefuck" because that was the funniest goddamn thing I ever heard someone call someone else), he pulled the most bastard moves of all bastard moves and, true to the first two syllables of his new first name, cocked his arm and punched her right in the breadbasket. This wasn't no pansy punch, neither. I'm talking full-on Jake LaMotta: spread the feet, bend the knees, turn the hips, and torso twist for maximum tension. He hit her so hard I was surprised he didn't punch straight through her spine. He hit her so hard even I got bruises.

Wildcat sucked in a great gasp of air and held it there for an hour. I thought she was going to die. Her face turned red, and the veins in her forehead popped out. When she finally caught her breath, she let out a raspy gasp, and took in great whoofs of air. Morty laughed and laughed. But Wildcat was a fighter, and after a full three minutes of wheezing and gulping, she finally caught her a good lungful, hawked up a full lunger, and spat it right in his face.

Morty didn't like that. He didn't like that at all.

I thought he was going to punch her again, but instead, he grabbed her by the face and whispered into her ear.

"You're gonna regret that, bitch."

"Not half as much as you're going to regret this," she said.

Then she sank them white and pearlies right into the meat of his cheek. Morty started screaming, high pitched at first, then higher and higher, like a pig at the butcher's block. He tried to pull away but that only made it worse. Old Wildcat, she bit all the way through the skin and tore herself out a nice chunk, whipping her head back and forth at the end there like the wild dog she was. Then, in a moment of brilliant word association, she spit it out onto the coals and said, "Oyster roast!" which was funny, you know, because of the definition of cockles.

She was pretty much done after that. Morty stumbled away, pressing his hand against the hole where half his face use to be, blood washing down his sleeve. Asshole, he lumbered forward, hands balled into fists, and clobbered Wildcat right in the temple. Her head rocked back so hard it hit the scaffold, so he got himself a twofer.

Then she slumped forward and hung there, dead or unconscious, I wasn't sure which. But one thing was certain.

I'd just met my new best friend.

Even if she didn't know it yet.

Holy shit.
Contagious.
Not contiguous.
That's what I meant to say before.
Asshole was laughing because her laughing was *contagious*.
Jeez.

THE JAGUAR

Wheeler awoke to the smell of something savory cooking. Her head ached. Her tongue was dry. Her body felt crushed. Pain radiated everywhere, and it was all she could do to stifle the moans that wanted to escape her lips. She let it wash over her, writhing, trying to ride it out. It finally receded from her core, coming to a fine point in the meat of her shoulder.

When she could think clearly, she realized that she'd been strapped down to a wooden table. The ceiling above her was cracked and dingy. Cobwebs hung in corners. The smell of mold and rot mingled with the smell of the food. An old woman's voice, husky and dark, sang from someplace nearby.

"What gat ye your dinner, oh Frankie my son?

"What gat ye your dinner, my stupid young man?

"I gat eels boiled in broo: mother make my bed soon!

"For I'm weary and fain wald lye downe."

Wheeler let her head roll to the side, and there in the corner hunched a cat tearing away at something large and shapeless. She flexed her wounded arm against the restraints, trying their strength, and immediately regretted it. A bolt of pain shot from her shoulder to her fingers, and she moaned and sucked in her breath. The cat perked up and looked at her, eyes glinting in the light. Its muzzle was matted with blood, and a strip of meat hung from the corner of its mouth. When it saw she was awake, it darted away, heading for the sound of the singing.

"Oh I'll swell and I'll die, mother make my bed soon.

"I'll swell and I'll die and my head it doe swoon."

The cat meowed.

"Fuck off, Demon, you little pest. I'm conjuring a brew for our damsel in distress."

Demon loosed an unending stream of yowls, punctuated by the old woman's periodic grunts.

"Okay, okay," she finally said. "Lead the way."

Demon continued to meow as he led her to Wheeler, and then the old woman was there, staring down at her.

"You must be a strong one," she said. "Strong enough to survive a tecuani bite, huh?"

Wheeler tried to speak but her throat was too dry, and the only thing that would come out was a hoarse croak. The witch clucked her tongue.

"Tsh tsh tsh. Don't talk. Don't talk. Let Mrs. Feldman do her work."

She shuffled over to an ancient hutch across the room, her wool skirt swishing, carrying in its folds secrets deep and dank. The drawers creaked as she opened them and rummaged around, muttering under her breath, head hung low, looking nothing like the stout figure that fought off that monster in the alley. The language she spoke was strange, sometimes harsh and guttural, sometimes sweet and melodic. Demon wound around her feet, and she hooked her leather boot under him and deftly lifted him aside.

"Where are you, you little sneak?" she said. "Ah!"

She returned to Wheeler, a jar filled with clear liquid in her hand. "Drink this."

She propped Wheeler's neck up and, before she could protest, poured the liquid into her mouth, then pinched her nose shut. It was thick and sweet, and when she swallowed, it coated her throat and spread warm and gentle into her belly. She felt fuzzy.

"Nothing like spug juice to coat the throat," the witch said, laying her back down. "You got you an ache here, huh?"

She pressed her thumb into the wound in Wheeler's shoulder and Wheeler screamed, the pain clearing her head.

"Uh huh, uh huh. That's what I thought."

She pressed her thumb in again, deeper this time, and again Wheeler screamed. When her vision went black in the corners of her eyes and she started to pass out, the old crone slapped her awake with her other hand.

"Don't be such a baby. It's just a sting. Maybe you shouldn't be drinking in the alley, huh? Not the best idea for a pretty girl. Me, maybe." She squeezed Wheeler's bicep, elbow, and forearm. "You feel that?"

Wheeler moaned a little, and the old woman slapped her again.

"You feel anything?"

Wheeler pushed through the pain and the wooziness to think. Had she felt that? Felt that at all?

"No," she managed.

"Uh huh. Uh huh."

The old woman turned around again. Wheeler reached out, meaning to grab her by the wrist, but her numb fingers wouldn't cooperate, and all she managed to do was hook her thumb in one of the folds of her coat.

"Gonna . . . gonna . . ."

"What? What's that? Speak up! I can't hear you."

"Get . . . you. Bitch."

The old woman recoiled. Her mouth worked and her face cycled through an array of emotions—anger, hatred, melancholy, bemusement—before settling, finally, on one she felt best suited her actual feelings on the matter. A smile. She burst out laughing.

"Bwah ha ha ha ha! Did you hear that, Demon? She called me a bitch!"

Demon merely sat, his blue eyes calm and expressionless. The old woman's mirth died with his lack of a reaction, and she grabbed Wheeler by the upper arm again, and again Wheeler writhed in agony. She shoved her wrinkled, leathery face up to Wheeler's smooth, healthy one. Her breath smelled like garlic and onions.

"I'm a witch, not a bitch," she snarled. Her warty lip curled in disgust, and she held it there, quivering. "But I might be a bitchy witch!"

She guffawed again, spittle flying out of her mouth and landing on Wheeler's cheeks. The old woman was too taken with her own joke to notice.

"You hear that, Demon! I'm a bitchy witch!"

Demon meowed.

"Don't you dare agree with me, you filthy animal."

Demon meowed again.

"You're damn right it's a good joke. I'm a funny witch! A funny bitch! A funny bitchy witch!"

Then she turned and danced back into her kitchen, singing, "A witchy bitch! A bitchy witch!"

Wheeler didn't care. The pain had returned, roiling through her body. She took deep breaths, willing it to subside. It was a trick she'd learned as a child when her father fell a little too deep into the bottle, grew a little too loose with his fists. It might take a while, but she learned that if she tried hard enough, if she focused on her breathing and not the pain, that she could go somewhere else, somewhere where she didn't feel anything, where she was still herself but not in herself. It helped when her face was bruised and swelling, and it helped with the cancer treatments, the fear and the nausea. Now, however, she couldn't make it work. Maybe the wounds were too deep, deeper than those her father used to make. Maybe it was the room, the crazy woman, the strange cat, the shapeless form lying in the corner. Whatever it was, the pain wouldn't go away. But she did grow calm. She did grow centered.

She was going to get out of this. The old woman, whoever or whatever she was . . . she'd seen her kind before. Raving in the streets. Pounding limb and forehead against the pink pads of the rubber room. They were frightening at first, that was true, but no different than any of the other fine specimens of humanity she dealt with on a regular basis. To be honest, the drunks were worse. Violent and unpredictable. The druggies and the mentally ill had hard definitions. She knew how to subdue PCP. She knew how to corral dementia. But the drunks turned on her, like her father, and even though she knew how to swallow the rage and the fear, it always crept up on her when she confronted one. A lump in the throat. A ball of energy in her chest. Freaked her out and angered her all at once.

But this old woman, well, it'd be easier if the roles were reversed, wouldn't it? Usually all it took was a shot to the arm to put one down. Thorazine for the truly violent. Ativan or Haldol for the merely whacked-out. But that wouldn't help now. Not only was the lunatic the one in charge, but she was in her own kitchen, with access to forks and knives and cutting boards and God knew how many other tools. Wheeler blinked the tears out of her eyes and let her head roll to the side again. The shapeless form in the corner, she saw what it was now. The forearm of the beast from the alley. Partially eaten.

The witch came back into the room holding a black iron kettle by the handle with two oven mitts dyed the color of blood. The kettle was etched with arcane runes, and unspeakable designs, and its contents boiled and snapped, smelling like rotting fish mixed with bleach. In the other hand, she held a long, thin, serrated knife. Perfect for carving meat.

"Tut tut, yer time is up!" she said, placing the kettle on the ground.

Wheeler jerked against her restraints, but they wouldn't give.

"Wait," she said. "Please."

The witch stared at her levelly for a moment, and Wheeler thought she might have read some pity there, as if in that one moment her feature's softened. But she was wrong.

"Oh my little dearie," the witch said. "How else we gonna get them little squirmies out?"

Then she jammed the knife into her arm and started to saw.

Wheeler came around sometime later to the sound of the old woman singing again.

"Buggies, buggies, come outside. No more flesh for you to hide." She felt something tugging around inside her. "C'mon, c'mon. Trying to hide, eh? Ah ha!"

Wheeler moaned, and the witch said, "Awake now, are you? Good. You'll want to see this."

She squeezed Wheeler's cheeks with one calloused hand and turned her head. The witch had cut her arm the entire length of the muscle, from her shoulder to the crook of her elbow. Jagged and torn, it looked less like a surgeon's cut and more like the kind a butcher might make. Not that she expected anything different. The only consolation was that she couldn't feel a thing. Her entire side had gone numb from the neck down. The witch pointed at the exposed meat.

"See that?"

Wheeler shook her head, and the witch frowned into the wound. She started to whistle, high pitched and atonal, and when that didn't give her what she wanted, she stopped and spat on the ground, disgusted.

"Little buggers is playing hide and seek." She wiped her hands on her dirty skirt and held up a sooty thumb and finger. "Looks like I'll have to pinch them out myself." Then she pushed them into Wheeler's arm. She poked and prodded, eyes rolled to the ceiling, tongue popping out, like she was rooting around for change between a pair of couch cushions. Finally, she snagged something.

"Uh uh uh," she said.

Wheeler felt a tug deep in the muscle.

"C'mon, get you here you little demon."

Demon meowed.

"Not you, Demon. This demon here. Ha!"

She pulled out a ball about the size of a marble and held it up to the brown light for both of them to see.

"Nasty little fucker, isn't he?"

Wheeler cleared her throat, smacked her lips. When she spoke, her voice was little more than a scratchy rasp.

"What is it?"

"It's a little squabby. Burrowing inwards to turn your innards into outards."

The relief came slow, but it did come. Her arm, still numb, seemed a little lighter. The witch put the squirming egg on the table, grabbed the knife, and pinned it to the wood. Then, picking up the cauldron, she gave Wheeler a brown-toothed smile.

"Now we'll show the cunt, won't we?"

She splashed a dollop of the boiling concoction onto the pellet, and it squealed, high pitched, louder than Wheeler thought possible.

"Aw, poor baby."

"Is that what made my arm hurt so bad?"

The witch steered the cauldron over her arm.

"One of many, dearie," she said.

Then she up-ended it into the open wound.

Later.

She awoke with a gasp, as if breaking the surface of a deep pool. The numbness had subsided, and a dull ache that ran deep to the bone pulsed in her shoulder. She looked at it and saw that she'd been branded. She couldn't tell what they were; the brand was too fresh, the skin too swollen, to see anything but puffy skin.

Something tickled her forearm, and she looked down to see Demon licking the gash in her arm. Or what was left of it. The skin had healed. Wherever the cat licked, the wound sewed itself up. He stopped abruptly, leaving a few inches open, and gave her a placid look, licking his chops and purring. Wheeler laughed a little. Then something in her arm disturbed him, and he backed away, his back arched, and let up a growl.

"Huh?" the witch called from the kitchen.

The cat yowled again, this time partially swallowing it at the end, and the witch bustled back into the room, wiping her hands on her coat.

"That's impossible. Let me see."

She shoved him off the table and leaned in to inspect Wheeler's arm, humphing and unsatisfied. She sniffed the edges, once, twice, then drew back, more intrigued than anything else. Then she eyeballed the dead egg pinned down by the knife.

"What's this then?" Then, to Wheeler, "Bad news for you, missus. Bad news for you."

She unbuckled the straps holding Wheeler down and helped her sit up. When she saw the last two inches of the gash still open, she tsked and shook her head.

"Demon! Finish the job, damn you!" and bustled back to the kitchen. The cat hopped back up on the table and started licking Wheeler's arm, and Wheeler, bemused and amazed, watched the last of the skin sew shut. When he was done, she said, "Uh, thanks?"

"Don't you thank that demon!" the witch cried from the kitchen. "He's the spawn of Lucifer he is. Turn your back, he'll slit your throat."

The cat shot a baleful look at the kitchen and hopped off the table, trotting over to the monster's limb in the corner to finish his snack. The witch bustled back in, a steaming mug in her hand.

"See, look at him now. He's a killer. Eat up, you monster, eat up!" She handed the mug to Wheeler. It smelled of lavender and mint.

"What is this?" she asked.

"What is it? What is it? Fuck you, that's what it is! You hear that, Demon? 'What is it?'."

Wheeler thought about smashing the mug against the old woman's head. It would give her at least a moment to grab the knife, get to the kitchen. And from there? Where was she? Did it matter? She needed to escape, and—

"Hey," the witch said, snapping her fingers. Wheeler blinked. "Don't you think I know what you're thinking?"

"I'm not—"

"Oh yes, you are. Yes, you are. I've seen your kind before. You're a tough missus, a tough missus. Grew up around brothers. And your daddy, he was none too kind, huh? Always a man to tell you what you can't do, usually with his fists."

Wheeler, though shocked at the accuracy of the comment, didn't betray it. She put her nose in the mug and sniffed.

"Uh huh, uh huh. You're a tough one. And smart. There's a knife right there. You got a mug filled with hot tea. And a kitchen filled with knives behind me. But I tell you what." She tottered over to a hook on the wall and took down a stout, black cane. The handle had been fashioned into a silver ankh and red runes were burned into the wood. "You do what you're thinking, it won't be long before the rest of the eggs work their way from your shoulder into your neck. They'll fill your throat. But that ain't the worst part. As you're lying there, wishing you listened to that crazy old bat instead of beating her up, you'll feel them eggs grow and grow until . . . pop! Bwa hahaha!"

Wheeler didn't know how to react. On the one hand, she'd seen an old woman draw an egg out of her own arm. She'd seen a cat sew up a massive wound by licking it. It was real. It happened. On the other, this whole thing was beyond belief. And the old woman was, at best, unstable. She wanted to run, felt the need to escape in the very marrow of her bones, but didn't know where or how to do it. She was too terrified to even start. And what if the witch was right?

"Demon!" the old woman said. "Come on you nasty brute. We gotta visit your favorite skhatet." Demon stopped gnawing on the arm to loose a defiant cry. "Ach! It'll be here when you get back."

The cat took another quick bite before the witch hissed at him and moved over to nudge him with her boot. He reared back on his haunches, claws out, ready to fight, but the witch only laughed her chuffy laugh.

"You think I'm afraid of you, monster?"

Demon grumbled and growled but lowered his paws. He licked some of the blood off his muzzle, glaring. The witch ignored him.

"You, girl. You gonna drink that tea or not? Time's a wasting, and them eggs is quick!"

Wheeler didn't move, and after half a moment the witch threw up her arms and said, "Have it your way."

Then she raised the cane over her head.

THE RABBIT

So yeah. That happened. People came and went. They died. Ain't nobody came to let us go, though. Fuckers left us hanging on them scaffolds like animals. Tragic. Tragic. Then, a few weeks after Morty and Asshole done what they done and had did to them what they had did, we was awoke by a most glorious sound.

I opened my eyes in the gray light of the pre-dawn city, and all was calm and still. No moans, no suffering, nothing but the skitter of leaves on the asphalt as the new day's breeze kissed the streets. That and the crackling flames from the poor fuck who got himself burned alive the night before.

First of all, I wasn't too sure I heard what I thought I heard. I mean I heard it, but when I looked around to see if anybody else did, ain't nobody did nothing but hang there, lifeless and broken. I guess they all thought, "Well, this is it. They're finally coming to get us," but it didn't confront me none. My time in that jail cell taught me a few things. I seen and heard stuff that wasn't real. Brutal monsters with eyes in their shoulders swarming a fortress in a swamp. Twitchers swarming a snider on the hot black tarmac that led to a silver skyscraper. Bugs swarming the floor after a rainstorm, a chittering, insectile carpet.

Wait. That last one was real. I dined me something special for a few days when that happened, I tell you true!

But all them visions eventually dissolved into nothing. The monsters, the Twitchers, the skyscraper, I seen them and didn't see them, couldn't unsee them, but they wasn't there no more. So it was with them voices. No sense in freaking out. They'd disappear soon enough. Might as well enjoy it, the ancient melodies and harmonies, the soft, poetic lyrics, some ancient shit, sounded both human and not human. Beautiful, beautiful. It was so beautiful that I popped a boner. It was so beautiful that even Wildcat lifted up her head and opened her eyes. That's when I knew it was real.

Then they came. The White Robes. Hundreds of them. Men. Women. Robes so clean that they glowed in the morning light. They turned the corner right when the sun crested the tallest building on the street, spotlighting the path from their feet to ours, like Ra himself willed it so. Or Apollo, or Sol, or Walus, or Horus, or Yoyu, or Ravi, or Huitzilopochtli, or Kinish Ahau, or whoever or whatever the fuck you worshipped. Oh that singing was so sweet. And they really made a production of it, too, walking slow and ceremonious like, picking around the abandoned cars and barriers, finally breaking upon the scaffolds and filtering through the rows.

"Ten bucks they eat us alive," I said.

Wildcat snorted.

"C'mon!" she screamed as they passed. She tugged on her restraints. "Come and get me! Come and get me!"

Two of them stopped, a tall black schmuck and a short little Asian chick. They caressed her swollen limbs.

"Yeah, that's it!" she screamed. "Just a little closer. I'll chew your eyes out."

Jesus. I knew she was violent, but . . . Jesus.

Then them to White Robes did something I never thought they'd do. They started to untie her. Really. First they loosened the knots on the straps holding her to the scaffold, then they they unlocked her chains. Wildcat wasn't having nothing of that. She snapped at them with her teeth, gnashing and laughing at the same time, generally living up to her nickname. They avoided her plenty skillful, almost like they'd done it before or something. I'd have wanted to smack her around a little bit, show her what's what, but they took the opposite approach, putting their hands on her cheeks, stroking the fuzz that'd just started to grow back on her scalp. Must've been magic hands, because Wildcat calmed down after that, so much so that when they cut the last chain, she slumped right into the arms of the big black guy and passed out. Then he cradled her against his chest and turned around, singing to her as he walked back the way he came.

"Hey, Asian chick," I said. "What about me?"

The Asian chick stopped and smiled. Look. She was a cute girl, her. Gorgeous, really. When she smiled at me, I felt a warm glow in my belly, the kind of glow I got whenever someone as gorgeous as her smiled at me. But there wasn't nothing gorgeous about what she done next, which was draw her fingers across her throat two times and say, "Phfft! Phfft!" Then she turned around to catch up with her partner. "The fuck's that supposed to mean?"

She wiggled her fingers at me over her shoulder.

"I ever get off of this thing, I'm going to lose my foot in your ass!"

This didn't seem to concern her none.

One by one, the choir took someone off a scaffold and carried him or her away until I was one of the few still left. That made me a little nervous, like a kid on Christmas morning who don't see no presents with his name on it. ("Heh heh, come on guys it's my turn soon, right?"). Right when my nervousness turned the corner from Butterflies Boulevard to Panic Parkway, I seen her. The last White Robe. Heading right for me.

I ain't sure how to describe her other than to say she was hot. What do you want me to say? Beauty's subjective, ain't it? What's good for one don't work for another. In the history of beauty, there ain't too many universals. Except for Jayne Mansfield. Or Dorothy Dandridge. Or Bridget Bardot. Or Cybil Shepherd. Or Tia Carrere. Or Elle Macpherson. Or Kate Upton. So imagine the hottest woman you ever seen, and that's what this one looked like. Equally proportioned, golden ratio and all that. She had teeth. She had hair. She was hot.

By the time I stopped thinking about her hotness, she'd already removed my straps and chains and picked me up off that scaffold all gentle. I was so light that she slung me over her shoulders, my head and arms dangling down her back, which was pretty funny because when she turned and started to walk back to wherever it was she was walking back to, I let my hand slip down her robe and squeezed her ass.

I had visions. Dreams. A mechanical dragon circling a great silver bullet. A school in the mountains blanketed by snow, with huge, shadowy forms slinking around in the surrounding woods. And then The Widow Mrs. Feldman showed up. Ugh. Remember all them hot chicks I just listed? Why couldn't it have been one of them instead? But it wasn't. It was her. She was all fucked up, too, more fucked up than usual. Busted legs, busted face. And she kept trying to say something to me but I couldn't hear her, and the more I couldn't hear her the more frustrated she got, screaming at me, pitching eight kinds of fits. I didn't know what she wanted me to do about it. I couldn't hear fuck all from fuck all, and then the next thing I knew somebody punched me awake, yelling, "Welcome to Hell, asshole!"

When I didn't move, he yelled, "Wake up! Now!"

So I did. I opened my eyes. Like I had a choice.

First thing I noticed was that someone'd spiffed me up in a gray track suit and trainers. Premium stuff. Not my style, but premium stuff. Second thing I noticed was my body wasn't all broken no more. No more stick-like wrists, no more concave chest. I was me again. Hale and hardy, just like when I was a young man, before them cops locked me away in that cell in the basement. Last thing I noticed was I had no idea where I was, but before I could think any more, whoever punched me awake the first time punched me awake again.

"I said get up, asshole!"

"I am up, asshole."

It was some goon, some run of the mill goon. I seen guys like him a hundred different times, only this one had his hair clipped tight to his head. Never seen that before.

"You gonna get up, or am I gonna have to punch you again?"

I opened my mouth and he punched me again.

"Fuck's sake," I said. "You keep doing that, I'll take that fist and —"

He punched me one more time.

"Get your ass up and get in line!"

Alright, so fuck it. I got up. I was in the top bed of a bunk, so when I sat up, I dangled my feet over the edge, a little surprised at the strength in my legs. Man. I felt better than I had in years. The definition in my muscles, the ability to actually sit up without getting woozy . . . it was like I was brand new. Whole. Unfortunately, whoever was under me didn't share these personal sentiments.

"Get your fucking feet out of my fucking face," he said. Then he punched me in the Achilles heels. Both of them, first the left, then the right.

Fuck's sake.

"Watch it with the punching," I said. "I just got them things back."

Old heel puncher, he didn't waste no time. Grabbed me by the legs and yanked me straight off my bunk. I landed hard on my ass, and the next thing I seen was teeth and fists and nails. Logically, the next thing I felt was biting, punching, and scratching. I wish I could have fought back, but it was enough work for me to cover my head with my arms let alone strategy myself out of the attack. Plus, my specialty was sneaking and cutting, two skills that didn't necessarily apply to that particular situation. Actually, I did try something. I tried to knee the bastard in the nuts, but that only made him laugh.

"Do it again!" he yelled, and I did, two, three, four times, but that was about as useful as a baseball bat at an orgy.

Actually, never mind. Try not to think about that last simile.

Meanwhile, all the other dip-shits in the barracks (and they was all wearing the same gray track suits and trainers I had on) surrounded us, screaming, yelling, generally behaving like people does when a fight breaks out, which is to say like idiots. Maybe one could've pulled the jerk off? I'd had enough already, that much was evident. I needed for one of them to H a BO, which finally somebody did, at which point I realized why my ball-kicking strategy didn't have no effect on his balls, because the guy didn't have no balls. And I don't mean that he was ball-less, like at one point in time he had him a set and then magically, poof! they was gone. First of all, that ain't the way things work. Nuts ain't like skin tags. They don't just fall off. Usually. I mean, I guess you could tie them off with a rubber band and some twine and after a while . . . . And I guess there's always a good pair of shears, but that takes persistence. Determination. A certain threshold for pain, maybe a little pinch of mania.

Secondly, that's not what I was talking about anyway. Ah fuck. I forgot what I was talking about. Fuck. Fuck. Fuck. Okay. Hold on. Balls. I was talking about balls. Nuts. The boys, the family jewels, kiwis, nards, nuggets, knackers, rocks, cobblers, goolies, gonads. And the fact that the guy who I kicked them in didn't have none. Because he wasn't a guy. He was a she. Like Lola. L.O.L.A Lola. Only opposite. She'd never been a he, not to my knowledge, at least. She was Wildcat, to be exact. Same cunt who'd been staked up on the scaffold next to mine. The one who bit old Morty's cheek off. Truth to tell, I was actually happy to see her.

"Wildcat!" I yelled.

"Fuck you!" she yelled back.

She looked real good. Strong legs and arms and back. Athletic build. Not too shabby in the face. The goon who'd woke me up pulled her off me and put her in a bear hug.

"Alright," he snarled, dodging a flash of teeth. "Knock off the grab-ass."

The barracks flooded with goons, about twenty of them, all bullshit and bluster, waving their black batons in the air and barking at everyone to "get the fuck out on the lawn, maggots!" And so we did, all of us. I couldn't help but notice that every neighborhood in

The Neighborhood seemed to have a representative or two in attendance.

There was Satan's Sultans, Satan's Suckers, Satan's Sufti's, Satan's Shahs, Satan's Sheik's, Satanic Assassins, Satanic Assistants, Secretaries of Satan, War Kings, War Barons, War Tsars, 9th Street Sinners, 12th Street Saints, Ministers of Mayhem, Marquises of Mischief, the Devils, the Dukes, the Disciples, Beakers, Breakers, Bleeding Boneshakers, Baker Street Boys, Boulevard Bobbies, Vampires, Viscounts, Dragons, Dragoons, Howzits, Northenders, Southsiders, Champs, Chumps, Puglies, Fuglies, Cock Block Cunt Kickers (CBCK), Penny Anties, Hateful Hooligans, Cheeky Bastards, Greedy Bastards, Bloody Bastards, Bonny Bastards, Regular Old Bastards, and about nine zillion other bastards I ain't got the time to list here because The Neighborhood was huge and ever expanding. They didn't discriminate neither. They got men and women, white, black, purple, orange. The pick of the Neighborhood's litter.

On the way out, one of them goons took it a step too far and a couple of Cunt Kickers tried to fight back. Had enough sack to take a few swings, even. Wasn't like they had a chance. Goons is goons, and these was military goons. So them Cunt Kickers got themselves kicked in the cunts. Also a couple of baton shots straight to the solar plexus That was some right shystery baloney right there. Don't get me wrong. I'm all for dirty fighting. Got a handful of sand? Grind it in your enemy's eyes. Palming a razor blade? Slice his mouth to shreds. But that's only okay if the people involved knew they was fighting, and none of us knew we was fighting. We'd all just been crucified, what, twenty-four hours ago?

I guess I must have paused a little too long, because one of them goons got right up in my muzzle and yelled, "Get your ass out on the lawn! Out! Out! Out! Out!" So I put up my hands and let him push me through the barracks and out the front door.

The lawn was exactly what it sounded like. A lawn. A long stretch of green right in the middle of a half-dozen barracks just like one I just got kicked out of, ringed by vine covered oak trees, with a few magnolias thrown in for flavor. To the right loomed a forest. At the end stood a stage. They lined us up in rows to face it, screaming and carrying on and such, and who'd they put next to me? Wildcat.

"You believe this shit?" I asked her.

"Fuck you."

"Fuck me? Fuck you."

"You think I give a fuck about you?"

"No I don't think you give a fuck about me. I was just saying."

"Well say it to someone else."

All the other barracks emptied out onto the lawn, too, and while most of them consisted of your standard minga, it looked like the goons had also plucked themselves an entire contingent of, how should I say this . . . brown people? Don't get me wrong. I ain't no racist. I hate everybody: mingas, moulies, slants, wetbacks, and abba-dabbas alike. But I don't call moulies moulies, or wetbacks wetbacks. I call them brown people. Didn't matter, anyway, because them brown people wasn't brown people. They was the pyramid people BG was talking about. I thought of them as Top Knots on account of the top knots some of them wore their hair up in. They preferred to call themselves the Tlek, which is pretty badass as far as I'm concerned. More badass than Top Knots. So that's what else I seen a lot of out there on the lawn, a shit ton of mingas and a shittier ton of Tlek.

The goons barked and snarled as they marched up and down the lines, occasionally clubbing some poor schmuck in the temple or knocking some other poor schmuck to the ground. Other than that, it was a nice day. The sky stretched out over us like it always done, baby blue, shot through and through with wispy strips of white. And that lawn? I gotta tell you, whoever they paid to do the landscaping deserved a promotion and a bonus and a couple of handys, because that green looked greener than any green I ever seen.

Little by little, the goons stopped yelling. Wasn't no sound at all. Not even bug sounds coming from the forest. And trust me, after all them years listening for even the tiniest twitter, I knew what to listen for. There should have been waves of cicadas singing their song. And in that kind of heat, and that close to the woods, we should have been slapping mosquitos and dodging bees. I looked around to see if anybody else noticed. Even city people had to know that a forest without insects wasn't no good. But guess what? Nobody did. None of them. Not one Cunt Kicker, not one Pugly, not one Fugly or Hooligan or any of them Bastards had a clue. I gave Wildcat a glance.

"Ain't no insects in the woods."

"What?"

"Ain't no insects in the woods."

"Jesus, do you ever shut up?"

"Sometimes. You hear what I just said?"

She didn't answer.

Then some guy took the stage. He was dressed for a night out, it looked like. Cream colored fedora, cream colored zoot suit, two-toned two-tones. He glared out at us all. One of the goons wheeled a podium with a microphone on it in front of him, but he didn't take it up. He waited there for what, I don't know, three hours? With the staring and shaking his head. Maybe they was plugging the P.A. system in. Then he finally took his hat off, snapped the sweat off his brow with a finger, and leaned into the mic. Ah Zoot. I'll never forget the first time I saw you.

"Howzit?" he said.

A few of the Howzits spread throughout the audience gave a tentative "howzit" in response, but when it became clear nobody else was doing it, they went mute. Zoot waited a beat, then he said it again.

"Howzit?"

Nothing this time. Not even the Howzits gave him a "howzit." That seemed to seriously piss him off. He threw his hands up in the air and turned around, jawing at his goons. The mic picked up a few choice words and phrases, like "morons," and "dumb bastards," and "Jesus fuck!" One of them looked like he was trying to explain something, but Zoot wasn't having it. He chewed the guy's ear off instead, finishing up with a ". . . the fuck you know what you're doing!" as he turned back to the mic. He put his hands on his hips, parting his jacket as he did so. Then he turned to the side and barked out a foul word. I'd tell you what it was, but I don't think I can print it in a family publication.

Hey guess what? I just remembered that this ain't no family publication. So the word he used was "cunt." Worst possible thing he could've said, right? Well, not worse than "cunt-fuck retard," like "can you believe how stupid these cunt-fuck retards is?". I guess "cunt-punch" or "cunt-fuck" or "cunt-snatch" is all pretty foul, too, but my point is there was a lot of cunts out there, and they're bad enough as it is by themselves, but in order to make them seem worse than the cunts they already is, you gotta add something to the root word, (cunt), and that ain't fair, at least not to the cunts.

"Okay you cunts," Zoot said. He held out his arms all dramatic, like he was about to make a big pronouncement, like this was the grand finale, the show stopper. He took a deep breath, let it out, and said, "Howzit."

A couple of the Howzits tried again, but everybody else still had no clue what was going on.

"The fuck's he doing?"

"The fuck he want us to do?"

"The fuck's going on now?"

Zoot slammed his hand on the podium and the P.A. shrieked out some feedback.

"Holy shit!" he snapped. "You all can't really be that stupid."

Someone in the crowd yelled, "Hey fuck you, asshole!"

"Who said that? Who the fuck said that?"

The crowd erupted with laughter, and Zoot looked over to some of his goons and made a quick motion with his fingers across his neck, "Phfft! Phfft!" Just like that, two of them darted into the ranks and pulled some jerk out of line. From the mashed up state of his nose and mouth, and the cauliflower ears and the wonky eyes, it looked like he was a Fugly. Or a Pugly. Never could get them two right.

"Get your friggin' hands off me!" he cried.

The goons dragged his ass right up to the stage, forced him down on his hands and knees, and held him there. Zoot took the mic off the stand and leaned over him.

"What's your name, son?"

"My name? My name's Fuck You, that's what my name is."

"Oh, well, hello, Fuck You. I'm Zoot, and you're screwed." He gave us a wide smile and a wink. "So, Fuck You. You're a Fugly, yeah?"

"Yeah, what of it?"

"You guys is known for, what, some pretty nasty shit, huh?"

"Watch it, old man."

"You like to fight dirty? Rip off the ears with the teeth? Punch in the nuts with a shiv? Sand in the eyes? Slice the Achilles?"

Fuck You seemed to relax a little.

"Yeah. So?"

"Well, for once your miserable life, you're gonna have to play by the rules. My rules. Got it?"

Fuck You opened his mouth, but Zoot read the room and cut him off. "Never mind. Listen. I'm gonna give you a chance to apologize for what you said. Can you do that? Apologize?"

"No."

"No? Why not?"

"Because fuck you, that's why not. You know who I am? You know what I done? What I could do to—"

Zoot balled up his fist and clobbered the guy in the jaw. Fuck You spit blood and showered the stage with a string of curse words, but Zoot ignored it and, even though nobody was clapping, he took a bow. Nervous laughter dotted the crowd. He turned, put the mic back on its stand, and gestured to one of his goons backstage, and when he turned back around, he was holding a huge battle axe. Fuck You changed his tune when he saw the blades on that thing gleaming in the sun, you better believe it.

"Whoa, whoa, whoa, chief. Wait a—" but before he could finish, old Zoot raised the axe over his head and cut the guy's head clean off. It bounced once on the stage and onto the ground, followed by the inevitable spurt of blood. The crowd erupted, especially the Fuglies. They was yelling and cursing and threatening, but Zoot, he didn't have none of it. He grabbed the mic and raised the bloody axe over his head.

"Any of you fucks wanna say something, you come on up here and say it to my face."

I ain't never heard no crowd quiet down as fast as we did right then. Seriously. Zoot stared out over us, waiting for somebody to fuck up, but nobody did. And then, out of nowhere, someone did the best thing anybody could have done in that situation. He farted. And not just any fart, but a fart with the volume and frequency of a million infants—a squeaker, too, long and loud, like whoever done it had been holding it in for hours. It sounded like letting the air out of a gigantic balloon. I was impressed.

Not with the farter, and not with old Zoot, though that was some impressive shit he done. If this was a job interview, I'd of hired him on the spot. Nah. I was impressed with the goons surrounding the goon who squeaked out that squeaker. Not a snort did they utter, not a peep did they mutter. If it'd been me next to him, my head'd be bouncing in the dirt, too, because that shit was funny, and I didn't think Zoot was in the mood for laughter. When the fart finally ended, he nodded, as if the whole thing had been planned.

"That's what I thought," he said. He ran his hand over his face, like he was exhausted or something. "Every time. Every time. You know, I don't even know why I bother with you anyway. We need cold cuts, not cooked cock."

I could hear the eyebrows furrow with that one. Ain't nobody was brave enough to ask, but I knew what they was thinking, because what they was thinking was what I was thinking: What the fuck's he talking about?

"Listen up, fuckos," he said. "It's this simple. When I say 'Howzit', you say 'Howzit' back. Got it? Howzit, howzit. So . . . howzit?"

The collective "Howzit!" we returned was so loud that it scared a few birds nesting in the gutters of the barracks.

Zoot looked like he didn't know whether to laugh or not. Finally, he lowered the axe and said, "Fuck's sake." He leaned heavy on the podium. "I'll make this simpler than I usually do because I think you're retarded."

He pointed the axe at the forest.

"Don't go in there."

He pointed the axe at the goons.

"Do what they say."

He pointed the axe at us.

"You fuck any of that shit up."

He held the axe in the air again.

"I'll kill you myself."

THE SNAKE

Cihuacoatl Coatl, the High General of the skhatet's imperial army, stood on the wall and looked out over an ocean of monsters. They swarmed the jungle and the fields, surging in from all sides, tearing up crops and houses and people—anything that got in their way. Where was his army? The warriors from the villages? He'd sent for them weeks ago, but they never came. The fact that they might have rebelled crossed his mind. It had happened before. They must have been overrun themselves. The men on the wall rained down arrow after arrow, spear after spear, but still the monsters came, ripping into the corpses of their dead brothers, using the bodies to climb higher and higher.

"Pour it on!" he cried. "More! More! More!"

He marched up and down the scaffold that ran the length of the north wall, rallying his men, shouting orders. When the tecuani piled too high, he sent a section to tip vats of boiling oil over the edge and cook the things alive. The archers in the tower would set it on fire with flaming arrows, and the beasts would retreat for a time, at least until they found another pile to mount, and another, and another.

Coatl paused for a moment. He'd been in some terrible clashes before. The tecuani had attacked one of the skhatet's last outposts in the Pitzola Swamp and wiped out an entire regiment. And the plics with their toponis had destroyed village after village, pushing them farther and farther back from the edges of the empire, reducing the once proud people to a shadow of its former self. But this. This was catastrophe. He'd never seen that many tecuani in one place. He'd never seen them so angry, so aggressive. And they kept on streaming out of the swamp in wave after wave. It was only a matter of time before the walls were completely overwhelmed.

What could he use? How could he win? The adobe huts were tiny and difficult to defend. The aqueducts positioned too low to the ground. The only option was the emperor's temple, with its majestic stones and churning amber floating above the peak. The emperor could wipe out the beasts with a thought, use the amber to burn them to crisps and save his people, but he wouldn't. Maybe they could lure the monsters closer to it? Maybe the amber would react on its own? He'd never seen something like it happen before, but he needed to think of something. The problem was the pyramid itself. The height alone provided an advantage, but the stairs and tiered structure cut that advantage in half. The skhatet's engineers were not thinking of tecuani when they built it; they were thinking of men. Men couldn't jump between the different levels. Tecuani could. With ease.

The people, the farmers, the merchants, at least those who had survived the barbarity of the fields, had already flooded the temple's base. They were all desperately wounded, some with gashes from the talons of the monsters, some writhing on the ground, fast in the throes of infection from a sting. There was no hope for these. Beyond the walls, the eggs could take hours, days to mature. If a tecuani infected a leg or an arm, all they had to do was cut it off. But the closer to the source of the amber a man was bitten, the faster the infection spread, and the sooner the monster hatched. He saw a woman burst, and a tiny beast shoot out of her side. A farmer with a club bashed it to mush, then fell to his knees, weeping, to cradle the woman's head in his arms.

Coatl suppressed the anger, forced himself to think. They needed to separate the wounded from the infected. They needed to find better weapons than clubs. He turned back to the battle, seeking out a section of men to start the process, but then a portion of the wall crumbled at the base of one of the wooden supports, and a tecuani talon punctured the adobe again and again. He grabbed an Onton as he ran past.

"What's your name?"

"Xiuloc."

Coatl pointed at the wall where the tecuani had now punched a sizable hole.

"Take care of that!"

Xiuloc cursed under his breath. He jumped on the ladder and shot down, his feet barely touching the wooden rungs. A hundred yards to the west, one of the tecuani climbed over the wall and fell upon the warriors there.

"Breach!" Coatl cried. "Hold firm! Fight! Fight!" Then a beast vaulted over the wall and struck him full force, sending them both flying over the edge of the scaffold.

He landed hard on his back, knocking the wind out of his lungs. The beast pounced on him, the stinger shooting out of the mouth in its chest, aiming for his eyes. With a gasp, Coatl dodged it, then pressed it away, shouting, hoping to get enough leverage to roll out from under it. But the tecuani was too strong, its massive arms too long. It slashed his chest with a thick, black talon. Coatl knew he couldn't hold it off any longer, but this wasn't the first time he'd fought a tecuani. He pushed both thumbs into its slitted shoulder eyes. The monster reeled back, blinded. The stinger waved in the air, fluid running from its tip. Coatl snatched his obsidian blade from his hip and slashed it in two. The beast roared, prepared to strike one last time, but just as it swung for him, a spear exploded out of its chest, and another, and another, and Coatl rolled out of the way as it collapsed. Behind it stood Xiuloc and two other men, jaguar warriors, blades drawn.

"The wall is done," Xiuloc said. "We have to retreat."

Coatl saw it as he got to his feet. Tecuani flowed over in droves, leaping on fleeing warriors and tearing them to pieces with their talons, sinking their stingers, putting their poison. The people fled to the temple, using the stairs that ran up all four sides. The archers atop the pyramid rained down more arrows, killing tecuani and humans alike, but it wasn't enough. In minutes they would all be dead, or infected, or both. Unless . . .

He took his death whistle from where it hung off his cotton vest and brought it to his lips. Xiuloc and the jaguars followed suit. It was answered by the warriors all around them, Ontons, jaguars, eagles, shorn ones, and the people were given a moment of fleeting joy—joy because their warriors were there to protect them; fleeting because they knew they were outnumbered.

Coatl snatched up a spear and shield from the ground, and he and his men waded into the battle. They slashed and stabbed their way through two tecuani, unseaming one, slicing the legs off the other. Two more sprang on them from behind, shredding the eagle warrior with its talons. Xiuloc lopped off its right arm. When it turned to sting him, he stabbed it through the mouth and ripped upwards, cutting it in two. Coatl grabbed a maquahuitl as he ran forward and threw it at the feet of a cowering farmer.

"You want to live? Fight!"

It was their only chance. If he could get as many of their people to stave off the invasion as long as possible, he could make it to the skhatet, and if he could make it to the skhatet, make him see what was happening, there was a chance that they might survive. All they needed to do was use the amber, use the eye. And so that's what he and the men did. They fought, they pushed forward, and when they could, they armed the people with whatever was at hand: broken spears, discarded arrows, rocks, clubs, anything. It didn't matter if it was an old man, a woman, or a child. If they could wield a weapon, they could fight. And when they came across an infected, they cut off the head and dismembered the tecuani larva wherever it bulged.

"Fight! Fight!" they cried. "For your wives! For your children! For your skhatet!"

And they killed tecuani as they ran.

It worked. For a time. The beasts had not expected such vicious retaliation this late in the battle. Their lines fell back, however briefly, which was all Coatl needed. He dashed up the temple stairs, followed close behind by Xiuloc.

Four Shorn Ones stood at the emperor's door, fully armed and armored. They leveled their obsidian lances at Coatl as he approached. Xiuloc took his side. Ontons were known for their ferocity and blood lust; he didn't care who or what he killed, just as long as he slaked his thirst. Shorn Ones were fierce, yes, but he'd killed them before. Coatl twirled the maquahuitl in his hand.

"We need to see the skhatet. We need to see Seka-Khayu."

One of the Shorn Ones said, "Coatl. I know who you are. But we can't let you in."

"Your people are dying. You're next. He needs to use the amber."

"But he strictly forbade—"

"I don't care what he said! Let us in!"

They didn't move.

"I'm sorry, general."

Coatl took a step forward, and the Shorn Ones centered their spears on his chest. He didn't flinch. Xiuloc stepped up beside him, and two of the spears turned to him. The old warrior smiled grimly.

A stale blast of cold air hit Coatl in the face as he pulled open the heavy, stone doors. Xiuloc followed behind, his grimace easily mistaken for a grin. The bodies of the guards lay in awkward positions behind them. The skhatet's chambers were darker, and it took a moment for Coatl's eyes to adjust. Details slowly emerged from the gloom. Whispers from his right where the Gallery sat in the elevated stone booths. They were ancient and proud, with their bone awl piercings, their labrets and their gauges, their brands and their scars. The ornate headdresses, the jaguars, the eagles, were the only color in the dim light. The Gallery chose to be there, having existed for millennia during the brilliant apex of the Tlek, when the pyramids of the people towered high above the land, and the blood of their enemies flowed from the hearts of the conquered. Now that their time was past, they receded into the shadows and became shadows themselves, offering what remained of their power to the amber eye above the temple of Seka-Khayu, the last skhatet of their kind.

Seka-Khayu was, in Coatl's opinion, a mad fool, his mind and body twisted by centuries of royal inbreeding and one hundred years of drinking the amber. He sat on his throne, a misshapen leg sticking out in front of him. His crooked spine forced him to lean to the left, shaping a lazy "L" out of his torso. His head was overlarge and bald, and his underbite gave him the appearance of one of the monstrous fish the farmers pulled out of the Isquite. The bodies of the plics taken in the last flower raid hung upside down from the ceiling, their chests open, their hearts removed. Coatl had led the raid himself, snuck into the metal city in the middle of the night to kidnap the men for the blood debt. They had known the tecuani were coming; the gods would feed on the sacrifice and stop the attack. It didn't work.

The skhatet's personal escorts stood in the four corners of the room, seven men wielding white willow staffs. They were simple poles, with the typical designs and knots burned into the surface, the huitzilo, the ouroboros, the tochtli, ending with a gold scepter shaped like two quarter moons, inside of which burned the amber itself. The men wore the traditional uniforms of the Tlek elite: jaguar suits fashioned from panther skin, and eagle warriors with bleached bone breastplates adorned with feathers. As fierce and skilled as they were, they looked bent and crooked, pale from years of amber exposure. Coatl felt the old queasiness rebel his stomach. His father had been an early supporter of the fluid, brought it into his own home, used it on his own family. He could still remember the metallic taste on his tongue, and the terrible pain and nightmares that followed.

None of this scared him, but the sight of that old woman, the Crone, dancing a jig at the skhatet's feet while the skhatet himself clapped and hooted with laughter was bizarre enough to give him pause. The Crone's demon, her mau, wound between her legs, delighting Seka-Khayu even more. A strange woman from the other side stood in the shadows. One of her sleeves had been ripped off, and the Crone had branded her shoulder with her sign. As he watched, she doubled-over and vomited yellow bile on the tiles. Coatl had seen it before. She was infected. In the skhatet's presence. But why hadn't the process sped up? What had the Crone done to her?

Coatl struggled to contain his anger.

"Seka-Khayu," he said.

The skhatet didn't even look up.

"Ah, Coatl. Coatl is here. And he's brought a friend. Isn't that delightful?"

He addressed the Gallery with the last sentence, and they whispered their response, their mouths immobile, their eyes fixed. It filtered through the air like moths.

Beware ware ware are . . . .

Seka-Khayu giggled.

"Oh Coatl, they do not like you."

Coatl clenched his jaw.

"Seka-Khayu, we must speak. The tec—"

"What is your friend's name, Coatl?"

"My friend?"

"Yes, the man behind you, your Onton. What is his name?"

Coatl paused. In the heat of the battle, he'd forgotten. The Gallery whispered again.

Insolence ce ce ce

"Yes, I quite agree," Seka-Khayu said.

He pointed his finger at Coatl, who went rigid, for this was the power of the amber. It worked through his muscles and into his bones, taking complete control. If he was smart, he wouldn't fight it. He'd seen men try before. They didn't last very long. Seka-Khayu smiled bitterly.

"Your friend, General? What is his name?"

Coatl struggled to get the words out. His jaw was locked.

"Xiu . . . Xi . . ."

Seka-Khayu's smile was replaced by a sneer, and he hooked his finger and flexed it. Coatl bent over. Seka-Khayu straightened his finger. Coatl was forced erect. Seka-Khayu opened all five of his gnarled fingers, and Coatl's arms and legs thrust out. Xiuloc watched, terrified. The Skhatet held the General there like that for a beat, all of the muscles in his body flexed and rigid, before breaking it off. Coatl fell to his knees. Pain radiated through his bones, as if tightening the marrow itself. He felt hollowed out, violated, but he would not show any sign of weakness. He would not surrender any more of his dignity. Seka-Khayu turned to address the old woman.

"You see, Crone, how pathetic my own people are? Here we have the great General Coatl. Hero of The Incursions. Such a mighty warrior. And he is unable to withstand even the slightest touch of the amber."

The Crone forced a smile.

"Is it any wonder why I want to be done with this place?" Seka-Khayu said. He turned back to Coatl. "Your friend's name, Coatl?"

Coatl struggled to his feet and stood there swaying. It was no use. He was too dizzy and sick. Xiuloc, horrified at what he'd seen, stepped forward.

"Xiuloc," he said. "I am Xiuloc."

Seka-Khayu wouldn't even look at him.

"Xiuloc. Do you know what your friend is? A snake. I have a snake in my temple."

Obscenity ity ity ity

"A snake and a crone. Short the Brotherhood, you are the two greatest challenges to my power, with pardons to The Gallery."

Coatl gathered his strength.

"Seka-Khayu—"

"I'm making the Crone dance, Coatl. Do you like it? Come, Crone. Dance!"

He twirled his finger at the old woman, who hiked up her woolen skirt and redoubled her efforts. Her mangled face was red, her black hair sweaty and matted to her forehead. Coatl had never seen such movements before. They were strange and offensive. She danced like someone who'd been touched, a kind of soft, shuffling step, at times smooth, at others not so much, and every third beat she flipped an ankle out to the side. She hummed an atonal tune under her breath, supplementing it with snippets of words.

"Hmmm mmm mmm." Shuffle shuffle flick. "Whar shall we gang and dine the day?" Shuffle shuffle flick. "I wot there lies a new-slain knight." Shuffle shuffle flick. "And his banes are bare and his nut is whyte."

The mau wove between her feet again, tripping her up, nearly sending her sprawling, and Seka-Khayu erupted in fresh whinnies. He signaled for Coatl to come forward, breaking his hold on the Crone. She put her hands on her knees, heaving for breath. The plic in the shadows vomited on the tight-fitted stone again. The sick swam with squiggling tecuani larvae. Coatl made a wide berth around it.

"Seka-Khayu," he said, eying it.

"Oh don't be such a baby, General." Then, to the witch. "My apologies, Crone, for the General's rudeness. He is a beast on the battlefield, but the mere sight of vomit sends him into histrionics."

"Skhatet, the tecuani—"

"Yes, yes, of course. The Crone here was just telling me how a tecuani attacked someone from her side of the door. So tragic."

"Skhatet, they've breached the wall. They're infecting your people."

A sneer crossed Seka-Khayu's lips.

"You mean those petty farmers out there?"

Coatl was struck. Petty farmers?

"Do you know what it's like, Crone, to be the leader of a dying species, and such a one as mine? Of course you don't. You've never had such a thing thrust upon you. It would be fine if my people were in any way advanced, but they're not. They're farmers. They farm. We've spent millennia putting seeds in the ground and watching them turn into plants. And the fights. So droll and tiresome. We fight each other over what? Patches of land. Titles. Perceived insults."

"Seka-Khayu, these are your people," Coatl said.

"Don't bother me with that," Seka-Khayu spat. "'My people. My people' you cry. My people are idiots. Have you not seen the great things on the other side of that portal? I have. I have seen wonders. Why have we not taken it for ourselves?"

"You know we can't. It's—"

"It's what? Has anyone ever tried?"

"But it's forbidden."

"A fool's argument, spoken by a true fool."

"Oh, great Seka-Khayu," the Crone said. "I don't wish to meddle in your affairs. I only need a small touch, you see. A small touch of the amber."

"Amber?" He gave the woman behind her a cursory glance. "For such a creature?"

The Crone smiled up at him, revealing her brown, crooked teeth.

"If you please, sir."

Seka-Khayu gestured at his leg.

"You know what it does. Why would you want this for her?"

"This woman was brave and fought well. Made a meal for my Demon."

"Demon?"

"My, er, my mau."

Seka-Khayu considered this.

"That is laudable, but she isn't one of us, is she? Surely you don't want to reward her with death?"

"Better, sir, than what awaits when those eggs mature."

"Oh crone, you poor deluded thing."

"There's something else, something I found. Inside her."

"How quaint."

The Widow Mrs. Feldman became less fawning, less obsequious. She cursed under her breath and said, "Seka-Khayu. You remember my husband?"

"Yes. Recall him very well."

"He turned me into this thing you see today. I'm not a vain person." She circled her face with her hand. "Not much to be vain about. Not anymore."

"Please, Crone. You're a lily among dandelions."

She smiled half-heartedly.

"Oh no. I'm immune to your charms. The old man cured me of that. He did me bit by bit, until the only thing left was my nose, and it was a lovely one, my nose. Perfect. He saved it for last on purpose, and that was it for me. The night he mashed my nose was the night I became what I am today."

"Oh, Crone, you do tell the most marvelous tales. Full of passion and imbroglio. But your husband wasn't that terrible."

"I knew you'd say that. You gave him what he wanted."

"Just a touch, as you would say. For his 'animations'."

The Crone looked horrified. Seka-Khayu shrugged, bored.

"I was intrigued by his ideas."

"Oh great Seka-Khayu. Beware that man. He is a cheat and a liar. Working all the time with his corpses. 'My family' he calls them. Pah!" She spat on the ground. "Abominations. Monstrosities."

"You need not worry. He was unable to deliver, so I locked him up in my dungeon."

"And you think that would hold him?"

"You'll find out soon enough."

The doors to the temple shook with a heavy blow.

"Seka-Khayu!" Coatl said. "The tecuani are coming."

Seka-Khayu smiled at him, but there was no benevolence in it.

"I know they are, General. I called them."

His guards, his loyal jaguars, gasped. They exchanged glances.

Had the skhatet just said what they thought he said? Their previous calm and sternness was replaced with doubt. Two of them took tentative steps forward, willow staffs leveled. The skhatet spread out his hands and all four became rigid. He forced them to surround Coatl and Xiuloc, each of whom readied their weapons.

The doors shook again, and Coatl calculated rapidly. He had to escape. The main temple, rooms used by the priests to drug and prepare their sacrificial victims, were dead ends. No other exits existed other than the one through which he entered, no higher ground save the Gallery, which was unreachable. The door shook again, and a crack formed in the thick stones. The Crone took a step back.

"Seka-Khayu, our time is done here," she said.

"Such impudence, crone," the skhatet snarled. "I decide when we're done."

"Oh brave skhatet," the Crone said. "My brave and wise leader. Old Mr. Feldman was the last man to talk to me like that. I sliced off his nose and fed it to my mau. If you don't give me a touch of the amber, I'll do you the same, but worse."

All of the happiness, the teasing mirth, disappeared from Seka-Khayu's face. The Gallery whispered.

The knife fe fe fe. The knife fe fe fe

Seka-Khayu opened his mouth to speak, to denounce her, but the stone door burst in wards, the rubble cutting down two of the guards, smashing their staffs to pieces. A dozen tecuani entered the chamber. They lunged at the men, ripping limb from torso, slicing their heads from their bodies. Some jumped for the hanging plics and sent stinger into flesh, infecting them. Seka-Khayu stood up, arms splayed.

"My children! My babies"

One headed straight for him, and he thrust his arm out, sending it flying toward one of his guards. The guard, released from his grip, tried to react in time, but he was too late. The beast landed on him, ripping his torso to shreds. His staff clattered to the tiles, and the scepter broke, leaking its amber out to hiss and spatter. The guard next to him, also freed, turned on Seka-Khayu.

"Not me, darling," he said.

He made a fist and the man folded in on himself, bones crunching, blood spurting. His staff bounced over to the Crone, resting against her foot. She snatched it up, gathered her skirts around her and backed away, cagey.

"For fuck's sake," she said.

The plic had passed out on the tiles and the Crone, seemingly unconcerned with the attack, waddled over and knelt down next to her. She bashed the scepter on the tiles, and, holding the woman's head, poured a careful drop into her mouth. Then she rose creaking to her feet, grabbed the woman by the foot, and dragged her through the arc that led to an ante-chamber and the door to their world. She could see it, fifty yards away, shimmering in the warm glow of the torches. A tecuani cut her off and she put her fingers in the air, spitting out a curt "Phfft! Phfft!" Its torso sliced clean in two.

"Where do you think you're going, Crone?" Seka-Khayu asked.

He pointed at the shimmering wall and it began to shrink. The Crone huffed and puffed as she dragged the woman behind her. She wasn't going to make it. The door was shrinking too fast. She threw a look over her shoulder. Another tecuani turned the corner, sprinting for her. Demon ran up from behind and jumped on its shoulder. He slashed at its eye. Distracted, the thing reached up and threw him off, then the Crone stopped, pointed at it, and muttered an incantation. One of its arms swelled and burst. The creature squealed but pushed forward.

The shimmering door was only twenty yards away, fifteen, ten, growing smaller and smaller as she lurched along, too small for both her and the woman to fit. She looked one more time over her shoulder. A monster fell from the ceiling and landed on Seka-Khayu's mangled leg. He screamed and fell back onto his throne. The shimmering door popped open wider, and she threw the woman through. Then it slammed shut, leaving only cold stone in its wake. The Crone paused there, momentarily shocked. She'd missed her opening. There was no telling how long she'd have to wait for another one. Demon wound between her legs, singing to her as the tecuani roared, throwing itself forward, closer and closer.

Seka-Khayu screamed in pain as the tecuani stung him again and again, putting the poison, planting its seed. He thrust his hand at it and opened his fingers wide, and the beast went rigid and its arms flew open. Then he drew his arm slowly back and flung it forward with as much force as he could muster, and the monster flew out of the temple, crashing on the stairs, its back broken. It was swarmed by its brothers as they flooded inside. Seka-Khayu ten thrust his fist in the direction of the Crone. A hole opened up underneath her feet, and she and her mau disappeared in it, followed by the raging tecuani.

He made a fist, and the stones reformed, locking them in the depths of the temple below.

Coatl picked up one of the staffs from the skhatet's guards and weighed it in his hands. He'd never used one before. It was forbidden. The Skhatet's guards were noblemen, tlatoani, bred from royal stock, chosen for their tolerance of the amber. Coatl was royalty himself, having come from a long line of military leaders, but he was no guard. He could not withstand the effects. He never could. It was what saved him when he was a child. His mother saw what it was doing to him and forced his father to stop forcing him to take it.

The tecuani surged into the chamber, an endless torrent from the fallen city, a deluge of teeth, talon, and stinger. They were so fixated on getting to Seka-Khayu that they didn't see the two warriors. Not yet. Coatl pointed the staff at the wall over the entrance and willed the weapon to work. Energy coursed through his body, an electric thrum that started in his loins and flowed up his chest and into his arm. It was pure power. The scepter burst with a honey colored beam, emptying all of its contents into the stones. The wall exploded and fell in a sheet. Coatl misjudged its power, but Xiuloc had not. He yanked the general back toward one of the side apartments before the wall collapsed entirely, crushing the tecuani still streaming into the temple.

It was a brave act, but futile. The amber in the guards' scepters grew low. The tecuani were too many. It was only a matter of time. The guards tightened the circle around their fallen skhatet, and the noose of monsters around them cinched close. As one they turned and thrust their scepters into Seka-Khayu's body, his stomach, his chest, his neck, his face. His body went rigid. The amber shot out of his eyes, his fingers, his mouth. It cut through his guards and severed the wall of tecuani as it fell upon the throne. The light coming from within his body grew brighter and hotter, engulfing everything around it, frying Tlek and beast alike, joining the thick beam of energy shooting down from the icon above the temple. The air was sucked from the chamber. There was a moment of silence. Then he exploded in a wave of amber light. Coatl and Xiuloc were carried into the apartment ahead of the blast. It rocked the temple in a nuclear tide, and any man or beast directly in its path turned to ash.

THE RABBIT

I know what you're thinking. You're thinking, "why the fuck did all of you guys stick around that place?" Well me, I had me an investigation to run, remember? "The old bat's missing and we think Zoot's got something to do with it." Yeah. On top of surviving Hell, I had to play Sam Spade.

But for the rest of them schmucks, I think that's a fair question. First of all, the gray track suits was the ugliest things I'd ever wore. Hot and itchy, too. And they didn't do justice to nobody's figures. On top of that, it wasn't like the powers that be went out of their ways to make us feel welcome, what with the yelling and the torture and the beheadings and what not. In fact, you wouldn't be the only one thinking it wasn't worth it, because on the night of the day Zoot cut Fuck You's head off, three Bloody Bastards, a Champ, and a Chump tried to run away. Wasn't too tough to do it neither, run away. Zoot didn't post no guards nowhere, and the only obstacle to getting out was the fact that ain't nobody knew where we was. All you had to do was wait until two or three in the morning, wrench open one of the side doors, and walk out, which was exactly what they done. But if the running away wasn't the problem, the escaping was. The most important one. Maybe them guys got far, maybe they didn't. All I know is they was back the next morning. Well, most of them was.

Here's what happened.

The goons woke us up at about thirteen past Way Too Fucking Early by blasting Frank Sinatra, which, when you think about it, is its own form of torture. Don't get me wrong. I'm just as loyal a fan of Old Blue Eyes as the next guy, but you try getting woke to the climax of "That's Life," with the horns and the drums and warbling back up singers, and see how much you like it. Nobody noticed nobody missing at that point, and even if we did we was all too busy being pissed off to care. But then the goons herded us out the door on the way to chow, screaming, banging on trash cans, the usual DI stuff, and what do you think greeted us right outside? Zoot's bloody axe leaning up against the last in a line of pine box coffins. And inside them coffins stood the corpses of the dumb schmucks who tried to escape the night before. It was actually kind of thoughtful. What wasn't so thoughtful was what they did to their heads, which is to say they didn't have no heads no more. Well, they did, but they was just tucked under dead guy's arm, like a helmet or something. Actually, never mind, that really was kind of thoughtful, considering what they could've done instead. Nobody said nothing as we passed by. We didn't need to. The message was clear enough.

You know what? That wasn't even the reason the rest of us didn't scram, even if it was a pretty persuasive argument not to. I mean, you know my situation. And maybe B.G. blackmailed some of them other schmucks similar, but the rest of them didn't leave because, well, look. On the one hand you got novelty, and then there's boredom. Think about it. More than a few of us was older than baseball; one or two rode rough with Teddy Roosevelt. I was a kid compared to them guys, and I was pushing seventy. But there's only so much life a body can take, so much killing or fucking he can do, so much booze he can drink, so much vengeance he can slake. Death was on the docket for most. The suicide solution. Eat a bullet. Slit a throat. Take the old skyscraper plunge or dance the extension cord boogie.

But even more wasn't quite ready to give up the ghost just yet, no matter how empty life got or how deep into the vortex it settled. Some of my fellow recruits'd already been fading away for years, lazing back in their lumpy recliners day after day, barely moving, not talking to a soul, thinking about all the death and destruction they'd caused and not feeling good about it, their minds a jambalaya of regret and pain, wishing for a chance to do it again without all the misery, wondering what they'd done to deserve such punishment. Maybe they'd suffered themselves an existential crisis. Maybe they was depressed. But I like to think they was searching for the answer to the age-old question: What do you get grandma for Christmas when she's got everything she needs? Apparently crucifixion, starvation, and decapitation, followed by BT. Now that, that was interesting. More interesting than any of the other options.

So they stayed.

And Zoot tried to kill us to death with cardio.

The problem was that none of us was really expecting it. The cardio, not the killing to death. The algebra wasn't difficult to calculate: Barracks times X over crappy mess hall food equals military training, and military training is pure torture. And torture us they did, three times a day every day, morning, afternoon, and night, with an extra session thrown in at midnight every now and then to keep us off balance. They loved to run us on that gravel drive that spanned the length of the forest we wasn't allowed to go into, and let me tell you, them trees upset me. Made me jumpy, like something was in there, watching. Running next to that forest felt like watching a spider dangling over a sleeping baby's open mouth.

It was always on our right, too, that forest, no matter how many figure eights and button hooks we ran. When they got tired of running us in one direction, they ran us in the other, *and that frigging forest was still on the right*. I couldn't reconcile that one. Ain't no harmony that fit it. Like toothpaste and orange juice. Not that I needed to worry about it. At least not yet. Some things you just got to accept, and if the forest that should have been on the left was on the right, well then on the right it was.

To mix things up, they run us backward. Then there was the wind sprints, the two hundreds, the fifties, the four hundreds. They made us jump on boxes, sprint up and down hills, and every day in between that, a five miler. Christ on a crutch. You know who loved it all? The Tlek. Goons said "Run!", they run. Goons said, "Gimmie a thousand sit ups," a thousand sit ups was given. It was like they was born for this shit. And the fighting, holy shit with the fighting. Hand to hand. Foot to foot. Dick to dick. It was fun for them. They'd gouge eyes and bite off digits. Craziest thing was that none of them took it personal. Two Tlek'd get into it, punch each other's nuts off, and as soon as it was over, they'd be shaking hands and patting backs, even with each other's blood dripping down their chins. Shit was fucked up.

Wildcat, though, she did not enjoy her time in Hell at all. We had us some other chicks in the barracks, and some of them wasn't bad to look at, but now that Wildcat'd recovered from Golgotha, I gotta say, she was hot. And when you're hot, you draw unwanted attention. Wildcat's was drew in the form of some CBCK schmuck named Artie. I knew his name was Artie because he talked about himself in the third person all the time. "Artie" this and "Artie" that. Friggin' moron.

For some reason, though, Artie didn't harass Wildcat about her hotness, he just took a disliking to her from the start, and I don't know why. The first time we ever went for a run, he horned in on her and started yelling.

"Hey! You! Artie knows you! Beaver, right? No, Squealer. Where's my fucking sword, you bitch?"

Wildcat had probably fought off horny bastards worse than him all the time, but still, a guy like that saying things like that to a woman like that don't make it nobody comfortable, especially the woman. So when Artie yelled at her she went blank in the face, clammed up tighter than a witch's clam. Looked sick, too, like she was about to puke or something. Playing the mouse didn't help her none, though. Guys like Artie see that and they pounce like a wolf on a burrito.

"You don't got no hot sauce with you now, do you?" he said. "Artie's gonna fuck you up good."

Wildcat pulled farther away, and he yelled, "Artie don't let shit like that lie. You'll see! You'll see!"

A couple of his friends held him back, saying, "Calm down, Artie."

"You know what that bitch did to me?" They dragged him off, hauling him to the back of the pack, but he kept jawing away. ". . . sent me over there to find this fucking thing and give it to her, and so I found it and . . ."

I pulled up next to Wildcat

"Hey, don't worry about that guy," I said. "I got your back if he —"

She still looked stricken, but she acted all tough and said, "Fuck off. I don't need it."

But oh she certainly did, because that night, in the cool dark of the barracks, as we all fell off into the black twists of our nightmares, Artie and his friends crept through the bunks and surrounded her on all sides. Two grabbed her legs, two grabbed her arms, and one shoved a sock in her mouth and strapped her forehead in a towel. Wildcat screamed and fought, but there was nothing she could do.

"Artie's here, Squealer," Artie said. He dropped a sock with a bar of soap in it by his side. "This won't be over soon."

"What the fuck?" I said.

"You shut up or you'll get ten times worse."

"I'm trying to sleep here."

Artie whipped that sock over his head and it thudded on my chest. It hurt predictable. Took the wind right out of me. Then he and his friends did the same to Wildcat. Over and over. Busted her up real good. Bruised ribs, bruised lungs, bruised legs. And when they were done, Artie knelt down next to her and said, "Don't fuck with Artie. You got that, Squealer? You fuck with him any more, he'll make you squeal so good. So good."

Oh if that didn't get my blood boiling. The midnight rib tickle I could live with, but the rape threat? Given my past, I think you can understand why I'd have a problem with that.

Wildcat tried to push through the pain the next day, but she just couldn't do it. I wish I could say that she laughed in their faces and doubled her speed when the training began, spitting blood the whole time, but she didn't. She lagged behind the whole morning, barely able to function. Before you go judging her, consider the fact that I only got hit once by one of them things and I could barely run. You think you're so tough, you try it. Seriously. Wake yourself up at three in the morning, beat yourself silly with soap in a sock, and see how far you can run the next day.

Bruno seen it, though. He didn't say nothing during training, but that night after chow, he came stalking into the barracks like someone just fucked his cat. He and his goons went through their routine, shouting and screaming and banging on shit until we was all up and standing at attention at the end of our bunks. Wildcat was green with pain, but she did her best to hold the pose. Once it quieted down, Bruno took the stage.

"Listen up! Seems like some of you think you can do whatever you please around here. Seems like some of you think you're in charge of your own destiny. Well, guess what? You are sorely, sorely mistaken. Let's make one thing clear: as long as you're in Hell, you belong to me! Every last one of you is mine! Property of Bruno P. Huntington, esquire, and I don't like people touching my shit without permission. You touch my shit without my permission, I'll rip out your eyes. You touch my shit without my permission, I'll tear out your lungs. Howzit?"

"Howzit!"

He stared us down.

"Now I'm going to give you one chance and one chance only. If anybody here knows who done what they done to—"

I pointed down the row at Artie and all his friends.

"They did it," I said. "Them fucks down there."

Artie came at me like a bulldog, yelling, "You motherfucker!"

There's all kinds of stupid decisions, from "fuck, I overspent" to "fuck, I fingered my sister." But reacting that way when you're accused of something, that's "fuck, I fucked the cat" stupid, and there ain't no worse stupid than cat-fucking stupid.

The first thing Bruno done was clothesline the guy. Seriously. I think Artie actually thought he was going to be able to do something to me, but the second he started his bum rush, Bruno jumped into action. Stalked down the line, aiming right for him, and at the last second he stuck out his forearm and took him out. Artie went down like a wet sack, clawing at his throat.

"Who else!" Bruno screamed. "I want names."

Well shit, Bruno. You want names, I'll give you names.

In the end, there was six more bodies stood up in pine boxes the next morning. Zoot's Ichabod Crane All Stars. Wildcat strolled up and down the line, looking at each one. She had that key that wasn't a key in her hand again and was flipping it between her fingers. I watched her for a bit before I approached.

"What's that?" I asked.

She stuffed it in her sweat pants pocket, quick and guilty.

"That guy . . ."

"Who, Artie? Don't worry about him. He was an asshole. Got what he deserved."

"Yeah, but . . ."

"But what?"

"He said he knew me. I never saw him before in my life and . . . do you remember anything?"

"About what?"

"About before."

"Before we got here? Sure."

She hugged herself, the fingers of her right hand tracing the brand on her left shoulder.

"I don't," she said. "All I know is I woke up here on that scaffold."

"Huh. That sucks. You got you a bad case of the anemia."

She didn't say nothing. Just stood there. After a while I got the sense that she didn't want me hanging around, so I left her alone.

She healed up fast. Record time, I'd say.

The rest of us didn't do as great. By the end of the second week, guys started pulling muscles, popping ACL's. By the end of the third week, reality set in. Half of us couldn't barely move. The rest just flat out couldn't. Pain's got a purpose, you know. It's the body's way of saying "knock that shit off." Only problem was Bruno wouldn't let nobody knock nothing off. Screamed himself hoarse trying to get us to produce, and we tried but there's only so much a guy could do when his parts won't work proper. The body don't give a shit about nothing but the body. It don't give a shit about politics, it don't give a shit about sports, and it certainly don't give a shit about a guy like Bruno P. Huntington, esquire. Once that left ankle popped, the overcompensation set in, and once the overcompensation set in, there ain't much more time before the that right ankle popped, too.

And that's what happened to us. One by one, the bunks emptied out, and one by one more pine boxes met us on the way to morning grub. Freaked everybody out, I'll tell you what. Nobody wanted to get injured in the first place, you know, but when the penalty for tweaking a calf muscle was decapitation, you better believe the stakes went from high to "oh fuck."

Them goons didn't make it no easier on us, neither. One day after morning sprints, one of them came up to a Pugly stretching her hip-flexors on the lawn.

"I tell you to do that?"

The Pugly, true to form, popped up from her stretch, ready to fight.

"No, you didn't tell me to do this," she said, her fists already balled up. "You don't think I know what's going on here? I spring a hammy and it's 'phfft phfft'."

"It ain't your hammy you need to worry about," the goon said, twirling his baton. "It's your knee."

"Ain't nothing wrong with my knee."

Snake bite fast, the goon cracked his baton on the Pugly's knee, and the Pugly crumbled predictable, screaming, holding said knee.

"There is now," the goon said. Then he sauntered away, twirling his baton and laughing.

Some other goons hauled the Pugly away, and the next morning, you guessed it, she was stood up in the pine, head tucked up under one arm.

Shit like that happened every now and then, capricious like, but mostly the injuries came natural. Numbers dropped so low that they started combining companies. My platoon went from thirty to fifteen, so they moved us over to another barracks, which dropped down to fifteen again, so they moved us into another one. Of the original three hundred or so who watched Fuck You get his nut knocked off, maybe one-third still took breath. Fortunately for whoever survived, by the time week four rolled around we was all of us healed up. No soreness, no strains, no sprains. As for me, I don't think I'd been in that good shape since never.

One night at the end of the first month, I got to feeling sick in the middle of the night. No reason why. Maybe it was something I ate. Maybe I caught a bug. Long story short, I rolled out of my bunk at about three in the morning and, knowing that there was no way I'd make it to the head in time, did the vomit trot out the front door, ran around the back of the barracks, and puked my guts out. I was just about to head back to bed when I heard two people arguing out on the lawn.

"Watch her head, dumbass."

"Shit, sorry."

"Sorry ain't gonna cut it if we bring her in damaged."

"What does it matter anyway? They're just doing what they're doing."

"Yeah, but—"

"Shit's fucked up if you ask me."

"Yeah, well, nobody asked you."

I waited a second before I peeked around the corner. Two goons was carrying a Sinner from my barracks between them, heading towards HQ. I seen her sleeping in her bunk as I stumbled out. They kept bickering like that until I couldn't hear them no more.

BG's words rang in my ears: "We think Zoot's got something to do with it." Well, yeah, BG. Zoot had something to do with something, but what it was I had no idea. The Sinner them two goons was carrying was one of our fastest runners. Delmonico steak. She was also true blue. Never showed no signs of desertion. They'd knocked her out, obviously. Dark thoughts clouded my mind, and the red veil descended. I swear to fuck, if they was raping her . . .

But then the reality of my situation set in. There wasn't nothing I could do. I guess I could've blasted them two guys, rescued the girl . . . but then what? Take her back to the barracks? We try to escape it'd be me *and* her in the pine when the sun came up. But I couldn't just let something like this slide, and like I've said all along, I'm a creeper and a sneaker, so I did what I did best. I creeped and I sneaked.

Wasn't too difficult, even in the light of the full moon. The goons was too busy huffing and puffing across the lawn to take notice. I kept to the trees that outlined the lawn, and whenever they took a break, I hid. Followed them all the way to the HQ behind Zoot's stage, where they swung around back to a door with a single, bare lightbulb hanging over it. I squatted in the bushes while they knocked.

"Think he's there?" one said.

"He's always there."

"Old guy gives me the creeps."

"Join the club."

"I tell you what me and Gus caught him doing to one of them corpsesickles?"

Just then I heard the door creak open, and a different voice, old and gravelly, said, "you got the soup?"

"Uh, yeah," the first goon said. "We got the soup."

"I told you to wait until five."

"So we're a little early? The fuck you care?"

"I have the stock. The lentils and beans. I have the onions, the bouillon. I am not ready for the meat."

"We are."

A long uncomfortable pause followed. Eventually, the gravelly voice said, "Okay."

The two goons grunted as they picked the girl up, then I heard the door close. Okay, that was weird enough, but when I turned around to head back to the barracks, the front door opened and out onto the front porch stepped none other than Zoot and Bruno. I hunkered down in the bushes. Zoot was already yelling as he left, gesturing with a lit cigar.

". . . don't give a flying fuck how you feel about it, Bruno! In case you ain't noticed, we got ourselves a glory hole's worth of problems more important than your feelings."

"The deserters and wash-outs I understand. They was dead meat anyway. I'd rather it be them than watch one of my guys get killed trying to compensate for one of their sorry asses. But these guys? They're born again hard."

"The fuck does that matter? They're cooked cocks. We need cold cuts."

"That might be easy for you to say, but I work with these people every day."

"Get it through your head, Bruno! They ain't people. Never was. They're fodder. We send them poor schmucks into the swamp and they get slaughtered. Them things is thanking us for it, too. We send hot meat out there we might as well be giving them incubators and permission to fuck us all in the ass."

Bruno didn't say nothing. Then I heard him sigh.

"It ain't right. You know it ain't."

"You know what ain't right? Them things taking over the fucking world, that's what ain't right. You want to stop them? This is the best way to do it."

"Twenty of my guys could do more damage than an entire hoard of the things he turns them into."

"Yeah, and all twenty'd be infected before it was over and it wouldn't mean shit."

"Yeah, but—"

"There ain't no 'buts', Bruno. It's my decision to make."

"No, it ain't. No offense, but I don't recall you clearing this with the council."

"Psh."

"Because I don't think they'd like this plan at all. In fact, I think they'd have some serious issues with what you're doing."

"The council don't know shit from shit. You know that. They ain't fought these things. They ain't seen what they can do."

Cue uncomfortable pause.

"You know I agree with you, Zoot. A little. But this wasn't the deal. You said 'run 'em harder' so I ran them harder. You said 'wash more of 'em out,' so I washed more of them out. But this is murder."

"Six to one, half dozen to another."

"The fuck that's supposed to mean?"

"Potato, Potahto."

"Jesus fuck, Zoot. Speak English."

"You know what your problem is, Bruno? For all the wars you fought, you don't know fuck all about war. You think there's rules? You think there's valor? I got news for you. War don't give a shit about rules. War don't give a shit about valor. You know what war cares about? War. Blood. Carnage. Whoever wins, wins, and there ain't no such thing as a fair way to do it. You want to kick your enemy in the balls, kick him in the balls. You want to pop his eyes out with your thumbs, pop his eyes out with your thumbs. War's just happy you showed up."

"You trying to lecture me about war? I been to war, Zoot. It's the reason you asked me to do this in the first place. But this ain't what I signed up for."

"Whatever you think you signed up for, you made up in your head."

They looked out over the lawn, Bruno angry, brooding. Zoot smug, smoking his cigar.

"Look," Bruno said. "We got a month until the Battle Royale, right? The whole council's gonna be there. All the big wigs, all the chiefs. Let me get them through weapons training and—"

"Hello? You been listening. There ain't gonna be any of them left for weapons training."

"Zoot—"

"Zoot nothing. I'm tired of this piecemeal bullshit. The old man wants them all at once. Once we get the numbers down enough where we can handle them . . . I told him yes."

"Oh man."

"The council's thinking conventional, and there ain't nothing conventional about this. They need to see what the Old Man's hoard can do. I stocked the colosseum's maze with some choice specimens. When the Battle Royale comes around, we'll show them exactly how this war's gonna be won."

I didn't have time to listen anymore. The basement door squeaked open and I had to jet before the goons caught me out there. I hightailed it back to the barracks and crawled into my bunk. Couldn't sleep a wink, though. The only thing I could think was "We're fucked. We're fucked."

A couple days later we was doing boxes on the lawn when a bright, yellow light flashed in the western sky. At least I think it was the western sky. (I'll tell you more about this in a sec.) It was so bright that for a moment everything stood out in stark relief, our shadows burned into the grass. I'd just jumped off a box when it happened, and if I could've stopped in mid-air, I would have, but ain't nobody can do that because of Newton. A concussion followed the flash thirty seconds later, a deep sonic boom, and that was followed by a blast of warm air. I thought, fuck's sake, someone's got the A-bomb over here? The sky'd been lit up like that for about five minutes when Zoot ran out of his office, staring up at it like the rest of us. He exchanged a look with Bruno, and then went back inside, Bruno hot on his heels.

The next morning, Bruno had us all line up on the lawn outside the barracks. No screaming. No running. Just line up and wait. His goons stood behind him, hands clasped behind their backs, batons on their belts, while he paced back and forth, back and forth.

"Listen up!" he said. "There ain't gonna be no more running, understand?"

Everybody let up a big cheer, but not me. Knowing what I knew, I wasn't too excited about what was going to happen next.

"I know you seen what we all seen," Bruno said. "We had to speed up your training. You've made it through Hell. Now it's on to The Battle Royale."

Someone in the row behind me said, "You gonna tell us what this one is, or are we gonna have to figure it out on our own again?"

Bruno pressed his lips together. He looked like he wanted to say something that he shouldn't. Either that or he had to take a dump. In the end he said, "Weapons training."

"Weapons training? What kind of weapons?"

Bruno ignored it.

"You're ready for this. You're in the best shape you've ever been in. Remember your training and you'll be fine."

And before anybody could ask another question, he gave his goons the signal and they barked us into formation.

He run us a different route than we ever run before, cutting through a little copse behind our barracks and ended up on a dirt road. I wish I could have knew which direction we run in, but the sun didn't follow the rules of the galaxy. It sailed all wacky. Some mornings it rose on the left, some mornings it didn't. Right then, Bruno run us right into it, and it looked bigger than it normally did, like I could see the flares off its surface if I squinted hard enough. And we was going to be doing a lot of squinting because it hit us right in the face. We let up a collective groan, holding our hands up to shield our eyes.

For the first time, Wildcat didn't jump out in front. The whole thing must have rattled her, or maybe she just didn't feel like screwing around that day. Whatever the case, she hung back in the pack. I picked my way through the crowd and pulled up next to her.

"What no wind sprints?" I asked.

"Psh."

"You spooked?"

She didn't reply right away, so I tried again.

"Where do you think this Battle Royale's at?"

She nodded ahead.

"There, probably," she said.

I followed her nod. Up ahead, the top of a stadium peeked out over the trees. The crowd inside let up a great big roar, like it knew we were coming, and then another, and another. The stadium disappeared from sight as we entered a long drive with trees on either side, then Bruno took a hard right and led us under a stone archway and into a long tunnel lit by torches. It emptied out into an open underground training area that was barred off from a dirt field—the killing floor.

"Wait here," he said, and jogged off to jaw at a couple of other goons.

We all strained to see what was going on out in the arena, but a load-bearing pillar blocked most of our view, and the iron bars made it difficult to follow anything. I seen a couple of fellow recruits out in the dirt, jabbing their broken spears at something we couldn't see. More weapons lay scattered at their feet: half a ball and chain, chipped morning stars, and the head of a battle axe that Zoot would've loved. Speaking of the dirt, did I tell you about the dark stains all over it, and how them stains was blood stains? No? Okay. There was dark stains all over the dirt, and them dark stains was blood stains.

I thought the same thought most everybody else in the same situation would have thought: *What did I get myself into?*

The crowd let up another roar, and under the stadium it was deafening. Then somebody out in the arena slammed into the bars, and the bars thrummed, deep and bassy. The poor schmuck was ripped away, and the next thing we seen was his body flying through the air, end over end, right towards two other guys in the middle of the arena standing with their backs turned to him. Whatever threw him must have been an engineer, because he flew in a perfect arc, arms and legs sprawling, and took both of them out. It would have been comedic if it wasn't so terrifying. Off in the distance, a different pair of recruits engaged in a different dance, only this wasn't no tango, and it wasn't no flamenco. The name of this dance was the "cut off your friend's arm with a long sword."

Wildcat sidled up next to me.

"Told you something was up," I said.

"Yeah. I know."

"Bet you didn't think it'd be that."

The guy who cut the other dude's arm off with a long sword was cauterizing the wound with a torch. This did not appear to please the guy with the bloody stump.

"I don't think anybody would've guessed that."

Wildcat shrugged.

"Guess we're next."

"Yeah. Guess so." She started to walk away and I said, "Hey, uh, sorry about that."

"Sorry about what."

"You know. My feet in your face the first day."

"What are you sorry for?"

"In case, you know." I pointed at the arena. "I don't wanna go out with nothing bad on me."

She thought about that for a bit. Or at least she seemed to. Then she said, "You can die all you want, but not me. Nothing's killed me yet, and I'm sure as shit not gonna let whatever's out there do it now."

That was a healthy attitude. A little unrealistic, but healthy. I made a note to think more positive. Then Bruno came back, and that idea went straight out the window.

"Listen up," he said. "This is the deal. Normally I'd have another month to train you, but we don't have another month. So here's the rules: there ain't no rules. They let you out all at once. Pick up what you can. Kill anything that ain't human."

There was a thunk, and then the iron-bars creaked and whined as they opened up.

"Good luck," he said.

Then he stepped aside.

"Fuck this shit," someone in the back said. "I'm not going out there."

The rest of the rabble agreed, shouting out other choice words I don't feel like repeating here because let's be honest, by this point you've probably had enough of all that. I was almost tempted to agree, but something came over me. I don't know what to call it other than a grand sense of the absurdity of the whole thing. The crucifixion. The military training. Whatever the whole 'cooked cocks and cold cuts' thing was about. It was followed by a surge of confidence, like even though I knew that something bad was going to happen to me, I didn't care.

So while everyone else, even the remaining Tlek or Top Knots or whatever, whined and carried on, I sacked up, spat myself a fat lunger, and went inside. That's right. Me. Pussyfoot McGee. For a guy whose preferred method of confrontation was a total lack of confrontation, looks like I had the biggest balls in the bunch.

Right before I breached the line, Bruno pulled me aside.

"Don't waste your time with the shit in the dirt," he said.

"What?"

"You wanna live? Head for the maze. Use it."

"Okay. Alright."

I tried to leave again but he grabbed my arm again.

"We're still a ways off from the temple, so if you get stung, cut it off."

"Stung? By what?"

"Anything. You get stung, cut it off."

"Okay. What if I get stung in the chest? Or the head?"

He thought for a second. Then he shrugged.

"Jesus, Bruno," I said, and he smacked me across the face.

"Don't use the Lord's name in vain."

"You think I don't mean it useful?"

And with that, I pimped out into the arena, arms extended, middle fingers flying. Seemed appropriate.

Oh I wished you could've heard the boos. The boos and the fuck you's. In fact, there was so many people yelling "fuck you!" or "fuck off!" or "fuck off, you!" that for the first time in my life I thought to myself, "maybe they oughta cool it with all the fucks."

It took a few for my eyes to adjust to the sun, which was, of course, still blaring, but when they did I found myself strutting around a colosseum straight out of the ancient Rome. The fact that goons and goombahs from all over The Neighborhood packed the stone stands (Zoots, Howzits, Cock Blockers, etc . . .) was a given. That didn't flinch me. The floor of the place, though, that freaked me right the fuck out. So, sure, weapons dotted the dirt like, uh, weapons. In the dirt. But did I mention that the dirt floor wasn't a dirt floor but a wood floor covered in dirt? And that only covered half the colosseum, too? The other half dropped down about twenty feet, in which they'd built a stone-walled maze that extended back under the dirt covered wood floor. And that wasn't the worst of it, neither, because in the middle of the whole thing, half in the maze, half not in the maze, stood . . . well shit, I don't know what to call it. A miniature castle? An Oracle? I'm gonna say Oracle even though I think that's wrong, mainly cause Oracle sounds better than "stone building."

And if that didn't beat the devil to Tuesday, sitting on a throne planted on top of the Oracle was the freakazoid of all freakazoids, a weirdo in a leather panther suit, black claws and open mouth head for a helmet and all. Couldn't see his face, just a strong jaw with a bone through the chin, and a pair of amber eyes glowing out from inside the big cat's mouth.

(Okay, I just realized that "weirdo in a leather panther suit" might be mistook for "weirdo in a leather pant suit." Granted, it'd be a weird thing to see somebody sitting there in a black leather pant suit but that ain't what I meant. What I meant was what I said: a weirdo in a leather *panther* suit, like a suit made out of panther skin. A leather panther suit. You gotta admit that that's more fucked up than just some plain old weirdo sweating it out in a leather pant suit. It just is.)

And the worst thing about the worst thing wasn't even the worst thing. That would be the animals running around in the maze, and the iron-bared compartments cut into the side of the Oracle with more animals banging up against them. What kind of animals? I dunno. Birds. Fucking kitty cats. What do you think what kind of animals? The kind of animals that liked to eat people. Lions, most of them. A couple of pumas.

I kept to the side of the arena, trying to do like Bruno said, make it to the edge of the killing floor so I could check out the maze. The crowd mostly ignored me, though a few of them threw food in my direction. Pretzels. Pizza. The lions and pumas and such didn't seem to be too interested, neither, occupied as they were with finishing off the previous round of cooked cocks, so my little jog out to the edge where the killing floor dropped down into the maze was relatively uneventful, junk food tossing notwithstanding.

When I got there, I peered out over the edge. The open part looked like a swamp with stone walls growing up out of it. Scummy water. Itchy plants. Willow bogs. Gators floated in the corners. Or maybe they was crocs. Or Komodo Dragons. What'd I know? Not too many reptiles in the city, you know, and what did it matter anyway? They was there, lurking, waiting to eat me, as things like that was wont to do.

An electric whine sounded, like somebody'd turned on a P.A. system, then a familiar voice filled the arena. It was BG.

"Hey, how's it going everybody?"

"HOWZIT!"

"Right, right. Look, I just wanted to welcome everybody to the five hundredth Battle Royale. There's too many of you from different gangs in here, and I ain't trying to deal with no turf wars today, so you better have followed our no-weapons policy. I catch any of you with a gun or a knife or any of them maqu-whatevers you Cock Blockers like to use, I'll cut your throat myself, yadda yadda yadda. As you can see, the opening act is done, and our best and brightest is already out on the killing floor."

92

The crowd let up a grand cheer, and BG motioned for them to quiet down.

"You hungry? Get you a hotdog or pretzel. You thirsty? We got some genuine Tlek pulque. You don't like that, we got some beer, too. So sit back and relax and take yourself a gander at what our boys and girls can do. After this is done, you'll know what I know, which is this: them tecuani ain't got nothing on us. They're dead. Every last one of them."

Amidst the roars of approval, I seen a flicker of something out of the corner of my eye and spun around. It was Wildcat.

"Ain't that something," she said.

She'd already armed herself with a spear, well, half a spear. She even picked up a legionnaire's helmet, you know the type with the cheek plates and the neck plates and the red horsehair crest? It had a hole in the temple, which kind of negated the whole point of wearing it, but whatever.

"Which part?" I asked.

She looked around.

"Everything."

I pointed at her spear.

"Bruno told me not to bother with that shit. Says what we really want is in the maze down there."

She looked out over the edge.

"Fuck that. I ain't going down there."

"Yeah," I said, and I gave it a worried glance.

More recruits stumbled out of the gate, squinting into the sun or spinning around, dumbfounded. One guy tripped over a broken shield sticking out of the dirt and sprawled face first into the ball of a morning star. His body shook once, twice, and then he lay still. The crowd pointed and laughed and jeered. Then the freak in the panther suit stood up, holding his arms to the sun, and they erupted in cheers again. I heard the clink and clank of metal on metal, the groaning whine of more gates opening up, and two lions, a bear, and a wild boar stormed out from under the Oracle.

"Oh shit!" I cried. Fuck Bruno. I needed something to fight with. I searched the dirt for a weapon, but there really wasn't nothing else remotely close to effective in my general vicinity. A broken hame. A few scraps of leather. I turned to Wildcat.

"Where'd you get your stuff?"

"I dunno. It was just lying around."

"Fuck me."

Fortunately for me, the lions and the bears occupied themselves with the eating and mauling and goring of the schmucks closest to them, but the wild boar sprinted straight for us, kicking up dirt as it ran. Wildcat jumped away and it zeroed in on me.

"What the fuck!" I cried.

"Fight your own battles!"

Something glinted in the sun to my right. A longsword, or the beginnings of one, stuck in the dirt at the edge of the killing floor, right where it dropped off into the maze and the swamp below. I ran for it, the boar on my heels, hoping to snatch it up and decapitate the thing, or at least dodge aside and let it run off the edge, but, you know, the best-laid plans and all. The first thing I done wrong was think the sword was whole, because it wasn't. It was a shard. Sharp enough and dangerous enough, but not what I was hoping for. The second thing I done wrong was not get out of the way of the boar fast enough. It plowed right into my knees, I flipped right on top of the stupid thing, and we both went over the edge. I don't know which of us screamed higher. I hugged it tight, the shard of a sword snug against its belly, and we landed in a pile, me on top. Hurt like a motherfucker.

Here's my review of the whole experience: I didn't like it. Judging by where the sword shard ended up sticking that wild boar, I don't think it had a very nice time, neither. How'd I know? When we landed, it squealed like a, like a . . . well, you know. Ain't no other sound like it. I dunno. I didn't really think about it right then. I didn't really have time. I rolled off, moaning, my hand covered in pig guts. I'd got the wind knocked out of me, too, which was unfortunate for a variety of reasons because remember that gator I seen before? Yeah. I rolled off just in time to see it come running straight at both of us, me and Richard. (Richard's the name I just gave the wild boar.)

"Jesus!" I screamed, and scrambled backward.

Fortunately for me, the gator got distracted by Richard's guts. Can gators smell blood? I dunno. Probably. Did it matter in this case? I dunno. Probably. All I knew was that it chomped it some prime pork courtesy of yours truly, which bought me the time I needed to pop up and get away. So thanks, Richard.

Unfortunately, getting away was not as easy as I assumed.

First of all, that gator wasn't the only thing in the swamp. There really was a croc *and* a Komodo monster in there, too, and they burst around their munch buddy taking out his day on Richard's ass and came after me. Watching a croc run next to a Komodo monster is actually pretty funny, unless the croc and the Komodo is running after you, at which point it goes from amusing to terrifying in about half a second. So what'd I do? I done what I was made for. I turned tail and ran, ran right into the maze under the arena.

It was at that point that I realized what all that cardio was for. I felt like a god, I did, my legs churning up the meters, faster and faster. I actually managed to put a little distance between the two things chasing me, and seeing as running things like me down and eating them whole was what they was made for, that's not saying nothing. Light filtered in through the cracks in the wood over my head, and dirt and dust, too, and I blinked and coughed as I ran. The ceiling here was lower, and I almost felt like I had to stoop when I ran.

First I ran through a straight alley with iron-barred cages on either side. I didn't get a great look as I was in the process of running for my life, but what I seen didn't give me no confidence about what them goons had in store. Lions? Bears? Boars? Crocodiles? Them was just the opening act. Claws gouged my arms, my legs, even my face. Something wet landed on my right shoulder and burned through my shirt.

I sprinted for the first turn. Twenty feet away, and some fuckwit with a barbed tail sliced through my ankle. Ten feet and another cocksucker stabbed me in the rib cage. I wasn't going to make it. The slicing and the gouging and the stabbing slowed me down considerable. The croc snapped at my heels. The Komodo hissed. Then a foot broke through one of the boards overhead about five feet from the turn, shining a beam of bright light into the maze. The leg fell all the way through (only the leg), and hit the dirt. I jumped for the hole, managed to grab it and, like a gymnast, swing out of the way of the monsters chasing me. The croc got all tangled up in the leg, and the Komodo ran into the wall.

"Ha!" I yelled.

Then some asshole stepped on my fingers and I dropped down right in front of the croc. Thank fuck that didn't matter. Crocs ain't no rocket surgeons, you know. Once it was preoccupied with the leg, it didn't care about me no more. It just stared at me with them cold, dead eyes while it chowed down, which creeped me out.

That dumbass Komodo, though, it was pissed off. I never seen no Komodo more pissed off than that one. Truth be told, I ain't never seen no Komodo at all, affable, angry, cheerful, or churlish, but that don't mean I can't tell if one's getting prickly or not, and this one, it was downright crusty. But it took the tunnel to the right, so I took the left one, trucked it straight for about fifty yards where I ran into a goon standing at one of them secret chutes. He had a tommy gun held tight in his hands.

Poor schmuck didn't even see me coming. I launched myself into the air and knocked him flat on his ass. I guess nobody never taught him how to brace his neck because his head rocked back and spiked itself on a rock sticking up out of the dirt. He was in the last stages of a death fit by the time I got to my feet. I took his tommy gun and snatched whatever he had hanging on his utility belt: a key, two knives, and three one hundred round tommy gun drums. Took me a sec to find the selector, but when I did I flicked it to auto, clicked the safety off, and squinted up into the chute that led back out into the arena.

Them fuckers was gonna pay now.

THE JAGUAR

Flashes of crooked, black teeth.

Yellow bile dotted with eggs.

A pyramid silhouetted by a pregnant moon.

An old crone, speaking without words, desperate and afraid.

A rusty shard of a dagger raised overhead, plunging toward her arm . . .

Wheeler awoke from these dreams with a scream. Her head was pounding, her body was sore, and she had no idea where she was. She looked around, trying to get her bearings. Dirty bricks, scummy puddles, a dumpster. Holy shit. She'd passed out in the alley.

The new day's light cast shadows as the sun rose over the tops of the bars and bodegas and apartment buildings. A car cruised by and honked. Somebody barked an obscenity across the street. Even farther off came the echoes of construction crews and other noises: buses revving, the clatter of the META as the trains began their morning commutes. The city was waking up.

Wheeler slumped back against the bricks. Ugh. Her swollen tongue, that taste in her mouth, and what was that smell? She looked down at her clothes and, of course, saw the dried crust of vomit clinging to her jeans. Her shirt was ripped at the shoulder, exposing her skin. Great. Just great. This was going to be a hell of a day. Her shoulder ached to the bone, and when she went to rub it, she felt a strange scar there, a scar she didn't have before. She looked at it, frowning. No. That wasn't a scar. That was a brand. A triple-spiral. It was thick, too, fresh.

What the hell?

Somebody had branded her in the middle of the night.

It made her sick, sicker than she already was. She felt hollowed out, violated. Someone did that to her and she hadn't even stirred. What else had they done? But no, her clothes were still on, and nothing else hurt. Just her shoulder. And her arm. And her abs. She patted her pockets and breathed a sigh of relief. Her phone, her keys, her wallet were still there. Thank you, oh thugs of the city, for not rolling this poor damsel in distress. Or raping her. Christ she was an idiot. Drinking until she blacked out was bad enough, but passing out in an alley? Jesus.

She checked her phone for the time, but the battery was dead. Judging by the position of the sun, it was about five or six in the morning. She still had a few hours to get herself together and get to the precinct.

She made it to work only twenty minutes late. Peña, her partner, was sitting at his desk when she trundled in and collapsed into her chair. He smirked.

"Rough night?"

"No. I'm just not feeling good."

"I can smell it from over here."

"Shit. I put on a gallon of perfume."

"Yeah, I know. I can smell that, too."

Wheeler groaned. She nodded at the captain's door.

"She in yet?"

"What do you think?"

"She ask for me?"

"Not directly. Better take off those sunglasses."

She did.

"Okay. Put them back on."

She did.

"We got anything this morning?" she asked.

"Oh yeah."

Wheeler sighed.

"What?" Peña said. "You think you could have it easy just because you got drunk last night?"

"C'mon."

He didn't say a word, just watched her as she shuffled the papers around on her desk and opened up one of her drawers, muttering about someone stealing her Advil.

"Did you take it?" she asked.

"You know, you can fuck up your own career as much as you want. You want to drink yourself to death, fine. But I got a wife and kids."

Wheeler leaned back and folded her arms over her chest.

"I know. I met them."

"I can't afford to screw up here."

"So don't."

"You know how this works. What you do affects me, too."

Wheeler opened her mouth to reply, but she couldn't think of anything that wouldn't sound like an excuse. She certainly wasn't going to tell him about the relapse.

"You done?"

"Get your shit together, Kate."

"Yeah, yeah."

"I'm serious."

Wheeler stood up and turned her back on him, flipping the bird over her shoulder in the process.

"Anybody got any Advil?" she asked.

Nobody had any Advil. Nobody had any Advil or Bayer or Prozac or Zoloft or Lithium or anything that might take the edge off, even though she asked as nicely as possible, which for Wheeler entailed not cussing and almost smiling. Unfortunately, her almost-smile looked more like a grimace (no matter how hard she tried, always a grimace), and people usually thought she was either being sarcastic or that happiness felt genuinely painful to her.

Peña was gone when she got back to her desk. She took out her phone and opened up the photo app. She'd taken a picture of the brand on her shoulder and wanted to inspect it closer. Three connected spirals. She typed that into the browser on her computer, "Three connected spirals," and as soon as she did, an image of a screaming old crone flashed into her mind. She grew dizzy and sick, and her arm began to ache from elbow to shoulder. It was so bad that she had to grip the edge of her desk. When it passed, when her vision cleared, she found herself staring at her monitor. The cursor was still blinking in the form field, waiting for her to press enter. That wasn't normal. That wasn't normal at all.

"What are you searching for?"

Wheeler nearly jumped out of her seat. She slapped her hand over her phone and whipped around. It was Peña, mug of coffee in his hand.

"Fuck, Peña. You trying to get shot?"

"Not a good idea in here."

She minimized the browser and he shrugged. He went around to his desk and picked up his jacket.

"You coming?"

"Where?"

"Got a call from the Bottom."

He looped his badge up and hung it around his neck. Wheeler automatically followed suit.

"What's up?"

He pushed in his chair and strode away.

"You coming or not?" he said.

She made him stop at a bodega to pick up some pain relievers and a bottle of water. He filled her in on the ride across town.

"Anonymous call for a 415 at the Bottom. Blues went into an old warehouse in the Industrial Section. Found two bodies. 415 is now a 187."

"Drugs?"

Peña shrugged.

"Maybe. It's the right area."

Wheeler took a long pull off her water.

"Sip it, don't chug it," Peña said. "You won't rehydrate if it goes right through you."

"Thanks, dad."

"That's not how I meant it."

"I know. I was joking."

They crossed under the railroad bridge and into the Bottom. Wheeler always thought it was funny, the fact that the Bottom was located literally on the other side of the tracks. Of course it was. Where else would a place like the Bottom be located? When she was little, it was just the place where she lived, where she went to school. The violence and the drug dealers were just a nuisance, something to be careful about, like the glass on the sidewalks and the needles in the alleys. Her mother always assured her things would change, that the chronic poverty and endless cycle of brutality couldn't last forever. But it did, and by the time she joined the force, it had actually gotten worse.

She looked at the burned out buildings as Peña steered the cruiser through potholed streets. The old brownstones with the thick, iron-gated doors. The graffitied bricks. They stopped at a light. A shirtless young man sitting in the doorway of an abandoned building stared her down. When Wheeler didn't look away he said, "Fuck you."

"Friend of yours?" Peña asked.

"Looks like he wants to be."

The young man got up and spread his arms.

"What?" he said. "What?"

The light turned green and Peña drove off. Wheeler watched the kid in the side view. He'd wandered into the middle of the street and was screaming at them.

"Your family's from this area, right?" Peña asked.

"Don't you ever get tired of this."

"I don't care what color your skin is. If you're from the Bottom, you're related to everybody from the Bottom."

"Kind of like all spics are wetbacks?"

"Hey. I'm third generation wetback. My parents went to Columbia."

"A wetback's a wetback."

In the distance, the scaffolding of a skyscraper under construction rose up over the skyline, towering above the tenements, warehouses, and mills of the Bottom. The silver metal of its foundation gleamed in the sun, marred slightly by the cranes and rusty iron stages.

"Big tech's moving in," Peña said.

"Single Corp, right?"

"They put one of those every major city in the country."

Wheeler thought about the ads she was watching the night before. Viddy Viewers™. Nimble Digits™. Barrel-arm Biceps™.

"Upload your consciousness to the net, right?" she said.

Peña nodded.

"That's some scary shit right there."

"I don't know. It'd be nice to live forever."

"You serious? It's a sin."

"Christ, Peña. Not everything's about religion."

"It is for me."

"Not everybody's you."

"You'd really be fine turning your soul into ones and zeroes?"

"To live forever? Sure, why not?"

"What if the server goes down? Somebody hacks it? What then?"

"First of all, you don't have any idea what any of that means."

"Doesn't sound good."

"And second of all, I'd wait until the end, right when I was about to die, before I did it. Nothing to lose then."

"Ese es el argumento del diablo."

"The devil's got nothing to do with it."

"That's what he wants you to think."

Wheeler took another sip of her water. The pain killers were doing their work, and her hangover, while still making its presence known, had abated just enough for her to feel slightly human. She needed a nap and a workout to get all the way there, but that wouldn't happen until after her shift was over. Until then, she'd have to tough it out. She watched the skyscraper grow closer as they drove.

"They're already calling it 'The Silver Bullet'," she said.

Peña didn't answer, and Wheeler thought about an article she read about the Single Corp and the singularity, and despite what she said to her partner, it scared her just as much as it scared him. Her generation's fixation with screens was bad enough, but now there were implants and augmentations, predictions of being able to beam a signal right into their heads. And then there was The Singularity as a term. It sounded evil, perfectly suited for a comic book villain's master plan for world domination.

They crossed over from the Bottom into the Industrial District, leaving the close city streets and endless Section 8 housing for smoke stacks and train tracks. The paper mill, with its sulfuric stench and mouse trap twists of steel tubes, pumped cloud after cloud of white smoke into the air, and the abandoned power plant, with its rusty storage drums and cracked and busted windows, hunched by the river, covered in creepers. A few minutes later, they arrived at an old textile warehouse.

Two marked cars were parked outside. The officers, four of them, waited patiently inside each one, enjoying the air conditioning. They got out as Peña parked and cut the engine. Wheeler didn't wait for her partner. She exited the cruiser and approached the men.

"What do we got?" she asked.

The officer in the lead, a former high school athlete gone to seed, answered first.

"Couple of meth heads. O.D."

"Are you in forensics, officer . . . ?"

"Kowalczyk. No. I'm not in forensics. But I know an O.D. when I see one."

"So what makes you think this is an O.D?"

"The vials. The pipes. The yellow shit all over their faces."

"Yellow shit?"

"Yeah. Like puke."

"Yellow puke?" A flash of amber eyes, bared, black teeth. Wheeler shook it off. "You see a lot of druggies with yellow puke?"

Kowalczyk laughed a little bit.

"Puke's yellow." He looked at his partner. "They're just junkies. You seen one, you seen enough."

"Yeah. I guess they all look the same, huh?"

"Got that right."

His partner nickered. Wheeler glared.

"You check the back yet, officer?"

"Not yet."

She lost her cool.

"What the fuck are you doing waiting out here?" Kowalczyk's mouth dropped open. "Are you a fucking idiot? Go secure the exits."

"Yeah. Okay."

Peña approached as Kowalczyk and his partner left, muttering to each other.

"Way to piss off our back up," he said.

The other two officers, younger than Kowalczyk and his partner, came up.

"Look," one of them said. "I don't know if it's drugs or not, but it's something weird."

"Weird?"

"Yeah. That yellow stuff—it didn't look like puke to me." He glanced at his partner. "I've never seen anything like this before."

The inside of the warehouse was predictably run down. Dirt coated the floors, broken windows lined the ceiling and walls, and rusting equipment hulked, dead and dormant, in the corners. Wheeler had expected it to be pitch black inside, but it wasn't. Light poured in through the huge windows, illuminating the particles and the dirt floating in the air. It smelled like dust with an undercurrent of mold. She found herself wishing for a mask.

They found the bodies wedged behind some machines in the middle of the production floor. The first, a man with long, stringy hair, lay face down, arms and legs splayed out in an X. His entire lower back was ruptured, the meat and bone ripped out as if something had exploded from within. The other was a woman, sitting propped up against the cinderblock wall, legs spread out before her, arms hanging by her side, palms up. She was dressed in 80's druggie chic: jean skirt, mud-crusted Adidas, fishnet stockings. Her eyes were rolled back in her head, her mouth wide open. A huge hole gutted her right side, the bones of her rib cage cracked out into the dirty air. One of the officers pointed the toe of his shoe at the body.

"Ever see something like that, detective?" Wheeler shook her head. "What do you think it is?"

She wanted to respond but images flooded her head again. A puddle of yellow bile. Monsters with teeth in their chests. Ancient warriors with white staffs. Someone put a hand on her shoulder, and she startled back to reality.

"Detective?" It was the police officer. He was young, with pretty blue eyes. He looked concerned. "You okay?"

"Yeah," she said.

She needed to get the lay of the place a little better. A metal staircase on her left ran up to an open second level. Offices, most likely. Perhaps more victims.

"You guys check up there yet?"

"Kowalczyk was first on the scene. We just responded to his call."

"He say anything about it?"

"Nope."

"Alright then."

She headed over to the stairs.

"I'll come with you, Detective."

"No, I'm good. You make sure they didn't miss anything else."

When she was just out of sight, she pulled her shirt down over her shoulder to look at the brand. The puffiness had gone down a little, but it was still there. She was amazed at the lack of pain and soreness. Somebody banged on the doors behind her, and she pulled her shirt back up, stifling a yelp. Two shadows stood on the other side of the dirty window. Kowalczyk and his partner. Had to be. Kowalczyk said, ". . . knock that fucking bitch off her high horse."

His partner chuckled.

"What she needs is a good cock in her mouth. That'd shut her up."

She saw their shadows as they moved on to the next set of doors, rattled them once, and kept going. It only took her a moment to decide against reporting him. The department made a lot of noise about sexual harassment, but like any big institution, it was slow to take action when it really happened. She'd known women whose entire careers were ruined by reporting some kind of abuse. Oh sure, the brass made noise and cleared their throats and checked all the right boxes, but in the end, it was the victims who were transferred to the most difficult departments, put on night shift, had their paperwork double and triple checked. Some dealt with it, put in their time, and transferred out of the city as soon as they could. But not everybody had that option.

"Wheeler, you hear that?" Peña called

"Yeah. It's just Kowalczyk checking the doors. I'm going to clear the offices."

She took out her gun and climbed the stairs, aiming it before her. About two-thirds of the way up, her eyes grew level with the floor. She stopped. There, about ten feet away, lay another body. Male. Face down.

"I got another one up here!" she yelled over her shoulder.

She trotted up the steps and knelt down to check his pulse. That's when she saw his lower back. It was bulging with a tumor the size of a soccer ball.

"Peña!"

At the sound of her voice, he gasped to life and grabbed onto her leg.

"Fuck!" she yelled, and stood up, yanking herself out of his grip.

He reached for her.

"Heeeeeelp."

"Peña call a medic!"

"What?"

"Call a fucking medic!"

The man went into convulsions, his back arching, his head banging against the aluminum scaffolding. Wheeler wanted to comfort him but the thought of touching him made her skin crawl.

"Peña!"

"I'm calling!"

The tumor on the man's back swelled larger and larger. His seizure stopped and he collapsed. Wheeler held her breath. She waited. Nothing.

"Peña!"

"I can't get a signal!"

"Well then go—"

The tumor exploded in a spray of yellow fluid, and . . . something . . . shot out. She didn't know how to describe it. The best she could come up with was a black ball of slime, a black ball of slime with legs and arms but no head. It landed on the metal grid of the walkway ten feet behind the (now dead) man. She took a step down to brace herself and fired three shots. They went wild, pinging off the frame. The creature snapped to life and galloped straight for her, leaving a trail in its wake. She fired again, but it zigged to the left. She squeezed off another four rounds, hitting it finally in its hindquarters. It yelped and stumbled but kept coming on, a small hitch in its step. Wheeler kept firing, took two more steps down, and then it was there, right in front of her. She ducked as it jumped, covering her head, closing her eyes and mouth. She didn't what whatever that yellow slime was getting anywhere near her. It sailed down the stairs and landed at the bottom just as Peña and the other officers ran up. They opened fire, and the beast crashed through the window and was gone. Peña turned to Wheeler.

"You okay?"

She stood up, checking herself for any of that yellow slime. It was spattered all over the rungs and railing, but she was clean.

"Yeah."

"What the fuck was that?"

"I think . . . I don't know what it was. It came out of that vic's back."

The slime crackled and hissed on the plates of the stairs, and she could see little round things squirming around in it. She edged around each one as she walked down, covering her mouth and nose with her hand. Kowalczyk and his partner blustered around the corner, red-faced and out of breath, guns drawn.

"What the fuck happened?" Kowalczyk asked.

Peña pointed up.

"We got another dead junkie on the second floor, asshole. I thought you said you checked the whole place out."

"We did."

"Obviously you didn't look too hard."

"Shit."

"Shit's right. Now go out front and call for the coroner's office."

"I thought you already called it in?" Wheeler said.

Peña held up his phone.

"No signal."

"I could have told you that," Kowalczyk said as he headed for the double doors. He stopped for a second, noticing the yellow slime on the window pane. "You see this?" he said, and leaned close to inspect it. A little too close.

"Don't!" Wheeler cried.

But it was too late. He winced and drew his head back sharply, barking out a clipped, "Fuck!"

He gave a powerful farmer's blow out of each nostril.

"Fucking shit went up my nose!" he said. He snorted and spat on the ground. "Goddamn, that's disgusting. What is it?"

"Christ, Kowalczyk," one of the other officers said. "You're an idiot."

THE SNAKE

Coatl felt the weight before he opened his eyes. On his right foot, his lower back, his left shoulder. It wasn't crushing him. Not yet. He tried to bite back the pain, but it hurt so ba—

Stop.

Tlek generals did not feel pain. Yes, he was trapped, but he could breathe. And the pain was nothing; nothing crushed, nothing broken. He would find a way out. He had to. First, he pulled his arms into his body, feeling the rocks that covered him shift and fall away. He wasn't as deep as he initially thought, was he? In fact, when he pushed himself up, nearly all of the rubble fell away, leaving only his right foot caught. He pulled on it twice, but it was stuck tight, wedged between two massive blocks. There was no way to free it without some kind of leverage.

He looked around to get his bearings. The archway was clogged with debris, completely blocking his escape, and the bulk of the chamber was filled with rolling mountains of limestone, sandstone, and chunks of wood. Two of Seka-Khayu's guards lay dismembered on top of it all, their staffs resting in their open palms, just out of reach. A half dozen other men were scattered about, some in pieces, some sticking out of the wreckage as if they'd been a part of the construction. The rest of the chamber, about a third, was untouched.

As he surveyed the room, a noise came from the other side of the arch. Tecuani. It had to be. Someone behind him groaned. Another guard, buried up to his chest. He opened his eyes, gasping, and Coatl waved his hands, trying to get his attention. The guard moaned again, louder this time, and the general picked up a rock and threw it, striking the wall. The guard looked up, surprised. Coatl held his finger to his lips. He pointed at the archway. Still in pain, the guard nodded. He understood. But another guard somewhere out of sight didn't. He came around and started to scream.

"Ahmo! Ahmo! Ximocahua!" Coatl hissed. *No! No! Stop!* but the man was out of his mind.

The noise on the other side of the arc grew louder, and something swept aside a swath of the rubble blocking the way. Coatl fell flat, his stomach pressing into a sharp rock. He swallowed the cry, sucked in his breath, and waited. Nothing at first, then the sound of one of the beasts as it jumped onto the debris and crunched over the stones, then another one, and another. He remembered his maquahuitl and felt along his belt for it, but it wasn't there. It must have fallen off in the blast. The staff, the guard's staff, was his only hope. He dared to lift his head and peek up over the rocks. There they were, three full-grown tecuani, stealthily picking over the wreckage, infecting whatever flesh they came upon. Once, twice, and double that again. Soon the chamber would be filled with their kind, the monsters' numbers replenished, and the destruction of the temple, of his skhatet, of the elders in the gallery, of anybody in the way of the blast of amber, would have been for nothing.

They were almost upon him. Wild ideas filled his head. He could throw a rock, hit the nearest staff just right so it would turn in his direction. He could snag a body with it, use it as a shield. Yes, and then the hummingbird would come down from the sun, crush his enemies, and elevate him to the skhatet himself. The tecuani in the lead jumped forward and landed right in front of him. Coatl closed his eyes, waiting for the sting, the sensation of the larva pushing into his body, but it never came. He opened them again. The monster had stopped at the corpse of the guard to his right. It's foul odor filled the air, mingling with the sour smell of sweat and blood. Slowly it leaned over and extended its stinger, piercing the dead man's skull, undulating as the eggs pulsed through. Coatl knew he was next. He put his hand under him, searching for the rock that pushed up into his gut, gathered his strength, quelled the fear in his belly. In his last moments, he would be strong and brave. He would die as a warrior.

Just as he was about to act, someone cried out, "Miquiz tetzahuitl!" *Die monster!*

It was the man behind him, the one buried to his shoulders.

The tecuani released its victim, zeroed in, and jumped for him. The commotion shifted the stones and jarred the infected body loose. It tumbled down the little slope, the staff bouncing along behind, heading right for Coatl. He would only have one chance. He rose up to his knees. He lunged for the staff as it clattered by, managing to snag it by the end. Then the body struck him on the side, and he almost lost his hold.

"Tepalehuiliztli!" the soldier screamed. *Help!*

Coatl's grip was tenuous, and he had to be careful and quick. If he pulled too hard, he'd lose it. If he waited too long, the man behind him was dead. Then there was the corpse leaning against him, the tumor in its skull swelling, pulsing.

"Tepalehuilizli! Aho! Aho!"

Coatl panicked and lost his hold. The cursed staff rotated away. It was too far now, but if he got it to turn to him . . . He lunged again, feeling something in his ankle pop, but his fingers swatted the wood and the staff rotated. He grabbed it by the neck and twisted his torso, aiming at the tecuani, willing it to life just as he did before . . . but nothing happened. No surge of power rushed up his arm. No amber bolt shot out of the scepter. The tecuani didn't disintegrate.

It reared back to strike the guard, who yanked his right arm out of the rocks, revealing the sharp end of a broken staff. He stabbed the beast in the leg, and it squealed and struck him in the face with its talons, nearly ripping off his entire head. He fell to the side, his dying eyes staring at Coatl, and with one last effort, he pointed at another dead guard sprawled next to him.

"Yeh," he gasped.

Then the tecuani fell upon him.

Coatl looked down. Of course! The guard's hand. He snatched it up and wrapped it around the staff, then he pointed it at the tecuani, already heading for him.

"Miquiz!" he cried, shoving the staff at it.

But again, nothing happened. Coatl's eyes went wide.

Oh no.

The tecuani lurched for him, and he ducked as it swiped at his head, it talons sheering the top of the staff completely off. The scepter smashed on the rubble, and the amber poured out of it, hissing and bubbling. Coatl grasped what was left of the staff in both hands and, just as the tecuani made its move, stabbed it right in its open mouth, using its own force to vault it over his head. The energy of the arc yanked him out of his trap. He tumbled end over end, stopping only when he slammed into a column on the other side of the chamber. He stood, shaking, barely able to put any weight on his right foot, which was swollen and bruised.

At the other end of the chamber, the last two tecuani eased themselves down off the pile, and behind them, three younglings burst out of the infected soldiers. Coatl yanked the staff out of the dead beast's jaws, then hopped to the wall at his back. The monsters crept forward, wary, testing him. He jabbed at the first one and it barely flinched. A second jab and it bared its teeth. It was toying with him. He tightened his grip. The beast on his left feinted and he bit, swinging for its head and missing by at least a foot.

It was all the first one needed. It pounced and tore into his right shoulder with its teeth. He screamed and plunged the staff into its exposed eye, stabbing over and over until it let go of his arm, then he launched his weapon into its open mouth. It stumbled back, squealing, talons hacking away at the willow wood. The second one moved in, stinger exposed, and pierced his calf. He felt it put the poison, the burning ball of larva shooting into his muscle. He screamed and beat the thing with his fists, but it was pointless.

Something hot and liquid splashed on his chest. The monster lay in two pieces on either side of him, its guts a steaming pile on the stones. Xiuloc stood on the other side, holding a maquahuitl. Behind him lay the other beast, also slashed in two. His smile faded when he saw the sting on Coatl's leg.

"General," he said. "No."

He batted aside a youngling and sliced the other two to pieces before returning to Coatl. The meat in his calf had already begun to bulge.

"We can cut it off," Xiuloc said.

"No."

"You'll live. I've seen it done before."

Coatl shook his head.

"I'll go to the hummingbird, not to Mitclan." He held up his hand. "Help me up."

Xiuloc did, and Coatl put an arm around his shoulders.

"Where are we going?" Xiuloc asked.

"Out. The farther away from here we get, the longer it will take, right?"

"Where, though?"

Coatl smiled.

"The river."

"The river?"

"Just take me there."

The river Isquite did not suffer war. She did not suffer disease, or death, or time, or strife. She simply was. Eternal. Ageless. She gave the Tlek water to drink, wood to build houses, and fish to eat. But she stole things, too. Her surface might have been as smooth and as glassy as the obsidian they used to make their weapons, but beneath her waters swam the horned messah, with its rows of teeth and strong jaws, and the swarms of pictlan, with their razor teeth and depthless appetites. The Isquite was beholden only to her husband, Sobk, and Sobk did not care about anything but her, and he did not change, which was exactly how they both liked it. As long as she ran through the jungle to its end in his black void, Sobk was happy. And when Sobk was happy, Isquite provided for the people who lived on its banks. The Tlek sent Sobk gifts to ensure this, wreathed flowers, totems carved from the driftwood she shared, and when someone died, an old man or woman, a mother, a father, a child, they put the body in a canoe carved from a newly felled torchwood tree and sent it to ride Isquite's tides and meet Mitclan.

When Coatl was a boy, hundreds of villages lined her banks, so many that they all seemed to merge together. It was not really so. Each village had its own chief, and each chief reported to a tlatoani from the city. They sent tribute to the great Seka-Khayu, food, incense, and when the time called for it, their own sons and daughters. Sometimes the villages fought one another, usually over trivial things, like whose crops were whose, or whether one village was purposefully overfishing its part of the river. If the violence ever grew too great, the nobleman responsible for the area sent in his troops, a jaguar or eagle unit, to keep the peace.

Normally it didn't come to that.

Coatl remembered friends and neighbors from the dozens of minor chiefdoms that surrounded his own, the boys and girls he played with as a child, the old men who took him hunting and showed him the ways of the jungle, the old women who sang to him and told him stories. All of them were gone now. Some were killed. Some took their own lives. Time moved both fast and slow on the other side, and though at different ages his people became eternal, they were not immune to disease, they were not immune to poison, and they were not immune to weapons. When the lung filled, when the snake bit, when the spear gored, the flesh corrupted.

And they were never replaced, for as his generation made its home here, so, too, did the plics, the pale warriors, with their tall city walls and houses that pierced the sky, and their weapons, the fast spears that they used to hunt and fight. When they came, the Tlek no longer bore children, for that was part of Huitl's design. It happened to the beings that came before the Tlek, the ancient race that introduced them to the amber. Once the Tlek appeared, they slowly died off too. So it was now with his people.

Xiuloc walked in front, clearing the brush with his maquahuitl as they walked along the bank, which was to Coatl's preference. He didn't want anyone to see him wince. The bulge in his calf grew larger. He could feel the thing inside of his leg, feeding on him. He tried to ignore it, to bite back the pain.

"Xiuloc," he said. "How did you know about the tunnels?"

"I grew up in the temple."

"Grew up there? How?"

"You remember after the Incursions when Seka-Khayu murdered Ka-Tiu's generals, his most trusted advisors?"

"He gave them mercy. He could have sacrificed them on the temple stairs. Instead, they conquered the seven gates and serve the skhatets in the shadow of the sun."

"Except he didn't kill them all. My father was an advisor to Ka-Tiu. Seka-Khayu spared his life but took me as his ward. Before I was trained as a warrior, I was a cook, a tailor, an attendant."

Coatl remembered. After the mutiny was put down, Seka-Khayu slaughtered thousands of his enemies. The stones of the temple drowned in blood for weeks as one by one he tore the beating hearts from the chests of the men responsible, and their wives and children, too. These were proud people. Fierce warriors, wizened leaders. Coatl might have fought against them, but he respected their bravery.

So Xiuloc's father was one of these traitors? Interesting. He must have been a chieftain of some minor village, though it was more than likely that he was just some old warrior who got caught on the wrong side of the conflict. He wasn't important enough for his son to live. To disrespect a skhatet was to disrespect the hummingbird himself, and such contempt could not go unpunished. Xiuloc should have been sacrificed. What was the point in letting him live? It only showed weakness.

A branch scraped against the bulging tumor, bringing the general to a halt. The pain was so great that it spread up his leg and into his belly, and he grew light headed and had to lean over and put his hands on his knees. The wound in his shoulder ached. His ankle throbbed. He'd lost a lot of blood. Too much blood. Xiuloc's voice cut through the haze.

"You can survive. I can cut it out."

"You know how it works. Its teeth are in my bone, sucking it dry."

"We're far enough from the amber. It's already stopped growing as fast as before." Xiuloc held up his weapon. "I can slice it in two. It will never mature."

"It will rot inside of me. My death will be long and painful."

"But—"

Coatl stood to his full height and took a deep breath.

"You're not cutting it out. You cut it out, the next thing to go is the leg. I won't let that happen. I'll meet Huitl whole."

"Yes, general."

"I just want to see my old home."

"Yes, general."

They continued along a path that ran parallel to the river. Coatl thought about his life as he limped along, what his father would have thought of him, his mother. They'd lived so long ago that he couldn't remember much about them, couldn't remember their faces. When had they died? Was it in a war, or did they become weary of life and pay the blood-debt? It saddened him that he couldn't remember.

He thought about the transformation. It was a capricious gift. For most, it occurred at some point in their youth, well after puberty but before the ravages of time took its toll. The very lucky stopped aging before twenty-five, when body and brain peaked, when the muscles were supple and forgiving and the mind absorbed knowledge and adapted with ease. Some, however, waited their entire lives for the process to begin, and many committed suicide rather than live an eternity in the throes of useless dotage. Very few never grew out of infancy. These were sent down to Mictlan as soon as their condition became known. It was seen as a grace.

For Coatl, it happened at the best possible age. Eighteen. Imagine possessing the strength and agility of youth and the wisdom and worldliness of age. Huitl wanted something from him, of that he was certain. It was why he trained so hard, killed so many: to serve his skhatet and please his god. But now he was worried. Would his life really end with the death of Seka-Khayu? How would he get through the seven gates if he'd taken part in the death of Huitl himself?

The river ran to their right, and before them wound the branches and roots of his childhood. He scanned the darkness for signs of his old village but found nothing. The jungle had swallowed it up, just like it swallowed up the rest of the villages. His leg finally forced him to stop, and he found a branch on the bank and sat. Behind him, illuminated by the light of the full moon, black smoke from the destroyed temple gushed into the night.

When he and Xiuloc escaped, when they slunk out of the temple like cowards, he'd seen the burned husks of humans and tecuani alike filling the streets, the doorways, and the alleys. He was glad they were dead, the tecuani for obvious reasons, but his own people, too. Some had been in the throes of infection, with up to five or six tumors bulging out of their heads, their necks, their arms, their stomachs. Seka-Khayu afforded them a kindness by killing them with the amber blast, and they died in battle, so they would not rest in Huitl's shadow. They would join him in the sun. He was never the best or most competent leader, his skhatet, but at least he'd done this, however unwillingly. Something rustled in the brush a few feet off, and Xiuloc sprang to his feet, gripping his weapon.

"Who's there?"

Nothing.

He looked at Coatl, who shrugged. The brush shook again and, angered, Xiuloc waded in, slashing at the branches. Then he drew back.

"Teh?"

Whatever it was darted away. Coatl couldn't see it in the darkness, but it was small and fast and brown. Xiuloc lunged to his left and snatched it up with one hand. It thrashed in his grip and slashed at his eyes, kicking and punching, and the brave warrior was almost overwhelmed. He held it at arm's length, dodging the blows as best he could, half-laughing, half-grimacing as he turned to present it to Coatl. Somewhere in the midst of the violence, the general finally understood what he was looking at.

It was a girl. A little girl.

At least she looked little. She could have been sixty years old for all he knew. As Xiuloc struggled back into the clearing, she bit his wrist, clamping down as hard as she could. He grimaced but didn't let go. Then another bush rattled and another brown blur sped out and jumped on his back. It was a boy, half as old as the girl. He pulled Xiuloc's top knot, yanking his head back, then placed a sharpened piece of obsidian to his neck. In one swift motion, Xiuloc dropped the girl, pulled the boy's arm away, and flipped him over his head. The girl picked up a fallen tree branch and hit him in the shin. He howled and hopped away.

"Ximocahua! Ixquich!" he cried. *Stop! Enough!*

Coatl would have helped, but the whole thing was too funny. He started laughing the moment the girl bit into Xiuloc's hand. She ran over to the boy and helped him off the ground, and they stood there, glaring at Xiuloc, who was still wincing. He leaned over to look at his shin.

"She nearly broke it in half!"

"The great Xiuloc!" Coatl said, still laughing. "Supreme warrior of the Onton! A credit to his tribe."

"Very funny," Xiuloc said. He looked at the bite wound on his wrist. "Broke the skin."

This sent Coatl into another gale of laughter. He turned to the children. They were strange looking, their skin lighter than his, but not entirely white like the plics. There was a slightly olive tinge to it, too, and it looked thick and pliant. Their faces were broad and flat, but their eyes were blue, and their hair was long and blonde and shaved one side. Their skulls were tattooed with an ouroboros: the snake that eats the sun. They wore white robes cinched around the middle, but their feet were bare.

"Come," Coatl said. "Sit. Anybody who can defeat an Onton soldier has earned my respect."

The boy glowered, mute, and girl shook her head, two, tight turns.

"No? Surely you can't be too busy to keep two old men company?"

"You're not going to hurt us?" the girl asked.

"Me? Hurt you? How could I do anything to harm such a fierce panther?"

She softened a little.

"We have to go."

"Go? Where?"

She pointed in the direction of the city, and Coatl sighed.

"I'm not sure you're going to like what you find there."

"We have to deliver a message from our chief, Ka-Bata."

"Ka-Bata?" Coatl said.

He hadn't heard that name in years. He was one of the early lords, from the time of the Great Exploration. Indeed, when his name was mentioned, they called him that. "The Explorer." "The Seeker." The other lords called him crazy, accused him at various points of being a coward, a madman, a genius, a seer—whatever label best fit their argument at the moment. All Coatl knew was that Seka-Khayu seemed both afraid of him and amused by him. As one of the few tlatoani who had not succumbed to the years and asked for the blood debt, he'd earned great stature and the skhatet's respect; as the only one who never traveled to the temple to pay tribute, he compounded his anger. And yet Seka-Khayu never sent his forces to drag the insolent old man back to the temple. Coatl appraised the little girl, wondering what her purpose was.

The Seeker was alive? If he was, and if he still had his army . . .

"I'm afraid you're out of luck," he said. "If you deliver your message, you'll be delivering it to the dead. Maybe you could tell it to me? I am a warrior."

The little girl's face fell. She looked panicked. The city? How could everybody in the city be dead? It was eternal. Seka-Khayu, the skhatet, the hummingbird and the sun, lived there.

"But our village—"

The boy interrupted her.

"Don't tell him."

"He's a warrior. He might be able to help us."

"What are you about?" Xiuloc asked. He looked at Coatl. "General, this is a snare."

She glared at him, and Coatl shook his head and patted the air with his hands. Don't. Let me speak to her. Then a bolt of pain shot through his leg and he automatically reached for the bulge, stopping at the last second. He grimaced back the pain. The girl whispered something to the boy and he nodded.

"Speak up, girl," Coatl said. "I might like you, but you'll keep no secrets."

She thought, calculating rapidly.

"Are all of the other warriors gone?"

Coatl nodded.

"If they were in the city, yes. There were a few garrisons in the jungle, but . . ."

She looked at Xiuloc, his maquahuitl, then back at Coatl. She pointed at his leg.

"The crone in my village can fix it."

Coatl pressed his lips together.

The girl shook her head and pointed upriver.

"What are you doing here, then?"

"We came for Seka-Khayu and his jaguars. The plics—" She broke off then, struggling to find the right words.

"Are all of your warriors dead?"

She shook her head.

"The plics—"

"The plics what?"

Keyn said, "Don't, Sehlah."

"Speak up girl.

116

Sehlah pointed at the bulge in his calf.

"If you come with us, if you help us, my crone can heal you."

"Nobody can heal me. It's only a matter of time."

The little girl nudged the boy.

"Show him."

"No."

"*Show* him, Keyn."

The boy, Keyn, turned around and pulled the loose tunic he was wearing up over his shoulders, revealing his bare back. A massive scar rippled the skin, a perfect circle from the nape of his neck to the base of his spine. Xiuloc whistled appreciatively.

"Were you punished, little Keyn? Didn't bring back the water fast enough from the river?"

Keyn let the tunic dropped and turned around, angry.

"I was bitten by tecuani," he said. "Two of them. They put the poison."

"You're funny, little boy."

"It's true," the girl said. "I saw it myself. Two balls, the size of my head. Bit into his spine. Come back to our village. My crone—"

Coatl leaned forward.

"Sehlah. Stop edging around the truth and tell me what's going on."

She shook her head, trying to deny it.

"No. Your leg. She can help."

"You don't care at all about my leg. You said it yourself: you came for men. Warriors." He gestured at Xiuloc. "We're just two, but we're warriors. Why do you want us to come back to your village?" She looked at the ground, ashamed at being caught. "Tell me."

When she wouldn't look up, Keyn spoke for her. "Fine. I'll tell. The plics. They came to our village. They . . . they're hurting."

"Hurting? They're in pain?"

"No. The women."

"Why don't your warrior's stop them?"

"They're gone."

"Gone? Or dead?"

Sehlah shook her head.

"Will they be back?"

"Ka-Bata says so."

Coatl and Xiuloc shared a look, and the former sighed.

"Well, Xiuloc," he said. "Looks like you got your wish." He held out his leg. "Huitl has work for me yet."

THE RABBIT

Not many people have ever seen someone's head split open like a watermelon. Or at all, really, like a watermelon or not like a watermelon. Count yourself Irish if you haven't because that's some disgusting shit right there. In the realm of the senses, there are certain things most of us consider pleasant. Massages. Chocolate. Lavender bath salts.

Picture this: it's summer. 5,000 degrees in the shade. You're sweating your taint off. Then someone hands you a glass of delicious sun-brewed tea, and it's filled to the brim with crushed ice (the best ice), and there's a fat lemon wedge wedged on the edge (no seeds, of course), and a little beach of white sugar duned up on the bottom, and you know that it ain't just any old sun-brewed iced tea, it's the flavored stuff, peach or raspberry or cherry or something like that. The premium ragoo. Jesus's nipple clamps. How it washes down your throat, and you can feel the cold make its way down, and when it spreads its fingers out when it reaches your belly.

Man, that's a great feeling.

You know what ain't a great feeling? Watching some poor fuck's nut crack open and his brains spill out like cranberry sauce.

So that's the first thing I seen after I got back out onto the killing floor. Boom. Split-head sundae. Then another guy got his arm cut off. Boom. Everybody who didn't get their head exploded or their arms cut off was running around like idiots. Not the best strategy. A few had picked up something that could be used as a weapon. Shards of knives. Half-spears. Broken swords. Some of them found these cricket bats with razor blades embedded in the sides, and I thought to myself, "Cricket's a lot more violent than I thought." But ain't none of them got nothing as deadly as my tommy gun.

And on top of that, none of that other stuff was remotely effective. As weapons, I mean. Not that anybody should be surprised.

We might have been a surly bunch, us recruits—tough, street-wise rumblers—but ain't none of us ever been trained to fight as a group, really, and all the goons taught us how to do was maximize our lung capacity. In formation. And maximize lung capacity many of them street-wise rumble-scrappers did. They scattered like rats around the killing floor, running from boars, and bears, and lions, and leopards. Problem was that man evolved using his wits and his tits; he ain't built to outrun things that evolved to outrun everything else. So the boars gored, the bears bit, the lions leaped, and the leopards, I mean Jesus fuck, the leopards outright toyed with people. I seen one pounce on a dude and tear a gulch down his back and then sprawl out on its belly and lick its chops while the poor fuck moaned in the dirt. When he tried to get up, it slapped a paw on the back of his legs to hold him in place. Look. I'm a cat person. I love me some cats. But anybody ever spent any time around one knows they can be real assholes, and that leopard just proved it right there.

Speaking of *genus felis*, Wildcat turned out to be the most useful out of everyone. Remember that guy in the leather panther suit sitting on the throne on top of the Oracle? Well, she climbed up there and took him out, her and about twenty other miserable jerks. The goons'd placed a crow's nest under the throne, and I guess they didn't think nobody'd ever try to take it from them, but then again I guess they never had to deal with someone like Wildcat. And that nest was stocked with all kinds of weapons: a tommy gun, ten drums of ammo, gasoline, spears, and more of them cricket bats I told you about. I didn't know all that then. Found it out later. Might've helped with the planning if I did, but I didn't, so fuck off.

A boar wheeled around the corner and headed straight for me, but I blasted some rounds in the dirt at its feet. That convinced it to run in a different direction. A bored looking bear lumbered by with two spears sticking out its side and two lions sweating its flank, biding their time. Didn't even give me a second glance, and I don't blame them. Bears got a lot more guts, and lions is hungry. A cheetah sprinted past but it wasn't chasing nothing, it was just running. Then some poor guy came screaming around the corner like a crazy person, which was understandable because he was completely engulfed in flames. Even worse was the fact that he headed straight for me.

"Back the fuck off!" I yelled.

He didn't. I leveled the tommy gun at him.

"I'm serious, asshole!"

That's the thing about being completely engulfed in flames: the normal conventions of polite society don't seem to hold much sway. He kept on running at me, screaming, so I unloaded on him in three short bursts. One hit his shoulders, twisting him to the side. One took out his knees and he dropped into the dirt. The third one didn't do nothing because I'm a terrible shot. (Them first two was just luck.)

"Ever hear of stop, drop, and roll?" I yelled, but he didn't say nothing on account of the bullets and the fire and such.

I caught a break in the slaughter and ran up to the base of the Oracle, staying within sight of one of the chutes built into the side in case anything weird came out. Wildcat was crouched down in the nest, looking around all wild eyed like, like a critter in a bush. I squeezed off a few rounds into the air.

"Hey! Wildcat!"

She ducked at the blast, but then stood straight up.

"The fuck you doing down there?"

"I just killed some guy tried to run me over. He was on fire, by the way."

"Huh. You got a gun?"

"What this? No. It's a dildo."

I squeezed off another blast. Wildcat was not impressed.

"You might want to save your ammo."

"I got three more drums!"

The crowd grew restless. I heard some booing. I didn't blame them. The animals was all full. No action going on anywhere. Wildcat leaned down into the nest and came up with her own Tommy.

"I got one, too."

"Yeah? That's fantastic."

Wildcat smiled for the first time I ever seen it, then she looked down at me, about to say something, and that smile dropped and her eyes went wide.

"Look out!"

I took the warning literal and spun around, ready to empty my load into whatever was attacking me, only there wasn't nothing attacking me because it was a joke. A goof. A prank. Like a "ha ha made you look." In fact, Wildcat even said that.

"Ha ha, made you look."

"Very funny," I said, waving the gun at her. "You want I should—"

"Oh shit, look out!" she screamed again.

"Bullshit," I said. "I'm not an idi—" and then I was knocked into the air and slammed into the wall of the Oracle.

The worst part of it wasn't getting hit or even slamming into the wall, even though that was some straight up bullshit right there, and by that I mean it hurt like a sonofabitch. It hurt like a sonofabitch with crabs. It hurt like a sonofabitch with crabs only the crabs was, like, super-crabs, irradiated super-crabs that, because of the irradiation turned into chlamydia, so what was once just irritating and a little itchy turned into fire shooting out of your dick.

So that's how hard I hit the wall. Chlamydia hard. And when I was able to turn over (hitting a wall like that tends to boost your wind), I seen the craziest thing ever. I can't even describe it without almost freaking out. All I can say is that it didn't have no head, its face was in its chest, it had two rows of teeth, arms like Goliath's, twenty-inch talons, etc . . . pretty much everything that'd make a monster a monster. Talk about a shock. Oh yeah, and I dropped my tommy gun when it hit me, dropped it right at its feet, which also didn't inspire me with confidence.

So yeah, both of them things simultaneous? Worse than getting hit.

Fortunately, Wildcat still had her gun, and when the thing, whatever the fuck it was, ran up to me, talons ready to gore, teeth ready to crunch into the cherry chocolate ball that was my head, she unloaded her entire drum into it. I'm telling you, she was a hell of a fucking shot. Nailed it right in the mouth, sent it stumbling back a dozen feet before it collapsed on its back, arms and legs splayed. That was kind of comical. I didn't have time to appreciate it though. In fact, I didn't have time to piss or say boo before another one of them crazy things came running up for round two of "fuck's sake does this shit ever end?" Only instead of coming after me, it stopped over the dead body of the thing Wildcat shot to pieces, extended a stinger from inside that fucked up chest-mouth, and slid it all gentle into its dead friend's shoulder-eye, like a lover. I didn't have a clue as to why, but if you've been paying attention at all you know what was going on, and I figured it out pretty quick a little while later.

What I'm trying to say is Wildcat's kill and the second monster's pausing to do its business gave me enough time to get to my feet and limp away. Yeah, that's right, I said limp because nobody who hits a wall chlamydia hard recovers completely in a minute. Everything hurt. Hurt to stand, hurt to run, hurt to breathe. Oh, and my pecker hurt, too, not that I needed to use it right then, but as long as I was making a list. So there I was for the second time in fifteen minutes, stuck in the middle of a slaughterhouse battle arena without a weapon, being chased by a thing what wasn't human. So what'd I do? I knew what was down underneath the stadium, and maybe that monster did and maybe that monster didn't, but it was my only chance.

I pushed forward as hard as I could, ignoring all the pain, even the pain in my pecker. After about ten yards, I shot a look over my shoulder, and the monster'd already disengaged from its friend and was sprinting for me. Wildcat finally reloaded and fired at it, but as good a shot as she was, we was too far away at this point. She ended up strafing the ground around me, so thanks a lot for that, Wildcat. I thought maybe that I'd run to the edge of the drop and then roll to the side at the last minute and the thing'd go right over me and hopefully get eaten by a gator or two, but then I realized that wasn't the greatest plan because have you ever stopped on a dime and rolled to the side? It ain't like I ran on a rail or something, like I could cut a sharp ninety degrees at will. The human body ain't made for that; I'd probably pop a kidney or something. In reality, I'd have to slow down at least ten feet before the edge, and by the time the stopping and the jumping was over, whatever was behind me would just adjust and follow suit.

So screw it. Jump it was. The more I ran, the more I regained my wind. My legs, my arms, my whole body remembered all that cardio. I don't mean to brag, but I booked it. I booked it faster than I ever booked it in my life. Mercury himself would have been impressed. The only problem was that monster was faster. And stronger. I pushed. It pushed. I pulled away. It gained. Nothing left to do then but book it harder, and I booked it right up to the edge, caught the lip on the ball of my right foot, and jumped like an Olympian, arms twirling, legs peddling the air.

I landed hard in the water, scaring the hell out of the croc sunning himself on the bank, which would have been funny if it wasn't so terrifying. It hissed and whipped around, and I lunged away. Then the monster landed right on top of where I'd just been, just in time for the croc to sink its fangs into its arm. That went on for a bit. The croc bit it and it bit the croc, and neither of them seemed too happy about the situation. One thing was for sure: all that grunting and growling and hissing sounded like the soundtrack to a psychopath's nightmare. I felt sure that any second something'd clamp onto my leg and drag me off, but it didn't, and I flopped onto the bank like a drowned cat, pushed myself up, and lurched away, heading back to the maze under the arena.

You might be asking yourself why I'd do something like that. Or not. I'm going to explain it anyway. Remember before when I knocked that guard out and took his gun and his ammo and that key? And all them weird things in the cages I passed when the gator and the croc and the Komodo was chasing me through the maze? Okay, good. Now you're getting the idea. So I limped over to the tunnels with plenty of time to spare, stepped right up to the first cage, inserted the key and . . . well, I was about to let whatever was inside out when it (whatever it was) slammed into the bars of the cage like an enraged ape. No, actually that was exactly what it was. An enraged ape. Enraged apes ain't the most reasonable creatures, hence the adjective. It shot its arm through the bars and I hit the deck and scrambled back. This did not please the ape none, and I wasn't in no mood to argue, so I snatched the key out of the lock and crabbed over to the next cage, which seemed empty.

I stood up and knocked on the bars with the key, looking over at the swamp where the monster thing was still grappling with the gator. It seemed to be getting the upper hand until another gator showed up, which made life a little more difficult. Specifically, the second gator bit the monster in the ass. Seriously. Right in the ass. Opened that tension grip mouth and chomped down. I seen a lot, but I ain't never seen nothing like that. I even chuckled a little bit, at least until I seen what was in the cage I crabbed up to, which was a pair of glowing amber eyes, followed by a rattle.

Perfect.

I mean, fucked up, but perfect.

I unlocked the cage and went to the next one, and the next one, and the next one and on and on until I did about thirty. Got myself bit and scratched up real nice but nothing too serious. When I got to the intersection, I turned around in time to see a few of the doors creak slowly open, a couple of furry paws creeping out, a few dozen tentacles waving in the air. I took the right-hand side this time, hoping to run into another guard so I could nick his gun, but no such luck, so I scrambled out the first side door I found and back into the arena. I ran around to where I could see the crow's nest, and there was Wildcat.

"Holy shit," she said. "You're alive!"

"Yeah," I said, putting my hands on my knees. "We're gonna have to get out of here in a minute."

"How do you think that's going to happen?"

As if on cue, a giant snake-thing slithered out of one of the chutes in the Oracle's side. Looked like a combination of a copperhead and a scorpion. Didn't pause to look around or nothing, just headed straight for the crowd. More followed. Flying things. Scrabbling things. Wriggling things. Things with dozens of legs. Things with dozens of dozens of legs. Things with big sharp teeth. Things with little sharp teeth. Some of them seemed concerned with us, but most of them were more interested in the buffet sitting unarmed in the seats, and that buffet screamed like pigs on a spit. Then they done what crowds of panicked people always done. They started trampling each other trying to get to the exits.

"That might help," I said.

And all them creepy monsters did what came natural. If it had a stinger, it stung. If it had talons, it tore. Pretty friggin genius if you ask me. At least until them stingers and talons turned in my direction. I beelined back for my tommy gun which was still lying in the dirt next to the first monster that'd come at me, the one with the chest mouth and shoulder eyes. Right when I reached for it, a black ball of slime burst out of the thing's head and rolled out into the middle of the killing floor. Took me less than a second to snatch my gun up, but by the time I did, the thing was gone.

I guess Wildcat'd had enough, because she showed up at my side, saying, "The fuck are you doing? Go!"

So we went. Me, then her, and whoever else managed to survive the most disgustingest battle royale I never wanted to be a part of. We sprinted for the gates. We didn't get ten steps away when a lizard with eagle wings and bear claws swooped down and snatched one of the stragglers into the air, followed by another one and another one. They aimed right for us, wings fluttering, talons snatching. Wasn't no way out of it, neither. We juked, they juked. We jived, they jived. Right at the last second, when them razor sharp talons was about to slice into Wildcat's neck, she half-spun and held her hand out in front of her, like that was going to help or something.

And you know what? It did.

Friggin eagle-lizards stopped in mid-air, froze in place. They looked about as surprised as I did. Wildcat was even more amazed. She was so amazed that she didn't even get pissed when I grabbed her by the elbow and pulled her away, yelling, "C'mon!"

We both looked over our shoulders as we ran to make sure the monsters wasn't chasing us, but them eagle-lizards kind of just flapped away, a little demoralized.

Oh, and did I tell you about them snakes with the spider legs? No? Well, there was snakes with spider legs. Kind of defeated the purpose of being a snake, them legs, but nonetheless they had them. One came scrabbling up at us from the right as an angry bear came lumbering up at us from the left, so I waited until the last possible second and then grabbed Wildcat and we stopped short. Then the two collided. Right in friggin front of us. That's comedic gold right there, ladies and gentlemen. Couldn't have asked for better. Even made a funny bonking sound, like two coconuts knocking together.

Anyway, the bear, upon getting laid out by a snake-with-legs, conducted itself predictable. It pounced upon one of them legs and ripped it right off. Then the snider (that's what I'm going to call the snake thing with spider legs from now on: "snider." Get it?) sank its fangs into the bear's shoulder. Things escalated from there. A cheetah ran down one of them monsters with the chest teeth, a baby one, picked it up, and flung it into the air, you know, for giggles. (See what I mean about cats?). A slithery something shot right at us out of nowhere and Wildcat mowed it down. Some poor schmuck's head landed in the dirt next to me, bounced right in my way. I kicked it like a soccer ball.

I nearly shat myself with relief when we made it to the gates, even though the thing was locked, which was rude. I thought maybe somebody might have seen what was going on and give us an out, but whatever. Just another pain in the ass to deal with. Good thing for me I got brains.

"Step back," I said, and shot the lock with my tommy gun.

By the way, shooting locks until they open? It don't work. Not unless you're in the movies, which we wasn't. Know what happens instead of the lock breaking? Bullets ricochet off the metal bars, that's what. One of them pinged off and caught an eel with a scorpion's tail right in the flank. Another hit some guy in the foot while he was in the middle of running from a snider. He went down.

"Christ, dude," Wildcat said, glaring.

She snatched a broken sword from the dirt and jammed it into the shackle. A couple of wrenches later and the thing busted off (the lock, not the sword). Then she slapped me in the chest with the flat end (the sword, not the lock) and yanked the gate open.

"That doesn't work in real life."

"Yeah," I said, jumping inside. "I got that."

The path outside was flooded with screaming goons. Puglies, Fuglies, Chumps, Champs, Vamps, Cunt Kickers, Topknots, the whole lot. Me and Wildcat melted in with the crowd and stampeded our way back up the path, heading for the barracks. Where we was going after I had no idea, but I thought it best not to run against the crowd. The next thing that happened happened so fast that I didn't even have time to think. The stampede made it out of the woods and onto the eggshell path, and we ran up a short hill, around a curve, down a hill, back up another, and around one last curve when lo and behold there stood Zoot himself and about fifteen other goons all strapped to the gills with tommy guns.

"Say goodnight, assholes," he said, and they all started firing.

The dumbasses in front got eaten up pretty quick, which was good for us because it bought us a few seconds to jump into the ditch on the side of the road. I guess they didn't count on anybody else firing back, though, which was what me and Wildcat started doing—glued our fingers to the triggers and swept the path back and forth, knee-capping everything that got in our way. Whoever didn't get knee-capped sprinted for the woods, the same woods Zoot said never to go into. When the smoke cleared and the din of the weapons faded into the day, the only recruits left alive was me and Wildcat and about a dozen others behind us. Some had been shot in the arm or the gut, but for the most part they was good. Except for this one guy. He'd been shot in the collar bone. Shattered it into a zillion pieces. He wasn't no good at all. I nudged Wildcat with my elbow.

"Get up and go see if they're all dead," I said.

"You look."

Before I could reply, someone screamed, "Hey! That you you fucks?"

Me and Wildcat shared a look. It was Zoot.

"Yeah," Wildcat said. "So what?"

"C'mere. I wanna show you something."

"Sure. I bet you got a bridge to sell us."

"No, seriously."

"Why? So you can shoot us down?"

"I won't shoot, I promise. I'm outta ammo anyway."

I looked at Wildcat.

"I think he's legit. Go ahead."

"We already been over this."

"Better hurry up!" Zoot yelled.

I glanced at the road behind me. Nothing yet, but he was right. Only a matter of time before all them things from the colosseum came calling.

Wildcat seen the look in my eye and said, "Look. Don't do it. He'll be dead in a minute."

"We ain't got a minute."

Then I stood up out of the ditch, holding my gun at the ready.

Zoot was lying on the other side of the path, toe up. He didn't shoot. I walked out into the middle of the road. He still didn't shoot. I circled around a little closer. Then I seen why he didn't shoot. His legs were tore to pieces, one so much that it was nearly severed from his body. He wasn't just out of bullets. He was out of gun. It sat on the edge of the path, way out of his reach. He didn't do nothing but lay there, one arm over his chest, staring at the sky, waiting. I walked over, shoes crunching the gravel, and he didn't move. I looked over my shoulder at Wildcat.

"You're an idiot," she mouthed.

In the distance, I heard the sounds of the approaching hoard. Snarls. Grunts. Roars. When I turned back around, Zoot was still lying there, motionless, breathless.

Then he picked up his head.

"Fuck!" I yelled, and squeezed off a burst. It ripped up the gravel to his left.

"Fuck you, you fuck!" he yelled. "I'm already dead and you wanna make it worse?"

"Sorry, sorry," I said. "You just scared me, that's all."

"Yeah? Good." He held up a little tin whistle between his fingers and smiled at me, like he'd been waiting to show it to me all along. It was kind of gross, too, because his teeth was all bloody.

"Nice whistle," I said.

"You know how long I been working this?"

"What? Killing everybody for no reason?"

"You know fuck all."

"What do you know about it? I heard you, Zoot."

"Heard what?"

"You and Bruno's little chinwag the other night."

This struck him serious. I could tell because a little of his attitude dropped.

"You heard that?"

"I heard that."

"Yeah, well. War is war. I did what needed to be done."

"What's all this 'cold cuts and cooked cocks' nonsense?"

"You ain't figured it out yet?"

"I've had my hands full."

He coughed, and a little blood dribbled down his chin.

"They're about to get a whole lot fuller."

Then he plunked the whistle into this lips and blew it as hard as he could. Over and over. Tweeeeeee! Tweeeeeee! Tweeeeeee! When he was done, he let his head fall back again and laughed and laughed and laughed.

"You're fucked!" he said. "You're really fucked!"

"Oh yeah?" I said, and blew his frigging brains out. "Who's fucked now?"

The calm that settled over the path felt like death. Maybe because a whole bunch of dead people was lying all over the place. The wind whooshed through the trees in the forest. I leaned over and picked Bruno's whistle out of his mouth. Who the fuck did he call with that thing?

"You hear that?" Wildcat called.

She stood up in the ditch, facing the forest. Some of the other escaped goons, the ones that didn't get dead, stood up too, looking around like they didn't know what to do with themselves. Couldn't blame them. You try escaping the shittiest shit show of all shit shows and see how clear your head is after.

"Hear what?" I said. Wildcat fell into a crouch, her eyes searching the trees. "Hear wh—"

And then I heard it. A high pitched whistle, as if mimicking the exact sound of Zoot's little tin toy, only more echoey and a lot more of it. Hundreds of them. Getting louder. Heading straight for us.

THE JAGUAR

The rest of the day went by fast, so fast that Wheeler nearly forgot how hungover she was. They had to seal off the scene, call in forensics, call in HAZMAT, debrief the officers. Peña made some calls to the city to find out who owned the warehouse.

"You'll never guess," he told Wheeler.

"Single Corp?"

"The one and only."

Then there was the paperwork. By the time she was done, dinner time had come and gone, and she was exhausted. She was so exhausted that when Peña made fun of her for saying she saw a monster burst out of the guy's back, she didn't bite. Not at first.

"I'm tired, Peña," she said. "Leave me alone."

"Who you gonna call?"

She flatlined him.

"Bill Murray!"

Fine. You want to fight?

"You saw it happen," she'd said, incredulous. "You saw it burst out."

"No, *you* saw that. I saw an animal loose in a warehouse."

"Then what about the other two? Both had exactly the same wound in different places."

"It was a wild animal, Wheeler! Thought it lucked into a couple of day's worth of food."

"C'mon, Peña. That sounds ridiculous—"

"*That* sounds ridiculous?"

"I saw what I saw."

Peña shook his head.

"You came to work smelling like a whiskey bottle. You'll pardon me if I don't necessarily trust your judgment right now."

She waved him off.

"I've got paperwork."

She worked until six, then went home and crashed. She'd never been so grateful for her bed, and even though it was hot in her apartment, she fell into a deep sleep. Her dreams were vivid but disjointed. A series of repeating images, really. Tableaus. An old woman gibbering at her. A puddle of squirming eggs. The triple spirals, spinning, spinning. The dagger, the pyramid, the moon. The woman, the puddle, the spirals.

She woke up sweating and hot, and when she checked her window unit, it was barely cranking out any cold air. She hit it and it kicked on. She put her face up to it and closed her eyes. She felt good. Fully refreshed. For the first time in a long time, she arrived at work early. Earlier than Peña, which was a near impossibility. Three manila envelopes sat unopened on her desk. Pictures of the warehouse scene, the toxicology report, and the coroner's report. She didn't find anything new in the pictures, and the toxicology report came back inconclusive, but something in the coroner's report struck her as odd. It listed three bodies, each one with roughly the same sized wounds, covered in animal bites. That wasn't the odd part. It was the description of the bites.

Canine. Possibly feline.

She read that line three times. Canine. Possibly feline. Who were they hiring these days? She picked up the inter-departmental phone and called the genius who performed the autopsy, but he wouldn't back down.

"We see a lot of stuff like that," he said.

"Animals that bite like two different species?"

"No. Dead bodies used as a buffet. We've got feral cats and stray dogs all over the city. Not to mention raccoons. Hell, I've even seen lion attacks—"

"Lion attacks?"

"Lion attacks."

"So the bites on the victims at the mill. They came from multiple creatures?"

"I didn't say that."

"So it was one creature."

"I didn't say that, either."

Wheeler sighed.

"Then what does 'Canine. Possibly feline' mean?"

"Exactly what it says. I don't know exactly what made those bites, but the dental patterns resemble two different species."

"How is that possible?"

"Not my job."

"Excuse me?"

He sighed.

"I can't conceivably tell you how something like that is possible. Science doesn't prove what you want it to prove. It just tells the truth, whether you like it or not."

Wheeler bit back an insult.

"Can you get me a report of all the similar types of attacks your office has logged in the past three months."

"No."

"No?"

"Detective, I've got a backlog of autopsies to perform here. My supervisor's on my back all day about it. I haven't seen the sun or my boyfriend in a week."

"Life's tough."

"You want that information, you can submit the form online. I'll send you the link. It takes forty-eight hours, pending approval."

"Forty-eight hours?"

"Pending approval."

Wheeler tapped her teeth with her pen.

"Can you—can you tell me whether or not there are any animals out there with both canine and feline teeth?"

"I can tell you that such creature has not been documented."

"Good, then—"

"But that doesn't mean they don't exist."

"Are you kidding me? What am I supposed to do with that?"

"I don't know, ma'am. You're the detective."

And then he hung up.

Lovely. Jerks like that made her job so much more pleasant.

She shuffled the pictures around on her desk for a little while longer, not getting anywhere. Then she took out her phone, opened up her Maps app, dialed up the warehouse, and added three markers to it. She stared at it, thinking about the night before last when she passed out in the alley. On a whim, she found it and put a marker there, too.

"You're here early."

It was Peña. He was standing behind her, two cups of coffee in his hand. He set one of them down on her desk and went around to his side.

Wheeler took a sip.

"Thanks."

"You look a lot better."

"Yeah, well . . ."

"What are you working on?"

"Clusters."

"Clusters?"

"Of animal attacks."

"Really?"

She held up the coroner's report.

"Don't start with me. I've got it right here. The victims were covered in bites."

"I'm not doubting that part. Call the hospitals yet?"

"No."

"Why not?"

"What am I supposed to ask them? 'Hey, you guys have anybody come in with bite wounds that look both feline and canine?'"

"What?"

She tossed the report over to him. He read over it.

"Who did the autopsy?" he asked.

"Don't get me started on that, either."

Peña leaned back in his chair and linked his hands behind his head.

"What about what's-his-name? You know, the EMT. The driver. The one who has the hots for you? Dirk? Deek?"

"Dell. And no."

Dell the driver. God. He'd been hitting on Wheeler ever since he got the job six months before. He was young and cute she had to admit, but everything about him screamed former frat boy, from his haircut to the body spray he bathed in. Peña opened up his laptop and started clacking away.

"It's your case," he said.

"It's our case."

"Yours now. I'm handing it off."

Wheeler grunted. She tapped her teeth with her pen, thinking. Shit. She was going to have to call Dell. And he was going to ask her out on a date.

Eight hours later, she found herself standing out in front of Well Street Station, trying not to look out of place. Or worried. She'd gone home to get ready, showered, changed out of her work clothes, wore something nicer, tighter. Even put on some makeup. If she was going to play the vixen, she might as well look the part. The letter from the oncologist was buried in some catalogs that came in the mail. She hadn't seen it until she was nearly out the door. Now it sat unopened in her back pocket. She didn't have the courage to read it. Didn't want to go through the mental preparation of planning time off, calling her sister to come and stay with her again, filling her phone up with podcasts and audiobooks.

Okay, stop. Stay on course.

Even though the sun was beginning to go down, the heat had not diminished. The weather report said it wouldn't break for a few more days. She decided to go into the restaurant before her make up melted. The hostess brought her to a table by the huge front window. She could see the Silver Bullet shooting up over the tops of the buildings like a missile. The upper portion was still under construction, with crews working under spotlights all night long. Cranes turned, sparks flew, and every now and then the shouts of the workers reached her ears.

The surrounding neighborhood was fully caught up in the gentrification spurred by its construction. Entire blocks were being renewed, squeezing out families who had enjoyed low rents for decades. That was bad, but it also got rid of the drug dealers and the pimps and the prostitution. Just three years before, Wheeler had busted a child sex ring in a burned-out brownstone across the street. The alleys had been littered with needles and vials, the streets potholed and crumbling, and after two fake fires during which three firemen were shot at, city FD stopped responding to any calls from the area unless accompanied by a police escort.

She marveled at the transformation.

Those same disgusting alleys had been scrubbed clean, the streets repaved, and several boutiques had moved in: Sweet Grace for Women, Single Corp UpMarket, Nordstrom, Bluebell, and Pettibone-Schyuler, "The City's Premiere Designer Grocery Experience." She felt safer here than she did at the precinct. In fact, she'd counted three blue and whites cruising by since she arrived. That never happened before. Ah, money. Ah, capitalism.

She checked her phone, partially hoping to see a text from Dell telling her he'd be late. Then she could leave. Oops. Sorry, couldn't wait. You blew it, loser! Except this wasn't a date. She needed him. And he wasn't late. He still had ten minutes. As she was putting her phone back in her pocket, a voice said, "I knew you'd get here early. Just can't wait to see me, can you?"

"Hey, Dell," she said, looking up.

She had to admit. He was cute. Tall. Not too skinny, not too bulky. He was wearing black jeans and a tight, black T-shirt that hugged his torso and muscular arms. He pulled out his chair to sit down, and she saw the curved bottom of a brand peaking out from under his left sleeve. He smiled at her as he scooted in.

"Damn you look good. You do that for me?"

"Um . . ."

"Mmm. Mmm. Classic metro chic. I'm jealous of your partner."

Just the thought of thinking of Peña in that way made Wheeler slightly ill. Come on, Katherine. Shine it on. She smiled.

"More like classic metro detective," she said.

He laughed a little too much at the joke.

And of course he knew everybody there. The hostess walked by and he said 'hi baby'. It would have been nice if she wasn't underage. He gave a shout out to the bartender. It would have been impressive if the guy didn't look confused. When the waiter arrived, Dell didn't even look at the menu, just ordered a water for himself. That, actually, surprised her.

"And for the lady?" the waiter asked.

"Um, I'll have a water, too."

He left, clearly disappointed.

"I would have thought you were a beer guy," Wheeler said. "Maybe even Jack and coke."

"Not me. I don't drink."

"AA?"

"Allah." He read her expression. "Don't worry. I'm not wearing a vest."

"I didn't—"

"It's okay. I get it."

"It's just the frat brand, and well, you."

"Frat brand?"

She nodded at his arm.

"Oh, yeah. Well, I was young once, too."

"Young? What are you, twenty-three? Twenty-four?"

He laughed.

"Damn, Katherine. I mean, can I call you that?"

"Wheeler's fine."

"Oh, okay."

He glanced out the window and caught a glimpse of the Silver Bullet. His smile faltered. Wheeler caught it.

"You don't like our corporate overlords?" she asked.

"The Single Corp? No."

"Seems to have done a nice job with the area."

"You mean pushing all the brown people out?"

Wheeler didn't disagree. She wasn't too sure about the Single Corp, but Dell was so forceful that she felt the need to argue.

"Aren't they hiring all those brown people?"

"Sure. For minimum wage jobs. Shift work."

"It's an opportunity."

"Not really."

The waiter returned with their waters and took their order. Salads. Both of them. He left even snootier than the first time.

"Do you know where the Single Corp is from?" Dell asked.

"Wall Street? Silicon Valley?"

"Not even close."

"Russia?"

He laughed.

"China?"

He shook his head.

"Nobody knows where it's from."

"Oh come on, Dell. That's impossible."

"Look it up. It's listed as a multi-national company, but there isn't a single point of origin. The CEO doesn't speak in public. Ever hear of Fox-Conn?"

She had. The slave-like working conditions. The suicide nets.

"Uh-huh," Dell said. He tilted his head at the Silver Bullet. "That's the kind of 'opportunity' they're offering."

Wheeler took a sip of her water.

"I didn't know you were such a social justice warrior."

"I'm a human being. And I don't like it when some faceless corporation takes advantage of people for power."

"Profit."

"Profit is power."

Wheeler looked out the window across the street. A few of the old brownstones were still standing, but they'd been roped off with yellow construction tape. Dell followed her gaze.

"All those historic places will be gone soon. Single Corp bought up the block. Where do you think all the people will go?"

Wheeler thought she knew what he was implying.

"You think they're going to build dormitories?"

"Just like Fox-Conn. You work for them. You live on their property. You drink their water, eat their food, wear their clothes, watch their programming. They own you. They own everything about you. What does that remind you of?"

Wheeler took it all in. Other than the effect it had on the neighborhood, which in her mind was positive, she hadn't really given what the company was doing any thought. Not as much as he had. The waiter returned and placed their plates in front of them with a flourish.

"Your salads," he said. He held up a pepper grinder. "Cracked peppercorn?"

"No thanks," Wheeler said.

He held up a dish with a spoon in it.

"Fresh parmesan?"

They both shook their heads.

"Of course not. Can I get you anything else? A cracker? More ice for your water?"

Wheeler tried not to glare.

"We're fine."

"Very well," he said, and left.

Dell mixed his salad up with his fork and took a bite.

"You're very quiet," he said after a moment.

"I'm sorry. It's just . . . you're not exactly what I expected."

"I get that a lot."

"I feel like I need to apologize. This isn't really a date."

"No kidding."

"You knew?"

"Look. Women like you don't call guys like me out of the blue unless they want something."

"Way to make me feel horrible."

"Am I wrong?"

Wheeler didn't know how to respond, so she told him the truth.

"No. You're not wrong. I'm sorry."

"It's okay. I know I come on a little too strong. I was actually surprised when you agreed to go out with me."

Wheeler blushed. She almost apologized again, but he cut her off.

"Don't. Seriously. It has to be important or we wouldn't be here, right?"

"Yeah. Yeah, it is important."

So she told him. About the warehouse. About the tumors. About the bites. Everything except the part about passing out in an alley and the dreams she was having. When she was done, he'd almost finished eating. She hadn't touched a bite.

"I can't believe you ate through all of that," she said.

"I'm an EMT. You won't believe what I've had to eat through."

"Fair enough."

"So what do you want to know? How can I have anything to offer?"

"Well, have you seen anything like this around town?"

"Animal attacks? Sure. Dozens. Dogs. Cats. Even had a lion attack once."

"I heard. So, did you ever have one where people got really sick?"

"Like rabies?"

"Maybe. Or tumors."

"Tumors?" He laughed. "Animal bites don't cause tumors."

"Right. I know. But could you check for me?"

"That's confidential stuff, Wheeler. Can't you submit a warrant?"

"I could, but it takes—"

"Forty-eight hours pending approval."

"Plus," she added. "Do you think a judge would ever listen to me about something like this?"

"Good point."

The waiter returned.

"I don't suppose we'll be ordering any dessert tonight, will we?" He glanced at Wheeler's untouched meal. "To-go box, madam?"

They laughed when he left.

"Do you really come here?" she asked.

"No. I was just trying to impress you."

"Well, I'm flattered. But I'm more of a burger and beer girl. And that guy's an asshole."

"Yes. Yes, he is."

"So what do you say? Can you do a little poking around for me?"

Dell thought for a moment. Then he nodded.

"Animal bites and tumors?"

"Animal bites and tumors."

He smiled.

"I'll do my best."

The heat did not dissipate when the sun set. If anything, the lack of sunlight made it feel hotter, as if the dashed expectations for the day to cool down somehow increased the temperature. She trudged up the stairs to her apartment, feeling the sweat run down her skin under her shirt, and when she opened her door, a warm blast of air rushed out of her apartment. Her window unit had totally died, and there was no point in contacting her landlady this late. She lived out of the city and wouldn't respond until the next morning anyway. So Wheeler took the two box fans out of the storage closet and put them in the windows. Then she reclined on her sofa, trying to relax without thinking about drinking. She read a romance novel cover to cover and took a shower. She lay in bed, letting the box fans stir a current over her skin. It was hot. Someone was cooking a late night meal on a grill. The smoke wafted into her window. She didn't think she'd be able to get to sleep in that heat until it snuck up on her.

The dead bodies smelled like cooked meat. They lay all around the base of a bombed out pyramid. Smoke poured from its interior. She couldn't tell if the bodies were human or not. The firestorm that killed them had twisted their bones into agonizing contortions. More choked the steps leading up the side. She knew she shouldn't go to it but couldn't help herself. She picked her way through the bodies.

Suddenly she was inside, winding around the chunks of adobe and limestone. More bodies lay inside, equally charred. Whispers from above, ghostly faces with mouths sewn shut staring back at her with black, hollow eyes. Before her sat a gutted man on a throne. Amber liquid bubbled out of his torso like molten gold. She watched as his belly gurgled more fluid, and then she was next to him, looking down into the cavity. The liquid wasn't flowing out, she saw, it was flowing back in, a thin trail siphoning up from the ground. His hand twitched and he opened his eyes.

The world turned upside down, and she found herself zooming through the floor. She landed in a cell far below. There were no windows, no doors. Just an open space. A single torch lit the room. Despite the depth and emptiness, she found herself growing hot, the heat emanating from the limestone floor. Sweat trickled down her back.

She felt the presence of the other before she saw it. It was standing in the corner, shrouded by flickering shadows. It breathed heavily, watching her. She crawled back as far as she could, stopping only when her back met the cell wall. Her heart thumped in her chest, and she wished she had her gun, a knife, anything because the thing in the corner was angry and it was her fault and it wanted to hurt her, to make her pay and she knew this because the dream logic told her so. She closed her eyes and willed the thing away.

"It's just a dream," she whispered. "Just a dream."

She whispered it over and over again and all of the sudden the air grew cooler. The tension lifted. She breathed a sigh of relief and opened her eyes.

The thing rushed her from the corner. A horrid old carcass with long, greasy hair and pasty white skin. It ran straight up to her face, screaming, "The key is the key! The key is the key! Let me out! Let me out! Let me out!"

Wheeler sat up in bed, screaming. Her bed was drenched in sweat. What was that? She'd had bad dreams before, but none so vivid, so real. The brand on her shoulder flared up and she winced. It was burning, like a signal, and when she looked at it, ran her fingers over it, she swore she saw a flicker of amber run along its slick surface. She brushed her hair out of her eyes, trying to make sense of what was going on, and the carcass, the thing from the dream, swooped down from the corner of her room and got into her face again.

"What are you waiting for!"

Wheeler sat up in bed again, screaming again.

She checked the corners of her room. Nothing there but cobwebs. She flopped back down, arms spread wide. The pain in her shoulder faded, and as it did she slowly became aware of the heat. Had it gotten worse? There was no breeze. Crap. Her box fans had crapped out, too. Maybe it was an electrical issue. She needed a drink. God she needed a drink.

Out on the street. Harvey's to the left. She'd thrown on her exercise clothes (tank top, running shorts, running shoes), totally intending to go for a walk. But the second she stepped out of the door to her building, she stopped. She fingered the pepper spray she'd clipped to her shorts, trying not to visualize the steps: the whine of the front door, the blast of air conditioning, the feel of the stool, the sound of ice in a tumbler . . .

Stop it. Don't think about it. You don't need it. She was determined not to go in, despite having finally read the letter from the lab, despite that horrible dream, and despite the fact that she could actually taste the whiskey on her tongue. She wasn't going to do it. She wasn't going to wake up in an alley again. She couldn't do that to herself. She just couldn't.

Wheeler took a deep breath, steeled her will, and walked slowly by the front door, taking purposeful strides, left, right, left, right, until she was one block away, two, four, eight and her heart rate was up and her breathing heavy but she was relieved, and all she wanted to think about was the next step, the next turn.

The city was alive in the summer heat, families and friends hanging out on front steps, entire blocks buzzing and alive with people trying to escape their stuffy apartments and townhouses. Wheeler power-walked through it all, intent only on tiring herself out. She did a figure eight around the block, waving at the people she knew, ignoring those she didn't. That quickly grew boring, so she expanded her circle, again and again, until she was out of her neighborhood entirely. From there it was easy to make the decision to just keep walking. She wasn't tired. Her feet didn't hurt. The exercise felt good.

The farther out she circled, the less people she passed. It was quiet. For the city, at least. The lights in the townhouses and row houses winked out. Traffic dwindled to the occasional car, and then to no cars. It wasn't until an hour had passed that she realized that she was in a part of the city that she didn't recognize, which was odd because, after a lifetime of walking its streets, she thought she'd seen it all. The houses were all dark, the stoops cracked and unkempt. She slowed her pace, taking care to look around. Wait. She had been there before, hadn't she? Her left arm started to ache, her bicep and shoulder. It was dull at first, then slowly built into a painful soreness, pinpointed on the brand on her shoulder. The pain peaked when she came to an old brownstone in the middle of the street, and she was going to push forward when something caught her attention and made her stop in her tracks.

A triple-spiral. Exactly like the brand on her shoulder. Flashing out at her from the front door. It seemed to blend into the wood itself, but when she started to walk again, it flared again, fiery gold with cold, yellow licks. It pulsed at her, called to her. There was a gate separating the stoop from the street. She unlatched it.

The next thing she knew, her hand was on the doorknob. She wanted to knock, call out, but something told her not to, that it didn't matter. A familiar melody popped into her mind, and she began to hum. Lyrics soon followed, and, though she wasn't one to break into spontaneous song, she couldn't help but recite the lyrics she knew went along with the tune.

"Singing in the sunshine, laughing in the rain. Hitting on the moonshine, rocking in the grain."

How did she know that? The name of the song escaped her. It was right there but she couldn't grab it. She hummed a few more bars and shook her head. Weird.

The smell of rot hit her full in the face as soon as she walked in. Something had died in there. She wasn't a rookie. She'd handled plenty of murder cases before, seen some pretty horrific things, and every time she went into a house that smelled that bad, horrific things were soon to follow. It was dark and hot, and the heat made the smell worse. She reeled. A quick flash of dizziness, an aural whomp flowing through her head like a wave. The brand on her shoulder ached, and she had to lean up against the wall just outside of the vestibule to gather herself.

"Man," she said, holding her hand over her nose.

She fumbled on the wall for the light switch, hoping the electricity worked but knowing it probably wouldn't. Her fingers found the panel, two antique buttons, on and off. She clicked the top one and was happily surprised when the chandelier glowed to life overhead, illuminating the entire grand entry.

This place. She knew it. She really had been there before. But when? Why? Who lived here? A stairway in front of her led up. To the right, a reception room. Before her, the hallway to the kitchen, and beyond that, the dining room.

She crept down the hallway, trying to breathe only through her mouth. Pictures hung on the walls, dozens of them. First portraits in oval frames, all of them of a beautiful woman wearing a brown dress and red belt. Her black hair was tucked up under a headdress, her face hidden behind a transparent veil. Then came more modern portraits of the same woman, the styles changing with the centuries. She'd grown older, more worn, but still beautiful. Always she stared out at Wheeler as if daring her to comment.

Soon she came upon a tintype, and now the woman was significantly older. Gone was the beauty of her youth, replaced by a fleshy face and an ugly scowl. She was joined by an equally old and equally ugly man. This was followed by early, black and white photographs. Children joined the couple, one, two, eight. The last picture looked like it had been taken at the turn of the last century, with the old man and woman dressed in stiffly formal clothes, standing on the top steps of the brownstone. Below them spread out a large, wide family, all of them bearing the same bold stare and serious expression, men, women, children alike.

She stopped at the cusp of the kitchen. The meager light from the chandelier in the entry illuminated very little there. The corner of the counter. A few knives scattered about a worn, wooden cutting board. The shells of rotting vegetables. The smell was worse here. The dining room lay beyond, dark and foreboding. She could barely make out the edge of a table in the dim light, and though she knew she should investigate, she didn't want to go any farther. She willed her legs forward but they wouldn't move.

Come on, Kat. Get it together.

She pushed through to the dining room and tried the switch, and as soon as the light flooded the room, she wished it hadn't done it. The rotten smell that Wheeler knew all so well was coming from a hunk of meat sitting just inside the doorway, an arm of some kind, covered in thick, black hair as sharp as porcupine needles. Flies buzzed around it, crawling through the hairs. She squatted down to have a closer look, using her pepper spray to poke around. The flies, disturbed by the motion, flew in her face. She brushed them away.

"Someone's been eating you," she said.

She waved away another fly and lost her balance, and when her hand shot out and grabbed the dining room table behind her, images flashed into her head. A warty lip. A pyramid. A dagger. She was immediately dizzy again, and even though she wanted to get away from the rotting meat, she had to wait for it to pass.

When it did, she stood up and inspected the table. It looked like it had been used for surgery. Civil War surgery. A serrated knife with a homemade handle sat next to what looked like a knitting needle with a hook on the end. A bowl of bloody water, dotted with more flies. White rags stained red. And a wooden stamp, with a bell as round as her shoulder and a metal pattern embedded in its surface.

The triple-spiral.

She was dizzy again, and sick. Sweat ran down her face. Images formed in her mind, memories, too, but no matter how hard she tried to catch them, they fled. She leaned against the table a little too hard, and the bowl filled with bloody water fell off and crashed to the floor. A second later, something slammed hard above her and she jumped. It sounded like someone dropped a bowling ball on the hardwood. Why hadn't she brought her gun? She wiped the sweat out of her eyes. A car honked on the street outside. Another noise from above, followed by thundering footsteps heading down the stairs.

She had her pepper spray. And the bloody knife on the table. Wheeler snatched it up. The footsteps pounded closer. Should she run for the door? The stairs emptied out into the front of the house, and whoever (or whatever) was up there might catch her before she made it out. She gripped her weapons tighter, her eyes searching the ceiling. Bam bam bam, another level. Whoever or whatever it was should have been almost to the front of the house, but it seemed to be getting closer to her. She traced its progress down and suddenly realized that there must have been another set of stairs, one that led to the back, a servant's stairway, perhaps. The footsteps pounded right above her, now just on the other side of the wall. All of the sudden a man ran out of the gloom, head down, barreling straight ahead, completely unaware of her presence. Katherine bent at the knees and held the knife and pepper spray in front of her, positioning herself so that the table was between them.

"Hey!" she yelled.

He looked up, surprised, and came to a stumbling halt. He was the easily the strangest looking creature she'd ever seen. He wore a wig and a top hat, and pantaloons and stockings with the bottoms cut out, and a leather bomber's jacket over a bare, tattooed chest. The tattoos were tribal, patterns mostly, Celtic knots. The letters CBCK ringed his collarbone in black. His head was shaved but for a single side knot that draped over his shoulder, and his eyes were painted black with kohl. In one hand he held a cricket bat with sharp, stone blades embedded in the side. He smiled at her, and she saw that his teeth had been sharpened to points.

"Hey," he said. "How's it going?"

Wheeler blinked.

"You speak English?"

"Yeah, Artie speaks English. What else would Artie speak?"

"I–I don't know."

He eyed the knife.

"You gonna stick Artie with that?"

"Maybe."

He adjusted his grip on the lethal looking bat.

"You wanna make you a deal?"

"Okay."

He gestured at his chest and stomach.

"You don't stick Artie anywhere." He swept the bat to his right. "You step aside."

Wheeler calculated. This was a B&E. She was a cop. Even if she was off duty, she couldn't just let him go. Of course, this wasn't her house, either. She licked her lips.

"Can't do that. CPD."

"The fuck's that mean?"

"I'm a detective." He stared at her. "A cop."

"I know what a detective is. Are you . . . Wheeler?"

Wheeler licked her lips.

"I arrest you before?"

"Nobody arrests Artie. Artie's been having nightmares. That friggin corpse screaming 'Find the bone! Make the key! Wheeler! Detective! Wheeler! Detective!' Driving Artie up the wall."

Wheeler felt the blood drain from her face.

"Artie can see. Wheeler's dreamed the same."

"Who is she?"

"Oh, you know. You know who she is. Same bitch what gave you that."

He pointed at the brand on her shoulder. Wheeler blinked a drop of sweat out of her eye.

"I-I can't let you go."

"Fuck you you can't let Artie go. Artie goes here. Artie goes there. Artie don't ask permission. Besides, seems like Wheeler don't live here, neither."

"Doesn't matter."

"Sure it does. Wheeler's not supposed to be here. Artie's not supposed to be here. Simplest solution? After Artie gives what he's got, Wheeler and Artie, they both scram."

"Not going to happen. Put the bat down."

"Bat? What bat?"

"Put the fucking bat down!"

He held up his weapon.

"What, you mean this? This ain't a bat. This is a sword."

"I don't care what you call it. Put it on the ground."

"Alright. Look. I can't take that old crone no more. On and on every night with that shit. So I got something for you."

He reached into his jacket pocket and Wheeler squirted the pepper spray right in his face. He dropped the bat, his hands flying up to his eyes.

"What the fuck!" he screamed.

Wheeler hovered around him, still holding the knife and pepper spray.

"Get down on the ground!"

"Artie's trying to help!"

"I'll hit you again!"

He bellowed and rushed her, arms swinging blindly. She pulled the trigger on the pepper spray again, but he was filled with adrenaline. Wheeler had seen this before. He wasn't going to stop. So she took a step back and kicked him square between the legs. Her toes hit something hard, and she felt them crack. Then he shoved her aside and ran through the kitchen, slamming into furniture, swiping the pictures and portraits off the wall. Wheeler hit the table with a grunt, then limped after him. He broke through the vestibule and out the front door. By the time she made it to the street, he was already on the other side, stumbling up the stairs of an old abandoned townhouse. He hit the door, struggled with the knob, and fell inside.

"Goddammit," Wheeler grunted, and hopped down the steps.

THE SNAKE

Coatl wanted to push through the night, but Xiuloc forced him to rest.

"You're injured," he said. "You can't just ignore it."

"Sleep won't make me better. Ka-Bata's crone will."

"Not if you never make it to her. You need rest and food."

"I'm fine."

"*I* need rest and food. A good leader keeps his men healthy, yes?"

"Yes. But Ka-Bata, if he's really alive, he has an army."

"I know, general."

"We can fight back."

"I know, general."

In the end, he relented. Keyn offered to fish the river, and Sehlah started a fire. They ate what the boy caught, then bedded down.

Coatl awoke with the sun. He hated to admit it, but the Onton was right. Though his body ached and his leg throbbed, he felt much better for all the rest. The children were already awake, itching to go, but Xiuloc snored as if it was the middle of the night, his mouth wide open. Sehlah whispered to Keyn, giggling, but Keyn frowned and shook his head.

"Fine," she said. "I'll do it."

She crept over to the warrior, pausing once when he snorted and smacked his lips, then she crouched down next to his head and picked up a little twig. She held it over his open mouth, waited until he inhaled, and dropped it in. Xiuloc startled awake, coughing. He spat the twig out into his hand, then stared at the girl, who was laughing behind her hand.

"Did you drop a twig in my mouth?" he asked.

She squealed and ran back to her brother.

They led the warriors farther downstream than they'd ever been. The river roared along beside them as they walked. Coatl felt it like a presence, and no matter how hard he tried to ignore the noise, he couldn't. When he was a child, if someone had commented on the sound he would have said, "What noise?" Now it tickled his nerves. Just before the sun reached its peak, Sehlah turned away from the river and deeper into the jungle. Xiuloc, who'd taken up the rear to keep watch, caught up with the general when they turned.

"I've never been this far west," he said.

"Neither have I."

"I didn't know we had any villages this far out."

"We don't."

"Those children. They're not Tlek."

Coatl nodded, thinking.

"I've never met Ka-Bata," he said. "His tribe didn't fight in the Mutiny, for your side or mine. But Seka-Khayu left him alone. Never punished him. Didn't make him pay the blood debt. I always got the sense that the skhatet was afraid of him."

"That symbol on their heads. The snake that eats the sun. I've never seen it."

"We can hear you," Keyn said.

Coatl and Xiuloc shared a guilty glance, and Coatl elbowed him. Apologize to them. Xiuloc swallowed his pride.

"We're sorry, Keyn. We're just curious. Your names. We've never heard them before. Where do they come from? What do they mean?"

"Sehlah means beautiful flower," the boy said, punching Sehlah in the arm and laughing.

She hit him back and told him to shut up.

"And what does Keyn mean?" Coatl asked.

Keyn glared at the girl.

"Don't say it!"

She smirked at him.

"It means 'gentle' and 'handsome'," she said. "He will have many wives!"

"Sehlah!" Keyn cried.

She ran off, laughing again, before he could hit her.

They passed through old villages, the remains of the adobe huts and old steam baths almost indistinguishable from the underbrush. Coatl tried to remember which village was which, but he couldn't. It had been too long. The path the children took fascinated him, too. He fancied himself a fair tracker, but they seemed to follow a trail visible only to them. Every now and then they paused to whisper to each other, using a strange language he'd never heard before.

Guttural at times, it was smoother than his own, more musical. His leg hurt with every step, and his limp became more and more pronounced. Xiuloc knew he was too proud to admit he needed help, so when they came across a thicket of bamboo, he hacked away at the sturdiest shoot for the general to use a staff. It was tall and thick, and it could be used as a weapon in a pinch. Coatl was grateful, but even with its help, his wound took its toll. The sun beat down, and the day grew hot. He needed a break. They came into a clearing, and he said, "Sehlah. Keyn. We must stop."

They did, frowning. He pointed at the drooping tumor. "I have to sit and rest. Please. Only a few minutes."

Keyn looked at the girl, his head shaking a little bit.

"This is a bad place," she said.

Xiuloc looked around, skeptical.

"It's a clearing. Look, there's even a few old logs to sit on."

"No!" Keyn said. "Those aren't logs. That's a witch house. An old one, an evil one from the ancient cities."

"Not much of a house anymore, is it?"

Coatl limped around the perimeter. The boy was right. Those weren't logs. They were made of some strange metal he'd never seen before. There were four of them, squared off at each corner, all of them in various states of decay. It looked like an outline. Now that he looked closer, they were charred and twisted in places. The air seemed to grow heavy. No birds flitted overhead, no insects buzzed in the brush. Sehlah looked around her as if she'd heard something.

"Sehlah, it's okay," Keyn said.

Coatl lowered himself to the ground with a grunt, letting his leg stick out in front of him. Xiuloc joined him and chuckled a little.

"Don't worry, children," he said. "We're fierce warriors. If any bad witch tries to hurt you—" he brought his maquahuitl down in a swift arc, expecting it to thock into the earth, but it merely bounced, chipping one of the blades. He grunted. The children were not reassured. They hovered at the edge of the clearing, fearfully eyeing their surroundings.

"This witch couldn't have been too powerful," Coatl said. He pointed at the logs. "Someone burned down her house."

Sehlah let her eyes rest on him.

"It was the white robes. They sought her out and spilled her blood on the ground where you're sitting. When they were done, they set fire to it."

"White robes?"

"Knights. The Knights of Salvation."

The two men shared a glance.

"Salvation is a myth, Sehlah," Coatl said. "A story to tell babies."

"It's not. We've seen it. What's left, at least."

"Of Salvation? The city?"

She nodded, and while Coatl wanted to laugh, her face set so solemn and serious that he didn't have the heart. Keyn must have read his doubt, because he said, "It's true. The plics took—"

"Keyn, quiet," Sehlah said. "They won't understand." She looked at Coatl. "Is your leg rested? We should get moving again. It gets dark early this time of year, and we still have a long way to go."

They walked on, the river's roar growing softer and softer until the sounds of the jungle finally overtook it entirely. After the remains of the witch house, they came upon no more old Tlek villages, no more adobes, no more steam baths, just hands and hands of untamed jungle.

"Ka-Bata was a crazy old fool for living this far away," Xiuloc said. Coatl shook his head ruefully.

"I'm not so sure. Look what happened to everybody who chose to stay close to the skhatet."

It was close to evening when the terrain began to change. The trees thinned out, and the brush grew lower to the ground until both simply disappeared, and they found themselves walking through tall grasses and boggy marsh. Then seemingly out of nowhere, they came upon a hand-bridge. Coatl had never seen anything like it. It was long and sturdy, with even planks and rope strung between the pilings, seven sets in all, evenly spaced, expertly measured. The wood was old and gray, stained green where they sank into the bog, but thick and stalwart. The bridge ended in a gatehouse made out of rough-hewn tree trunks, anchored into a tall battlement, also wood. Ka-Bata might have been unpredictable in his politics, strange in his beliefs, but he was no fool when it came to the dangers of this world.

The bridge was accessed by an elaborate entrance, an archway made from adobe that stretched back several yards to form a box. It was covered in a vast net of iron thorns, making it impossible to climb. Any enemy wishing to access the bridge would have to win the box or wade into the water. A wooden door blocked the way, the circular handles fashioned to look like snakes, of course. Carved pieces of wood hung from the roof, knocking against each other in the breeze and producing a rhythmic musical sound. Anchored on either side of the door were wide, copper dishes in which the guards (for Coatl could only imagine that the structure had been built with guards in mind) probably burned coal or oil, something to work as a beacon or a warning signal. Or a weapon. They were dead and cold now, but the fires must have been quite impressive when properly tended.

"A silly contrivance," Coatl said, meaning the entire structure. "Impressive, but useless."

"Ka-Bata built it," Sehlah told him. "It keeps our enemies out."

"They can just swim across the bog."

The girl regarded him thoughtfully, then she turned to Keyn. "Show him."

"With what?"

"Use your twists."

"But I only have a couple left!"

"Just do it, Keyn."

He groaned and reached into a little pouch hanging from the belt of his tunic, taking out a twist of dried meat. Then he walked over to the bog's water line, gnawing off a bite along the way.

"Watch," he said, and threw the rest in.

Nothing happened for a moment, then the surface started to boil, and a swarm of fish erupted from the depths, fighting over the piece of meat. Pictlan. They snapped and gnashed their razor sharp teeth, tearing each other to pieces. When the meat was gone, they devoured their own dead and disappeared, leaving a red stain in the green water.

Sehlah smiled at Coatl.

"They could try to swim across the bog," she said.

The door to the bridge opened with a whine, leading into the guard's room. Stashes of weapons lined the walls. Atlatls. Maquahuitl. Spears, clubs, lances, bows and arrows, and, leaning by itself in the corner near the door, one of the plics' weapons, old and rusted and useless. Xiuloc found a spear. Then he opened up a chest that had been anchored to the wall. Dried fish and clay pots of water sat within. He picked up a pot and sniffed it. It was fresh. He drank and handed it to Coatl, who finished it off. He put the pot back in the chest and watched the children as they walked across the bridge.

"I think you should stay here," he told Xiuloc.

"Why?"

Coatl didn't answer him at first, didn't know how to explain his feelings. He trusted the children. He believed them. But . . .

"Xiuloc, don't you think that if the village was really overrun by plics, they would have attacked us by now?"

Xiuloc considered this.

"There are no plics," he said. "Or it's a trap."

"If it is, Ka-Bata's dead. And if he's dead, whoever goes in there is next."

"Then we'll take them on together."

Coatl held up his injured leg.

"If it's like that, then I'm done. But the tecuani are still out there. In the swamp. Replenishing their numbers. There must be some of our people left, some warriors somewhere. Someone needs to find them. Rally them."

Xiuloc clenched his jaw. It wasn't right.

"What if there aren't any left? What if we're it? I'd be leaving you to die."

"That's a risk I'm willing to take. Stay here. Let me do it. Maybe the children aren't lying. Maybe their crone will be able to help."

Xiuloc looked like he was about to argue. He didn't like the idea of leaving this man alone, not injured. Coatl was a great warrior, a celebrated general. He deserved his help, his respect. But in the end, they barely knew each other, and though he was a general, he owed the man no allegiance. He'd already saved him twice. He grunted.

"Okay," he said. "More food for me."

Coatl leaned heavily on the bamboo staff as he crossed. His ankle ached. The tecuani larva sagged, pulling on his bone, and though Xiuloc had done a good job killing it, pierced it straight through the heart and brain, its teeth remained fixed. It felt like his skeleton was being pulled out of his skin. He wished they could just cut it out, but the risk of infection was too great. He'd seen what happened to men who tried it on their own. Their legs rotted. They died in horrible pain.

He distracted himself by taking note of his surroundings. The bridge was long and old, but sturdy and well-maintained. More symbols had been carved into the pilings, variations of the ouroboros, but some different ones, too. A triple spiral. A circle divided into four quadrants, with a half-moon resting on top. Three vertical lines, the one in the middle slightly longer than the two on the outside, joined together at the center by a horizontal spear. The children touched each one as they passed.

"What are those?" he asked.

Sehlah said, "A message."

"What does it say?"

She pointed at the ouroboros, the snake that eats the sun. "This is Ka-Bata's. It means he returned."

"Returned? From where?"

Coatl looked up at the wall as they approached. It should have been crawling with plics, their weapons ready to mow down any enemy, Tlek or tecuani alike, but he didn't see any. In fact, no guards were posted at the door, no soldiers walked ramparts, and no fires burned, either in welcome or in warning. All was still and silent.

They were about twenty yards from the front gate when it opened with a crack and a whine. All three paused on the walkway, waiting. Then a figure in white stepped out, tall and lithe, with long, flowing blonde hair. Coatl flipped the club in his hand, readying himself.

The children, however, did not seem concerned.

"Mor!" Keyn shouted, and broke for the form. Sehlah followed, somewhat uncertain.

"Keyn, wait!" Coatl called after, but it was too late.

He limped after them, his ankle throbbing with each step. How fearsome he must have looked. The figure disappeared back into the village before Keyn even reached her, and he called out for her again, "Mor! Wait!"

"Get back here!" Coatl yelled. "Keyn!"

The boy made it to the gate well before him and ducked inside, followed by Sehlah, who was yelling for him to stop. Coatl, winded and limping, finally reached it, surprised at how much energy it took for him to run such a short distance, and so slow! The wound must have drained him more than he realized. But there was no time. He pulled the gate open so he could fit inside, took two steps, and stopped.

An entire village was arrayed before him. Adobe huts with thatched roofs, a granary, an empty cattle pen, stilted rooms for food storage. But nothing else. Nobody else. It was entirely empty. Even the children had disappeared.

"Keyn!" he yelled. "Sehlah!"

Nothing. The gate closed behind him, and he closed his eyes. They might take him, but it wouldn't be without a fight. He heard the footsteps behind him, felt the nervous energy. He spun, lashing out with the club. But his attackers were not as inexperienced as he thought, and as he spun, waiting for his club to connect, already swinging the staff to land a second blow, his head exploded with pain and his vision went momentarily black. He collapsed, halfway conscious. He'd dropped his club. He didn't know where the staff lay. He slapped the dirt, hoping to land on either, but all he found was more dirt. Something stepped on his wrist, something cold and hard. He finally opened his eyes.

A man stood there. At least Coatl thought he was a man. He was covered in the strangest armor he'd ever seen, from the hard, silver shoes he wore on his feet to the helmet covering his head. He picked the general's club up and swung it back and forth a few times, as if taking practice swings. Then he stopped and seemed to consider the intruder at his feet.

"Your leg is infected," he said. "I can't have that in my village."

The strength it took for Coatl to smile up at him made him dizzy, but he did it anyway, he showed his blood stained teeth and said, "Zan miquizpantiizah."

"The only thing you get in death," the man said. "Is death."

"Teh," Coatl said. "I'll see you there and kill you again."

The man in metal stopped swinging and paused. Then he leaned over so that Coatl could see his eyes glimmering from inside the helmet.

"General Coatl," he said. "Is that you?"

Coatl snorted into the dirt. Then he started to laugh, even though it hurt his head.

"What's so funny?" the man asked.

Coatl barked out another laugh and then gathered himself.

"Nothing, Ka-Bata. Nothing," he said. "I wish I could say I'm happy to see you, but . . ."

"No?" Ka-Bata stood up straight and flipped the club in his hand. "This won't make you happy, either."

When Coatl woke, he was lying on a pallet in a room that looked exactly like the one from his childhood. The stone walls, the rectangular windows, the wooden door. Not everybody had a room to himself, but his father, a member of Seka-Khayu's inner-council, held a large amount of power. The Tlek did not measure wealth so much in material belongings. They measured it through power and influence, and the way to gain those was through military might, prowess on the battlefield. A large dwelling was more of a side benefit. Valuable but not coveted. Anybody could build a large compound. All it took was the will to do so. But Coatl had grown up wealthy. In victory after victory, his father and his uncle rose through the ranks until Seka-Khayu granted them titles and seats on his council. When his time came, Coatl followed.

He wondered if there was a garden on the other side of the door, just like his old house. Would there be a steam bath on the far end, too? But there were other items in the room, things he didn't recognize. An ornate table with a checkered, stone top. White pots fashioned into the most magnificent shapes. A three-paneled screen with images of the gods Tepotz, Tezchat, and Queza printed on its leather face. The combination was unnerving, and it made his head swim.

His head. Oh, his head. It throbbed and ached from Ka-Bata's blow, and when he felt his temple it was swollen and tender. He'd been hit like that before, and he knew how to handle that kind of pain. But he'd never been stung by a tecuani. Not many people did and lived, and the fear of the unknown, of what was going to happen to him next, increased his suffering. So that's why, when he sat up and looked at his leg, he was amazed to see the tumor gone, the tecuani larva removed. A discolored flap of skin hung off his calf, the excess from the tumor, and now that he was more awake he realized that all of his pain was localized, that it no longer radiated up his leg and through his bone, but that it only seemed to hover around the area of the wound. Obviously, Ka-Bata had ordered the operation, but why? Why knock him out only to save his life?

The door opened and an old woman, the oldest woman he'd ever seen, hobbled in. She was dressed in a sleeveless tunic, her shoulders and chest branded with the triple-spiral, the sign of her cabal. She was carrying a tray with a kettle of steaming water, a poultice, and an obsidian blade. She paused when she saw he was awake.

"Don't think about running," she said. "Not on that leg." Then disappeared behind the screen.

Ka-Bata's crone. The crone that removed the thing from his leg. It had to be. She shuffled out from behind the screen, and three neatly folded white cloths were now stacked on the tray, as well as a little spool of black thread. She sat the tray down on the ground next to his legs, squatting with more ease than he thought possible from a thing so ancient.

"You're very lucky," she said, carefully arranging her instruments.

"Lucky, you say."

"Very lucky indeed. The little tecuani's teeth weren't fully mature. Very easy to take out. Very easy. I've seen them pierce the bone all the way through, like a lance. Yes. You are lucky."

She dipped the poultice in the hot water.

"What's the blade for?" Coatl asked.

"Have you ever seen a tecuani wound heal? No, of course not. Of course not. Filthy creatures. Very filthy. Even the babies."

She grabbed his leg with a gnarled hand, and he hissed and tried to remove it from her grasp, but it only made her clamp down harder.

"Stop it."

She picked up the blade and brought it to his leg.

Coatl said, "Wait."

"That's what they all say," she said, and started cutting.

He fell back onto his pallet, swallowing the cry that threatened to break loose. He was a warrior, a general. He would not show weakness before anyone, not his men, not his skhatet, and certainly not a crone. She hummed as she cut, a simple tune, adding words every now and then to the melody. He focused on the lyrics, which were in that same, strange language the children had used.

"Hmm hmm-hmm hmm-hmm-hmm, I can hear the ocean's roar . . . . Used to sing on the mountains; has the ocean lost its way?"

When he finally had enough, he reached out and grabbed her hand. She stopped, watching impassively as he gulped the air. Then she waved the knife at him.

"If you think that hurts, wait until I stitch it."

"A moment, please. Just a moment."

Was that a look of reproach on her face? Such a brave warrior, a celebrated general, now whining like a child. Men were so weak.

"A moment, then," she said. "But then I go back to work."

The pain faded a little, and he said, "What is that song?"

"Oh, it's just an old rhyme."

"I've never heard it before."

"You wouldn't have. You've never visited Gabriel."

The word was strange and difficult for him to pronounce.

"Who is . . . Gab-rul?"

"It's pronounced Gabriel. Gay-brie-el.

He sounded it out and she nodded.

"Close enough," she said.

"Where is he."

"What?"

"Gaybrie. Where is he?"

"Gabriel's a place, not a person."

"Okay, but—"

"Hush now. Let me work."

When she was done and the excess skin had been removed, the crone used the black thread to stitch the wound. Coatl wavered on the edge of consciousness, the pain of the surgery mitigated by the relief of having the monster out of his body. The old woman put the bowl, the knife, and bloody towels and everything else behind the screen and left for a while. Coatl slept, waking only when she returned hauling two dirty blocks, one in each hand. She braced his leg with them and he gasped. They were freezing.

"What is that?"

"Ice. For the swelling."

"Where did you get it?" he asked.

The crone stared at him, a flash of anger crossing her features. She opened her mouth to speak, but then the door flew open and into the room bounced a bear in a white linen robe. Coatl had never seen such a hairy man. His head and face, his chest, his arms, even his feet were covered in the thick, coarse stuff. Ka-Bata? Could it be? Gone were his piercings, his feathers, all the symbols of a chief. He looked more like a plic than a person.

"General Coatl! Ha ha! As I live and breathe! In the flesh! Ha! That was a pun! Oh, pardon me, madam."

The crone glared at him.

"Ka-Bata. He is very sick, and very—"

"Lucky to be alive, of course, of course."

His crone stared at him until he lowered his eyes and tucked his chin to his chest. When she didn't say anything, he cleared his throat.

"Make sure he doesn't move that leg," she said, poking him in the chest with her tray. "And no pulque, Ka-Bata."

"I wouldn't think of it, madam."

"I'm serious."

"As am I."

She gave Coatl a pointed look, then glared at Ka-Bata again as she scooted out the door, her tray in front of her. Ka-Bata smiled impishly and raised his eyebrows at Coatl as she passed. When he was sure she was gone, he peered around the door, once, twice (just to make sure), then drew it closed.

"She's gone," he announced. He pulled a strange container out from inside his tunic. "Drink?" Coatl stared at him, baffled. "No? More for me then." He unscrewed the top and took a long drink. "Ah. Nectar of Mayel."

"Ka-Bata, what is this? Where are we? Why are you dressed like that? And why did you club me in the head?"

"So many questions, General. But what else should I expect from the son of a councilman? Tell me. How did your father react when you decided not to follow in his footsteps?"

"How did he—"

"I'll wager he nearly exploded."

He looked at Coatl expectantly. Finally, Coatl said, "He was not pleased."

Ka-Bata erupted in laughter.

"I knew it! I knew it!" He took another swig from the container. "Your father, he was a great man, but he was wound tighter than a stingray's ass. Do stingrays have an ass? Who knows." He groaned as he squatted down on the ground. "If I pinched a reed between my thumb and forefinger and tried to insert it into your father's ass . . . he'd probably cut off my arm!" And with that, he broke out into fresh gales of laughter.

"Give me some of that," Coatl said, reaching for the container.

"Yes! Yes, general! Have some. Have yourself a nice long swig."

He handed it over, and Coatl took a gulp. Coatl had tasted alcohol before. He was a warrior, after all. His father had an agave garden and allowed his servants to make pulque to sell and trade at the market. But this, this was much stronger than any he'd ever tasted. It burned his throat and spread out into this belly. He choked and coughed, his eyes watering and his face turning red. Ka-Bata laughed so hard that he couldn't breathe.

When the general could speak, he said, "What is that poison?"

"Poison!" Ka-Bata said, snatching the container back. "How dare you? That's my best batch of whiskey yet!" He took another swig and tucked it back into his tunic. Just in time, too, for seconds later the crone came back into the room. Ka-Bata looked over his shoulder as she disappeared behind the screen. He rocked on his heels.

"Forget something, madam?"

She didn't answer, reemerging a few seconds later with her knife and bowls. She was about to leave when something caught her attention. She sniffed the air.

"Ka-Bata, I said no pulque in here!"

"Madam, I swear on the hummingbird we have shared no pulque."

She peered around the room, seeking out any evidence of drinking. When she didn't see anything, she poked him in the shoulder.

"Don't touch anything back there."

"I wouldn't dream of it."

Then she left for the second time. Coatl, in the meantime, had leaned back on his pallet again. The whiskey. Is that what Ka-Bata called it? Yes. Whiskey. It did its work. Dulled the pain. His feet throbbed pleasantly. A warm glow suffused his body.

"I'll have another drink, if you don't mind."

Ka-Bata smiled and reached into his tunic.

"Now you see, yes? Now you see."

"Yes. I see," Coatl said, receiving the container. He took another swig and held it up. "What is this thing called?"

Ka-Bata suppressed a grin.

"A flask."

Coatl held it up appreciatively.

"I like it. It's strong." He gripped it, impressed. "Where did you get it? And that suit you wore at the gate? What is it made out of?"

Ka-Bata took the flask back.

"I don't know. They're just a few of treasures we found in Gabriel."

He leaned back against the wall, resting his head against it.

"There are strange things in that city, old things. Fantastic devices. Marvels. But dangerous, too. Look at this."

He rolled up his sleeve and showed Coatl a long, shiny slug that reached from his wrist to his shoulder.

"They almost killed me. Tried to take my arm, they did! Would you like me to tell you about it?"

THE RABBIT

When I was a kid, I seen this scary movie once. Actually, when I was a kid I seen a lot of scary movies, not just once, because when I was a kid we didn't have no TV, we only had movies. I'd hit the theater on a late Saturday morning after helping pop with the newsstand and nobody wouldn't see nothing of me until later that afternoon. I loved the horror shows. *The Picture of Dorian Gray. The Golem. From the River's Depths. Life Without Soul.*

Nosferatu? Fuck's sake that freaked me out. And Nosferatu from *Nosferatu?* Fuuuuuck me. Them long-ass fingernails and them pointy, gnarled-up teeth, not to mention the bugged out eyes? Reminded me of one of them things on the bottom of the ocean that looked like it could bite off a bull's leg. But none of that, no werewolf, no black lagoon, no bull's-leg eating ocean dweller, scared me as much as what came flying out of that forest.

First it was nothing, just that whistling noise, which actually made it worse. Built suspense. Ramped up the tension. On top of that, we could hear the monsters rumbling toward us from the arena. Nothing too terrible, just screams and growls and people screaming "oh my god please don't tear my guts out!". That kind of thing. For the nine billionth time in a long string of nine billionth times, I didn't know what to do. We couldn't go back. Obviously. And we couldn't run to the barracks, neither, because what good would that do?

Our only option was to make a break for the woods, but that didn't feel like a good idea, both because Zoot seemed dead serious when he told us not to go there and because, you know, of the noise coming out of it. Speaking of which, whatever was whistling toward us got louder and louder, followed by the sound of cracking sticks and, I swear to god, bullets thunking into the trees. One of the survivors (I'm saying it was a Cock Blocker, but he could've been a Champ, a Chump, or a Bastard for all I knew) took a few tentative steps toward the tree line, listened for a sec, then turned to me and said, "What is that?"

I shrugged. Why'd he think I'd have that information? We'd been together the entire time.

Wildcat displayed the best judgment out of us all. She grabbed an extra drum off a stray tommy gun, ran back to the ditch, and jumped in. Good thing, too, because that Cock Blocking Cunt Kicker? The Cock Blocking Cunt Kicker who asked my opinion of the noise whistling through the trees? He tried to ask it one more time but only got about half way through the sentence before . . . well, here. Watch:

"Seriously," he said. "What is tha—"

And then a silver slicer, like an arrowhead made out of super sharp space metal, slammed into his chest and burst out the other side in a spray of blood. He looked down at the hole like it'd just asked him to solve for x. Then he fell over, dead.

So I joined Wildcat in the ditch.

I barely made it back before a whole slew of slicers shot out of the trees, hundreds of them, thousands, plunging into anybody still caught out in the open. They burst through heads, they burst through necks, they burst through chests, anything, any part they could, zipping through the air like supersonic missiles. It was over in seconds, and then they sped off into the distance. Wildcat started to crawl out of the ditch, but in a rare fit of near genius, I grabbed her by the back of the shirt and pulled her down.

"Get off me," she said.

"No way. Just wait."

"For what? Them things to come back?"

"Yeah. That's the point."

"Dude."

"Shh!"

I cocked my head while she frowned at me. The whistling faded into the day, replaced by the sound of the monsters getting closer and closer. Wildcat bounced with anxiety.

"We gotta get out of here!"

"Pleaseshutthefuckup!"

Out of the corner of my eye, I seen the first monster turn the corner in the road. It stopped at the sight of all them dead bodies, drooling like a fat fuck at a pig roast. Goodness me, where to begin? The decision was made for it, I guess, when six more of its friends came up behind and knocked it out of the way and started sinking stingers. Cue disgusting slurping noises. They swarmed the corpses, the jackals, snapping and growling, tearing off limbs. Here a crunch, there a crunch, slurp, smack, munch munch.

If prior experience served me correct, in a few minutes the place would be swamped with little baby monsters, and they'd be looking for a meal, too, in which case we was dead, me especially. I ain't bragging or nothing, but I imagined myself quite the tasty treat.

The monsters got closer.

A tumor on a Fugly's stomach started to form.

Wildcat hunched down in the ditch, gripping her gun.

Then I heard it again. The whistles.

The friggin slicers was heading back our way, just like I predicted. Beautiful and terrible. Wildcat heard it, too.

"Holy shit," she said.

Had to time this right. I counted to ten, twenty, thirty, and the whistling sound got louder and louder. The monsters heard it, too. Stopped infecting every body part they could see and turned as one to the source of the noise. It was the first time I ever noticed a speck of intelligence in their features. Their eyes were in their shoulders, and they didn't have eyebrows, and the mouths that took up their chests hung permanently open, but if they did have eyebrows and if they could do anything other with their mouths open, them eyebrows would've knitted and them mouths would've clamped shut. One even turned and looked at the others, just like that Cock Blocker did a few minutes before, like he was asking a question.

What is that?

Beats us.

Well, motherfuckers. You were about to find out.

At fifty seconds, the whistling peaked and I ducked back into the ditch. One of the slicers zipped so close over my head that it chunked into the path. Fucker was aiming for me. Then the rest of the wave shot through the air, tearing the monsters to pieces. I'll spare you the details. I'm sure you can imagine it. Six thick bodies of muscle and teeth mowed down, chopped to bits in a split second. It was actually even more brutal than the first wave, as if the slicers had learned or something, started bunching up in groups of three or four. They tore through their victims and shot off into the forest. Branches cracked. Trunks exploded.

Somehow the seventh beast escaped any harm. It stood there, shocked, maybe even amused. A few more of the baby monsters popped out and rolled around in the dirt. I started counting again and only got to fifteen when the whistling sound returned. Branches cracked, trunks thunked, and at twenty-five the slicers (and there were less of them now) shot back out into the path, zeroing in on the last beast. They did what they needed to do, and then there was one more heap of meat laid out on the road.

"They're getting smarter," I said.

Wildcat laughed.

"No shit."

"And the space between attacks is getting shorter."

"No shit."

"What do we do?"

I heard a shout and peeked up over the edge of the ditch. A handful of us, at least twenty, were running for the woods. Wildcat said, "Better than staying here," and followed suit.

Oh well, what the hell, I thought, and jumped out and ran along with her.

I ran like I was running from—well, there really ain't no comparison for what I ran from. At least not in the animal kingdom. So I ran like there was a billion space-metal arrowheads zipping through the air behind me, each one intent on turning my insides into fertilizer. The whistling peaked as I put on an extra burst of speed, and if I'd cared to throw a look behind me, I'd have seen hundreds of them flattening out into a line two feet tall and about three feet off the ground.

Maybe I could have zigged, maybe I could have zagged, but I didn't think there was no point to it. All that would've done was slow my sorry ass down. Best strategy was to sprint straight ahead. The most important fifty-yard dash of our lives. Beeline it for the trees and get as deep into the forest as possible. Use all the . . . oh shit. That's what all the cracking and the trunk thunking was.

I passed Wildcat and ran right into a tree branch. Forehead shot. Even made a funny bonking sound. Hurt like a sonofabitch, too, but not as bad as the switches that whipped my eyes and cut my arms while I attempted to keep moving forward. Then I stumbled into a spider web so thick that I heard it rip the bark off the trees it was stuck to, which set me to twirling, coughing and choking, trying to wipe the web off my face. I ain't afraid of spiders (see chapter one), but the thought of one getting stuck in my hair or crawling into my mouth made me gag. If anything, that should tell you how much I'd recovered from my thousand year stint in solitary. Wildcat sprinted by.

"What are you doing?"

I opened my mouth to tell her what she could do with herself and inhaled something. Went right down my throat. I think it was a rat. Then a Tlek with a top knot zipped by, ducking and leaping like he'd been born for it, which, considering the fact that the Tleks lived in the jungle, was probably pretty accurate. He eyed me as he passed, a faint look of disgust on his face, and I waved him away, coughing, trying to smile, just in case he was thinking about stopping to help. He wasn't. All he done was frown and kept running, jumped over a thicket of thorns and disappeared into the brush.

I heard the slicers crash into the woods, thocking into the trees, cutting into the branches, cutting down anybody with the bad luck to be behind me. A few goons hit the deck. Maybe they thought the slicers'd fly right over, but that plan backfired some kind of spectacular. Maginot Line spectacular. I'll give them credit, though, because it wasn't a bad idea, and it looked like it might work, but the slicers on the bottom adjusted and shot straight down ninety degrees, skewering their necks and spinal cords, blasting through their brains. I thought, phew, one line of slicers down at least, but then they burst out of the earth and rejoined the hunt. Awesome.

Some numb cunt angled himself right in front of me, you know, because he only had to run faster than the guy behind him. I weaved, he weaved. I cut, he cut. So fuck that. Some of the slicers'd gone rouge, broke the line and started mowing us down one at a time, so I waited until I heard the whistling get real close, and right at the last second, I dodged. Thing didn't even swerve. Piked the guy in front of me in the back of the neck and lodged in his skull. He fell flat on his face like the worthless sack he was, and I spat at him as I ran by.

Still, he was on to something, so when some other numb cunt started to catch up, I wove in front of him at the last second and thunk, down he went. This, I decided, was my best shot at survival. High pitched whistle, cut to the left, thunk. High pitched whistle, cut to the right, thunk. Whistle, cut, thunk. Whistle, cut, thunk. Then a slicer pounded into the tree to my right. A chunk of wood shrapneled my ribs. Splinters peppered my face and neck. Hurt like, uh . . . . Well, it hurt like getting shards of wood shot into your body, that's what it hurt like. I'll let you guess which one felt worse, the rib chunk or the face splinter.

Okay.

In the interest of pacing and general good manners, it now becomes necessary to think of the next five images as a montage. Action adventure. Two seconds each.

Heavy breathing. Blue black woods. A tree to the left explodes.

Wildcat trips, and a slicer whizzes overhead, adjusts too late, slams into the earth.

Shot of an ankle. A sliver blur. Blood spews predictable.

A hand splayed out, trying to block the silver terror. It don't work.

An old man standing on the deck of a log cabin in the middle of a clearing, beckoning.

We was down to fifteen. Fifteen sad sacks running for our lives, but at least we had a destination. That old man had to be protected somehow. All we had to do was get inside his house. Why else would he be waving us over like that? Unless he was just screwing around, in which case fuck that guy. I chose to believe he wanted to help. The clearing was about fifty yards away, and I reached into whatever reserves I had to try to make it. Didn't speed up, but didn't slow down neither. Twenty yards. The head of a Bastard to my right exploded; a shower of blood. Fifteen yards. The wall of slicers mowed through the woods. Ten yards. The whistling got louder and louder. Five yards. I could feel their heat tickling the hair on the back of my neck. I gritted my teeth, striving, striving and then, bam! I burst into the clearing like I'd just won a marathon, eyes closed, chest out, arms wide, waiting for the slicers to do their bloody work, shred me like a wood chipper.

But it didn't happen.

I kept running anyway. No way I was going to stop, not then, not after what I seen what them things could do. Here's a tip: if you ever want to try running with your eyes closed, don't. Inevitably you're gonna trip and fall, which is exactly what I done. My shin hit a stump, sending me tumbling headlong, end over end, and let me tell you something, falling that way ain't fun. Only an asshole fell like that, or a geek in middle school, or a stunt horse in a war movie. I bounced once, got the wind knocked out of me, and slid a few feet before I finally came to a stop. Then I just lay there, gasping.

Weird electric noises filled the air, like a bug zapper in Miami. When I finally got my wind back, I rolled over and saw the most amazing thing. The slicers were hitting some kind of invisible shield and evaporating, burning up in a shower of silver and electric blue, millions of them, zap zap zap zap zap. It would've been beautiful if I hadn't been so terrified.

"Fuck's sake," I moaned. "Fuck's sake."

My head ached, my ass ached, and my ribs was on fire. I mean it was literally on fire. Not like a metaphor. Must've been the wood shards. Gave me a nice thirty-degree burn on top of that puncture wound. It also worked in my favor a bit, because, after all the burning flesh, the flames cauterized the wound, like searing up a nice hunk of steak. My ribs was still busted and there was still a chunk of a tree in my side, but at least it was kind of clean, so, yay irony.

Turned out only four of us made it: me, Wildcat, that rude Tlek top knot I told you about, and some random dude I ain't never seen before. The slicers continued to hit the shield, lighting it up like fireworks, but I guess even the shield had its limits. Three burst through and tore into that poor random dude I ain't never seen before. After they took him down they didn't go after any of us, though. They kept plunging in and out of him like they'd got stuck in a loop, his body shaking each time they punched through, gut, head, back, legs, over and over, bits of metal shearing off until he wasn't nothing more than a bloody pulp and they wasn't nothing more than angry pebbles. The last one came to rest on his chest and rolled off.

I looked at Wildcat, standing a few feet away with her hands on her knees, and at the Tlek, who wasn't put out at all. In fact, he looked ready to run again. We was all in great shape, but that was a brutal run. The least he could do was sweat a little. He had a birthmark on his calf, too, or an old wound: a huge, red blob that reached from his ankle to his knee. Whatever it was that got him must've been big.

The slicers finally stopped hitting the shield, and the silence that followed felt a little unnerving. I sat up, half expecting something worse to come bursting out at us, but for once in my life that didn't happen. Instead, we got invited over for lunch.

The old man was still on his porch acting like nothing happened. He waved us over.

"Hey," he said. "You guys want some soup?"

THE JAGUAR

He disappeared. The strange man, the one with the CBCK tattoo across his collarbone. Wheeler followed him into that abandoned townhouse. She watched him melt into the living room wall. Fall, actually, his foot peeking out onto the hardwood.

"Fuck's sake, what happened to you?" somebody on the other side said.

"Fucking bitch sprayed me."

He pulled his foot over the border.

"You found her?"

"Yeah, but—" and then the opening closed up and was just a wall again.

Wheeler scoured the place, but it was just an abandoned townhouse. The rooms were bare, the windows cracked. Mold in the ceiling. The basement door was locked, and no matter how hard she rammed it with her shoulder, it wouldn't open. Her foot was killing her anyway. Probably busted a few toes. She limped back across the street and picked up the strange man's bat, making sure to hold it by the leather strap, then limped all the way home. It was one in the morning by the time she got back. Exhausted, she collapsed into bed and fell right to sleep.

The next morning two of her toes, her pinky and the one next to it, had swollen to the size of sausages. She couldn't even put her full weight on that foot, let alone walk. It was her day off, but she didn't want to sit around by herself. If she did that, she'd start thinking about the letter, the hospital visit, and she wasn't ready to do that yet. She needed a distraction, so she popped a few ibuprofen and showered, and went to work. Normally she liked to walk, but that wasn't going to happen with a busted up foot, but there was a bus stop on the corner. She stopped at the door on the way out, eyeballing the cricket bat she left leaning against the closet.

What the hell, she thought, and took it with her.

A thick envelope was sitting on her keyboard when she gimped to the precinct. She sighed as she sat down, happy to get off her feet, and put the cricket bat on her desk. Then she opened the envelope.

Holy shit. Dell came through.

She filtered through the contents. Hospital reports. Dozens of them. Hospital reports that contained every and any mention of an animal attack within a ten-mile square radius of the old mill. She spread them out all over her desk and took a deep breath. It was going to be a long morning.

"What are you doing?"

It was Peña, just getting to work.

"Detecting."

"On your day off?"

When she didn't answer, he leaned over his desk to see what she was reading.

"10-91's?"

"Good eye. I didn't know you could read."

"Is this about the mill?"

Wheeler grunted, trying to focus. Peña pulled a different manila envelope out of his bag and tossed it to her. It skidded across the surface, took out a few pens, and landed in her lap.

"Thanks, Peña."

"You going to read it?"

"Depends on what it is."

"Reports."

"I gathered that."

"Of animal attacks."

"No shit, Peña. Really?"

"You seemed to think it was important."

"It is important. Thanks."

She cleared room for it, uncovering the cricket bat.

"No problem." He pointed at the bat. "Is that?" he said, hurrying around to her side. "Where did you get that?"

"Uh."

"Do you know what that is?"

"A cricket bat?

"A cricket . . . can I?"

"No. It's evidence."

"Then why haven't you dropped it off at the lab."

"I'm going to."

"When?"

"Later."

She tried to ignore him by reading the reports, but he hovered there, inspecting the thing.

"You can pick it up by the strap," she said.

"Yeah, I know." He pulled it off her desk, taking more papers and pens with it.

"Thanks again," she said, leaning over to pick it all up.

He whistled.

"This is a macuahuitl. Pretty old, too."

"Family heirloom?"

He didn't dignify the remark with a response.

"Where'd you get it?"

"B & E."

"When?"

Wheeler looked up from her reading.

"Are you going to let me get to work?"

"Fine, fine," he rested the weapon against her desk. "Better get that down to evidence."

She kept reading.

"Okay. Fine. I'll leave you alone."

Peña didn't just leave her alone; he left his desk altogether, mumbling something about a meeting. Wheeler read and took notes until lunch, then took a break to bring the bat down to evidence and grab some carry-out from the Chinese place around the corner. She plunked her lunch on the corner of her desk and sat down. The precinct computers were almost a decade old, and even though she left hers on when she went out, it had crashed when she got back. She turned it on again and let it go through its updates, and by the time the OS finally loaded and all of the background functions stopped, she'd finished eating.

She cleaned off her desk, gave it a cursory wipe down with the palm of her hand, and spread out Dell's reports. After reading a few of them, she opened up the maps app and started in, plotting each canine attack with a red marker and each non-mammal attack (there were a disturbing amount of snake bites recorded) with a green marker. When she finished, the screen was covered in red and green with no discernible pattern or cluster, no radiating circles, nothing that resembled any kind of organization at all.

"Shit," she said.

She leaned back in her chair and stretched, the bones in her shoulders and elbows popping and cracking. Had to stop hunching over her desk like that. She rolled her neck in a slow circle and let out a sigh. The interdepartmental phone rang and she picked it up.

"Wheeler." She listened to the voice on the other end. "None at all? No, he didn't have any gloves on. I'm sure. Because I was there. Alright. Thanks."

She hung up.

No prints. No prints on the macua-whatever. Maybe he shaved them down.

The clock on the screen read 2:16. On a hunch, she filtered through Peña's police reports, looking for the one on the mill. She searched the entire stack twice, first flipping through, looking for a last name, then more carefully, organizing them by date. It wasn't there. The report on the mill hadn't been filed. She picked up the phone and punched in a few numbers.

"Hey, Steph. Wheeler. I'm good. Listen, can you get a hold of a trooper for me? Last name is Kowalczyk. Stan, I think. He responded to a 187 two days ago and I don't have his report yet. Yeah, I'll be here, thanks."

She hung up and turned her attention back to the screen. How else could she think about this? She set up a filter to eliminate any of the attacks that happened the month before. Nearly all of them disappeared, all except for two clusters: one in the Bottom, and one in the industrial section. Good. She filtered out any that happened two days ago, and the clusters tightened. One centered around her neighborhood and the other over the mill. She applied one last filter, this one to allow only attacks that occurred over a month before. All of the markers in her neighborhood and over the mill warehouse disappeared. Bingo. At least she had a timeline. The phone rang, making her jump a little. She picked up the receiver.

"Wheeler. Oh, hey Steph." She listened for a moment, then said, "How long?"

Kowalczyk lived in a predictably working-class neighborhood across the bridge in South East. Almost a century before it was a thriving area. Property values were solid, families built equity, schools were top notch. That was before the triple punch of recession, globalization, and tech robbed people of their production jobs. In short: after the last time the economy collapsed, businesses turned once and for all to AI and automation, cutting thousands of jobs and outsourcing the rest. Most of the dwellings in the area, the row houses, single family homes, brownstones, redstones, graystones, were barely maintained. Dilapidated fences lined overgrown lawns. Roofs drooped over listing porches. Concrete stoops cracked. Iron-gated doors rusted. The only thing that wasn't dirty or in need of repair were the American Flags hanging on outrigger poles. They shifted in the gentle breeze.

The next thing she noticed when she got out of her cruiser was the silence. A few cars passed by, and in the distance she heard honking horns, the rattle of construction, a boom as a truck drove over a plate in the road, but everything in front of her, the sidewalks, the porches, the tiny squares of lawn, was empty. Families still lived there, public servants, mainly. Police. Firefighters. Social workers. At three o'clock in the middle of the summer, the streets should have been thrumming. Children playing pick up games. Mothers gathering together, sipping ice coffee. Where were they?

She checked the address on her phone. 1308 South Ave, SE. There it was. Two doors down to her left. Two levels and an unfinished basement. Kowalczyk probably drank beer on the porch, listening to the game with his buddies. Budweiser in an Igloo cooler. An old fashioned transistor radio.

The iron grate rattled when she knocked on the frame of the Kowalczyk's front door, echoing in the empty neighborhood. She waited a beat, looking down the street to her left and right. Still nothing. Nobody. She knocked again and tried the handle. Locked. She rang the door bell a few times, not expecting anything, then went over to the windows to her right and put her forehead up to the glass, shading her eyes with her hands. She didn't see anything unusual. The outline of chairs and lamps. A hutch. Stairs to the left. She caught movement in the reflection, like something coming up behind her and she gasped and spun around, hand already on her gun.

Crap.

It was just the flag, flapping as a hot gust blew dead leaves and trash down the gutters.

Calm down, Wheeler. You're spooking yourself.

When she turned back around, a woman was staring at her from the other side of the window.

"Jesus!"

The woman was pale and sweating, hugging a thin, rumpled robe to her slouching frame. Deep, dark pouches hung under her glassy eyes, and her hair was plastered to her forehead. But that wasn't what

Wheeler focused on. What she focused on was the tumor, the size of a softball, pushing out of her neck.

"Ma'am, sorry. I didn't think there was anybody home."

The woman stared dead-eyed at her for a second, then turned and disappeared back into the house.

"Wait!" Wheeler said, banging on the pane. "Hey!" She peered into the window, cupping her hands around her eyes. The woman was walking up the stairs with slow, even strides, that blank expression still on her face. Wheeler banged again. "Ma'am! Hey, Mrs. Kowalczyk? I'm . . . damn!"

She tried the iron-barred door one last time, but all it did was rattle. Those things were built to keep people out. What were her options? She could break the window. Which was questionably legal. Shooting the lock only worked in the movies. There was a door on the side of the house, so she limped around to it, barely registering the pain in her foot. It was locked, so to the back it was. The back yard was littered with children's toys, footballs, baseballs, dolls, big-wheels. She cussed as she tripped over a tricycle on the way to the screened-in deck and had to take a moment before she could walk again. Damn, that hurt. But the screen door was unlocked. So was the back door to the house.

She gagged when she stepped inside. Something was rotting somewhere. Again with the rotting. The kitchen looked like it hadn't been remodeled since 1954. White fridge with rounded edges. Gas range. Two sinks. No dishwasher. No microwave. When she saw the puddle of yellow bile lying on the floor outside the cellar door, she pulled her gun out of her shoulder holster and tried to breathe through her mouth. She crept over and, making sure to step around it, was about to try the handle when she saw the nails someone had pounded through the door and into the jamb. They were crooked and cockeyed, overlapping each other as if the job had been completed in a hurry. Then she saw the dent in the middle, like something had tried to punch its way out. She backed away. The floorboards overhead squeaked, followed by the sound of a door closing. A few seconds later she heard the pipes groan and the shower start to run. She moved to the bottom of the stairs, aiming the gun up.

"Ma'am?" she called. "Mrs. Kowalczyk? I'm Detective Wheeler. CPD. I work with your husband."

A window unit kicked on, and Wheeler thought she heard something behind her. She whipped the gun in that direction, but it was only one of the curtains blowing in the living room. Another door closed above and she whipped back around to the stairs. She was going to have to go up there. She winced every other step, the wood creaking as she climbed. At the top, she turned and found herself looking down a short hall. The bathroom was immediately to her right. Three bedroom doors lined the hallway, all of them closed. A child's drawing was taped to the one at the end, a blobby, brown shape. The one on the left had a State College football pennant tacked to it. Wheeler checked the rooms, but they were empty. Beds unmade, toys scattered on the floor. The other door, the one that had to belong to Mr. and Mrs. Kowalczek, was locked from inside. After jogging the handle a few times, Wheeler turned to the bathroom. Steam poured out from under the crack. She knocked.

"Ma'am?"

The shower continued to run.

"Mrs. Kowalczyk? Are you okay?" She waited. "Ma'am, I'm coming in."

A wall of fog poured out when she opened the door, shrouding everything, but it quickly cleared. A double sink, a toilet. The shower curtain had been drawn tight. Behind it stood a motionless shadow.

"Mrs. Kowalczyk?"

The woman didn't move.

"Can you hear me?"

Wheeler reached out and pinched the edge curtain. A drop of sweat ran down her face. She let out a short breath. Just do it. She yanked the curtain aside. Mrs. Kowalczyk stood there, facing her, naked, a straight razor gripped in her hand. Her shoulder had been mauled, leaving an open wound so raw and ragged that a flap of flesh hung limp against her arm. The bone was clearly visible, the flesh purple and black up to her neck, out of which bulged the tumor. Water rushed over the wound, cleaning it out, sending an endless flood of blood down the woman's arm and side. It had to be painful, but she didn't even blink.

"I'm going to call an ambulance," Wheeler said. "You'll be okay. I'm—"

Mrs. Kowalczyk mumbled something.

"What? I'm sorry, I didn't hear you."

"Don't."

"Ma'am—"

"Don't call!" Shocked by the outburst, Wheeler said nothing. "He said it was just a headache. That he just needed to lie down."

"Your husband?"

Mrs. Kowalczyk nodded.

"Do you know where he is?"

"I let him sleep until dinner. It was so unlike him. Stanley's usually up doing something. Working on the yard or on that stupid car in the garage."

Wheeler blinked water out of her eyes. The heat and the steam pressed down on her.

"Mrs. Kowalczyk? I just want you to put the razor down, okay? Can you do that?"

"I didn't start to worry until I put the kids to bed. It was a hard night. Mark was being difficult, and Marcy wouldn't eat her broccoli. I thought he must have been down with the flu or something. Something he caught from work. But it's summer."

Wheeler knew she was going to have to wrestle the blade out of the woman's hand. Either that or shoot her in the arm. She took a step to the left to get a better angle. A faint smile crossed Mrs. Kowalczyk's lips.

"I know what you're doing. It won't work."

"Let's get out of the shower, okay? Then we can go downstairs and talk."

"I should have known something was wrong. When I opened our bedroom door, I should have known. Stanley snores like an elephant, but he was totally silent this time. For a second I thought he'd gone out to his workshop. His big screen's out there and his recliner. He smokes cigars. He thinks I don't know, but I do. Then I flipped on the light and saw it." She let out a shuddery breath, her tears mingling with the water from the shower head. "His face, his face . . ."

A pit formed in Wheeler's stomach.

"Mrs. Kowalczyk? Where are your children?"

The woman finally looked her in the eye.

"Don't go into the basement."

Then she brought the razor up to her neck.

Wheeler went into the basement. She already knew what was down there. After that, she went into two more houses before finally calling for back up.

Later, after all of the houses had been checked, and after emptying the contents of her stomach out into the street, Wheeler washed out her mouth with an old bottle of water that had been in her car for about a week.

Twenty-six.

Twenty-six dead.

Men. Women. Children. All of them with holes in different parts of their bodies, as if something had exploded from within. Most were in their sides, their legs, and their arms. A few had them in their backs or stomachs. Just like the junkies in the mill. Only these weren't junkies. They were teachers, city clerks, therapists. Families.

Kowalczyk was the worst. His face had burst open, leaving an empty cavity where the front of the skull should have been. She remembered what happened at the mill. He said the yellow stuff went up his nose. Did he die fast, or did he know what was happening to him? She couldn't fathom what it was like, the tumor swelling, the pressure in his head, his skull cracking, splitting. That he was an asshole there was no doubt, but even assholes didn't deserve to die like that.

The press had already arrived and set up on the perimeter, the blues more forceful than usual in keeping them and the gawkers at bay. Some of their own had gone down. It wasn't funny. It never was. Peña showed up. They watched as the coroners loaded body bag after body bag into their vans.

"Where were you?" she asked.

"Paperwork. I heard it got pretty rough. Cop's family?"

"Yeah. That guy from the mill. Kowalczyk."

"You alright?"

"Fuck off."

"One of the blues told me you lost your lunch."

"Didn't want it anyway."

He leaned up against the car next to her, folding his arms over his chest.

"I think you should see psych."

"I'm fine."

"No, you're not, Wheeler. You're not fine. You were bad enough before this, but witnessing a suicide—"

"Do me a favor and shut up, okay?"

He held out his hands in surrender.

"Okay."

The news outlets caught the action with their own cameras, pointlessly, she thought, as there were ten times as many civilians filming it on their Viddy Viewers™ and posting it for the whole world to see.

"You hear that Single Corp bought out the city's IT servers?" She glared at him and he shrugged. "Just trying to make conversation."

One of the coroners stumbled while wheeling a body down the front steps of a house to their right, and the bag fell off and landed in a forsythia. The crowd let up a gasp as dozens of Viewers™ zoomed in on it. The scene supervisor started chewing out the kid who spilled the corpse, and he and his partner struggled to get the body back on the gurney. Peña chuckled.

"Lead investigator's gonna love that," he said. "How's your foot?"

She frowned. She hadn't thought about it. She put her weight on her toes. Huh. They still hurt, but nowhere near as much as before. Maybe they'd only been sprained.

"Good," she said.

"Alright, well get it together. We have to go."

"Where to this time?"

"More bodies in the Bottom. Same description. We're on it. I'll drive."

"I'm on this one."

"That's the thing," Peña said. "Whoever called it in? Get in the car. I'll play it for you on the way over."

Wheeler listened to the message three times. It started with a burst of static, old radio sounds winding up and down the frequency spectrum. A distorted voice in the background was yelling, but she couldn't hear exactly what it said. Then she heard her name.

"Wheeler . . ."

Peña said, "How many times you need—"

"Shh!"

More static, more whining, then the voice came through again. The number of the apartment building, the street name. Then, ". . . is key . . . girls . . . use the key." One last burst of static, and finally the voice came in, clear and undistorted, "What are you waiting for!"

Wheeler put her phone down.

"Weird, huh?" Peña said. "You recognize that voice?"

Wheeler did. It was the woman in her dreams, the witch in the dungeon.

"No," she said.

"Whoever it is, she knows you."

"Or not. Could be some old kook looking for attention."

"Or something worse. Blues already checked out the house. Three bodies."

It was starting to get dark by the time they pulled up to the apartment building, a turn of the century brownstone with a bar at street level and two floors above it. A single patrol car idled at the curb. The officer sat inside, enjoying the air conditioning and filling out some paperwork. Wheeler went up to the cruiser and tapped on the window. The officer glanced up.

"On duty, lady," he said, and went back to his work.

She knocked again, holding the badge hanging from the chain on her neck.

"Roll it down, officer," she said.

His eyes went wide and he hit the power window button.

"Oh, jeez. Sorry, Detective."

"Are you the only one here?"

"Yeah. Lot's of calls tonight. Full moon. City's gone nuts. We're spread pretty thin."

"Okay. What's going on here."

"Three bodies. Second floor above the bar."

"You clear it?"

"Yeah. Talked to the bartender. He don't know about any renters. Said there hasn't been any for months."

His radio went off with a burst, and he turned his head to listen to it.

"I got another call—"

"Go ahead."

The bar was full but not crowded. Typical Bottom joint. Shotgun deep. Scuffed hardwood floors. Popcorn machine at the end. The bar took up half the place, with just enough room for the patrons to squeeze by or stand along the wall. Speakers anchored into each corner of the ceiling played classic rock hits. Hendrix. CCR. The Beatles. It smelled like booze and popcorn, with an undercurrent of wood soap and bleach.

The bartender was chatting with a few old timers at the other end while he filled up empty bowls with popcorn. He was on the late side of forty, with short salt and pepper hair and a square chin. The tight white t-shirt he wore tucked into his blue jeans made him look like a sailor, the muddled tattoo on his forearm adding to the effect. Wheeler thought he might have scowled when he saw them walking toward him, but then she realized that that was just how his face rested. He put the bag of popcorn down and wiped his hands on the back of his jeans.

"You here about the dead kids?" he asked.

The old timers shared a look and turned around on their stools to lean back against the bar.

"Yeah," Wheeler said.

"Good. 'Cause they're starting to stink. Bad for business."

"I bet. Do you know anything about what happened?"

"I already told that other guy everything I know."

"Good. Now you can tell us."

He leaned on the bar, flexing his triceps.

"You remind me of my daughter."

Great. Was this some kind of twisted pickup line?

"She's tough. I'm proud of that kid." He glanced over at Peña then back at her. "What do you want to know?"

They peppered him with questions.

No, he didn't hear anything strange. No, he'd never seen them before. He didn't know anything had happened until he noticed the smell.

"It's worse back there," he said, nodding at the end of the building. "The popcorn covers it up pretty good. For now. You let them marinate any more, though, they'll leak through the ceiling."

"You own the building?" Peña asked.

The bartender scoffed.

"Me? No. I can barely afford the rent. Owner lives out of state. Send him a check every month. Never seen him. Don't fix nothing."

"He rent the upstairs?"

"Up until last year. Tenants left. Don't blame them. Place is a dump. Leaky pipes. Drafty windows. I've had to chase a few squatters out since then. Kids like to come in from the suburbs to party. I called it in at first, but nobody came by."

"Yeah," Peña said. "We're a little busy."

"Guess so."

"Isn't it locked?" Wheeler asked.

"Yep."

"How do they get in?"

The bartender shrugged.

"How do they always get in?"

Wheeler entered the apartment first. It was dark and musty, with blankets tacked up over the only two windows, and a few pieces of overturned lawn furniture scattered around the cracked hardwood floor. The drywall in the ceiling had been torn out, exposing the joists, copper wires, and PVC piping. A few ragged scraps of old insulation hung from it like tongues. A stairway, leading up, separated the room from the kitchen.

The bodies lay in various positions; two curled up next to each other, one alone near the door jamb. Same scene as before. Three burst tumors. Puddles of yellow stuff on the ground. Drug paraphernalia lay scattered on the floor. Vials. Lighters. Spoons. She squatted down to get a better look. Two girls and a guy. The girls were heavily made-up, high heels, tight-fitting dresses. The boy wore designer jeans and expensive boots. All three had what looked like hearing aids in their ears. Single Corp Cochlear ConNext™. Wheeler saw something metal flash through a rip in the boy's shirt.

"He's got a brace," she said. "Barrel Arm Biceps™, I think."

"Net implants. Body mods," Peña said. "Rich kids."

Wheeler took a flashlight from her jacket pocket and shined it on the boy's hand. There was a wet mass gripped in it, with coarse black hair sticking out of a fleshy pulp. The hair stuck into his palm like needles.

"Looks like he fought back. Tore something off whatever did this."

"Whoever did this, you mean."

Wheeler grunted. "The hair is . . . thick. Like knitting needles." She poked at the dead boy's palm.

"Don't. We've got to wait for the techs to get here."

"Which ones? They're all tied up."

She put her flashlight between her teeth and pulled the boy's sleeve up over the metal brace.

"Wheeler," Peña warned.

"I'm just getting a better look. I haven't seen one of these Barrel Arm things up close yet. Have you?"

A sigh.

"No."

"Check this out."

Peña squatted down next to her, reluctantly interested.

"Is it bolted into his arm?"

"No, look." She pointed at the metal exoskeleton. "It really is just a brace. Strong as hell, but still just a brace. The harness is up here over his shoulders, runs down here to the glove."

"He just slips it on, huh?"

"Yep. They adjust for your comfort."

"Expensive."

"This is the budget version," Wheeler said. "For four thousand dollars extra, they'll make it look like a part of your body. Ten percent off if you use your ConNext™ to buy it."

"How do you know so much about this shit?"

She shrugged.

"Saw an infomercial."

Something banged on the floor above them. Both Wheeler and Peña stood up with a jolt.

"Christ," Wheeler said. "Fucking blue didn't check upstairs."

Another bang, this time hard enough to shake dirt into their eyes. Peña took his gun out of his shoulder holster, staring at the subfloor above.

"Doesn't sound like it."

Wheeler shined her flashlight at the doorway leading to the stairs. A wet, yellow trail glinted off the floor.

"Oh, shit. Peña, look."

"What the fuck is that?"

"What the fuck do you think it is?"

Peña aimed his gun at the subfloor above and squeezed off a round. The pounding stopped. They watched and waited, breathless. Then the pounding renewed, louder and more violent this time, cracking the joists, shaking the whole apartment. Both Peña and Wheeler fired at will, over and over, but the pounding continued until a hole formed in the wood.

A taloned hand, green-gray, shot through it and ripped out the rest of the boards one huge chunk at a time. Then a monstrous mouth appeared, all teeth and gaping, black hole, and it loosed a roar that deafened their ears. The detectives aimed for it and fired, bullets chipping the teeth, thunking into meat, but it just seemed to enrage the beast more. It shoved its way through the floor, carving rivulets in its rubbery skin, and landed on all fours in the middle of the room, right on top of the dead boy, severing his arm from his body and cutting off their exit.

"I'm out!" Peña yelled.

"Window!"

Peña tore the blanket down, letting the muted light of the street lamps enter the room. He was just about to kick the glass when the beast ripped him around and plunged its talons into his stomach. Wheeler fired into its back, stepping closer, emptying her clip, but even though the bullets riddled its torso and arms and legs, and even though it went down to one knee, it didn't let go of her partner. It lashed around at her with its free arm and connected. The force was unbelievable. She went flying back into the wall, her gun clattering off somewhere in the darkness. Momentarily free, the beast sank its teeth into Peña's neck and tore out his throat. Wheeler shook off the blow and scrambled around for her gun but couldn't find it. She did, however, find the dead boy's severed arm poking halfway out of the Barrel Arm Biceps™ brace. She looked around for the monster. It was hunched over her partner's dead body, gorging itself on his stomach. She was momentarily forgotten.

Getting the brace off was more difficult than she thought. It was so tight that she thought it might really be bolted into the bone, but after a tense minute of pulling and straining, it slipped off. She put her arm in it like she was putting on a jacket. There was a power button on the back of the glove, and when she pushed it, a little mechanical sound wound up and the brace tightened, snug but comfortable.

Wheeler turned around to face the thing that had killed her partner. It was still eating, its back turned to her. She walked stealthily up behind it and raised her fist over her head. The brace, sensing the action, whirred to life. She felt the energy, the power of it surge through the metal. When the noise reached its peak, she brought her fist down and slammed the monster in the back. It collapsed on top of Peña with a canine whelp. Wheeler brought her arm up over her head again, making the fist, waiting for the brace to power up, but as she did, the monster flipped over, its chest-mouth wide open. A stinger shot out. She dodged, and the next thing she knew, she was flying out the window.

THE SNAKE

Coatl weighed his response. He was in too much pain to care about Ka-Bata's story, but this was a tricky situation. Ka-Bata, judging by his expression, really wanted to tell it to him. To say no would be insulting, and Coatl needed Ka-Bata's army. Ka-Bata, fortunately, misread his silence.

"You don't like the room?" he said. He glanced around. "I don't blame you. I don't like it either. Hold on."

He opened the door again and peeked out.

"Okay, we're clear. Come on."

He moved to help Coatl up.

"Ka-Bata—"

"You want a nicer place? "

"It's not that. Seka-Khayu. The temple."

"Don't bother me with news of that madman!" Ka-Bata yelled.

Coatl was taken aback. Ka-Bata recovered, shaking his head.

"I'm sorry, General," he said. "I'm not angry at you. I know it's heresy, but I have no love for that fool. If you'll allow me, I'll explain. Come. Let's go."

"Go where?"

Ka-Bata put a friendly hand on his shoulder.

"Do you trust me?"

"No."

"Ha! Good! Good! Now come with me. I'll show you something that will make you trust me."

The general blinked in the sun, holding his hand up to shade his eyes. Ka-Bata led him by the arm into a beautiful garden the likes of which the old warrior had never seen. An adobe path wound throughout sculpted bushes and colorful flowers. Birds flitted from tree to tree, and a three-tiered fountain burbled in the middle of it all. They passed a little patio with strange chairs surrounding a fire pit.

They passed a sculpture of a plic in winged sandals posed to run. A lush lawn spanned the garden wall to wall. Coatl marveled at it all. Ka-Bata smiled.

"You like my garden," he said. "You'll like this even more!"

He steered him around a screen, and there, standing in an entryway to the garden, stood Xiuloc, his back to them, staring out over a wondrous expanse of pale desert. Another piece of furniture, similar to the one in Coatl's room but smaller, sat between them, with thick pillows arranged around it. Coatl, though he was happy to see the soldier alive, responded with an "Oh."

Ka-Bata's smile fell.

"Aren't you excited to see your friend?"

"Well—"

Xiuloc, thinking the question was meant for him, turned around.

"Ah, General Coatl," he said. He nodded respectfully.

Ka-Bata noted it and threw up his hands.

"I have totally misread the situation. I thought the two of you were intimate associates. I thought . . . well, never mind what I thought. The garden is nice, yes?"

Coatl didn't hear him. He was too interested in the desert beyond the walls of the garden. He'd heard stories of it, but never really considered its existence.

"Is that . . . ?"

"Ah, yes," Ka-Bata said, happy to find something interesting to tell his guests. "That is the great Jeshimah. Desolate and dead, it stretches all the way to the sea, and the cities of Salvation and Gabriel."

Coatl remained silent, as if he knew what the crazy old man was talking about.

"It wasn't always like this," Ka-Bata continued. "If the book is to be trusted. It was once covered with grasses from here to the cliffs. But the people of the cities misused it, sucked the life from the soil."

"What book?"

"The book of the genesis of the world. We found thousands of copies in the cities."

Two servants approached holding clay dishes filled with food. Squash and beans and corn tortillas and some kind of meat. They placed the dishes down on the table and scuttled away. Ka-Bata gestured to the feast.

"Please, sit. Eat. And I will tell my tale."

You think I don't know about my reputation as a madman, but I assure you I do. Yes, I don't—didn't—pay the blood debt to the skhatet, and yes my people do not pay tribute to me, but there is a reason for this. We are not faithless. We are not heretics. Quite the contrary. As you know I am one of the oldest of the original tlatoani still alive, older even than you, Coatl. When we first came to this place, when our time was done on the other side, it was not unusual for someone to want to explore. In fact, we encouraged it! We spread out and settled, from the jungle surrounding the Isquite all the way to the valley in the shadow of the Caxcal.

Look around you. This house and garden, that desert, for the longest time this was as far as my people would explore. We didn't share the eastern pull, for in that direction there was a final point, the mountain itself, an enticing, mysterious dead end. And though we had fallen in love with the life of the nomad, we were not yet ready to brave the Jeshimah. We explored north and south, and in every new place, we learned amazing things; with each new discovery, our minds expanded. We became addicted to it, sought more and more. There were people here before us, Coatl, did you know that? I know you don't believe me, but it's true. I've seen their work. These people were godlike. No, I didn't say gods. I said god*like*. They made things more magical than even the plics, though I think they were plics themselves. They were from a different time, a time both far into the future and long, long ago.

But in our absence, we lost contact with the skhatet and the other tlatoani. We didn't know about the tensions that were brewing. We heard rumors, of course, but we were too busy, too enamored with our new knowledge to care. What did their petty bickering have to do with us? We never even knew when the war broke out. No messenger was ever sent, so we continued with our mission. We explored, we traveled, we uncovered new wonders. That's why when Seka-Khayu called the council and settled the peace, I was not there.

Then one day he arrived at the borders of our village, angry at my absence, demanding tribute and an audience with me. My people were confused. We'd forgotten our place. Some were outright hostile. At least that's what I heard. I was here with my own tlatoani, planning our next expedition, the greatest one yet, an exploration of the Western Desert, when a servant came running up to us.

"Ka-Bata," the man said. "The skhatet. He's—"

"I am your skhatet," I said. "What do you want?"

"No." He gasped for breath. He must have run all the way from the bridge. "Seka-Khayu. The skhatet Seka-Khayu. He's here."

What was this fool talking about? I had to think for a moment before I understood what he was saying. Skhatet? Seka-Khay—

Oh no.

By the time I reached the wall, he'd been waiting longer than any ruler should have had to wait.

"Open the gates!" I yelled. "Open the gates!"

My guards, bless them all, winched them open with mingled expressions of fear and confusion. There stood Seka-Khayu with his entire retinue, jaguar and eagle warriors, representatives of the tlatoani, and several of his concubines. I kneeled immediately, my forehead resting on my knee. My people looked on with horror. What was their Ka-Bata doing? This was his village. Those were his walls.

Seka-Khayu would not move until he was sure all of my people had seen me. Then he motioned to his warriors. They fanned out around him and into the village. There were dozens, more than I anticipated. I realized that he knew something like this might happen, that there was a good chance that we'd forgotten about him. He could have easily overwhelmed the guards on the battlements, but he chose to wait. He wanted to make a point.

"Ka-Bata!" he exclaimed, smiling down at me. Then he turned to my guards and anybody else unlucky enough to have been caught at the gates when he arrived. "I require a blood debt for this."

Later, we feasted under torchlight in the garden. You know Seka-Khayu, how he is. He demanded the blood debt be paid immediately, and when it was done, his servants and warriors staked the bodies around the perimeter so I would be reminded of who he was and what he could do. The sweet desert winds breathed strong and sure from the west, mercifully wiping the smell of blood from the air and keeping the flies and insects at bay. Seka-Khayu held his face up and inhaled deeply. Then he gazed out upon the majesty that is the evening. The hunter's sky, streaked with orange clouds, the yellow sand. A rash of stars bored out of the heavens, silver holes in a violet pool.

"I can see why you like it out here, Ka-Bata."

I grinned, trying not to look at the bodies on the stakes. Inside, I was fuming. How dare he come to my village unannounced then punish my people for not being ready? I prepared my words carefully, ready to accept the consequences of what I was about to say, whatever they may be.

"Skhatet—" I began, but he held up his hand and cut me off.

"No need to apologize. I am a gracious leader, but you know that, of course."

"Gracious?"

"There is no need to worry."

"I'm not worried, my skhatet."

"Good. Do you know why I'm here, Ka-Bata?"

To be honest, I hadn't even thought of it yet. In the initial shock of his arrival, of being torn from my task and thrown into the midst of a madman's birthright, I had not, surprisingly, even begun to wonder why he had come. For a moment, terrible thoughts entered my mind. Had the great temple been overthrown? If so, by whom? Was it a revolt by the tlatoani? Was I the last of his loyal men, even if by default? If that was the case, was he going to stay? Indefinitely?

Amidst all of this mental uproar, I managed to say, "No, my skhatet."

He put a coy hand on my forearm.

"Please, Ka-Bata. This is your home. Here, I am a guest. You are the lord. You make call me Seka-Khayu."

"Thank you, Seka-Khayu."

"Tell me something, Ka-Bata."

"Anything."

"Why."

"Why?"

"Tell me why I shouldn't take the blood debt out on you and your family, too?"

He seemed to relish my shock. My eyes wandered as I searched for a response. How could I dissuade this madman from taking what was entirely his right to take? I would sacrifice myself. Me. Take me, I thought. Leave the rest alone.

"Skhatet, I don't—"

"Seka-Khayu."

"Yes. Of course. Seka-Khayu, I don't understand. If I'd known you were coming—"

"You've heard, no doubt, of The Mutiny?"

The expression on my face told him the truth, and he seemed amused rather than satisfied.

"No? Hmm. Well you didn't fight on their side, but you also didn't come to my aid, did you?"

I scrambled for an answer. Finally, I said, "We never received word."

"I sent a messenger."

"He never arrived."

"That's hardly my problem. Where is your envoy?"

"Envoy?"

"You no longer keep one, do you?"

"I don't think we ever—"

"Ka-Bata, I've been keeping tabs on you. I'm smarter than you think, yes? That's the problem with the tlatoani: you think you know everything. You take one look at my twisted body and scoff. You remember my father and mother, and their father and mother, the straight line back two hundred years, and think "he's mad." I might be. But I'm not stupid. You stopped keeping an envoy decades ago when I made him pay the blood debt just to see how you would respond. Do you remember what you did?"

"I didn't even know."

"Exactly. You did nothing. That more than anything else proves your lack of fealty."

"We've . . . been . . . very mobile, skha—Seka-Khayu. An envoy wouldn't have known where to find us. Even if we had one anymore."

"Ah, yes. Your adventures. The life of the lazy wanderer." He looked around my garden. The flowers, the plants, the bodies on stakes. "It seems to suit you well."

My anger rose up in me again. Lazy wanderers? Is that what he thought of this? Yes, we loved it, but it was by no means easy. The endless quest, the weeks in the desert, the scratching for survival. We stumbled across information that made us question our existence. How little we knew! How much there was to learn! With each new artifact, each new breakthrough, our ignorance was wiped clean. But constant discovery led to constant change. Our lives were in such a never ending pattern of adaptation and metamorphosis that it drove men mad. We came to understand that in order to survive, we had to put our certainty (about life, existence, purpose) on hold and leave open the window of enlightenment for anything we found. But how could I relay that to a man such as Seka-Khayu?

"Seka-Khayu," I said. "May I show you something?"

He smiled at me, benign and threatening. Rather than speak, he only nodded, a bare movement of his head. The guards on either side of me took a clipped step back to allow me to stand.

"I'll return in a moment."

Imagine, Coatl, the next scene from Seka-Khayu's point of view. A once trusted noble disappears for several minutes, leaving you alone to sit silent and tense in a garden at—as far as you're concerned —the end of the world. When he finally returns, you are agitated and hiding it poorly, but the rules of civility and your own breeding prevent you from doing anything more than just staring. And stare you will because the fool is carrying some kind of strange contraption made out of wood and metal. The bottom is a box with a lever sticking out of the side. An enormous bell blooms like a flower into the space above. The box is decorated plainly enough, but the bell, which is fashioned out of some kind of strange alloy, is etched with intricate patterns, flowers, and other imagery.

He sets it on the table next to you with a plunk, and you jerk back, offended. Then, as if to further insult you, the noble, a brave man who once defended your temple, who vanquished enemies on your behalf, who personally explored and mapped the new world into which you were expelled, places a black disc on the surface of the box, grabs the lever, and starts to crank like a madman. The disc soon begins to spin, faster and faster.

"Put the needle on the edge," I said, ignoring Seka-Khayu's clear dismay.

"What?"

"The needle," I said, nodding at the box. "It's on that arm. Pick it up and put it on the edge of the disc."

Seka-Khayu leaned over and peered at the machine. He lifted the needle and looked at me, a question in his eyes. I nodded. He dropped it on the edge and it bounced, landing a centimeter away with a scratch. Music poured out of the bell, right into his face. He gasped and scrambled backward out of his chair, knocking it to the ground. Even his guards seemed astonished.

"Don't worry," I said, still cranking. "It's strange at first, but just listen."

I watched his face as he struggled to comprehend, just as I had done my first time. The music was loud and angular, with distorted instruments and a pounding rhythm that drove straight through the middle of it all. There were drums, but drums that sounded nothing like ours, and no rattles, no flutes, no horns. A man sang over it in a voice both high and gritty. I didn't understand the lyrics entirely, but they were beautiful and aggressive, oddly poetic.

"Singing to an ocean, I can hear the ocean's roar/Play for free, I play for me and play a whole lot more/Singing 'bout the good things and the sun that lights the day/I used to sing on the mountains, has the ocean lost its way?"

I cranked and cranked while Seka-Khayu rose to his feet. He circled the device, staring intensely. He put his hand in the bell, and once he saw that nothing would hurt him, he put his ear up to it. Then he laughed. The guards did, too, sharing a glance. He took a step back and listened, and when the song was over he clapped, and I stopped my exertions.

"What do you call it?" he asked.

"I don't know."

He circled it again, traced the designs burned into the wooden box.

"You found this out there?"

"This and many more wonders like it."

From that point on, Seka-Khayu's attitude changed. He asked to see, and I showed him everything we found. Strange mechanisms, weapons we could not understand, furniture covered with unusual cloth, armor, tools, packages filled with liquid.

"Look at this," I said, holding up a cylinder made out of the same metal as the bell of the music device.

I took a knife and cut it in half on the table before him, revealing the beans in water within. He gasped.

"Are those—"

"Beans. Yes."

He snapped at one of his guards and pointed at it.

The guard paused, reluctant, and it wasn't until Seka-Khayu said it again, harsher this time, that he scooped up a tiny amount and put it in his mouth. His eyes lit up and he chewed and swallowed. He turned to the other guard and said, "good."

Seka-Khayu waited for the guard to show signs of being poisoned, and when he didn't, when he was certain the beans were safe, he took his own taste. His eyes lit up as well, and soon he was scooping more and more into his mouth. After that, he fell into a deep silence. Thinking he was angry, I withdrew into a corner of the garden and waited, waited for the inevitable. I had no idea why he had fallen so sullen. A few moments before he was delighted.

"Ka-Bata," he finally said. "I don't expect you to understand, but believe me when I tell you that I'm tired of ruling these people. The petty squabbles between tlatoani, the sad mewling of my 'people', the idiot farmers. Not once in a thousand years have I been interested in anything that's gone on over here. Until now. You have shown me many things. Many amazing things. Do you know where you can find more?"

"I think so," I said, shocked at his gravity.

"Then why haven't you gone there yet?"

I explained to him the problem of the desert, the miles of wasteland stretching from the threshold of my garden.

"My scouts report sightings of birds," I said. "Miles and miles away. A sure sign of the sea. Though they never saw it."

Seka-Khayu was unimpressed. He stood abruptly and his guards snapped to attention.

"Find these places, Ka-Bata," he said. "Bring back to me treasures such as what you've shown me tonight, and I will erase your family's blood debt."

The sun set red over the desert, and Coatl's stomach grumbled.

"Ah-ha!" Ka-Bata laughed, "I see my story has stirred your appetite. Would you like some of the beans I described?"

"I don't care what you bring me. Just bring me something."

Ka-Bata laughed and excused himself.

"I'll be back with a feast," he said.

When he was gone, Xiuloc turned to the old warrior.

"He's lost his mind," he said, nodding at the desert. "Too much time out there, under the sun."

"I don't know. He seems excited, but not crazy."

"Where are the items he described? The music maker. The weapons."

"Maybe Seka-Khayu took them already?"

Xiuloc frowned.

"I can see why the skhatet would want the weapons, but the other things . . ."

"He was the skhatet," Coatl said, and left it at that.

"General. What are we doing here?"

"We need his army."

"Look around you. Do you see any men other than servants?"

Coatl thought on it.

"No. But that doesn't mean—"

"What does it mean then?"

"I don't know. But Ka-Bata's a strange man. I think he might be trying to tell us something."

"What? That he has no more army? That much is apparent. We need to—"

"Here we are!" Ka-Bata called.

He was leading a team of servants carrying trays laden with food. Fruit and vegetables, cooked meat, beans, wild rice, tortillas. To drink, they presented casks of wine and clay pitchers filled with pulque. Xiuloc gave Coatl a meaningful look, and Coatl shook his head gently. Not yet.

They feasted, and Coatl, once weary with his wounds and unable to even think about eating, now found himself unable to stop. Ka-Bata bit into a tortilla filled with beef and wild rice

"That's a good sign," he said. "The eating."

When they were done, they sat back in their chairs, sated and content. The servants cleared the dishes and lit the torches anchored into the garden walls, stacked logs in the fire pit. Ka-Bata offered Coatl his shoulder to lean on, and the three walked across the patio and settled into some comfortable lounge chairs surrounding it.

"Are you still feeling well, Coatl?"

"Better than before."

"Good. Then I will tell you about what we found in the desert."

At first, nothing. We traveled west for days, then north, then east, meaning to zig zag across the sand to cover the most amount of space as possible. The days blazed with unimaginable heat, dry and draining, unlike the humidity of the jungle. We took to traveling at night when the temperature dropped and sleeping during the day beneath our open canopies. As we ventured, first west and then north, we began to discover things of interest. An oasis brimming with green trees and grasses, the water cool and dark. We camped there for days, enjoying the break from the constant sand and heat. We even found a field of dates and figs that had clearly been planted and farmed, but which now was overgrown and wild.

Then there were the skulls and the skeletons, bleached white over the years. These were not the remains of any animals we'd ever seen. Some of them we would now recognize as tecuani, but we found others, long, serpent-like spines with misshapen heads, exoskeletons of massive spiders with scorpion tails, a rib cage as tall and wide as the skhatet's temple! Even stranger were the pieces of metal embedded in the bones, threaded with wires fused to each limb. We were amazed, but the more and more we found, the more unnerved we became.

We kept the more manageable bones as souvenirs, but those discoveries, as wondrous as they might have been, were not the types of treasures Seka-Khayu wanted. As the days ticked by, we found nothing but sand and bleached skulls. My men grew bored, then frustrated. I considered turning back, but Seka-Khayu's threat hung heavy over me. My men didn't feel the same way. Whispers of mutiny began to reach my ears. I took the blood debt from one of the loudest, and while it put a stop to the whispers, their hostility grew. I truly thought that they would kill me and return.

Then one evening as we slogged through the endless sand, we came upon a monolith built on a high dune. We stopped in our tracks, uncertain as to how to proceed. We'd come across nothing like it in all of our days in the desert. I didn't want to risk losing any more of their confidence by appearing afraid or indecisive, but I had no idea what it was.

I need not have worried.

One of my men, a jaguar named Djhar, ran straight for it, yelling, "Ya! Ya! A miracle!"

Once he went, the rest followed. Soon they were dancing around it, knocking on its sides; it made empty, metallic sounds wherever they struck.

I heard Djhar cry "A door!" and watched his black form disappear inside. "Come on!" he yelled from within. "It's safe!"

And that's how we found the first of the outposts. They were all built the same way: square and tall, made out of thick, strong metal. My men, suddenly intrigued by the discovery, forgot all talk of mutiny. Many of the outposts were military in nature, stocked with weapons and supplies, but some were different. Did you come across any remnants of old houses in your journey to my home? I see you did. You did indeed. It would seem that many of the citizens of Gabriel and Salvation had chosen not to live in the safety of their walls. Or were expelled. In those that still remained intact, we found other items. The skeletons of the furniture upon which we now sit. More music boxes like the one I showed Seka-Khayu. Weapons not unlike those that the plics use today. Other devices of all sizes that seemed to have no purpose, scattered throughout the rooms, hanging on the walls.

The first of the iron boxes appeared in the sub-basement of the third outpost. A jaguar named Mahu found them under a trove of swords and arrows, sixteen in all. The basement was ice cold, but the boxes were warm to the touch. If one of us held our hand on it too long, it began to burn.

"Can I open it?" Mahu asked.

I nodded, though I was still uncertain.

The lock was old and rusted, and it didn't take very much effort for him to prise it open with one of the swords. As he did, the basement was flooded with a warm, amber light. It illuminated his wide eyes.

"It's beautiful," he said, gazing at it.

Inside of the box was a pool of liquid, amber, just like the light it produced, thick and full and filled with energy. The room warmed as we all crowded around. Mahu leaned forward, his hand outstretched, and it was as if I saw it in slow motion. I knew what he was doing was dangerous, and I wanted him to stop, but I couldn't tear my eyes away from it. Finally, right before his finger grazed the surface, I said, "Don't!" but it was too late.

The liquid leaped out of the container, covering his hand, his forearm, his shoulder. Mahu screamed and shook the affected arm, trying to rid himself of the poison, but it flowed out of the box like a river, and soon he was covered in it. It consumed him, head to toe, in seconds. And then it funneled its way back into the box, where it pooled just like before, waiting for the next victim.

We stood motionless, shocked. Then I grabbed one of the swords and used it to close the lid.

"Don't ever do that," I said, looking at the rest of the men.

They nodded solemnly.

The next morning, we developed a rotating system to tote everything we found back to my village, especially any of the iron boxes, to save for the Skhatet. We fashioned poles to slip through the handles on the sides so we could carry it without touching the metal. Once every seven nights, two would carry the treasure back, while two more returned to take their place.

The problem, my friends, was not the bravery of the men or the will of their leader. The problem was the desert. Have you ever traveled across it? No, of course you haven't. Until the plics laid down those iron bars for their great machines to travel on, nobody had. There's a reason why, too, and it isn't because of the heat or the distance. Any fool can find water in the desert if he knows where to look, and we knew where to look. No. As you probably already guessed, the problem came in the form of the live versions of the skeletons we found. Upon finding and looting the fifth outpost, and after sending two men home with the usual cache, we discovered them.

There were twenty of us, including myself. Djhar had proven to be quite reliable, and I came to trust him as a second in command. Whenever we discovered a new outpost, we made it a habit of sending out revolving patrols: to search for more oases, to map the landscape, to scout for enemies. When one returned, another left. Djhar took to the task with enthusiasm. Guileless and happy, he reminded me of myself before the years stacked up, along with the deaths, the pain, the sadness. I longed for that feeling again, when life was an adventure and I trusted my elders simply because of their age. That is the bitterness of wisdom, for once you gain enough, you realize that men are mere men, flawed, arrogant, vain, and, yes, capable, caring, and charitable, but mere men nonetheless. This is what I have learned. And let me tell you something else. A truth more important than any of the others. If anything else, the desert is the great equivocator, and while the skhatet may take the blood debt from me for saying so, know this: in the desert, no one man is better than the other.

One night, several months into our journey, I was awoken from my sleep by the cries of the guards standing on the battlements atop the latest outpost in which we'd taken up residence. The outposts had been brilliantly constructed, with four different floors accessible only by ladders and hatches. They'd built a basement and a sub-basement in each, the basement clearly meant for survival (as the metal magnified the heat of the day and remaining in the middle of the structure could spell a boiling death), and the sub-basement for food storage. It worked so well that among the containers of beans and corn and fruit, we found whole sides of meat (I didn't recognize the animal) still frozen in storage boxes anchored in the sandstone.

I had retired for the first time in almost a day and a half, choosing to take my rest in the hottest part of the afternoon. It felt like I'd just dropped off when I heard the guards, but when I climbed to the top of the monolith, the stars shone out of the midnight blue sky, and Khosh'iu blessed the sands with her pale light.

Two men were running toward us from over the dunes, as fast as the sand allowed. Khosh'iu was so bright that I could see the shadows of their footprints. The one in the lead was yelling and waving his hands, but he was so far away that I couldn't understand him.

"Can you hear him?" I asked the guard.

"I think."

"What's he saying?"

"He's just repeating himself. 'They're coming! They're coming!'."

I looked out over the desert, but all I could see was the dark outlines of the dunes.

"What's coming?"

The sand seemed to ripple underneath the surface several paces before the running man. He must have seen it, too, or felt it, because he stopped and held out his hands. Then something huge burst out of the wasteland, showering the air with sand, and he had just enough time to scream before it collapsed on him and then he was gone. We saw a writhing mound of flesh and scales, the scrabbling of millions of feet, and the flick of a long tale as it burrowed back underground.

"That," the guard said.

The second man didn't even slow down to look. He ran right through, making a straight line for the outpost. It was his only hope. Behind him, the sand began to ripple. I looked around the battlements. There, in the corner. An atlatl. I snatched it up.

"Get out of the way," I said, backing up.

The guard scooted to the side, and I took two steps and launched the spear to the left of the running form. I snatched another one up and threw it, too, aiming a little farther to the left. The ripple changed direction slightly, but when no more spears hit the sand, it zeroed in on the man again. He had almost reached us. The guard suddenly understood, and together we threw spear after spear out into the night, trying to cluster them as tightly as we could.

It worked.

The beast veered off, and our man (I could see now that it was Djhar) made it to the base of the outpost. We stopped throwing the spears and the beast veered back toward us. Djhar opened the metal door with a whine; I heard it crash close and the bar slam shut. The ripple sped toward us, faster and faster. At the last moment it burst out of the desert again, and again I saw the rippling of flesh and the scrabbling of thousands of feet. It slammed into the middle of the outpost, and the guard and I were thrown to the floor. The building shook and boomed but did not budge. I scrambled up and lunged for the edge, peering over the side. The monster had fallen back into the sand, dazed. A few of the guards threw spears at it, but they glanced harmlessly off its twisting body as it slithered away, finally burrowing back into the sand and disappearing with a flick of its tail.

Down at the base, Djhar had collapsed just inside the door. Someone had given him a container of water, which he held in a hand that seemed as if it wasn't attached to his body. His clothes were shredded, and several deep wounds cut canyons in his arms and torso. One eye was so swollen that it closed shut. I knelt down in front of him, trying to catch his one eye, which rolled around, unfocused.

"Djhar. Djhar. You're here."

His eye finally settled on me.

"Ka-Bata," he said.

I smiled.

"Yes. Ka-Bata. Take a drink. Take a drink."

He looked at the cup as if he didn't know what it was, then brought it up to his cracked lips. We are a dark skinned people, you know this, and we are accustomed to the heat and the sun, but he was burned and peeling all over his face and arms and legs. In some places it was so bad that it shone raw and pin. He took a sip and coughed, then took another.

"We have to leave," he said, catching his breath.

"No, we're fine. That thing is gone."

He shook his head.

"No. No. It's not. There are more."

I paused, pondering this information. Was he delirious? Delusional? How could there be more when in all our travels we hadn't even seen even one? I decided to humor him. It wouldn't help to argue.

"How many?" I asked.

He fixed me with his good eye and held my attention.

"Thousands," he said. "And they're coming for us."

THE RABBIT

At this point in the narrative, it becomes important for me to explain why anybody in his right mind would think going into a cabin in the middle of the woods was a good idea. I don't care when you was born: nineteenth century, twentieth century, a hundred and twentieth century—accepting an invitation into a cabin in the woods from a creepy old man was about as smart as taking a pine cone and shoving up your own ass. Even if he offered you soup. Not that there's not a market for that. (The pine cone in the ass, not the soup.)

But look, in a lot of ways, sometimes a creepy old man is just a creepy old man. Nothing else. Creepiness ain't a bellwether for psychopathic behavior. It just means someone's a little weird. Socially maladjusted. And social maladjustment is the battle cry of homo sapiens. It's so tangled up in our DNA we might as well add it to high school biology textbooks. Because only a species with severe social maladjustment issues would do the kinds of things human beings do to one another, like murder and torture and stealing each others babies and bombing entire races into the dust without an ounce of regret or remorse or repentance or contrition or censure or fear of castigation. So if the creep offered us soup, so much the better, because after the morning I'd had, with the wild boars and the alligators and them things in the arena and the silver slicer chase, I was friggin starving.

"You want some soup?"

Fuck yeah, I want some soup.

The other guy, the Top-Knot with the sprinter's lungs, he didn't look too sure. Neither did Wildcat. When I stood up and started limping for the front porch, she said, "You really that stupid?"

"No. I'm not that stupid. I'm hungry."

And I went inside.

The old man's cabin was decorated predictable. One level house. Open floor plan, hearth on the left, living room stocked with cargo furniture in the middle, basement door to the right of the kitchen. The kitchen ran along the back wall: fridge, sink, wood stove. A big, wide bump-out window overlooked the dark forest beyond. Apparently the old man liked wood, because other than the appliances, everything in the place was made out of hickory. Hickory ceiling, hickory walls, hickory floors, hickory furniture. I bet he even had a hickory toilet. Then there was the stuffed animal heads mounted over the fireplace. Nothing huge. A bunny. A raccoon. Something I didn't recognize because the skull was all fucked up. I liked the antlers he screwed over the door. Oh, and the framed poster of a kitten hanging from a tree with "Hang in there" printed under it? Choice decision there, old man.

The old man himself was standing in the kitchen with his back to me, stirring a pot on the wood stove. Savory smells filled the air. Pepper. Basil. Oregano. Cumin. Pretty soon Wildcat came in, followed by good old Top-Knot. I guess they thought it was better to be inside than not inside, and since they didn't hear me screaming when I entered the house, they must've figured it was safe. Plus, soup! Maybe it was chili. Or Thai curry. Steam from the pot plumed as the old man stirred.

"Have a seat, have a seat," he said. "My family will be here momently."

"You mean, like, moment by moment, or soon?"

He considered this. Stopped stirring. Seemed to think. Then he said, "Yes."

"Makes sense."

"They're so slow sometimes. The old bones creak, the dirt in the joints."

"Man, you're not kidding," I said, limping over to the table. "Ever since I hit twenty it's like whoa."

Wildcat and Top-Knot joined me, staring all around them. The place felt homey enough, I guess, but Wildcat looked like she didn't trust none of that shit. I ain't never seen her more jumpier, twitching at every little sound, eyes like flies. The old man banged something around on the stove and she nearly leaped straight up in the air like a cartoon. I half expected her to end up upside down, claws puncturing the ceiling. She didn't do that, though, because of physics, but she did throw him a look like she wanted to rip his head off. I gotta say that I didn't feel the same way. I was tired, and wounded, and my friggin knees hurt, so when I pulled out one of them chairs and eased myself down, I groaned with relief.

"No offense, mister," I said, stretching out my leg in front of me. "But them slicers did a number on all three of us. You got any band aids? Or whiskey?"

I checked the wound in my side, prodded around the edges of the burn, picked a few little chunks out. Hurt like a sonofabitch. My official diagnosis was this: it was fucked. The old man didn't respond or nothing, just stirred the pot, stirred the pot. Wildcat and me traded glances, Wildcat seeming to say, "See, I told you so." She splayed her palms on the table and leaned over it.

"Let's get out of here," she said.

"You didn't want to come in, why'd you come in?"

"I don't know. It's . . . " her hand trailed up to her shoulder, the one with the brand on it.

Top-Knot shook his head. Made a zipping noise with his mouth and mimicked the slicers slicking through the air with his hand.

"Amo."

"Exactly," I said.

Wildcat wasn't convinced.

"I'll take my chances," she said.

The chair she was sitting in scraped across the floor when she got up, and the old man turned around and said, "Any of you ever have any children?" he asked.

We stared around at each other. Okay, so that was a weird question to ask. What'd kids have to do with anything?

"Who me?" I asked. "No, I don't. Or maybe I do. Who knows? I made sex with a lot of women."

The old man seemed to chuckle, and I didn't blame him. I'm a funny guy. Or maybe he was laughing at the idea of me being a father, which was unsurprising. I'd be as good with kids as I'd be at nuclear engineering, with similar results.

"Children are a blessing," the old man said. "You'd be wise to have some of your own."

"You ever hang around me for more than a minute?"

"No doubt you're a strange man. A very strange man. But no man is so strange that his own child won't change him. I've seen it happen before. Brutal men. Irresponsible men. Drunk men. All of them transformed into rational, loving human beings all because of one thing. A child."

"Yeah? And I seen me plenty opposite, too. Rational dudes, happy dudes, loving dudes, all turned into stone cold bastards because the cooze they was with trapped them with a baby. Babies ain't nothing more than money draining shit factories. Then they grow up and turn into assholes. I know this because I was one of them once. A baby, not an asshole. Wait, no, actually, I was both."

The old man turned back to his pot to stir his soup. Must've been his favorite thing in the world, stirring.

"What is that, beef?" I asked.

"Life in the forest isn't easy," the old man said. "It requires muscle. And fortitude. And moral fibre. Takes weeks to clear the trees, chum the stumps. Months to cultivate the soil."

"Okay, let's talk about this now."

"The early years were difficult. We starved."

"Yeah, well, you tried to plant crops in the forest. That don't sound like to smart an idea."

"My wife, that bitch—"

"Whoa, whoa, dude—"

"'We'll have children,' she said. 'Big strapping boys. Girls with wide hips and strong backs. They'll help us. Help us clear the trees, sow the seeds.' Pah!" The old man spit on the hardwood.

"I thought you just said kids was the best thing to ever happen to you?"

"They turned against me."

"Yeah, that's what I said." There was something in the way the old man spit that reminded me of someone, someone from my youth shilling news papers and chocolates at my pop's newsstand. "Hey, you wouldn't happen to have lived in the city at one point, did you?" The old man chuckled, a harsh, chuffing sound. "Like you wouldn't have knew someone named Mrs. Feldman? We use to call her 'The Widow Mrs. Feldman' on account of the fact that her husband was dead."

The old man finally stopped stirring and, leaving the spoon in the pot, he turned and looked at us again.

"How'd you think I ended up stuck in this hell-hole?" he said.

Then he turned back around and resumed his stirring.

"Holy shit! You're the Widow Mrs. Feldman's husband? You're Mr. Feldman? But you're not dead!" He didn't say nothing. "Oh man, guys. You don't even know how amazing this is. The Widow Mrs. Feldman, she was this crazy witch who lived on my street. Like, she was a real witch, warts and all. Wore a black, wool skirt, even in the summer. Had a, uh, a cat. Called it Demon, I think." Wildcat'd gone pale. "I know what you're thinking," I said. "And I don't blame you. But how do you think old Mr. Feldman feels? That poor guy had to sleep with her. How disgusting is that? Hey, Mr. Feldman? How'd it feel to have to do it with such a revolting old wench?" He didn't respond. "Yeah, that's what I thought. I'd go mute, too."

Wildcat? She got progressively whiter and whiter. She swayed and sat down hard, and when Top-Knot put his hand on her shoulder to steady her she didn't freak out like she normally done when anybody touched her. She just closed her eyes.

"Hey, Mr. Feldman. If you was out here, you know, farming in the middle of the woods with your kids, why's The Widow Mrs. Feldman living in a brownstone in the city? And why's she call herself a widow?"

The old man slammed the spoon down on the stove and leaned on the counter like he'd finally had enough of my mouth. (I seen that reaction before. This fact should not surprise nobody.) Then he turned around and raised his chin, revealing the thick white slug of a scar running ragged across this throat, from one side of his spine to the other.

"Phft, Phfft," he said, slicing left and right with his finger.

Oh shit. Friggin Wildcat was right. Time to skedaddle. I got to my feet, wincing.

"Listen, uh, thanks for your hospitality and all. The electric force field. The nice soup. Is that chili? Because it smells like chili. No? So, yeah, but you're making Wildcat real uncomfortable, like, and uh . . ."

"You can't leave yet," the old man said. "My children are coming."

"No offense, old man, but fuck you, and fuck your kids."

"You can say that, you can say that," he said. And without another word, he turned and walked over to the basement door, opened it up, went inside, and closed it behind him. We heard a bolt click, one, two, three of them, then his footsteps slowly descending down, down, down into the basement.

"The fuck?" I said.

Top-Knot went over to the pot and took the lid off.

"Cococ," he said, looking up at us. "Cococ."

"What's that? Cocks? Jesus."

Something caught his attention in the window over the stove, and he leaned forward and peered outside.

"Oh." He turned to face us. "Mimic."

When we didn't respond, he said it again, only more urgently.

"Mimic! Mimic!"

"So?"

He started to stagger around, rolling his eyes in back and moaning. "I ain't got no idea what you're talking about."

He jabbed his finger at the window, so I ran up to the window to get a look. You ever do something and then immediately wish you ain't done it? That's how I felt right then. Because out there in the woods stood hundreds of dead people. Judging from the gray sweat suits and trainers they was wearing, they was recruits. And judging by their torn up stomachs and sliced necks, not to mention the dark, hollow eyes and the missing limbs, they was dead. Something bobbed to the surface of the pot of red sauce I was leaning over, and I frowned down at it. It was a finger. Cleaned and skinned, but obviously a finger.

"I don't think old Mr. Feldman's been farming vegetables out here," I said.

Whether or not we had experience fighting an army of the dead wasn't at issue, because really, it wasn't that difficult to figure out what to do next. Well. Maybe it was. Wildcat ran for the basement door where old Mr. Feldman disappeared and yanked on the handle.

"Open up!" she screamed.

She pounded on it a few more times, then backed up and started to kick the knob. Top-Knot joined her. Stood to the side, and kicked the knob once, twice, three times. It bent, bent, and then shot off, and when the door didn't open, he just started kicking it, too, over and over. He managed to kick a nice sized hole right through the middle of it, then he stuck his hands through and started tearing it apart bit by bit.

Ain't none of us was prepared for what we seen next.

I know what you're thinking. You're thinking, "you numb cunts. You just opened the door to the monster cellar." And really, I'm with you on that one. It could have easily happened. The last chunk falls and

—zombies flood out of the opening, all rotten flesh and broken bones. We turn to run and they swarm us.

—tentacles shoot out of the darkness, wrapping each one of us in them slimy plungers and pulling us back in.

—millions of rats fall out like a wall. Fucking rats. Predictable swarming/eating ensues.

—nothing at first. We all just stand there, staring into the void, waiting. Then a stench blows out of the blackness, and that's when we see the door is a mouth filled with stumps of broken teeth. It crunches down through the frame and sucks us all in.

—three kittens sit doing that thing where they lick their paws and clean their ears. Cute little fuckers, them. Top-Knot leans over to pick one up and a huge cat claw flies out of the back and impales him.

—a single butterfly flutters in the opening. Top-Knot, he ain't stupid. He won't be fooled twice. So he tries to back away, but the butterfly flies into his mouth and he swallows it down. Seconds later it erupts out of his body, fifty times its original size. It impales Wildcat with that tube-like tongue.

—A fat, pulsing sack of pus throbs in the frame. Black and shiny, shot through with dark red veins. It swells and explodes, covering us all in triple rectified acid-pus. We melt to the bone, screaming. Then the bone melts, too. You know, just to rub it in.

Fortunately for us, none of that happened. You wanna know what did happen? The exact opposite. He tore the door apart, and there stood . . . another door. Top-Knot grabbed the knob to that one and it was unlocked, and when he ripped it open, another door blocked the way, this one made made out of metal, with a handle made to look like a triple spiral. The lock didn't look like no lock I never seen, neither. Anti-climactic, I know, until you consider the fact that Old Mr. Feldman just went through it a few minutes before, and unless the laws of physics was different here than anywhere else in the universe, there was no way that he could've built three doors all at once.

"They're on the front porch," Wildcat said.

She was crouched down at the sill at the front of the house, peeking out from behind the window treatment. (Yeah. Old Mr. Feldman had window treatments.)

Top-Knot, standing on the other side of the stone hearth, snatched at my sleeve. I looked at him and he pointed up.

"Xontlachia," he said, looking up.

Me and Wildcat joined him, and sure enough there it was, a staircase leading up to a second floor. A second floor where there wasn't no second floor before

"You go first," I said, giving him a little shove.

He frowned at me, then at my hands, like he was contemplating cutting them off.

"Sorry," I said.

He shook his head and started up the steps. When he got to the top, he turned around and waved us on.

"Tonatiuh."

I guess that meant light, because when we got up there that's all we seen, a light at the end of a long hallway. Top-Knot jogged down it and what the hell, we followed. The hall was dark, but there was doors on either side, all of them shut tight and locked up. Wildcat kept trying to open them, but on the third one she yelled, "motherfucker!" and started kicking it but nothing happened.

"It's probably all just bricks anyway," I said, which didn't make her feel any better.

Top-Knot made it to the end of the hall and stopped.

"Xontlachia," he said, pointing down

He disappeared down another set of stairs, and then I heard him bark out something that sounded like a cuss word. Wildcat and I followed him, and then we seen why he was so upset. The steps brought us right back down into the living room again, standing on the other side of the stone hearth looking up at the same staircase that led to the hall we just run through. Turned around, there was stairs. Looked in front of us, there was stairs. Top-Knot ran back up again. A few seconds later we heard his footsteps and then he showed up on the steps behind of us. It was a loop.

Great.

Fists punched through the front windows. More pounded on the door. One of the dead thrust its head and torso through the open frame, impaling its neck on a shard of glass, and I recognized who it used to be. Artie. His face was all torn up, but it was Artie. The things behind him pushed forward, crushing his hips against the house.

The door cracked, followed by the jamb, then it fell and the dead poured in. They swarmed the furniture, reaching out for us. And I recognized all of them. The dude who ruptured his achilles in the second week of Hell. Good old Fuck You, his head inexpertly reattached to his body. A half-dozen Tleks. And another, and another, and another, hundreds of them, goons, goombahs, and brown people, all dead. Cold cuts. That's what Zoot meant. Cold cuts is zombies.

There wasn't no place else to go, so we did what anybody else would've done. We ran back up the stairs. Them zombies wasn't fooled, though. Good thing they didn't know how to use them. Stairs that is. The one's in front tripped and fell, but that didn't confront their friends none, because their friends used them as a handicap and trampled over them and up to the next step, where they promptly fell, and the ones behind *them* used their bodies as a handicap, and up and up and up. Not the most efficient way of climbing stairs. I seen old diabetics better at achieving that particular goal. But if you got yourself a somewhat inexhaustible store of meat to use as your own personal stepping stool, why not?

"We're fucked," I said. "We're fucked, and I didn't even get to eat no soup. Fuck this place. Fuck this whole thing. BG lied to me."

Wildcat didn't seem to hear me. She seemed to be thinking. Then she pulled that bone key out of her pocket and stared at it for a second. Then she looked behind her, thinking again. Without a word, she ran off.

The dead came on, crested the top and tumbled into the hallway. The ones in the lead stumbled forward, reaching and moaning. Nothing left for me and Top-Knot to do but back away. Not like it'd help; we'd just end up where we was to begin with. Downstairs. In the living room. With the zombies. Maybe they'd be impressed with our sudden appearance, at least shocked enough to give us a second to make a run for the exit. But probably not. They didn't seem like the white knuckle type. So we backed to the other end of the hall, and the dead followed. We backed down the stairs, and the dead followed. They made it to the edge and teetered there.

Wildcat was busy with the basement door, trying to shove that bone key into the lock.

"What the fuck are you doing?" I yelled.

"Shut up."

"Is that what that fucking key is for?"

"I said shut the fuck up!"

She twisted it, turned it, but nothing happened. The dead pressed in, closer and closer, and I thought, *Great. This is how I buy the farm. Torn to bits by a bunch of assholes who couldn't even make it through basic training.*

"Any time now would be nice!"

Wildcat kept turning the key, turning the key, and all of the sudden it slipped all the way in. Thunks sounded from the other side, like a vast mechanism had been spurred into action, and then the door flew open and a black form tumbled out and fell face first on the floor.

"Oh praise the goddess!" it said, and started to weep, big, back heaving sobs.

Fuck's sake, I thought. That wool skirt. That frizzy black hair. And that smell—salami mingled with garlic and cigar smoke.

"Is that the Widow Mrs. Feldman?" I said.

As if to answer, her cat, Demon, came yowling out of the door. He took one look at the zombies about to collapse upon the old woman and, you're not going to believe this, but he transformed into a, well, a man cat. Like a cat the size of a man, only with fur and ears and claws like knives. It charged the zombies and laid them out flat, just demolished them, sliced off their heads, sliced off their arms, sliced off their legs. I never seen nothing so filled with rage. Carved a nice big circle out of them zombies, enough to give us a little room to breathe. But it didn't last very long. Nothing like that could, right? And as fast as he transformed into something bigger, he shrank down into his old self again. Then he went over to The Widow Mrs. Feldman, who was still lying there, sobbing, and licked her ear.

"Leave me alone! Leave me alone!" she moaned.

And finally, inevitably, and kind of sadly, the zombies teetering like puppets at the top of the stairs cascaded down toward us. Sounded like luggage. Top Knot pushed me out of the way. Wildcat jumped the other. And the flesh wave poured down after us. Man did it stink. You ever walk into a closed room filled with a bunch of hungover teenaged boys? I'll just leave that one there for you to consider.

Didn't take long for them to recover, and the ones on the other side of the living room, those that had not yet climbed the stairs or gotten shredded by Demon's claws, heard the commotion and slowly turned in our direction. The Widow Mrs. Feldman stopped sobbing. She got to her knees and stared around her. The zombies in the lead moaned as one, reaching for us.

"Oh no you don't," The Widow Mrs. Feldman said. She drew her fingers across their knees, saying "Phfft! Phfft!." Their legs cut in half and they toppled over. She turned and did the same to the ones coming at us from behind, catching them across the middle and cutting them in half. The ones behind them kept coming, trampling the fallen. The Widow Mrs. Feldman was unimpressed.

"Oh for fuck's sake," she moaned. She cupped her hands into a ball and muttered under her breath. A yellow sphere of energy formed between her fingers, growing larger and larger. The zombies were only five feet away, two feet. We huddled together, back to back.

"Close your eyes!" The Widow Mrs. Feldman said.

I don't know if them other guys did it, but I didn't. She held her hands over her head and hurled the ball of energy on the floor where it exploded in a sonic wave, sending rings of energy into the horde, cutting them to ribbons.

"I left mine open!" I said, and she gave me an irritated glare.

"What did you idiots do?"

"What'd we do?" I said. "What are you doing here?"

Demon wove through her legs, singing his song.

"Shut up, you filthy beast. You're lucky I didn't eat you while we were stuck in that—"

He meowed at her, then bit her on the leg.

"Ach, you little demon!"

The old lady looked around at the dead things at her feet and sighed.

"I told him and told him. Don't do it. You're sick. But did he listen? No." Demon meowed. "Oh sure, blame me, will you?"

Wildcat said, "You hear that?"

"Hear what?"

She cocked her head.

"Listen."

"I don't hear—"

"Shh!"

And then I heard it. Far off at first, but getting closer by the second. The pop pop pop of gunfire. Then explosions, closer and closer, rattling the walls, shaking dust down from the cracks in the ceiling. Machine gun fire came next, then men shouting.

All of the sudden in walked BG followed by Bruno, both of them holding tommy guns. BG looked around at the mess, the blood and the bile, the body parts. And them zombies, they don't die just because they got cut in two. Most of them were rolling around on their backs like turtles, but more than enough had recovered and was crawling toward us again, trailing their entrails like half-stomped slugs.

"Jesus what a mess," he said.

A whole bunch of zoots in zoots came in after, and when they saw the crawlers, they loosed a hail of bullets unlike nothing I never seen before. And when it was all said and done, when the bullets was all used up, when the dead was deader'n before, BG looked at me through the smoke trailing up out of the barrel of his gun and said, "I guess you figured out what he was up to, huh?"

Then he nodded at The Widow Mrs. Feldman.

"Hey, Mrs. Feldman. How's it going?"

THE JAGUAR

Wheeler had been hit many times during her training at the academy. In the face. In the stomach. In the kidneys. It taught her how to take a punch, and taking a punch came in handy (no pun intended) during her days on the street as a blue. She didn't like it; nobody does. Getting hit hurt. One of her dipshit instructors dislocated her jaw. But never before had getting hit felt the way it did when she came around in the alley. She gasped awake awash in pain. It seemed to imbue her entire body, soak into her frame. Her skull felt like someone had pierced it with an awl, her ribs felt each one had been cracked in half, and her knees felt like they were on the wrong side of her legs.

She rolled over on her side and threw up.

After a while, she felt slightly better, good enough to test her limbs. Feet, check. Hands, check. The fact that she could think clearly was promising. Where was Peña? Oh no. Peña. The attack. She sat up and regretted it.

A little girl was standing in the alley next to her. Blonde hair, blue eyes, flawless, white skin. Dirt streaked down her face. She was wearing a sleeveless white sundress with yellow daffodils in the print. It was smeared with red and green blobs, and, judging by the thick lip of mud curling up from under her formerly white pumps, she had been spending a lot of time playing in the gutter. Or a cow pasture. Her shoulder had been branded with the triple-spiral. Wheeler groaned. Now she was seeing things. Great.

"Oh Bella, is it her?"

Another little girl suddenly appeared wearing exactly the same thing, only she wasn't wearing shoes. Her feet were so dirty that they were nearly black.

"I don't know, Ella. Isn't she pretty? Don't you like her?"

"Oh Bella, I like her a lot. I do, I do. Did you find her yourself?"

"She fell out of that window up there."

"My goodness that's a long way up. Why did she do that?"

"I think she might have been thrown out."

Ella tsked.

"Who would throw such a pretty woman out a window?"

"I don't know. What should we do?"

"Daddy told us to find her and give her the key."

"Did you hear him cussing the crone last night?"

"Oh my goodness, his language was foul!"

"He called her a 'bloody cunt' and told her to get out of his head!"

The girls squealed with laughter, ending by chanting "Bloody cunt! Bloody cunt! The crone's in a rut!" over and over. Finally Bella said, "But is it really her? Check her shoulder."

Ella stepped around and reached for Wheeler's arm and Wheeler batted her hand away. Ella's hand flew to her mouth.

"Oh, Bella, she's so tough! I love her. I love her so much. Daddy would, too. Don't you think?"

"I feel sorry for Daddy. He's so lonely."

"But he has us, Ella. And Logan and Lucas, and Byron and Bryon, and Hayden—"

"And Aiden."

"Oh yes, oh yes. I'd nearly forgotten about him. Daddy certainly is angry with Aiden."

"Wouldn't you be? He hurt Coraline bad. She's not normal anymore, no no no."

"Coraline was always not normal."

"Not like this, though. Did you see what she did to that poor rabbit?" Bella put her hand over her mouth, giggling. "It's not funny, Bella! It's not, it's not!"

"Oh Ella, do let's stop."

Wheeler, who'd been following the whole exchange with mounting irritation, said "Yes. Let's do."

Strange how everything hurt, but nothing seemed broken. Her head screamed when she got to her feet, and her legs were stiff, and there was a knot in her back where she'd landed, but everything worked the way it should. And her foot. Her broken toes. They didn't hurt at all anymore.

In fact . . .

She took a single, lame step forward. Then another. Then she stopped and patted her pocket. Her phone was there, but when she pulled it out the screen was cracked in a million pieces. She pushed the button a few times, but it didn't turn on. She turned around.

"Where did you get that?" she asked, looking at the brand on Bella's shoulder.

"What? My arm? I was born with it."

"The brand. On your arm."

The girl ran her fingers over it.

"It's my cabal, silly."

A cabal. Sounded right.

"You have one, too," Bella said.

"How do you know that?"

"Daddy said you would. He told us you'd be here." She adopted the gruff tone of what Wheeler could only assume was the girls' father. "'Go find that daft bink and get her the key.' He said you'd be in an alley next to a bar. And you are. Can we see it?"

Wheeler paused, then thought, *why not?* She pulled her sleeve up and showed the triple spiral. The girls gasped.

"Oh Ella, it's so bright and fiery! Do you see it? Do you see?"

"I do, Bella. I do, I do."

"She's the one! She has to be!"

"Who are you?" Wheeler asked, tugging her sleeve down. The girls giggled, covering their mouths with their hands. "Bella? Ella? Those are your names?"

"I'm Bella and she's Ella. What's *your* name."

"I'm Wheeler. *Detective* Wheeler."

"Ooooh, Ella, she *is* a police. Just like Daddy said. I bet she's killed a man before!"

"Oh, yes, Bella. Oh yes."

"Have you? Have you killed a man, *Detective* Wheeler?"

Wheeler couldn't stop the smile from creeping up on her. Such odd little creatures.

"What are you doing here?" she asked.

"I just told you. Daddy said–"

"How long was I out like that?"

"We don't know. We only just got here. Daddy said, 'Go find Aiden at the whorehouse first'." She grew sad. "But Aiden wasn't at the whorehouse."

"Whorehouse? Where's your mother?"

Bella laughed out loud.

"Mother? We haven't seen her in decades."

"Decades?"

"Oh yes," Ella chimed in. "Not since Daddy had her executed. She was doing the thing with another man."

"Poor Nathaniel. I liked him oh so much."

"He wasn't very nice to Mommy."

"Yes, he was! He loved her. He told me."

"But he was always making her scream so loud."

Wheeler frowned at them. She couldn't tell if they were being honest or just putting her on. She shifted, suddenly aware of an itching deep in her body, like she needed to scratch her bones. She tested her bad leg again. It no longer hurt. She could put all of her weight on it. She brushed a lock of hair out of her eyes.

"Is your dad nearby?"

"Not too far," Bella said, slyly. "Will you take us to him? We're lost, ever so lost."

"Uh-huh." Wheeler glanced up at the broken window. Two stories up. She was lucky. Luckier than Peña. What was that thing? They'd emptied their clips into it, and . . . "Shit."

She loped around the alley, looking for her gun. And that contraption. The Barrel Arm Biceps™. Where—?

"What's she looking for, Bella?"

"I think she's looking for this."

Wheeler looked, and Bella was holding her gun, pinching it by the barrel.

"Give me that."

The girls retreated, giggling.

"Bella? Ella? You need to give me that. I'm a—"

"Detective!" Ella squealed.

"I don't have time for this." Nothing. "Hand it over." They smiled at her. "Now!"

"Oh Ella, she's pretty and smart *and* brave."

"Daddy really will like her."

"Goddammit!" The girls' mouths dropped open. She took another step forward. They took another step back. "Girls! Give me the fucking gun!"

Their eyes widened and then, instead of running or freezing or doing anything else that might have been age appropriate, they laughed.

"She said 'fuck'! She said 'fuck'!"

"Fucking fuck! Fuck-e-dy fuck!"

And together: "Fuck-e-dy fuck! She fucked up!"

Then they grabbed each other's hand, turned, and sprinted out of the alley.

"Girls!" Wheeler yelled.

She cast a quick glance back at the window.

"Dammit," she whispered, and started off after them.

The first few steps were difficult, but it was easier to run than she thought. The girls teased her along. They would sprint away, giggling the whole time, and then stop and stick their tongues out. Once she got within ten yards, they sprinted away again. When they realized she couldn't catch them, they started to skip, still holding hands, swinging their arms back and forth. Bella held the gun out to her side, still pinching it by the barrel, and Wheeler was sure she'd drop it and it would go off. About a block after the chase began, they started to sing.

"When I was young and just a bad little kid/My momma noticed funny things I did/Like shootin' puppies with a B B gun/I'd poison guppies, and when I was done/I'd find a pussy cat and bash its head!"

"Girls, you need to stop right now!"

They mimicked her: "Girls, you need to stop right now!"

"I mean it!"

"I mean it!"

The Silver Bullet lorded over them, the construction lights in the scaffold reflecting off its shiny metal shell. Sparks flew like fireflies. Wheeler hadn't realized how close they were to it. With a squeal, the girls let go of each other's hands and ran across the street, ducking into an alley on the other side. Wheeler gritted her teeth and pushed forward. By the time she got there, the girls were already at the end of the alley. Bella was holding up a sewer grate for Ella, who disappeared into the hole.

"Hurry, hurry!" Bella cried. "The sniders! The sceels!"

Wheeler stopped, too tired to continue on. Her body might have felt fine, but she was out of breath. She leaned against the bricks, linking her fingers over her head.

"Girls," she said. "Enough already."

Ella popped her head back up.

"Mommy, please do hurry! They'll tear us apart, they will."

"Don't call her that, Ella."

"Why not?"

"She's not our mommy. Not yet."

"But Daddy will love her. She's oh so wonderful."

They giggled one last time, and then Ella disappeared back down the hole, followed by her sister. Wheeler sighed and weighed her options. She didn't have to chase them. She didn't have to do anything at all. It would look bad, losing her weapon, but all things considered, she thought it'd be easy to explain. It was time to turn around. Turn around right now and go back to that apartment. Peña was there. At least his corpse was. Christ. What was she doing? Then the gun went off, followed by squeals of delight, magnified by the acoustics of the sewer.

A blast of warm air tousled her hair as she clambered down the iron-runged ladder. A voice floated up from below.

"Come on, mommy! What are you waiting for?"

"Ella, I told you not to call her—"

"Oh shut up, Bella."

A reptilian rattle echoed through the tunnels, and the girls gasped.

"It's coming! It's coming!"

Wheeler heard their footsteps splash away.

"We left the key for you at the bottom! It's on the torch!"

Wheeler pressed her forehead on one of the rungs and whispered to herself. She looked over her shoulder. Only about ten more feet. She could make it.

She rested at the bottom, spent, too spent to worry about the fact that she was sitting in a sewer tunnel in near darkness. Near darkness. Yes, she could see. Just a little bit. Once her eyes adjusted, she could make out lichen coating the concrete walls, providing a low, green light. The tunnels were huge, large enough for a car to drive through. A small stream of water ran the length of the tube where she was standing, but she could hear the rush of a much larger torrent echoing farther down the way. It split into two channels to her right, both dark, empty, and foreboding.

"A torch at the bottom," she said, and slapped around the base of the ladder for the flashlight. Her hand hit something soft and squishy, trembled over a shard of something sharp and glassy, before finally knocking something over that clinked on the concrete. The flashlight. She picked it up, impressed at its size and weight. It was tactical. Where had they found a tactical flashlight? Never mind. She didn't want to know.

A key hung from a little leather strap on the end, if she could really call it a key. It was thick and heavy, shaped like a plus sign with a quadruple chambered backward 'C' hanging off it. It looked like it had been carved out of bone. She yanked it off the strap with a snap and put it in her pocket. When she pushed the flashlight's ON button, a feeble, brown light emanated from the bell.

Great.

"Thanks, girls!" she called.

A wild giggle echoing from the tunnel to the right. She sighed and glanced back up at the open hole above her.

Okay. Alright.

The stream started as a trickle, but as she crept forward, the water grew deeper and deeper until it rose up to her ankles, and then her calves, and then she took a step out into nothing and plunged waist deep. She let out an involuntary yelp. It was colder than the water behind her, sharper. She stood there for a moment, elbows kissing the surface, a grimace frozen on her face. The flashlight flickered and went out so she smacked it, but instead of flickering back on, a spring-loaded knife popped out of the bottom. She ran her finger along the blade. It was sharp and serrated, about six inches long. The flashlight flickered back to life, a little weaker than before. The girls called out to her, their voices even fainter.

"Come on, mommy! Come on!"

"The sceel will be here soon!"

"Sceel?" Wheeler said to herself. Then, louder, "What's a sceel?"

Nothing for a while. Then, "You'll see!"

The tunnel curved to the left, and then she faced another fork. She shined her dying light into both holes, but the beam didn't penetrate farther than a few feet. All she could see was blackness and the faint shimmer of water.

"Which way did you go?" she called.

The girls' voices were now barely audible.

"Go straight!"

"I'm at a fork. Which side do I take?"

The plink of water in the distance. Her boxy breath in the tunnel. Then, very far off, ". . . sceels . . . run . . . ."

Shit. Left or right? Left or right? Something splashed to the left, followed by the rattle, louder this time. At least she thought it came from the left. It was difficult to tell; everything echoed, bouncing off the concrete. Crap. Don't freak out, Wheeler. Remember your training. You're a detective. Use your skills. So she did.

She guessed.

She chose the right side. Mainly because she was right handed.

Twenty feet in, the tunnel turned to the right, and the water grew deeper. She waded on, finding comfort in the slight weightlessness. It didn't decrease the fear though, of the dark, of the water. Then something rubbed against her leg, something long and smooth and heavy. She had no time to think before it grabbed her by the foot and yanked her under the water. It released her just as soon as it pulled her down, and she bobbed back up to the surface, gasping and gagging. It brushed by her again she plunged the flashlight into the water, knife pointed down. There wasn't much she could achieve. The water was too deep, but at least if the thing, whatever it was, got too close again, she could stab it, slice it, somehow get it off of her.

It didn't come back, and without a second thought, she shoved forward as hard as she could, scooping at the water with her one free hand. The tunnel grew wider, the water shallower, and up ahead she thought she saw the low, warm glow of yellow light. She strove for it, plunging ahead, and the tunnel twisted in an S—a hard turn to the left, a hard turn to the right, the yellow growing brighter, the sound of rushing water louder, and the current stronger until all of the sudden she wasn't in control anymore, and she was carried along, faster and faster. The next thing she knew she flew out into the air and landed hard on her knees on a concrete surface, skidding forward until she came to a stop against a solid barrier.

She stood up, soaking wet, breathing heavily. She'd landed on a concrete island, maybe one hundred square feet in diameter. Behind her, the water emptied out of a tube into a dark space somewhere far below. Before her, a dam blocked her way, easily five feet high and twice as deep. A variety of weapons lay scattered about its base. Swords and daggers, rusted long knives. There were guns, too. Police issued Glocks. An AR-15. A couple of 30-06's. Two scepters stuck out of the dirt at the bottom, their crystal heads filled with a luminescent amber light.

The base of the dam was made out of dirt flecked with bleached white bone. That gave way to a layer of skeletons, then a layer of skulls, then rotting flesh. On top rested the body of a young boy, arms splayed, skin ice white, eyes staring out into the void. On his left hand he wore an old baseball mitt, the kind Wheeler had only seen in museums or old pictures. Even worse than that, worse than the smell, worse than the green film growing on the boy's bare arms, were the toys. Stuffed animals, action figures, baseballs, plastic dolls, Hot Wheels cars, slingshots, the kinds of things children carried with them when they went out into the world to play, to grow, to learn, to live, now reduced to so much detritus moldering away under a dead body in a sewer tunnel.

Wheeler ached for something more lethal than a blade sticking out of a flashlight, which was why, rather than backing slowly away and trying to get back into the tunnel that spit her out onto this hellish place, she crept toward the funereal mound, hoping that one of the guns was still operational. But the closer she got, the more she realized that the guns were unusable; almost all of them were covered with rust and mold, or half-buried in the base. A bright sword leaned up against the skulls, looking like it had fallen out of the open palm of the corpse of the boy on top. It was long and silver, with an ornate handle and delicate designs etched into the metal. Even more interesting was the blade. A fleur-de-lis with blood gutters and upturned spikes where the base met the handle. She picked it up and weighed it in her hand. The leather grip was worn but comforting, and the sword's balance was impressive.

Something splashed behind her, and she whipped her head around, listening intently. The sound of the water falling out of the other tunnel masked everything. Maybe that's all she heard. She waited longer than she needed to, spooked by the memory of whatever had brushed against her before, the thing that had pulled her under the water, testing her. She didn't want to turn her attention back to the dam until she was sure it wasn't coming back for her. But that would never be the case, not down here, and every second she stalled was another second she gave whatever it was to slink closer. Then she heard another splash and she turned for the dam. She had to get out of there.

In a moment of sheer desperation, she pulled on the leg of the dead boy and it shifted and rolled and tumbled down the front, revealing a shining Magnum in perfect condition.

Wheeler gasped.

Then the pile shifted again, and a black form scrabbled to the top, revealing a massive eel with a scorpion's tail and eight spider's legs. It scrambled over the weapon and raised a stinger nearly the size of her fist, dripping with venom. Sceels. Scorpions mixed with eels. Now she got it. She took a step back, raising the fleur-de-lis with both hands.

"Try it," she muttered.

Two more scrambled up next to it, smaller but just as lethal looking. They followed her with their beady black eyes.

"Okay, okay." She adjusted her grip on the sword.

They scrabbled down, dirt and bone sifting to the concrete, and Wheeler crouched, readying herself to strike, wondering how much damage she could do before one of them stuck her. They came for her and she swung, missing by at least a foot. The beasts paused, rearing up, their legs waving in the air. She tightened her grip and steeled herself for another strike, but then they turned and retreated back up the corpse dam, one by one, creeping over the dead boy until she was alone again.

Wheeler smirked and relaxed, letting the sword hang by her side.

"That's right," she said. "You better run."

A rattle sounded from behind her, echoing in the tunnel, bouncing off the concrete walls. She slowly turned around but didn't see anything. Shadows at first, hiding in the crooks where the amber glow couldn't reach. Beyond that, the ebon darkness of the tunnel. Then inked into that blackness, darker than dark, blacker than black, the outline of a terrible thing appeared. It was long and coiled, with a cobra's hood and an eerie green glint in its eyes. It filled the opening of the tube.

It uncoiled and spit at her, and she dodged the glob. It struck the boy's corpse and hissed and melted through the body with an evil, chemical cloud. Wheeler swung the fleur-de-lis, slicing into the scaly skin just under the monster's head, sinking deep into the meat. The beast squealed and writhed, backing out of the tunnel, shocked and panicked. She saw her chance. She turned and ran for the dam, lunging for the Magnum still sitting on top. Its metal grip felt oddly warm and heavy in her palm, and when she tried to pick it up, it stuck to the flesh of the dead thing beneath it. Just as she was about to pry it free, a black flash, faster than fast, struck out from the other side, and her hand exploded in pain.

She fell back, dropping her weapons and landing hard against the wall. Her hand was already swelling, and her forearm and bicep. It made her sick. It was too fast. Too much. The sceels scrabbled back atop the dam, their stingers poised and ready. Another surge of pain flooded through her, and her body seized, arms flying open, back arching. She didn't have time to think before the blackness began to take over. She seized again, gasping for breath as the poison strangled her lungs, and her left hand smashed the glass motif on top of one of the scepters sticking out of the bottom of the dam. The amber liquid leaped onto her outstretched arm and flooded over her, coating the wound, draining into it. It burned worse than the poison at first, the amber filling her up, filtering into her pores, fusing with her tissue, her veins, her tendons, her bones.

Inside of her, stemming from her hand and flying up her arm and into her chest, she felt a surge of power, a warm energy that burned away the poison and overtook her chest, coursing down into her belly and bowels. A final shock seized her muscles, and she felt it pulse out, radiating brighter and brighter, glowing white hot. She became less and less, disintegrating in the heat. She wanted to scream but had no voice in the rush of the energy, and then she was nothing. Just an idea, a bodiless soul, floating in shapeless white energy.

Forms appeared. The outlines of buildings. A street in the middle of a city. Skeletal shapes hanging from crucifixes. And she was one of those shapes, her arms spread wide, her hands nailed to the ends, the wrists bound to the wood by rope. There was something in her hand, a strange, white key. Her clothes were bleached white, torn and burned and tattered. Her body was hers and not hers. Two men wearing cream-colored suits and fedoras and two tone shoes. They were speaking, but she couldn't hear them, their mouths moving soundlessly. She managed to catch the edge of a word.

". . . got a match?"

She started laughing. She didn't know why. She didn't know what was real anymore. She didn't know who she was. Her name. Her past. It all swirled around her, just out of reach. Faces and places swam before her eyes, but she didn't know who or what they were or what they meant. They were important. They had to be. But she couldn't figure it out. She rubbed the key between her fingers. A comedy routine, of all things, bubbled into her mind. Two men. One fat. One skinny.

"Look you've gotta have a first baseman, right?"

"Certainly."

"Who's playing first?"

"That's right."

"When you pay off the first baseman every month, who get's the money?"

"Every dollar of it."

"All I'm trying to find out is the fellow's name on first base."

"Who."

The two men standing in front of her were just like the routine. One tall and hulking. One short and stocky. It made her laugh harder, even harder than before.

"The fuck you laughing at?" the stocky one asked.

"Yeah, I gotta match," she said, smiling with her teeth. "My ass and your face!"

THE SNAKE

Ka-Bata stopped speaking. He seemed pensive, digging into painful memories. After a moment, he looked up and noticed the darkening sky. The wind that drove across the barren desert beyond turned cold, so he ordered his servants to add more torches and refresh those that had gone out. He added more logs to the fire, stoked the flames they were so high that Coatl and Xiuloc had to move back a few feet. Ka-Bata swept his arms into the air.

"A good fire is a gift from the hummingbird!" He waved a hand in the air. "Let me finish my story. But first, more to drink!"

He clapped and called out to his servants, who hurried forward with cups filled with pulque. Ka-Bata gulped his down, spilling some in his beard, then motioned for more. An old man tottered forward with a clay pot and Ka-Bata glared at him.

"Not that. The other brew. From the city."

The old man blanched at his error and bowed as he retreated.

"Come, come!" Ka-Bata called. "Bring me the special brew!"

A young woman came out from the building holding a pitcher. She glanced up at him coquettishly. A smile tugged at the corner of Ka-Bata's mouth.

"You may put that down, my dear," he said, and she did, bowing a little.

He watched her swish back across the garden. She knew he was watching, and exaggerated her walk accordingly. He took a final swig before turning back to his guests. He leered at them, gesturing at her retreating form with his cup. Some of it sloshed over the edge. He appeared a little put out when he saw that Coatl had not touched his drink.

"You don't like it?"

"Forgive me, Ka-Bata, but I'm still feeling weak."

"Of course, of course. But maybe it's too sweet. Here, you must try this." He picked up the pitcher. "Dump that, dump that. In the plant." He looked around him, guiltily. "Quick. My gardener is a beast. If he sees you—"

Amused, Coatl dumped his cup in the plant next to him. Xiuloc merely finished his.

"Ha ha! Xiuloc is a man who likes to drink. Here. Hold them out."

They did as they were told, and Ka-Bata filled their cups with a thin looking liquid, amber in color. Coatl held his up to his nose and sniffed. It didn't smell bad, but it was strong. He and Xiuloc each took a tentative sip, then held the cups out in front of them, pleasantly shocked.

"Ha ha! Yes! Different, isn't it? I don't know how to describe it. Bitter, fruity, spicy, and delicious!"

Coatl took another drink, a larger one this time. The flavors played on his tongue exactly the way Ka-Bata described it. He held up his cup as a salute and put it on the adobe under his chair. Ka-Bata watched, disappointed. He recovered quickly.

"You'll drink when you're ready. I drink too much! Or so that witch keeps on telling me. So! Now I will finish my tale." He took a seat on other side of the fire, which had died down some. "Djhar. The beasts. That terrible night." He paused, templed his fingers and tapping his lips. "If that night was terrible, the next day was worse. I tell you now, knowing what I know, knowing what we found in that cursed city, I wish we'd never found them."

Djhar insisted that we head back to the last outpost.

"We will arrive after dark, but we'll have to risk it."

"Risk what?" I asked. "You said they sleep in the day."

"They do. But they are awake. They can track our movements."

"Djhar. You're not making sense."

"These creatures, they don't eat. They are gods. The children of the hummingbird. They only need the sun."

"I thought you said they were only active at night."

"They are. They eat the sun like we eat meat. They drink the rays like we drink water. But while they're doing so, they don't move. I don't think they can. They hide beneath the sand, always leaving a part of themselves exposed. It's their one weakness, and they know it."

"You know this and you didn't kill them?"

Djhar wouldn't meet my eyes. He kept shaking his head.

"It's not that easy."

He began to shake again.

"Djhar. It's okay."

"No, no, no."

I didn't know what to do. I'd never seen a man in this state before. I put a hand on his shoulder and he completely fell apart, weeping and sobbing. The men surrounding us looked away, embarrassed. I realized I had a responsibility here, not for Djhar but for them, for us, for our survival. I had to stop him before his hysteria spread, so I slapped him hard across the face. I did it again and his eyes found mine.

"Djhar, you are a warrior. Not some child. Do you understand me?"

He nodded once, a short, clipped action.

"I've never seen anything like them, Ka-Bata," he said. "They're ruthless. They stalk us and run us down, and they never stop."

"How is that any different from the jaguar? Or the cipac?"

"The jaguar hunts for food. And the cipac. But these, they only want to kill. To tear our flesh. It excites them. I've seen it. They go into a frenzy, and they . . ."

He started to hiccup, his eyes going wide and round. I shook him by the shoulder.

"Steady, Djhar. Tell us."

"The way they kill. I think they're using us."

"Using us? How?"

"To make more of themselves."

I know what you're thinking. Just like the tecuani. That's what I said.

"We'll slash them down."

"No, Ka-Bata. We have to run. We have to get out of here. They will kill us all."

"Djhar—"

"We found a city."

"A city?"

"Yes, a city on the shore of a grand sea."

"Were there people?"

"I don't know. We only saw it from a distance."

"Where? How far away?"

"Not long. Half a patrol."

I stood up, resolute, and held out my hand to help him off the ground.

"Then we'll explore it ourselves," I said. "But not before we kill some of these sun demons."

We traveled light, with only our weapons, our shields, and water. Djhar insisted we wait until the sun rose firmly into the sky before we set out. We headed into it at first before veering to the north. As light as we packed, we were not used to the heat. Many of us were already exhausted, having grown to our nocturnal schedule. This was the time of day when we often clambered down to the lower levels of the outposts to sleep. We took frequent breaks, resting in the shadow of a dune. Djhar pushed us onward, insisting that we keep our down time short "if we meant to live." The sun perched directly overhead, beating merciless and hard upon our uncovered heads and bare shoulders. We grew more and more fatigued. Djhar, however, separated himself from the group more than once, and more than once I thought we were lost until we mounted some high dune and found him waiting at the top, eyes searching the barren wasteland. It was atop such a dune that he implored us to stop and wait.

"Why here?" I asked, draining the last drop of moisture from my container.

He didn't reply. He stared out into the desert as if waiting for a sign or a signal. Finally he squeezed his eyes shut and looked away, grimacing.

"You shouldn't stare to long out into the desert, Djhar. You know that is—"

"Ka-Bata, come stand right here."

He motioned to me with one hand, rubbing his eyes with the other.

I did as he asked.

"I found a nest," he said.

"A nest?"

"Where they sleep."

He pointed out into the desert, still rubbing his eyes. I looked but saw nothing.

"Just wait," he said, anticipating my question. "You'll see."

I did. I waited. And waited. I noticed that we were looking down into a valley of sorts. High dunes that formed a U-shape. We stood at the opposite end of the opening. I was on the verge of asking him what I was waiting for when a bright flash of light coming from the middle of the U blinded me. I squinted and held up my hand, trying to block it.

"Is that them?" I asked.

"Yes. It's a nest."

"Then what are we waiting for?" I drew my maquahuitl out of the sheath on my back, but he put his hand on my arm.

"Not yet."

One by one, more flashes of light shot out of the sand below, first dozens, then hundreds, then thousands, the glare from the sun reflecting off them so bright that soon it was impossible to look without shielding our eyes. The men muttered to each other, amazed, afraid. I shushed them, trying to comprehend it. The beasts were packed together, vulnerable but for the huge dunes around them. They must have chosen the spot on purpose.

"We stumbled into a nest like that two days ago, at dusk," Djhar said. "We thought it was more treasure, something the plics left behind that we could give to Seka-Khayu. They devoured half of us almost immediately. By the time we made it to the lost city, it was only me and Sebk. You saw what happened to him."

I did. I watched that massive worm burst out of the sand and devour him whole.

"If those are the little ones," I said. "Where do the big ones sleep?"

As if to answer me, the sand beneath our feet shuddered, and a huge eye-shaped hole formed at one end. One of my men, an eagle warrior named Anen, fell into it. I leaped for him but Djhar held me back.

"It's too late," he said.

The sun struck the empty hole, and a burst of energy shot out, a hundred times more powerful than those that reflected off the sea of creatures beneath us. The ground rumbled awake, the sand shifted, and we were all sent flying. I landed on my back and tumbled down to the plane below, and as I watched, I understood the nature of the dunes all around us. They were the guards, the big creatures, at least ten of them, arranged to protect their children below. The one we were standing on uncoiled slowly, a screech erupting from its depths. It was a massive dragon. It impaled one of my men on its teeth and gulped him down. There was nothing left to do but run, but as I stood to do so, Djhar held me back again.

"Watch," he said.

The creature wavered there in the air, it's eyes opening and closing. Another sound came out of it, a sound I'd never heard before. It was high-pitched at first, full of energy, but gradually it wound down into a deep grumble, and as it did so, the creature lost its power. It crashed to the sand, shaking the earth.

"Have you seen that before?" I asked.

Djhar nodded. He pointed at the sun.

"They've just begun to rest. They need more time."

"How much more time?"

"The big ones need the whole day. The little ones, though, they could be ready soon."

So we ran for the city. It took longer than Djhar remembered, and once or twice he got turned around and had to recalculate his path. As the day waned and the sun fell lower in the sky, he grew more and more nervous.

"We can't be out here," he kept saying. "They'll feel our footsteps. Where is it? I swear I thought it was in this direction!"

There was nothing to do but continue. Djhar kept throwing looks over his shoulder as the day wore on, we all did, waiting for the end, for those things to rage across the sand like a plague and mow us down, but they didn't come. Finally, up ahead, one of our faster men cried out.

"There! There!" he said. "I can see it!"

Indeed, on the horizon I saw the outline of tall city walls, dark and dead as the sun set behind it. The barbican, the battlements, the bulwarks, all flying the ragged flags of a people swallowed up by time. Djhar laughed out loud, relieved. He turned around to say something to me, and the laughter died on his lips.

"They're here," he said.

I turned to look too.

Behind us, the sand rippled as the monsters drove towards us, cutting a swath hundreds of hands wide and thousands of hands deep. Behind them, I saw the shadows of larger bulges. We ran as fast as we could. As we grew nearer, I saw the sea beyond, beautiful and red from the setting sun. The city was built on a cliff that overlooked it, and a strong, cool wind kicked up from the direction of the water, riffling the tattered flags, bringing with it the fresh smell of salt, soil, and wood.

The ground grew harder, and the beasts in the lead burst out of the sand to run along behind us. Free of the friction of the earth, they gained speed. One flew up behind me, aiming for my heels, but I took out my maquahuitl and slashed at it, cutting it through the middle. It made an strange zipping noise and burst into flame.

Another one shot for Djhar, nipping at his feet. He led it on and, at the last possible second, cut to the right. It dug into the earth and tumbled as it tried to correct it's course, giving me ample time to hack it in two as I ran up from behind.

Djhar rounded out his turn and headed back my way. One of the men in front of us fell, and I went to help him, but Djhar cried "No!" and with good reason, too. In seconds he was overrun by the beasts, his cries cut off as they swarmed his body. I felt a rush of wind part the hair on my left, and then the soldier in front of me exploded. Those things. They were firing at us. Arrows of some kind. Another struck city wall, the shards cutting down another man. One by one we were taken out, until it was only Djhar and me, running for the gate. Our pursuers knew they had one last chance to attack, and they sent a volley several lines deep.

It's odd how time will slow down in these kinds of situations. I've heard it so many times before, experienced it myself in the middle of battle, and each time, after the bodies were buried and their souls moved on to the seven gates, after the wounds of the survivors healed, I could still see the details of the fight as if I were still in it. The slashed throats. The gutted bellies. The hacked limbs. Worse were the expressions of the men I killed, a mingled twist of anger and fear, each one of them unbelieving as they paid their blood debt. Even now as I talk to you, years after our flight from the strange monsters in the desert, I can see every last feature of the gate: the riveted surface, rusty and stained green, the lichen and moss growing out of the cracks in the stones, swaying in the wind, the walls streaked with salt and brine, and, as I ducked inside to the black void that awaited inside the city, the look of pure terror on Djhar's face as one of those monsters hit him from behind, and the white heat that consumed his body and turned him into so much dust.

"He's asleep."

Coatl heard the voice from depths of his own exhaustion. It was Ka-Bata, and at first he thought the reference was toward him. But how could he be asleep when his eyes were open? How could he be asleep when he could clearly see Ka-Bata's lips moving?

"I'm awake," Coatl said. He blinked hard, trying to focus.

Ka-Bata seemed irritated.

"Your friend isn't."

Xiuloc was snoring lightly in his chair, mouth open, head thrown back. The cup he'd been drinking from dangled from his fingertips, and as they watched, a few drops of liquid pattered on the ground beneath and it slipped off and hit the adobe with a ting.

"He's fine," Coatl said. It was a little touching, really, to see a grown man so utterly in the grasp of sleep. "Your story. You haven't finished it. What happened in the city?"

Ka-Bata weighed the question, tapping his fingers together. For the first time since Coatl met him, the old man seemed uncomfortable. His servants hovered in the shadows of the garden as if awaiting an order. Such is the strength of the man, Coatl thought. At such a late hour, to have his servants still alert, attuned to his next whim. Ka-Bata took a deep breath and shook off whatever was bothering him. He flashed a smile at his guest.

"My story. Yes. The city's name was Gabriel. I learned this later on. At the time, I thought only of the safety of its walls."

I squeezed myself through a crack in the gate. You laugh at that now, yes, but I was on patrol back then, my body a fine tuned instrument. Now, though. Too much pulque. As tight as that squeeze was, I still had to figure out how to close the gate or the beasts would follow. As if to confirm this, two of them burst into the crack through which I'd pushed myself, sending chips and chunks of stone flying through the air, peppering my arm and side.

The city looked like it had been abandoned for a long time. Sand piled up in corners of the walls. The windows of the buildings around me, if they weren't cracked or shattered, were covered in a glaze of dirt and slime. An iron wheel had been set into the barbican to the right, green with age. I had no idea if it would even turn, but I had to try. I threw my body into it, but it wouldn't budge. More explosions at the crack. Sparks and shards flew. Panicked, I lunged again and again, and finally the mechanics gave a tight groan, and the gate shut a few more inches but stopped short.

The crack was now too small for anything else to enter, but any breach in a wall was a weakness, and I knew those things would figure out a way to exploit the flaw. The wheel would turn no more. I was not strong enough, so I searched around me for something I could use as a lever. There. Sitting under what looked like a fallen shelter. A long, metal pole. I snatched it up and jammed it into the spokes, using my body weight to hang from the end. I jumped and pulled and screamed, yet nothing happened. The gate shook as the beasts struck it again and again, but it was strong and held firm. Their attack must have rattled something loose, though, because something cracked and the wheel spun half a turn and the gate closed another inch.

It was almost completely closed now. I could see little paws scrabbling into the space that was left between the gate and the wall, the razor sharp claws of my enemy. I readjusted the pole and yanked again and again, using all my remaining strength, but it wouldn't move. The pounding of the monsters on the other side grew more fierce, the percussions rattling the frame, sending dirt and chunks of rock showering down up on me. When the first big hit came, it sent me flying. A paw as big as a tree forced itself through, and a mighty mechanical noise filled the air. The gate squealed and opened a foot. Two creatures shot inside. I scrambled back, striking out with my maquahuitl, deflecting the one zipping for my head. The other latched onto my arm and tore it open. More flooded in and I thought, "This is it. This is the end of Ka-Bata."

Then a thunderous noise erupted from behind me, as if a thousand boulders were falling all around, and the creatures fell to the ground, squealing in fits, or exploded where they were. The thunder continued, and amidst it I struck out with my weapon, unsure of whether or not I did any damage but determined to help my unexpected savior, whoever or whatever it was.

The tree-sized limb receded, and I lunged for the lever, yanking it down. The gate slammed shut, cutting the smaller beasts still flowing into the city in half, smashing them into the jamb. I fell to my knees, exhausted. After the percussion of the attack and the crashing died down, and the only sound was the rush of the beasts as they swarmed outside the door, I finally stood up and turned around to see who had saved me.

It was a handful of men the likes of which I'd never seen. Their skin was white, and they were wearing the strangest clothing. Stiff, formal things that looked uncomfortable and restricting. On their heads were clapped dressings that matched their clothes; their feet were covered in shiny, heeled skins. Plics.

We know what they are now, but back then . . .

The one in the lead spoke first.

"Who the fuck are you?" he said, though at the time, I didn't understand him.

I started to explain to him what had happened, but he obviously didn't understand me. The rush of the battle had infused my limbs, and in an effort to try and clarify myself, I stupidly raised my maquahuitl and pointed behind me, pointing to the desert, and took a step toward them.

They all took a step backward.

"Whoa, whoa, whoa," the leader said.

I continued on, trying to tell them "We came from the outpost. Those things killed all of my men," but they raised their voices in warning again. And when I wouldn't stop moving toward them, the leader hit me in the head with the butt of his weapon.

Ka-Bata stopped.

"Plics," Coatl said.

"Yes. Plics. This was years and years ago, mind you. I had never seen one before. Never seen their weapons or heard their language. I didn't know. I didn't know what I was getting into."

"What you were getting into?"

Loud voices came from inside the adobe, followed by laughter. Ka-Bata stood up, turning briefly toward it.

"Coatl," he said. "I'm sorry. You must forgive me. But without them, we could never have survived."

A group of plics entered the garden, as disorderly and obnoxious as any ever was. They were all dressed in the uniform of the Brotherhood—cream-colored suits, fedoras, shiny black patent leather shoes, or two-tones. The one in the front held out his arms when he saw Ka-Bata.

"Ka-Bata! Long time no see, huh? How's it going?"

When Ka-Bata spoke, it was in the halting language of the white men.

"Very well. Go very well," he said.

"Go very well, huh? Look, it'll be less painful if we *nahuatlatoa*."

"I agree."

The plic looked over Ka-Bata's shoulder at the wounded Coatl and the slumbering Xiuloc.

"I thought you said you had some prime meat for me? All I see is a gimp and a drunk."

"These are good warriors. Excellent fighters. This one is a general."

The plic looked dubious. He pushed Ka-Bata aside and stepped over to Coatl, stooping over right in front of him and putting his hands on his knees. Coatl watched, amused, as the white man inspected him as if he were an animal.

"Good shoulders. Good build. What's up with that gash on his leg?"

"Battle injury. My crone fixed it."

"You mean that weird woman. Your crones creep me out." The plic stood to his full height. "Alright. I'll take this one, but not sleeping beauty over there. Him and the ones you got in the cell." He spit in his hand and held it out for Ka-Bata to shake, and when the deal was made, he straightened his suit and tie and sauntered off. "Pick up the merchandise, boys."

The other plics surrounded Coatl, who was too confused and weak to fight back.

"I'm sorry, Coatl," Ka-Bata said.

"But the tecuani . . . we need your army."

"Then you're in luck, my good General," Ka-Bata said. "That's exactly where the plics are taking you"

THE RABBIT

After the whole zombie situation, BG let us hit the barracks to pick up anything we might have left behind, which equated to clean socks and a fresh pair of trainers for each of us. Then he drove us out to a train station and put us on the 9:10 to "The Hell Out Of This Place." That was cool for two reasons:

1. The obvious.
2. I fucking love trains!

I love the sound of the tracks clacking away, I love the feeling of the cars swaying, and I love the chuff of the engine. In fact, I love trains so much, that's what I think this book should be called. "I Fucking Love Trains, a novel by Asshole Jones." Got a nice ring to it, don't you think? This particular train was a beaut, too. Looked like it came straight out of the old west, with it's iron engine and the steam whistle blowing (yeah, the Brotherhood still used steam engines).

It was a cute little thing. Three cars. An engine, a coach, a caboose. Top-Knot nearly leaped out of his skin when it arrived. I actually had to turn around and tell him it was okay, not that he understood a word I said, but he got the gist. We was all three of us so exhausted that we each took a seat without a word, leaned back, and went right to sleep.

I woke up to a voice saying "Hey BG. What time we supposed to get there?"

"3:30," BG said. Then, as I sat up, "Good morning, sunshine."

He was all open faced and goofy grinned, like I'd shown up late to a family reunion. He looked natty in his peaches and cream, his triple worsted vest, his Eldredge-knotted tie. His fedora was sitting on the table between us, and I bet if I looked under that table, I'd've seen his favorite pair of two tones planted firmly on them U-boats he called feet.

"Howzit," he said.

"Everything fucking hurts, thanks."

"Get used to it."

"Used to it?"

"You're going to war, asshole. Shit gets hurt in war. You want something to eat?"

"Got any lobster?"

"This guy. Hey Tommy Trigger. Two steaks. Medium rare."

He snapped his fingers, and Tommy Trigger, who'd been cooling his heels in the back across from Wildcat and Top-Knot, rose to his feet and glared at me, like I was the one who'd made him do something he didn't want to do.

"Right away, BG," he said, and left using the back door of the car. BG shook his head.

"That's Tommy Trigger. He's a bit of an asshole."

"Yeah?"

"Yeah."

"He must be one hell of a deadeye with a name like that. He your sharpshooter or something?"

"Tommy Trigger? Nah. He ain't got no skills. In fact, he's the worst shot in the Neighborhood. Six to one before he can hit anything. So he likes to kill people by pulling the trigger. A lot."

"Huh. So listen, BG. Can you answer me something?"

"Sure."

"What the fuck is going on? I knew you wanted me to figure out what Zoot was up to, but the fucking crucifixion, the cardio, them things in the maze? What the fuck?"

He ticked it off on his fingers.

"Golgotha, Hell, and The Battle Royale."

"Battle Roy—are you fucking kidding me with this?"

"Nope."

Tommy Trigger came back into the car and sat down on the bench across the aisle. He leaned back against the window and put his feet up, reminding me of every surly teenager I ever seen in every cheap matinee trying to look tough. All he needed was a toothpick sticking out of the corner of his mouth. Or cigarette between his lips. And what'd he do? Took a cigarette out of a pack in his breast pocket and plunked it between his lips.

"Don't you light that shit up in here," BG said.

"What, this?"

"Yeah, that."

"You smoke, too."

"Not that turkish crap. Smells like burning cow shit."

"C'mon, BG."

"You want to smoke? You take it outside."

"We're on a moving train."

"Exactly."

Tommy Trigger didn't do nothing. Just stared at BG, mouth hanging open.

"Broom!" BG snapped, and Tommy, sighing, got up and headed back the way he came, muttering to himself the whole time. BG watched him go, then he said to me, "Look, sorry about not giving you all the details. That was wrong. But I figured you had enough to deal with at the time, what with your crazy head and whatever. You didn't weigh nothing but a nickel over ninety, neither. Putting something like this on your shoulders might've broke your back."

I couldn't disagree, but still.

"Would've been nice to know, all things considered."

We sat for a while in silence, staring out the window. The landscape was dark and bleak and barren. Forms lurched around in the night, some of them big, some of them small, ain't none of them friendly. Tommy finally came back with the steaks and potatoes, the reek of his tobacco mingling with the savory smells of the food. He put the plates down in front of us, then pulled some silverware out of his back pocket, two steak knives and two forks, and slapped them down on the table.

"You want anything else?" he asked. "Salt? Pepper? Handy?"

"Get out of here."

"I meant a napkin."

BG smiled at him with his teeth.

"Okay, okay," Tommy said, and left.

After all the bullshit of the past few weeks, I gotta tell you that that steak was gorgeous. Like a blow job after ten years of not getting a blow job. Or a rim job. Or a hand job. Any kind of job that'd result in the inevitable. Only different because I was eating. What I mean to say is that steak was like an orgasm in my mouth. Wait. That didn't sound the way I wanted it to sound. Eating that steak, it was, like, all salty and juicy and it melted on my tongue so good, first hard and tough, but eventually not so hard and tough, and, uh, and that's where the similarities end, because I was the one who felt good, and in that analogy, it's the other guy popping off down my throat, and giving head ain't nothing like slurping a hot slab of meat between your—

Ah fuck it.

Never mind.

It tasted good. That's all I meant to say.

One thing I learned being a killer and a wanted man was that it was never a bad idea to have an option. Run out of bullets, better have a knife. Knife blade breaks, better have another knife. So after we finished, I snuck the steak knife on my lap, you know, as an option.

Two goons in pinstripes came in and cleared away the dishes and such. Then they came back and stood there, one of them little and wiry, the other one as big as an ape. The ape had on a white shirt and gray tie, but the wiry schmuck was wearing a valentine button up and pocket square, with a silly skinny white tie. Security detail, I guess, hovering nearby in case I decided to do anything stupid, which was smart considering right then I felt downright retarded. The ape looked predictable stupid, and the little one had one hell of a scar on his cheek, and—

"Holy shit," I said. "Morty and Asshole!"

Asshole gaped. Morty sneered.

"Ah, fuck," he said. "You? You made it?"

"Yeah, me. Hey nice scar. Sucks to be an asshole, don't it?"

Morty took a step toward me, his hand reaching under his jacket, but BG put his hand up. He looked at me quizzical.

"He tried to rape my friend," I explained.

BG's eyebrows shot off his forehead.

"When?"

"Remember when you crucified me?"

"Oh." He pulled two fat cigars out of his breast pocket. "You want?"

"'Oh?' That's all you got to say? I oughta take that fuck's gun and open him up a third eye."

Morty pressed his lips tight, vibrating with anger.

"You go ahead and try it," he said.

"Calm down, Morty. I ain't gonna do it right now, not when you got a hard on for me."

"BG! C'mon."

"Cool it, Morty," BG said. When Morty didn't cool it, BG gave him a look and the guy backed off. BG lit his cigar with a match.

I said, "What about all that shit you gave Tommy about the smell?"

"This don't smell," he said. "Here."

I took the cigar, and he struck another match, and we both leaned in so he could light mine. I took a puff. I won't make no analogy here because of what happened the last time I tried, so all I'll say is this: tasted great.

After we was done, BG spread this map out all over the table. It was old school, hand drawn, like something out of an old book, or what you'd find framed-up in an antique store.

"What's this?"

"It's a map."

"I know it's a map. What's it a map of?"

"This is where we is."

"What, like America? That don't look like no map of the states I never seen."

"Well, it ain't quite America."

"Is it or ain't it?"

"It ain't."

"Jesus."

He bipped me upside the head.

"Don't take the Lord's name in vain."

"Sorry. Christ—"

He hit me again.

"Using the last name don't make it better!"

"Alright, alright. I didn't know you was so spiritual."

"I ain't. But there's some shit you can say and some shit don't say. Saying 'Jesus Christ' is one of them what you just don't say, just in case you didn't figure that one out."

"Fine."

"You wanna know what's going on here, or you want me to throw you and your friends back into another situation with fuck all intel?"

"They're not really my friends. I mean, Wildcat's alright, but she punched me in the foot. The other guy I don't barely know."

"Jesus Christ, this guy. Look at the map."

So I looked at the map.

"I can't read it."

"You can't read?"

"I can read."

"You can't read English?"

"I can read English. I just have a hard time doing it upside down."

You ever get one of them looks, like when you're being a schnook and someone looks at you kind of droll and disappointed, as if to say, "I've had it with you, asshole"?

BG shot me one of them looks. Then he turned the map around so I could see it.

"Better?"

"Oh yeah. I can read it real good now. Thanks."

This is what I seen.

First, a great big gash of green running down the middle of it, and in the middle of that, a great big gash of blue. A jungle and a river. Closest to me was a regular old street map, separated from the jungle and the river by a dozen dozen miles. Streets and landmarks. Parks and cemeteries. The Neighborhood, laid out in all its glory. Whoever done it even drew a whole bunch of crucifixes on one block, and right in the middle he'd cleared out space for something he labeled "The Neighborhood Boneyard."

Best part of it, though, was the wording. The streets was named correct. You got your 15th and Dixon, you got your 29th and Jefferson, you got your Fleetwood and Sumner, you got your Geddy and Collins. But the mapmaker also added a whole bunch of personal landmarks, too, like "Fucked Molly May In The Ass Here," and "Kicked That Cunt Barry Fischman's Teeth In Here." Shit like that all over the place. Oh, and "Dixon Street"? You can imaging how he spelled it. 'Dixon'. He also wrote down all the territories of the gangs, with the Top-Knots being closest to the jungle, and the Fuglies being over near the Industrial sector.

So, yeah. That was the Neighborhood.

Just outside the jungle he'd drew another city, only this one was much smaller. A temple shaped like a pyramid in the middle, with little roads and such running criss cross all over the place. Nothing'd been labeled, just the word "TLEK" stamped on the pyramid. On the far side of the map, past the river and the jungle and the desert, he'd made an arrow pointing off the edge, with the words "SWAMP" and "SPUGS" under it.

"Nice map," I said.

"Thanks.

"I like the way you burned the edges. Gives it a real antique feeling."

"I think you're missing the point."

"And what is this, coffee? You stain it up with french roast?"

"You gonna take this serious, or am I gonna have to sock you one?"

"You sock me one and I stick my foot up your ass."

"Your foot?"

"Maybe both. You got a big ass."

Morty took a step forward and Asshole, after he realized what was going on, followed. I tightened my grip on the knife, and they pulled their jackets back to expose their heaters, two each, holstered under each armpit. I've taken out dudes with less than a steak knife before. Wasn't easy, but I done it. BG seen the look in my eye and he held up his hand again. Morty looked like he was going to burst. Didn't stop eyeballing me but didn't make no more moves neither. Not that he could have stopped what was coming.

I knew BG was talking to me. Seen his lips moving, heard noise coming out of his mouth, but all I could really do, all I could really think about, was the next five steps:

Knife in Morty's throat.

Dive out the booth.

Slice Asshole's achilles.

Knife in BG's heart

While they're writhing around or bleeding out or what have you, take their guns and blow out their brains.

I seen it laid out before me like an instruction manual, like blueprints. Boom boom boom boom boom. Wasn't no guarantee it'd work. Instructions ain't always precise. Architects forget to carry a decimal. Buildings fall apart. All I knew was that if I got past step four, I was golden. Step four was the clincher. But I knew my limits. Fortunately for all of us, every moment nothing happened, every second nobody acted, nothing happened.

BG said, "It's gonna be okay, okay? Morty and Asshole is just gonna back off—back off guys. Do it!—see, they're backing off. And you're gonna put that knife down, right? Everyone's just gonna relax, okay? Put the knife down. There you go. There you go."

Put the knife down? Ah shit. I showed my ass, didn't I? Didn't even know I'd taken it out, but out it was, gripped in my right fist. In fact, both hands was balled up on the table, knuckles as white as a corpse. BG searched my eyes.

"You okay?"

I relaxed my grip.

"Yeah."

"Morty?" he said, pointing behind him but not even looking around. "You and Asshole. Put them heaters away."

They didn't do nothing at first, just stood there, gripping their guns. BG snapped his fingers.

"Now!"

They did it.

"You want something to drink?" BG asked me.

"Water."

"You sure? You look like you could use a belt."

"Scotch and water."

"Morty, get him a scotch and water."

"Aw, BG."

"Do it, asshole."

Asshole frowned.

"You want I should do it? Or Morty?"

Morty cussed under his breath. He slapped Asshole on the chest with the back of his hand.

"C'mon. Let's go."

"Okay, Morty."

I pointed at the map.

"You want to tell me about King Tut and his monsters or what?"

"Not Tuts. Tleks. Tuts and Tleks? Two different species."

"Yeah, I know from Tleks. I was being a dick."

"You got that right."

Morty came back and plunked my drink down on the table in front of me, and I took myself a good, stiff snort. When the liquor ran its course down my throat and into my belly, I was ready to talk.

"Shoot," I said.

And he did.

First thing he told me was that this place, the Neighborhood, the pyramid, the training ground, the forest, the river, the mountains, the arena, this train, this wasn't nowhere near America.

"No shit."

"Shut up and listen."

Apparently, there'd been four sentient species on planet Earth. One way before the dinosaurs, one way after the dinosaurs, and one way after way after the dinosaurs. He ticked them off on his fingers: the spugs, the Tleks, and us. The Tleks didn't call the spugs the spugs. They called them tecuani, which meant "wild beast." Remember them crazy things with the face in their chests and the two rows of teeth and them big, long arms? Yeah. Them's tecuani. Then he started talking about the myth of the Tleks. How they was aliens from another planet that got left behind.

"You mean like the Aztecs?"

"Eh, kind of."

"Fine, like the Mayans, then."

"Eh, kind of."

"The Egyptians?"

So basically what it came down to was this: most of every species evolved regular. They lived. They died. They turned into plant food. But in each one there were always outliers, members that didn't follow the rules. Them was us. The Brotherhood. And the tecuani. And the Tleks.

"This place here," he said, motioning at the map. "Is kind of like a refuge for us things and them things. We can come and go between here and Earth as much as we like, but only when we're the dominant species. After that, we're stuck here."

Permanent. No more Earth. Just this place. Didn't sound too bad to me, except for the fact that once we was on this side, ain't nobody or nothing made no more bodies or no more things.

"Wait, like, we can't fuck?"

"No, you can fuck."

"Okay, good. I like fucking."

"You can fuck until your balls is empty, but you just can't make babies."

"Even better!"

"Maybe for you, but not for the species. Being over here in this place, it's a nice way of the universe saying 'fuck off and die' without actually having to fuck off and die."

"Okay. Look. I get it. The Tlek. The Spugs. The training. The arena. You're building an army. Seems a little stupid."

"Stupid? You want we should just roll over? Seka-Khayu might have died, but he ain't dead yet."

"That don't make no sense."

BG swept his hands over the map.

"None of this shit does."

"Good point."

"Look. I don't expect you to totally get it all at once. It's a lot to absorb, and you just been through hell. All you need to know is Seka-Khayu's been drinking the amber for centuries. Nobody who drinks the amber for that long dies that easily."

"I'll take your word for it."

"So he's coming back, and he's looking to invade our world. And we gotta stop him."

"If you need to stop him so bad, why'd you let Zoot do what he done?"

"We didn't. That's what I sent you for. To figure out what he was doing and stop it. Nice job, by the way."

"Thanks."

"I was being sarcastic."

"I got that."

He took a sip of his drink.

"I gotta say, now that I know what he was doing, I kind of think it's a good idea."

"Seriously?"

"A little bit. But . . . in the end, the dead don't take orders too good. We need cocks in jockstraps. Boulders in bras. We'd hoped your group'd push us over the edge to be able to fight, but I guess Zoot took care of that."

He looked at his watch and got up.

"It's getting late," he said. "You guys is gonna need some rest before—"

Something crashed into the side of the car, and he stumbled over into the other booth. The car rocked and righted and he snapped at Morty and Asshole, who jumped into action.

"Get the ladder," Morty said.

"For up there?"

"Where do you think?"

Asshole peered out the windows into the dark night.

"But Morty, it's dark."

"I know it's dark. It's nighttime."

"Oh, okay."

Asshole didn't move. Morty slapped him upside the head.

"Get the ladder!"

"Oh yeah!"

Asshole reached up and pulled the ladder down from the ceiling. Morty climbed up, unlocked the trap door and disappeared onto the roof. Cold air filled the coach. Asshole peered up after his friend.

"I'm scared, Morty," he said.

From the roof of the car, Morty said, "That's okay, Sam. So am I."

That seemed to work, and Asshole, whose real name was Sam, apparently, and whose shoulders was as wide as the Nile, pushed that big head of his up through the square opening. Then his shoulders, then his legs, and then he was through, and the trap door shut and latched closed. Seconds later, I heard sound of machine gun fire. The steam engine picked up speed.

"What's going on now, BG?"

"Sniders."

"Snyders? Like the pretzel?"

"No, like the snakes mixed with the spiders. They're out there. Like to come out at night."

"That's what hit us? Them's some big sniders."

"Big as a semi."

I let that one sink in for a bit. After a while, all I could think to say was, "Fuck's sake, BG. Fuck's sake."

THE WIDOW

The Widow Mrs. Feldman leaned her elbows on the sill. The aches and pains of her ordeal pinched and menaced her. Every joint seemed to tweak no matter what position she adopted. She should lie down, take a break. Just a day. Let herself heal. Snort. Sure. And a billion gold coins should rain down on her front stoop.

Those things were still out there. If she let her guard down even for a day . . . there were already enough over here as it was.

She pulled a cigar out from the folds of her skirt and lit it with a snap. The sun began its slow descent, casting shadows of the townhouses across the street. She watched the old abandoned town house, waiting for the shimmering. A minute passed. Ten. Just as the sky turned from blue to pink to red, it happened. A tear in the fabric of the two worlds.

The Widow Mrs. Feldman blew out a thick plume of smoke.

"Demon!" she cried. "D—"

Demon meowed as he jumped up on the sill, taking his place before her. The old woman scratched him between the ears.

"Time to sing for your supper," she said.

A NOTE FROM BONESAW

Hey. How's it going? Look, I don't know you, so I ain't about to pretend to know what it's like to live your life. But you know what? I know the author, old Jimmy whats-his-name, and boy howdy is he a piece of work. Loves to take naps, him. Mouth like a sailor. Charm of a, uh, guy without any charm. Like a mattress salesman.

Anyway, Jimmy makes a living off his books, see, and one of the things that helps him out is if his readers leave reviews. Even if you don't like it, leave a review. It ain't like it's difficult these days. Just hop on Amazon or Goodreads or whatever and dial up your two cents. It really helps!

ACKNOWLEDGMENTS

Thank you to the many authors who wrote books about indie-publishing, specifically Tim Grahl, Joanna Penn, and the Sterling and Stone crew. Without their books and information on marking and the creative mindset, I would never have felt confident enough to take the leap to authorpreneurship.

Also thank you to my beta readers. Without their hard work and excellent feedback, the book would have been significantly less entertaining. Angie Noll, Sandra and John Fedowitz, and Duane Pye were particularly helpful! Their notes and feedback helped me develop the third act and create a tighter, more controlled, less capricious experience.

ABOUT THE AUTHOR

James Noll is a freelance writer, an educator, a musician, and a novelist from Fredericksburg, VA. He's published three other books: *A Knife in the Back, You Will Be Safe Here,* and *Burn All The Bodies. The Rabbit, The Jaguar, & The Snake* is his fourth novel and the first in The Bonesaw Trilogy. When he's not writing, he takes long naps. When he's not napping, he's probably thinking about it.

Check out his work at www.jamesnoll.net